# THE DEVIL CARD

## THE 3RD HIDDEN GOTHAM NOVEL

### CHRIS HOLCOMBE

**BOOKS
LIKE US**

Published by Books Like Us, LLC

90 State Street, Suite 700, Office 40, Albany, New York, 12207

"Yes, Sir! That's My Baby," Words by Gus Kahn, Music by Walter Donaldson, Published in 1925 by Donald Publishing Co. and WB Music Corp. Public Domain.

"It Had To Be You," Words by Gus Kahn, Music by Isham Jones, Published in 1924 by Jerome H. Remick & Co. Public Domain.

"Masculine Women, Feminine Men," Words by Edgar Leslie, Music by James V. Monaco, Published in 1925 by Clarke & Leslie Songs, Inc. Public Domain.

Published in the United States of America

Print ISBN: 978-1-7364458-2-2

Ebook ISBN: 978-1-7364458-3-9

ALSO BY CHRIS HOLCOMBE

THE HIDDEN GOTHAM SERIES:

*For John Mainieri aka "John with the Pugs" and his husband Michael Schilke, neighbors forever.*

# ACKNOWLEDGMENTS

The author would like to thank the invaluable assistance of the following people:

David Bishop, for (once again) enduring several Author Crises of Faith with grace and aplomb; Mary Louise Mooney, editor and history-fact checker extraordinaire; Robin Vuchnich for yet another fabulous cover; "The Boys" Ricky Milburn and Rob Karwic for being my cheerleaders and happy hour buddies; Claire Fruscello for the wisdom and council; Sonoko Jacobson and April Rodriguez for their love and support; Michler Bishop for the book about spiritualists (I finally got around to using it!); my neighbors who are (to quote the indomitable Tina Turner) "Simply the Best,"; and you, the readers—we have a Book 3 because of you!!!

# THE FIRE

A stinging slap jolted Isabella Delucci from her wine-soaked slumber.

She sat upright in bed, eyes blurred and crusty, thoughts groggy. Her head felt congested, heavy and thick, and her throat ragged and sore when she swallowed. *Porca miseria!* Was she coming down with a cold? That damn Vito. Keeping her out all night in the chilly air while he bored her mind and pawed her dress.

A muffled voice called her name. She looked around. Why was everything so smokey? Papa and his friends? That couldn't be. Mama didn't allow Papa to have them over anymore on Saturday nights. She said she couldn't stand their poker games. All those stinky cigars clenched between yellow teeth, all her food going into someone else's bellies. All their money going into someone else's pockets. Surely, he wouldn't disobey her. Disobeying Mama was taking one's life into their own hands, and those were odds not even her Uncle Atty would bet on.

"Bella!"

Her name again. Clearer this time.

She turned and saw a darkened shape standing beside her threadbare mattress.

Mama's voice, loud and cutting, shouted, "We go! Now!"

She ripped off the bedcovers, revealing Isabella's tattered nightgown with Mama's clumsy stitches at the hem.

"Come! Come!"

The darkened shape left the bed and disappeared into the dirty haze.

Isabella's throat protested the cloudy air, and she erupted into chest-wracking coughs. Still coughing, she swung her feet onto the floor and followed Mama. The fiercely hot floorboards scolded her bare feet just as she scolded herself.

*Not cigar smoke, you stupid girl. Fire!*

She slowed to a stop.

"Mama!" she called, desperately searching the smoke-filled room, the gray air too thick, the space too dark to see anything. Her eyes stung. Tears spilled down her cheeks and rolled off her chin. "Mama! I can't see you!"

The shape returned. "Keep your head down! This way!"

Mama grabbed her hand. They bent at their waists and stumbled forward, coughing uncontrollably. The air's immense heat bit into Isabella's skin, its teeth sharp and relentless, and the black smoke obscured everything. This was their home and yet, nothing was recognizable, nothing familiar.

Mama's shape stopped.

Isabella heard a wrenching sound and splintering wood followed by cold air blasting her skin, chilling her to the bone. A window. Something hard hit her hands, and she looked down. A pair of leather shoes. Men's shoes. Papa's.

"Put these on and go!" Mama said. "Take the ladder down! Wait for me on the corner!"

Mama pushed her towards the rectangle.

Isabella turned around. "Come with me! Mama, please!"

"I must get your brothers! Their door won't open!"

"What about Papa?"

"He is not here. Go, Bella!"

"Mama!"

But the shape was gone.

Isabella hesitated before putting on Papa's shoes, finding them much too large for her feet. She panicked.

*How am I to walk in these, Mama?!*

The smoky room provided no answers.

She turned to face the window. Distant voices yelled outside, followed by clanging bells and sorrowful sirens. She ducked underneath the sash and stepped onto the fire escape that seemed to vibrate from all the commotion. Or was that just her pulse pounding? She looked down. Fire trucks, police cars, and ambulances covered the street, over four floors away. An enormous crowd stood by and watched in their overcoats and bathrobes.

She steadied herself and began her shaking, halting journey down the fire escape. The metal shook with every movement, and she tried not to think of the fall should it give way. Black smoke surrounded her. Orange sparks crackled and popped beside her ears. Now and then, a fleck of burning ash grazed her skin, causing her to jump and hastily brush it off, lest her nightgown catch fire.

*Dear God, help me out of here!*

She concentrated on placing one foot in front of the other. Slowly but surely, she navigated her way down. When she got to the last level, she froze.

Full-bodied flames, red and furious, roared out of the first-floor windows below, blocking the fire escape ladder that led down to the sidewalk. Blocking her path to freedom. How was she to escape now?

Male voices yelled for her.

She turned her head.

The firemen.

Confused, she looked to where they were gesturing. A second set of firemen held a circular jumping sheet below where she stood. The sheet was white with a red dot in the center, like one of those games at Coney Island. Throw a dart, shoot a pistol, win a prize.

More yelling.

She didn't understand what they were saying, but she knew what to do.

Her hands reached for the bottom hemline and found the loose stitching. She pulled and ripped the edge of her nightgown all the way around. With her teeth, she tore the strip into two jagged rags. She wrapped them around each hand and gripped the metal banister of the fire escape. The heat burned through the nightgown fabric.

She clenched her teeth and hoisted herself over the railing. Papa's shoes almost slipped off her feet, but by the Grace of the Madonna, she kept them on. She steadied herself on the edge by holding on to the railing with all her might.

"Turn around!" shouted one of the firemen. "Turn around and jump, girl!"

She pivoted to rebalance her weight. Her right hand, despite being burned by the railing, tightened its grip. She turned on the ball of her right foot and swung her left foot and her left hand to the other side. The briefly untethered palm and heel hit the landing and the railing with a loud *clang!* Her torso started falling forward, but she jerked herself upright, arms spread wide in aguish, like Christ on his cross. The jumping sheet lay below her, a good fifteen-foot drop.

The fireman, who called to her the first time, caught her eye. "Listen to me, girl! Aim for the red dot! When you jump, land on your bottom, alright?" He patted his own in case she didn't hear or understand him.

She nodded.

"Are you ready?"

She nodded again. The railing seared into her palms, and she couldn't bear one more moment of this.

Before she knew it, she was airborne.

She fell so fast she hadn't realized she'd left the fire escape until she hit the jumping sheet. The impact knocked what little air there was out of her lungs. Firemen staggered, then gently lowered her to the ground. The man giving her the instructions yanked her up. They fled to the middle of the street, where they met with a man in a suit.

"Why the hell isn't the water on?!" he bellowed to the fireman.

"Damn screw on the hydrant's busted!"

"Jesus Christ. The entire building's gonna collapse before too long!"

They left her there.

She gazed around in amazement: trucks, axe-wielding men, and robed figures, all illuminated by the fire's glow.

A man dressed in white appeared next to her. "Come with me, *signorina.*" He gestured towards an ambulance.

She wouldn't follow him. Instead, she pointed back to the inferno she'd just escaped. "Mama's in there! So are my brothers!"

"*Signorina.*"

"No!"

She turned and gasped in horror.

Her building, her *home*, was being eaten alive. Flames gnawed at the windows, chewed at the walls, and clawed at the roof.

Her eyes darted around, searching for Mama and her brothers through the thickening black smoke. Where were they? *Oh caro dio*, where *were* they?

There! Two boys, aged eight and eleven, were making their way down the fire escape in their nightshirts, the youngest leading the oldest. Of course. Rocco was braver, Emiliano more cautious.

Isabella held her breath as she watched her younger brothers.

The ambulance man grabbed her arm. "This way! We need to treat your burns!"

"Damn your treatments!" she snarled.

*"Signorina—"*

"Get off me!"

She twisted herself free and charged towards the area where the jumping sheet lay. The man in the suit and the fireman were still arguing.

The fireman broke away, saying, "Miss? Miss? You need to stay back!"

"I need to help my brothers!"

"Miss, you can't—"

She held up her hand, silencing him, then pointed to the two boys.

He followed her line of sight and nodded. He went over to the jumping sheet. "Men, get ready! We got two more jumpers!"

The firemen mobilized, picking up the rounded contraption and carrying it to the fire escape. By now, Rocco and Emiliano arrived at the third level, but the second level —from where she jumped—was now blocked by the intensifying flames thundering out of the second-story windows. Emiliano held onto Rocco to keep him from charging downwards. Their voices rang out, wordless but terrified.

The fireman gestured to them. "Come to the edge! Over here!"

The two boys walked over to where he pointed. They were a good twenty-five, maybe even thirty feet from the ground.

*Will they survive that?* Isabella thought. *Can* anyone *survive that?*

They didn't have a choice.

The fireman gave them the same instructions that he had given her. He added, "The little one goes first! Got it? The little one goes first!"

Isabella tugged at the fireman's sleeve. "Make the oldest go."

He half turned. "What?"

"The oldest is more afraid. His name is Emiliano. If he's up there by himself, he won't—"

"I got it, miss, I got it." He leaned his head back and yelled up, "Emiliano! You go first! I promise we'll catch you! Get to the very edge! Understand? The very edge!"

Emiliano threaded his way through the bars of the fire escape, then clasped them with tightened knuckles.

"Good! Very good, Emiliano! Are you ready? On the count of three! One, two, three . . . !"

Emiliano stood frozen.

"Come on, son!" The fireman beckoned with his hand. "You need to jump!"

An explosion thundered from the bottom floor. A swift hand of heat forced Isabella backwards, and she fell onto her side. The gravel of the street bit into her burning palms and her exposed calves. Her heart pounded against her breastbone.

*No . . . No!*

She looked up. The boys remained on the fire escape, with Emiliano still clinging to the spokes.

*Please, Emil! Be brave, be brave!*

"Emiliano!" called the fireman. "We're running out of time, son!" Once more, he beckoned with his hand. "On the count of the three! One . . . two . . ."

Isabella took the biggest breath of her life. "Rocco! Push!"

The little boy placed his hand against Emiliano's back. Before the older boy could protest, he was in the air.

The falling shadow landed on the jumping sheet with a *whoompf!*

Isabella staggered to her feet. "Emil!"

She was on her way to the sheet when the fireman held her back. "Wait here, miss!"

"But—"

Before she could further argue, a tiny shadow darted towards her. "Bella!"

Emiliano ran into her arms, his nightshirt soiled with soot. She held him tight, muttering assurances despite her panic.

The fireman glanced upwards at the building. "Rocco! It's your turn! Get to the edge like your brother! . . . Thatta boy! . . . On the count of three! One, two, three!"

Isabella glanced up to see her youngest brother fall through the air and land on the jumping sheet with the same *whoompf!* sound.

Agonizing seconds went by.

Then the little shadow bounded towards them. Rocco

joined his brother and sister in their embrace. Together, they sobbed, their words unintelligible, their relief too much to bear.

The moment didn't last.

They were short one family member.

Isabella pulled away from her brothers' embrace and asked them, "Mama. Where's Mama?"

Coughs interrupted Rocco's reply. "She was . . . right behind us. . . She told us . . . to go."

Emiliano nodded. He, too, was coughing. "She couldn't breathe . . . but she . . . shoved us out."

Isabella looked up at their window and saw nothing but the thick, black smoke.

She disentangled herself from her brothers and went over to the fireman next to the jumping sheet, pointing upwards again. "Mama! My mother! She's still up there!"

"Miss, you need to stay back! This place is about to go!"

"But Mama—"

A shuddering groan followed by snapping pops silenced them. The fireman glanced behind him and cursed. Before Isabella could protest, he grabbed her and her brothers and ran them across the street. Behind them, a sickening crumble and roar soon followed by shouts of alarm and pounding feet. Spectators shrilled with terror.

The fireman threw Isabella and her brothers behind one of the fire trucks. Black smoke mixed with gray dust and unbearable heat engulfed them. Isabella shut her eyes, holding onto her two brothers with all her might.

The roar subsided as quickly as it came.

A moment trudged past.

When Isabella's eyes first opened, she could see nothing. She coughed so hard it shook her back and rattled her spine. She turned her head away from her brothers and spat phlegm on the ground.

The dense smoke began fading into a gray, hazy mist. Shapes slowly came into view. Silhouettes of trucks and people.

She looked down and checked each of her brothers. No major cuts that she could see, minor burns on their palms. Must've been from them gripping the fire escape, as she had done. Their faces were smudged with charcoal, the sight causing her to reach up and rub her own cheeks. When she brought her hand back, she found it stained black.

A horrible realization.

*Mama!*

She ran around the fire truck and halted abruptly when she saw what remained of their home.

The building was gutted.

Floors collapsed. Brick, glass, plaster, and wood everywhere. Firemen, ambulance workers, and policemen pulled each other up from the wreckage, coughing, covered in gray-white ash. Smoke clogged the street, and burning cinders floated all around them like fireflies. Someone had finally opened the hydrant, and water from hoses arced upwards, in vain, to the pile of smoldering rubble.

The world was strangely quiet. Not even the pounding of the water hoses, the yelling of the firemen, or the crackle of the fire could reach her.

The only sound she heard was her own ravaged voice calling for Mama . . .

1

The last witness was here, Dash Parker knew it.

The thought sped up his heart and twitched his fingers. He bounced on the balls of his feet, anxious and yet strangely reluctant to enter the building looming before them.

Finn Francis, who stood next to him, murmured, "I said it before, and I'll say it again. This is a curious choice for our McElroy."

Dash glanced up at the five stories of sporadically lit windows. The sight resembled the many gap-toothed jack-o'-lanterns adorning the city in honor of Halloween in exactly one week from tonight. "What exactly is this place again?"

Finn replied, "The American Seamen's Friend Society. A sort of flophouse for bell bottoms to make sure they don't get into trouble—staying at sleazy hotels, visiting speakeasies like ours, dropping coins and trousers at houses of ill-repute, that sort of thing."

"I see."

"Mind you, being here doesn't stop them from going to

such places. Men shall be men and goddess bless them for it."

Dash nodded as he spied an enormous tower perched on the far corner of the property. It overlooked the black ribbon of the Hudson shimmering in the moonlight. The water ran fast in between New York and New Jersey, like a pickpocket escaping through a busy crowd.

"You know how to get us in?"

Dash had already asked Finn the question before they left their apartment, but his nerves were getting to him. The anticipation of finally erasing McElroy's threat and feeling that long-sought-after release was almost too much for him to bear.

Finn scoffed. "Why you doubt me is a mystery for the ages. Of course, I do!"

Dash sighed. "I apologize, Finn, it's just—"

He turned and looked at his friend. Strange, seeing Finn without his "Finn-ness." No mascara, no eye shadow, no lipstick. No flamboyance of any kind. Just an unadorned, unembellished oval face with wide blue eyes, long curly lashes, a pointed chin, and an upturned nose.

Of course, neither one of them looked like themselves. Dash wasn't in his usual black tuxedo, the one tailored to his trim six-foot frame. Instead, they were both dressed as dock-workers: scratchy, long-sleeved white work shirts, thick brown work pants with wide suspenders, and heavy brown boots. Flat caps covered all of Finn's short-cropped dark hair and most of Dash's own misbehaving brown strands.

Dash adjusted the brim, bringing it lower over his hazel eyes, and continued his thought. "It's just I want this to be it, Finn. The last witness. The finale to this hell McElroy has put us through. God knows we've been through enough this month."

"Ah, yes, finding all the other witnesses he claimed to have of that ill-timed argument between you and that hideous Walter Müller."

"McElroy *had* those witnesses, Finn. No claims about it."

*Until we paid them or otherwise convinced them to forget what they saw and heard.*

Dash pulled at his shirt collar, trying in vain to adjust it.

Finn reached over and smacked his hands. "Stop picking at it."

"This cut is most unfortunate. How can you stand it?"

"It's all part of the dock experience, dearie. Coarse clothes getting you in the mood for rugged men with calloused, but surprisingly adept, hands. I didn't think this was your first night at the docks. Or has Joe and his prowess erased those memories?"

Joe was their other roommate and speakeasy partner. He was also Dash's lover.

Dash ignored the comment. "We've been lucky that McElroy's witnesses despised him as much as we do. It made negotiations that much easier." He returned his gaze to the Society. "I hope this Peter Fraker feels the same."

A silence settled between them. In the distance, unseen waves struck the pilings in a constant rhythm—*slap spray, slap spray*—and a cold, biting wind brought with it New York City's perfume of progress: burnt coal, spilt diesel, and discarded ash, underlaid with the faint, but unmistakable, whiff of rot.

"Well, fear not," Finn replied. "I know exactly how to get us past the guards." He leaned in close, spilling a secret. "I was here most recently with a lovely bruiser of a man named Borden. His name means 'den of the boar.' Isn't that just delicious?"

Dash groaned. "Finn—"

"Don't be such a Grundy; it's a fabulous story. I was at this bar doing a little basketeering. That means seeing which bell bottom best fills out his trousers—"

"I know what basketeering means, Finn."

"Pardon *moi*! It's been so long since you've last been on the prowl. I figured you'd forgotten it."

"Finn, the story."

"Well, I don't mean to brag—"

"Yes, you absolutely do."

"—but I *did* snag the biggest basket in the room that night. Boar, indeed. I thought I had finally found the rough in 'rough trade.'"

"Good heavens," Dash muttered.

"Don't look at me like that! Sometimes a lady likes to get thrown around a bit. Be shown whose boss. I quickly learned, however, the goddesses have a sense of humor, for he turned out to be the gentlest of lambs instead of the beastliest of boars. Not what I expected, but enjoyable, nonetheless."

Dash shook his head.

*What am I going to do with you?*

"What's the point of telling me this?"

Finn sighed. "The *point*, dearie, is that because of my dalliance with Borden, I know the front deskman on the Sunday night shift." He gestured towards the Society's entrance portico. "Shall we?"

Dash nodded. "After you."

Finn was first through the double wooden doors with Dash quickly on his heels.

The lobby was a cramped, yet still impressive, space. Multiple square-shaped columns in fancy green-painted tiles decorated the entranceway. Mode brass chandeliers hung overhead, their light bulbs buzzing with Edison's precious electricity. The yellow walls were punctuated with taxidermized animals, including a deer's head and—Dash did a double take—yes, that was an entire peacock preening over them.

No Halloween decorations in sight. Finn had said before that bell bottoms were a suspicious lot; Dash supposed it wouldn't do to have witches, devils, and skeletons all over the place.

The front desk was encased in dark heavy wood, with pale pink wallpaper above it like the blushing sky during sunset. It was tended by a man dressed in a red uniform with gold buttons and gold thread, head down, showing off his matching hat. He appeared to be reading.

"Follow my lead," murmured Finn before strolling up to the front desk, impish grin in place. He tapped the bell on the corner, its shrill ring echoing throughout the lobby. "Good evening. Is that George Talbot? George, how are ya, doll?"

The man looked up. Dash thought he resembled an owl: square head, big eyes behind oval glasses, round shoulders, slightly puffed-out chest.

"Finn Francis?" He adjusted his glasses, as if by touching the rims he could bring his eyes into focus. "As I live and breathe. I didn't think you'd be back here."

Finn placed his hands on his hips. "And why would you think that, George?"

"Because of—" George leaned forward and dropped his voice. "—because of the incident in the bowling alley."

Dash raised his eyebrows. There was a bowling alley at this place?

Finn waved George off. "They should've known not to bet against *moi*."

Dash cut in. "What was the bet?"

George nodded towards him, murmuring to Finn, "Is he Jake?"

"Oh, Jaker than Jake; he's practically a Jill himself," Finn replied, then explained to Dash, "A bunch of Scottish bottoms thought I couldn't hit a strike whilst doing the splits."

George jerked his thumb towards Finn. "He did it not once, but twice."

"Which was *not* the original wager. I should've collected double! But I was gracious instead, and what did I get for extending grace?"

"Chased out of here like a fox outrunning the hounds."

"No good deed goes unpunished."

"Did they ever catch you?"

"What do *you* think?"

"I think if anyone caught you, it was that stevedore with the thick neck." George bounced his eyebrows up and down. "Did he feel the tickle of fairy wings that night, Finn old boy?"

Finn placed a protective hand over his chest. "Why George, a lady *never* kisses and tells."

"Good thing I'm not one, then. I tell everyone what gospel I've found. Sadly, it's been months since I've last had a good testimony. Speaking of testimony." He held up what he'd been reading: *The Daily News*, a torrid tabloid heavy on lurid details and light on facts. "Have you seen the latest developments in the Hall-Mills murder case?"

"Of course I have! I've read every word ever since that dirty young Reverend Hall and his chippy choir singer were discovered dead in a field back in 'Twenty-Two. In New Jersey, of all places. Please, goddess, let me die anywhere *but* in New Jersey."

"What's the latest news?" Dash asked.

Finn arched his thin brow. "They're exhuming Eleanor Mills's body."

"The chippy choir singer."

"The very one."

George tutted. "I can't imagine what the prosecution thinks they're going to find."

"Probably a lot more than what the original medical examiner found. He came off as an incompetent ass. Gunshots to both and some lacerations on Eleanor. Lacerations, please! We all know the poor woman almost had her head taken clean off!"

"Hell hath no fury like a woman scorned," George said solemnly. "Why it took the police so long to arrest the Reverend's wife and her thuggish brothers, I'll never know. When are they finished with the grand jury hearings?"

Dash cleared his throat.

Finn straightened up. "Oh. Right." He snaked his arm around Dash and pulled him close.

Dash cut his eyes to the little man, but allowed him to snuggle up.

"Enough about murder." Finn's voice thickened to the heavy syrup that precedes a request he shouldn't make. "Do you have any free rooms tonight?"

George adjusted those owl-like glasses of his again. "Is he of the sea? You know the rules, Finn."

"Of course he is! You think I'd ask you to commit offenses against the Society?"

"He looks like a land animal to me."

"*Former* land animal. He's working to be more of a marine one, aren't you, dearie?" Dash missed his cue, causing Finn to shake his arm. "*Aren't* you, dearie?"

Dash replied, "Yes, yes, that's right. I got sick of working in the factories. Dusty, noisy, didn't know what time of day or night it was. Thought I might as well have some clean ocean air while I work. Sun on my face, spray in my hair, that sort of thing."

"Too much," murmured Finn.

George arched one eyebrow. "If you saw a single day in a factory, I'll eat my hat."

Finn batted his lashes. "George, hon, this is aboveboard, I promise." He leaned his head against Dash's arm. "Besides, you don't want to stand in the way of true love, now do you?"

George watched the two of them for a moment, then sighed the weary sigh of all of Finn's friends. "What am I going to do with you?"

"Encourage me, I hope."

George rolled his eyes and placed a metal key on the desktop.

Finn picked it up, giving it a once-over. "Now George, there's a friend of his," he said, nodding towards Dash again, "that just got into town. He might've checked in within the last day or two. We were wondering if he's still here."

"You know I can't comment on guests, Finn. We only give out names to the police, and that's only because those elephant ears would love to find a reason to shut us down."

"Not to worry, this man is good friends with the police, isn't he, love?" Finn said, raising his eyebrows at Dash.

Dash nodded. "It's true. Has a connection through family, or so I'm told, with one copper in particular. A Cullen McElroy?"

He and Finn looked at George expectedly.

George kept his face neutral, his voice mild. "Is that name supposed to mean something to me?"

"Well," Dash replied, "sometimes he likes to show off,

you know? My friend, that is. Bring around someone to impress. His name, by the way, is Peter Fraker."

George gave his head a slight shake. "No one here by that name."

"Oh, well," Finn said, "sometimes old Pete likes to play games. Loves those spy stories and mystery novels. Such a card. Any chance a man came in with a copper recently? I can't imagine there would be *that* many who do around here." He laughed self-consciously.

George's mouth stretched into a brief, tight smile. He took the room key from Finn's hand. "You'll be wanting the Captain's Suite. Plenty of privacy, a gigantic bed, and an outdoor patio."

"A patio? George, in *this* weather?"

"You might want some fresh air after you, uh, make use of the bed. And as it so happens, we have just one left." He reached beneath the desktop and held up the new key. "I think you should take it."

Dash and Finn looked at one another. The suite must've been the more expensive room of the two.

Dash looked back at George. "We shall then."

George laid the key onto the front desk and brought out a metal lockbox that rattled with coins.

Dash fumbled in his trouser pockets. "How much?"

George replied, "Two dollars per night."

*Good lord!* Dash thought.

He found two bills and placed them on the desk, sliding it towards George, who glanced down at it.

"Per guest."

"Ah." Dash reached into his pocket again. He held up a fin.

"Exact change, if you please."

"Right." Dash's fingers dove once again into his trouser

pocket. Tucked into the bottom crease that always seems to hide whatever it was you were looking for were the blessed two one-dollar bills. He laid the second set of bills on the desk.

George snatched up the four dollars but—and Dash couldn't swear to this—only two of the four dollars made their way into the metal lockbox.

"Elevator is around the corner. Enjoy your stay. And as for your friend, Mr. Fraker is staying with us as Jonah Collins. He's in room 3C."

Dash slid the room key into his palm.

Finn tapped the front desk. "You're a dear, George." He pulled at Dash's arm. "Let's go. I've always wanted to see a captain's suite!"

As they rounded the corner away from the front desk, Dash muttered, "I think your friend double-charged us."

"It's New York," Finn muttered back. "Let's be thankful he didn't *triple*-charge us."

They found the elevator operator, another man dressed in red and gold, also reading a tabloid. He folded the paper as they entered and nodded at them as if he hadn't been caught.

"Third floor, please," Finn said.

The operator closed the brass gate, and with a wrench of a lever, they ascended. The brass box hummed and vibrated.

"Can you believe they're digging up the choir singer's body?" the operator said, holding up the tabloid. "I hear the killers near took that Eleanor's head clean off." He drew a finger across his throat to emphasize his point.

Finn nodded. "She sure sang from the wrong hymnal."

The operator wrenched the lever back to its original

position, shuttering the box to a stop, and pulled back the gate. He'd overshot the floor by a good six inches.

Finn turned and gave him a baleful stare. "I don't mean to criticize, dearie, but really?"

The operator shrugged. "It's temperamental and they won't fix it. Have a good evening."

Finn sighed, shaking his head with disgust as he leapt down.

Dash had to duck to keep from hitting his head on the top of the elevator doorway.

They entered a long, narrow hallway surrounded by more dark, heavy wood. Electricity buzzed from the wall lamps, their shades sporting scorch marks from when they used to cover oil-fueled flames instead of glass bulbs. Male voices murmured behind room doors and walls, the consonants soft, the vowels fuzzy, as if Dash were underwater. The effect was otherworldly, almost ghostly.

When he remarked as such, Finn replied, "I don't doubt that spirits live in these halls. They housed the survivors of the *Titanic* here, you know. It wouldn't surprise me if those lost in that tragedy found their way to this place."

Dash tugged at his shirt collar and his shoulders.

"Quit that," muttered Finn.

They'd turned a corner, and Finn held out his hand, stopping them both. He nodded to the door in front of them. 3C.

"This is it," Dash said. "The last witness."

"May the odds be in our favor."

"Amen."

"A-*woman*."

Dash took a deep breath, stepped forward, knocked, waited, then knocked again. He had barely lowered his hand before the wooden door swung open.

2

Peter Fraker was a man who long ago must've admitted defeat.

Dash saw he was slight in stature and curved in posture, as if God tried to draw a straight line and allowed himself to get distracted. Blond hair curled at his forehead, his ears, and the nape of his neck. A large nose dominated a thin face with sharp cheekbones. He wore a sleeveless undershirt that exposed stringy muscles and pale skin. His blue-and-white-striped pajama bottoms trailed across the floor.

Finn surprised them both by pushing into the room, saying, "Excuse me, Mr. Fraker, but we need a moment of your time."

Dash hesitated for a second, then followed suit.

By the time Peter registered what had happened, he and Finn were already inside the room, which was the narrowest Dash had ever seen. (And that was saying something, given his experiences with Greenwich Village apartments.) The space was just over six feet wide, if that, with a closet on one side and a wooden bunk bed, thankfully empty of another occupant, on the other.

"This is . . . cozy," Dash said.

"They're made to resemble a ship's quarters," Finn replied.

They both turned to look at Peter Fraker. Fear blanched the man's face an even whiter shade of pale. He kept his hand on the doorknob, the room door still held open.

"Who are you?" he asked, his voice thin and reedy. "What do you want? I don't have any money, if that's what you're after."

"Fear not," Finn said, "we're not here to rob you. Or cause you harm in any way. We're your fellow Villagers."

"Be that as it may, I'll have to ask you to leave. It is very late and I'm quite tired and, well, I don't mean to be rude, but you have no right barging in here—"

"Mr. Fraker," Dash said. "We're here to discuss Officer Cullen McElroy."

Peter immediately shut the door. "Who are you?" he asked again. "You coppers? Or—" He glanced around as if there were other men who were listening in on them. "—you the Feds?"

"Neither," Dash said.

"Oh, no. You're not working for *him*, are you? I already promised I'd keep quiet and stay hidden. What more does he want?" His worrying brow worried even more. "And how did you find me, anyway?"

Finn replied, "We were at the Greenwich Village Inn yesterday complaining about ol' Officer McElroy—a favorite activity of ours—when your neighbor, who was also there, joined in, telling us all how that damnable man was packing you up against your will. And how you slipped your neighbor a piece of paper that said where you'd gone and to please forward your mail. Bold move, Mr. Fraker."

"But why should you care about me?" Peter asked. "What do you want with *me*?"

Dash stepped in. "Because we're also victims of Officer McElroy. He's claimed he has witnesses that link us to a man who's disappeared. We've been finding them one by one—"

Finn yawned. "Truly exhausting."

"—and reasoning with them not to work with McElroy."

"Surprisingly easy, by the way."

"But then two days ago, McElroy bragged he had one last witness and because he knew we'd been, to quote him, 'sniffing around,' he hid this witness in a place where we'd never find him."

"And then there's your neighbor," Finn said, "telling us yesterday about your forced eviction." He held out his hands. "We took a chance and now, here we are."

Peter nodded. "Yes, alright, I see how—how this came about." Just then, his eyes widened. "Wait a minute. Wait just one minute." He shook a finger at Dash. "I recognize you! You're the tailor he's been asking about."

"Yes, sir."

"He wanted to know if I ever saw you with a fellow named Walter Müller, and I said I had. You two were arguing one night in front of your shop. It was a nasty thing. He called you all sorts of uncouth names. And then he fell, and you tried to help him." He lifted his chin. "I was the one who told you to get him off the street before he hurt someone. And you said it was more likely he'd hurt himself." His brow wrinkled. "Say, whatever happened to him?"

*Believe me,* Dash thought, *you don't want to know.*

Finn stepped forward. "Mr. Fraker. Peter. Or is it Pete?"

This caught the nervous man off guard. "I, err, um, Pete is fine."

"Wonderful! Pete, dearest, we are in a conundrum and only you can help us. Officer McElroy is trying to make our lives rather difficult."

"He tends to do that."

"Yes, he does! And to be perfectly frank, you telling him about the argument has put us in quite a bind."

Peter tilted his head slightly. "Did something bad happen to that German fellow?"

The images of that August night came rushing back to Dash. Overturned furniture slashed and tossed on their sides. The front door ripped off its hinges. A summer storm lashing the street outside, lightning popping like tabloid cameras. And there was Walter Müller, pistol in hand, barrel aimed at Dash's chest. Walter hadn't noticed that Prudence Meyers, the attorney whose law firm he had just ransacked, was creeping up behind him. She inched closer and closer with each lightning flash.

"*It takes strength to pull the trigger,*" Walter said to Dash.

Pru's response as she brought up her blue-steel Remington to Walter's temple was just as simple and to the point: "*You got that right, mister.*"

Walter's body jerked as if electrocuted. Blood, bone, and brain exploded from the side of his head . . .

"Did something happen to him?" Finn said, repeating Peter's question and rousing Dash from the memory. "How do I put this . . . ? You see . . . it's a bit complicated."

A lie finally sprang from Dash's lips. "Mr. Müller owes Officer McElroy sugar and is hiding to avoid false imprisonment, violence, or both."

"Oh. I see," Peter said. "And you know where he is? You

do, don't you! And Officer McElroy is trying to pressure you into giving up his location!"

His location was a potter's field after being tagged a John Doe.

Finn replied, "It's an oversimplification, Pete, but it'll do for tonight's purposes."

"Tonight's purposes? But—"

"Mr. Fraker," Dash said, "Officer McElroy has threatened us with charges of kidnapping, even murder, if we don't turn over Mr. Müller." The first part of his statement, to his credit, was the truth. "And now, with your, ah, eyewitness account, he has even more leverage to use against us."

Peter nodded slowly. "I *see*. Because I can put the two of you together. Yes, I can recognize what a situation I've put you in. Unfortunately, I don't know if I *can* recant. To tell the truth, I didn't even *want* to tell him. I absolutely loathe the man and told him I didn't know what on earth he was talking about. We Villagers need to stick together."

"A-woman," Finn replied.

Peter gave Finn a curious look, but continued. "But then he came back about a week later and he . . . he threatened me as well."

Dash and Finn flicked their eyes towards one another.

"Oh?" Dash said, stepping towards Peter. "What has he threatened you with?"

Peter's pale cheeks flushed red. "I don't see how that pertains."

"It might, if we can help you get out from under his thumb."

"After all," Finn added, "we bohemians need to stick together. You said so yourself."

"Yes, well. I—I—" Peter ran a hand over his brow, smearing the beads of sweat that had suddenly materialized across his forehead. "W-w-well you see, my wife's away for two months in Argentina and it's such a long time and the apartment is so quiet and I . . . oh damn it all, I made a mistake! I admit that, but McElroy, he—he"—Peter was full-on handwringing now— "he found out somehow, I guess he followed me to the hotel I liked to visit on occasion, and he photographed me and . . . another woman. In the lobby."

"Ah," Dash said.

"And going to the hotel room. And . . . leaving it. Together."

"I see."

"And McElroy said he could get the front desk's logbook."

Finn laid a hand across his own chest. "Please tell us you didn't use your own name."

Red patches now formed on Peter's neck. "I didn't think I had to! I've never really done anything like this before."

"Adultery 101, Petey, *always* use a fake name! Or at least someone else's. I myself use the name of a nasty priest who once told me I was going to hell. Ha! Not if god checks the registry at the Waldorf Astoria and sees Father Patrick O'Grady signing in with dozens of married—"

Dash interrupted. "Mr. Fraker, what was Officer McElroy's threat?"

Peter took a shaky breath. "McElroy threatened that he would turn those photographs over to my wife when she returns from Argentina and to my boss, who is very much on the straight and narrow and expects his employees to be as well." His panicked eyes flicked back and forth between Dash and Finn. "I'll be divorced, fired, and ruined! Ruined, I tell you! That's why I'm here, even though I don't want to be. He told me to stay in this room and to see no one. I couldn't very well tell him no, could I?"

Dash put on his friendliest smile. "Mr. Fraker, did Officer McElroy happen to mention where these photographs are?"

"No, only that he had them in his possession."

"I wonder . . ."

Finn narrowed his eyes. "Dearie, what are you scheming?"

Peter blew out a sigh. "What does it matter? None of us can do anything about this! I can't take back what I saw, and you can't turn over an innocent man to someone like Cullen McElroy."

*My dear boy,* Dash thought, *if you only knew how guilty Walter Müller truly was.*

"We might be able to assist you," he said slowly, as the idea began to take shape. "If McElroy no longer has the photographs, then he can't force you to say what you saw, correct?"

"I—I—well, I suppose he can't."

Dash turned to Finn. "Then the answer is simple. We'll just have to steal them."

Peter was aghast. "*Steal* them?!"

Finn grinned. "Oh, I do love a good theft. Dash here is a marvel with locks and I'm like a mouse, able to fit through any doorway or window, quick as you like."

"If we help you, Mr. Fraker," Dash said, "will you help us in return?"

Peter looked from Dash to Finn and back again. "If you can truly get rid of those photographs, then I'll—yes, yes, I'll help you." He clenched his jaw. "*Someone* must stop this man, this lousy, crooked no-account!"

"Good! Glad to hear that," Dash replied. He reached over and patted Peter's shoulder. "Not to worry, my friend.

We'll all soon be free of this misery." He glanced over at Finn. "It seems our good luck still holds."

A sharp knock rattled the door in its frame.

"Open up!" said a familiar voice.

The three of them all looked at each other, eyes wide with panic.

The voice belonged to McElroy.

## 3

Finn rolled his eyes at Dash. "You jinxed us, dearie."

Dash turned to Peter. "What's he doing here?"

"He said he'd check on me," Peter replied. "Throughout the day and night, to make sure I'm still here."

Dash checked his wristwatch. "This late? It's nearly midnight."

"Open up, Fraker!" called McElroy through the door.

Finn muttered, "You should've left when you had the chance."

Peter panicked. "Where could I go? He'd certainly find me again! And he'd make my life worse, much, *much* worse."

"He's right, Finn," Dash said.

The door rattled again, McElroy getting angrier by the second. "Fraker! Ya better not be playing me any tricks or you're gonna regret it!" Another fierce round of knocking. "Don't make me break the goddamn door down!"

Dash looked to Finn. "We've got to get out of here."

Finn agreed. "Fire escape. Behind you."

Dash turned on his heel and saw a narrow window cut

into the far wall. He hoped they wouldn't find the sash painted shut.

He squeezed past Finn and unlocked the window. The sash squeaked its way upwards, and cold, damp air rushed inside like flood water. The metal fire escape tacked its way downwards three floors to the darkened alleyway below.

He started angling his body into the window and out onto the fire escape. He held his breath, hoping the contraption would stay bolted to the side of the building. One never knew when and where the landlords skimped on their building "improvements." The metal vibrated but withstood his weight.

Finn, quick as a whisper, crawled through the window after him.

Dash glanced back inside. "Close the window and give us to the count of ten and then open the door," he said to Peter. "Tell him you took a sleeping powder and were dead to the world."

The meek man nodded and pushed down the sash.

"Let's go, Finn."

They made quick work of the fire escape. On the second floor, there was a ladder that should've been able to drop into the alley below with the pull of a lever. After a few tries, it was clear to Dash that the lever was rusted stuck.

"Goddess-damn this city," Finn breathed.

Dash glanced upwards. Two shadows crisscrossed in front of the window. Peter and McElroy, probably having an argument. No one was looking out the window and down at them—not yet.

"Forget the ladder," Dash said. "Jump!"

Dash lowered himself into the hole where the ladder would've dropped, gripping the bottom of the fire escape before dangling his body below. It was only a three-, maybe four-foot fall, but it still gave his heart a lurch. He landed on his feet, bending his knees like his older brother taught him.

He backed away and let Finn drop as well.

"That was a close one," Dash said, helping Finn stand upright.

"You got that right."

That was when a throat suddenly cleared behind them.

Dash and Finn both jumped, startled.

They nervously eyed one another before slowly turning around.

A large man stood only a few feet away from them, dimly light by the second-floor windows. Tall and big, with a shaved head, his broad shoulders and large biceps strained against his white shirt and black vest. Thick hips and thighs threatened to tear his wool trousers. He had an elongated oval for a face with thin brows arching high over dark eyes and a large nose made slightly askew by a bump in its center. A long cigar smoldered in his hand.

"Didn't mean to startle you," the man said, his voice deep as timber while his lilting accent caressed his words. Not European. Tropical. The West Indies, perhaps?

"Our apologies," Dash replied, getting his breathing under control.

The man pointed at the fire escape with his cigar. "Is there a fire?"

Dash looked up to where the man pointed. "Fire? Oh no, no. No fire. We—we're sneaking out."

"Sneaking out? Why? It's not a prison."

Finn jumped in. "Our captain is in the lobby, making sure we don't get into trouble." His voice turned coy. "I trust you'll keep our little secret? It's just hitting a speak before we spend the next six weeks at sea. You know what they say about 'all work and no play.' Good evening, sir."

"Good evening," Dash repeated.

They turned away from the man.

"Wait a moment!"

Dash and Finn stopped, looking over their shoulders.

The man stepped towards them. His brow furrowed, then brightened. "Finn?"

Finn turned around to face the man, tilting his head to the side like a cockatoo. "Borden?"

The man's thick lips spread into a smile, revealing bright white teeth. "Finn . . . Francis, yes? It is so good to see you!"

Dash watched as Borden spread his large arms and engulfed Finn in a hug that lifted him off the ground. His friend nearly disappeared inside the large man's embrace. Borden laughed, a joyful snuffling sound, before setting Finn back onto his feet. They parted, Borden all smiles, Finn all blush.

"B-B-Borden," Finn said. "What on earth are you doing here?"

"My ship is here for the week. What about you? What trouble are you into?"

Dash couldn't help but smile, which caused Finn to wag a finger at him.

"Not one word," Finn said to Dash. He looked to Borden. "Dearie, we're not up to anything. Honest!"

"Honest? Yes, yes, telling me tales about sneaking out the back. Don't think I've forgotten that you've a talent for courting mischief."

"Not my fault mischief is more fun. Then again, you know all about that, don't you?"

*Not now, Finn,* Dash thought before hearing a window

sash squeak above them and McElroy's voice braying, "I heard ya lift and close this thing! Who was out here, Fraker?"

Peter's meek voice replied, "I—I was just getting some air."

Dash said, "Finn, I believe we should stay out of view of a certain window." He nodded his chin towards a space on the brick wall of the building that was bathed mostly in shadow.

Without a word, Finn pressed himself against it.

Dash did the same, keeping his face averted. He didn't dare look up, which would risk showing McElroy who he was.

"Mr. Borden, is it?" he said over his shoulder. "Can you tell us if someone is in a third-floor window looking down at the alley?"

Thankfully, Borden didn't question the request.

Dash heard an intake of breath.

"Yes, there is. Big fellow with a round face?"

Both Dash and Finn cursed.

McElroy's voice rang out. "You! You there!"

Dash's heart leapt up into his throat.

"Did you see anyone come down?"

Dash heard Borden reply, "Are you talking to me?"

"No, I'm talking to President Coolidge. Yes, I'm talking to you! You're the only one standing there! You see anyone come down from this fire escape?"

Borden paused.

Dash held his breath, preparing himself to run as fast as he could if Borden gave them up.

Borden exhaled, and Dash smelled the tarry smoke of the cigar. "No, sir. All I've seen tonight is you poking your head out, trying to wake everyone up."

"Uh, huh. You stay there! I'll be right down."

Dash made a move to go, but Borden murmured, "Be still. He won't fit through that window."

McElroy's struggling voice hissed a series of curses and epithets that echoed throughout the alley. Agonizing minutes passed, yet Dash didn't hear any heavy footsteps on the metal fire escape, only more growled profanities.

Another window sash squeaked above them, and a second voice joined the fray.

"Will you knock it off?! Some of us are trying to sleep!"

McElroy growled, "Don't talk that way to me, sonny. I'm an officer of the law."

"Oh yeah? Well, I'm an Officer of Shut-The-Fuck-Up."

"Why you—"

A third window went up. "Will you two keep it down?"

"It ain't me, it's this loudmouth so-called officer of the law!"

"I don't care if it's Jesus Christ—"

"I'll arrest the both of ya's if you don't show me the proper respect!"

The three men argued for a bit before McElroy—presumably failing to crawl out of the narrow bedroom window—shouted a series of expletives. A window sash slammed down hard and rattled in its frame.

The second voice said, "Uh, huh. Officer of the law, my ass."

The third voice replied, "Can it, will ya?"

"Yeah, yeah, yeah."

The other two windows closed.

Borden said, "They're all gone."

Dash and Finn left their places on the brick wall.

Dash turned and looked up at Borden. "Thank you, sir."

Finn added, "Yes, thank you, dearie."

"You don't have much time," Borden replied. "He'll be down here soon."

Dash looked at either ends of the alleyway. "What's the fastest way out of here?"

Borden pointed with his cigar to Dash's left. "I would go that way."

"Let's ankle, Finn." Dash set off in the direction showed by Borden.

Finn stayed put, causing Dash to halt himself.

"Borden?" Finn said. "There's a man in room 3C by the name of Peter Fraker, though he's on the logbooks as Jonah Collins. If you could keep an eye on him for us, I would be forever grateful."

Borden frowned. "Who's this man?"

"No one like *that,* I assure you," Finn replied quickly. "Just someone we need to keep safe."

Dash hissed, "We have to go!"

Borden took forever considering this request before nodding. "For you, Finn, I will."

Dash tried to push off again, but was once more held back by Finn.

"And it should go without saying that if anyone asks, you never saw us, savvy?"

Borden crossed his arms over his enormous chest, making his rounded biceps swell even more. "That depends."

Dash muttered his own string of curses that rivaled the ones McElroy spat into the alleyway.

Finn turned coy. "Depends on what?"

"Do I get to see you again?"

Dash didn't think it possible for Finn to blush any harder, but here he was, watching his friend's face turn the same shade as a tomato.

Finn stammered a few incomprehensible words before Dash said, "Of course you will. Say goodbye, Finn."

Finn barely got the words out before Dash yanked on his arm, pulling him away from Borden. They ran like bandits down the alley.

"Where the *bloody* hell have ya been?"

Dash and Finn had returned to their block on West Fourth Street between Sixth and Seventh Avenues. He was reasonably certain they hadn't been seen or followed by McElroy. Or anyone else, for that matter. They had just passed Jones, one of two tiny streets that dead-ended into West Fourth, when Joe O'Shaughnessy came into view and his booming voice called out to them.

"Evening, Joe," Dash replied, walking up.

Joe stood on the darkened stoop of their speakeasy's front, a tailor shop called Hartford & Sons. Both of his hands rested on hips tightly clad in brown trousers. Even in the darkness, Dash could sense the man's features: fiery red hair falling in tumbles around a red-stubbled face; emerald eyes glinting like jewels; broad shoulders and wide chest straining against his white work shirt; solid torso pulling his brown suspenders taut. Despite the autumn chill, Joe had his sleeves rolled up. Dash knew once he was close enough, he'd see those naked forearms covered, like the rest of Joe's body, in flaming red hair.

Joe continued his tirade. "First, ya don't even take me wit' ya to the goddamned Sailor Society or whatever. Then, ya take yer sweet time gettin' back, leavin' me wonderin' if somethin' bad happened to ya."

*Ah, we're in that mood tonight,* Dash thought.

Joe's brogue became the thickest when he was agitated.

"Apologies," Dash said. "Things didn't quite go as planned tonight."

Finn came to his defense. "And before you give yourself a heart attack, O'Shaughnessy, we found our witness *and* discovered a way for him to lose his memory."

"Not to mention that Finn here might rekindle an old flame."

"Quiet, you!"

Dash laughed in response.

The two of them stood in front of Joe, who was not amused.

"I'm glad ya both had a swell time. Not only did ya worry me, but then Atty didn't show up and I couldn't open the bloody club. Had to spend all night on this stoop turnin' blokes away."

It took a moment for Dash to comprehend the message. He looked past Joe and gave his shop the once-over. The placard announced HARTFORD & SONS TAILOR and the two large windows surrounded the front door, same as always. The left window held a display of men's suits; the right showcased a sewing machine. Atticus Delucci, their club's lookout, should've been sitting behind it.

Atty's job was to do the alterations Dash measured for during the day. This gave the illusion that Hartford & Sons was a legitimate tailor shop while also providing some extra spending sugar for the four men. He was also to listen for the secret knock on the shop's front door.

Those who knew it were let inside, so they could walk over to the changing area mirror to push it open and enter the club hidden behind it, a "degenerate" speak called Pinstripes. Those who didn't know the knock were told to get lost. And anyone who flashed a badge caused Atty to press a button wired into the side of the sewing table. A red light would flash inside the club, indicating a possible raid.

Atty was essential to Pinstripes's operation, which was why Dash understood Joe's decision not to open the club tonight.

"Something's wrong," he said. "Atty has never missed a shift before."

"Only that time he got ill from eating those clams," Finn corrected.

"Yes, but he *told* us he would not make it." Dash looked at Joe. "Did he leave any messages for us?"

Joe shook his head. "Nothin' slipped under the door here or at the apartment."

"That's not like him."

"To be fair," Finn said, "he's not the sharpest tool in the shed."

"He's not inconsiderate. Atty may not be a lot of things—"

"An excellent shot, a snappy dresser, a quick study—"

"Finney," Joe warned.

"—but loyal and dependable," Dash continued, "he is. Do we know where he lives?"

Joe nodded. "Aye, in the Latin Quarter on the Lower East Side."

Finn said, "They don't say 'Latin' anymore, Joe. They say 'Italian.'"

"For the love of Mary—Latin is wha' they bloody spoke

in bloody Rome, which, in case ya didn't know, is *in* bloody Italy!"

Dash stepped in before the two could escalate their argument. "Let's pay him a visit to make sure everything's Jake."

Finn was aggrieved. "At this hour?"

Joe, for once, agreed with Finn. "Finney's right, me boy. It's almost one o'clock in the mornin'. Too late to go knockin' on doors. He'd probably think we're burglars and shoot with tha' bloody pistol o' his."

"And with our luck, he'd hit something for once," Finn said. "And while I'm looking forward to the day when I meet all the goddesses, I'm not in any hurry to do so."

"And whatever caused him to miss his shift, lassie, we won't be able to do anything about it tonight."

"Especially if he's dead."

Joe smacked Finn on the shoulder. "Tha's not gonna help calm Dash's nerves one bit!"

"I was *trying* to illustrate that there's nothing that can be done!"

"For cryin' out loud—I oughtta wring yer neck."

Dash held up a hand. "Gents, please." He let out a slow breath. "Alright, I concede, *but* I will head over there first thing tomorrow morning before I open the shop."

Joe patted his shoulder. "I'm sure he's fine. Probably ate more bad clams."

Finn shook his head. "You'd think he'd learn after the last time. I told him, 'Atty, dear, if the little lumps are still gray, avoid them like Times Square.'" With a flutter of his hand, Finn changed the subject. "Enough about that. Let us in, Joe, and pour us something strong. We need to figure out how to steal some photographs."

Joe squinted. "Steal wha' now?"

The next morning, Dash quietly dressed in a bright blue pinstripe suit he accentuated with a red-and-blue plaid bow tie.

*How patriotic of me*, he thought.

He grabbed a light gray fedora and an umbrella and left a snoring Joe in their cramped, dusty bedroom. He passed by a mewing Finn on a rollaway bed in their hallway—which, according to their landlord, was the "guest bedroom." It wasn't even the most absurd thing Dash had heard a landlord claim.

He exited a door next to the Cherry Lane Playhouse entrance on Commerce Street, taking in his surroundings. Another gray, cloudy day thanks to the remnants of a hurricane that hit Cuba and had been stumbling up the coast. It seemed to Dash it had rained at least once a day every day this month. Leftover hurricanes, sudden storms, and good old-fashioned downpours. He was sorely tired of wet trouser cuffs, grimy shoes, ineffectual raincoats, and dripping umbrellas.

He glanced back at his home.

Their "two-bedroom" apartment was above the Playhouse, with Dash and Joe's bedroom wall backing up against the dressing rooms. They were often treated to the show's constant melodramas: the perceived slights and jealousies, the sabotages and backstabbings, the hot-blooded lust and secret affairs—especially the affairs. The lead of the most recent show, a cad named Reggie, had been working his way through all the women (and some men) in the cast. Even Finn had a turn! If the show itself had had half the plot points onstage as it did off, it might've sold better than it did. As it was, the show closed, leaving behind a rare peace.

Until the next one, that is.

Glancing around their quiet, narrow street, Dash removed the Playhouse's skeleton key from his pocket. Finn had kept it from the days when he and Reggie were fooling around. (Apparently, one of Reggie's favorite spots to make whoopee was the box office.) The torrid details Finn espoused were immaterial save for one: he and Reggie, during a vigorous bout of lovemaking, knocked over and almost broke the box office's telephone.

The telephone was what Dash wanted.

Last night in Pinstripes, the three of them believed McElroy had three options to hide the evidence of poor Peter Fraker's act of adultery: a bank vault, a safe deposit box, or McElroy's own apartment.

If it was the first two, they were sunk.

If it was the last option, they were in business.

Just one problem: they didn't know where McElroy lived. And it wasn't just their own ignorance. They'd been asking around the Village for the officer's address, thinking they could follow him to his witnesses. No dice. No one in their neighborhood had a clue where McElroy laid his greasy head to sleep.

Hence the need for a telephone.

Dash took one more look around. He seemed to have this end of Commerce all to himself. He walked to a small door under the Playhouse awning, inserted the key, and entered. One more door and one more lock, and he was inside the tiny box office.

The room was dark, the shades drawn, covering the front window and shielding Dash from passersby. A calendar of forthcoming shows hung from the wall, including yet another version of Charles Dickens's *A Christmas Carol*.

"Great," Dash muttered to himself. "We'll be hearing 'bah-humbugs' incessantly for the next two months."

A narrow desk with drawers stood underneath the glass window, where the teller would take payments and issue tickets. On the right side of the desk laid a small notebook notating ticket tallies. On the left side of the desk stood the telephone, a tall, black contraption that looked to Dash like an iron daffodil. He picked it up and had the operator connect him to McElroy's precinct. A bored male voice answered the phone.

"Hello there," Dash said into the receiver, using his best stuffy, bureaucratic voice. "Can I speak to Personnel?"

"What's your name? What's your purpose?"

"Max Bennett," Dash replied, using his common alias, which was his older brother's first and middle names. The two hadn't spoken in years since the family found out Dash's nature, and Dash reveled in using his pompous brother's names in all sorts of illegal activities. "I work for Lowry Properties, doing a check on a potential tenant. Tenant says he works for the NYPD, and I need to verify his employment."

"Hold, please."

Dash held.

Eventually, the line picked up.

"Personnel," said a nasal female voice.

Dash repeated his speech.

"What's the name?"

"Cullen McElroy. M-C-E-L-R-O-Y."

"Hold, please."

The line crackled while he waited.

"Yes, he works here. You want dates of employment?"

"Sure, why not?"

"He's been on street patrol at this precinct from February 14, 1922, to present October 25, 1926."

"Will ya look at that? He started on Valentine's Day. Bet he's a love."

The woman sputtered a laugh. "Wouldn't count on it. None of 'em are worth the salt on the street. And this one was a transfer. Used to be in midtown working in the detectives' bureau."

"Detective? And now he's on foot patrol? Sounds like a demotion."

"You didn't hear that from me. Anything else?"

"Yeah, what's his latest address?"

"He didn't put it down on the form?"

"It appears not."

"Must've forgot. He's on Downing Street." She gave Dash the building and apartment numbers.

Dash reached over to the small notebook of ticket tallies and tore off a blank page. With a pencil found in one of the desk drawers, he scratched down the address.

"Thank you so much," he said. "You're a peach."

"Mind your manners, mister. I'm a tomato, the juiciest, plumpest on the vine and don't you forget it."

Dash laughed as he hung up the receiver, pleased with himself. He returned the telephone and the notebook to their rightful places and left the office and then the Playhouse proper, locking up both behind him. He accomplished one part of their plan. Now they needed to determine how easy it would be to break into McElroy's apartment, which called for a little surveillance.

But first, Dash must pay a visit to Atty. A small pang of worry twisted in his gut. He sincerely hoped nothing terrible had happened to his friend.

## 5

"Yo, mister," the cabbie said, "am I letting ya off on the corner?"

A crosstown cab was expensive, but Dash didn't want to solve the calculus problem of using public transportation to get from the Village to Little Italy. (The Sixth Avenue el times the Houston line divided by the Third Avenue el raised to the second power because of inevitable delays and pocket-picking transfers, now solve for x.) Forget that. He made straight Cs in math.

He leaned forward on the cab's bench seat. "The corner's Jake."

The cabbie pulled off to the side of Hester and Bowery. He glanced back as Dash counted out the fare. "Did you hear that old Reverend Ed was passing love notes to Eleanor using the church's hymnals?" Even the cab drivers were up to date on the Hall-Mills case.

Dash nodded. "They found a bunch of those love letters strewn all over the crime scene, if I recall."

"That should be enough to incriminate Mrs. Hall right there. Crime of passion. I've been saying that ever since they found the bodies. Ya don't shoot a man and his mistress and then try to take her head off unless you're seriously angry."

"That's an understatement."

"And a woman who's being cheated on? Mister, I've seen nothing scarier. A pal of mine made that mistake and when she found out, she threw his mother's vase at his head! He barely ducked in time before it shattered on their bedroom wall."

"Oh, my."

"She made her point, though. He stopped dallying, and she got rid of, and I quote, 'that hideous vase from your insufferable mother.'"

"Two birds with one throw. Keep the change, my friend."

"Thanks! You need me to stick around?"

Dash shook his head. "No need."

The Third Avenue elevated trains roared and rumbled as he stepped out of his cab. A shower of orange sparks fell to the street below in sudden, bright bursts. Dash's grandfather once told him that in the old days of New York, when the trains were steam, the hot embers from the coal-fed stoves would float down to the pedestrians, setting the occasional suit or dress on fire. Now New Yorkers had to watch for the sparks of a train slamming on its brakes or squealing around a curve. Dash wondered what these Italian immigrants first thought when they saw these daily firework displays in an iron city full of flash and noise.

A pungent, burning odor offended his nose. Was there a fire somewhere? He glanced around. Nothing was blackening the cloudy sky. Perhaps it was from the tracks—sometimes the wheels on rails created that hot, metallic smell—but this seemed different.

Dash shrugged off the thought and turned to face the building overlooking the tracks. According to Joe, Atty lived above the hardware store. A narrow, unmarked doorway stood just off to the right of the store's entrance. Dash strolled up to it and pressed the buzzer.

It took two tries for Atty to answer.

He looked the worse for wear. The short, balding man built like a boxer looked defeated in the harsh morning light. Muscles sagged in his white undershirt. His brown trousers had a patch on the left knee, and his suspenders trailed after him like a bridal train.

When Atty saw Dash, his eyes first widened with panic, then drooped into a resigned wariness.

"Hiya, Boss," he said.

"Good morning, Atty."

"I can explain 'bout why I wasn't at the door last night."

"Atty—"

"I apologize. It won't happen again."

"Atty—"

"It's just that something happened two nights ago, and I had to take care of a few things, and I didn't have the time to send word. That's all. I'm sorry, Boss."

Dash gave what he hoped was an understanding smile. "Atty, it's Jake, whatever it is. But you had us worried. Are you alright?"

Atty looked off to the side, contemplating his answer. His face darkened and his hands clenched into fists.

"Atty, you can tell me. I'm more than your boss—at least, I hope I am. But something is clearly troubling you and if I can help . . . ?"

One of Atty's hands unfurled, and he rubbed his face with an open palm. A mighty sniff followed.

*Was he crying?* Dash thought with alarm.

"Boss," Atty said with great effort. "There was a fire last night. My brother and his family, they lived in the building."

*That was a fire I smelled!*

Dash's heart sunk. "Oh, Atty."

"The children made it out, and my brother wasn't there, thank God, but his wife Maria? Their mother? She . . ." He couldn't finish the sentence. He shook his head and took a shaky breath. "Who would burn down a building full of people, Boss? Full of families? Innocent people just going about their lives. And poor Maria trapped in it when it came . . . when it came . . . " A sob threatened to break through, but he sniffed it back. "My brother and my niece and nephews, they're staying with me now. They've lost everything. The entire building burned to the ground before those useless firemen could do anything. Why the hell couldn't they get the water on? Huh? Much as we pay in this damn city, why the hell don't it work?"

Dash reached out and placed a hand on Atty's shoulder. "I am so sorry."

"Thank youse, Boss." Atty looked down at his untied shoes. "I'll be there tonight, though. I promise."

"Atty. If you need to take some time, I can watch the door myself."

"I appreciate that, Boss, but we both know you can't operate that sewing machine, and I—I needs the money."

"I'll pay you, regardless."

A firm hand went up. "No. We Deluccis carry our weight, we don't let nobody carry it for us."

Dash was about to argue with him, but then thought better of it. "Is there anything you need?"

Atty considered the request. "There is—" His throat was too tight. He cleared it. "My brother, he's broken by this. He's not thinking clearly. He's saying crazy things, things I don't understand, and now he's locked himself in the bedroom. I can't get him to come out. I'm worried about him. Can youse get him to come out? Maybe . . . maybe youse know the words to say that I don't."

Dash considered the request and thought of the nail files he always kept with him. "Or failing that, my friend, I can always pick the lock."

Atty's apartment featured rounded archways, dusty walls, and cracked plaster ceilings. Cheap wooden furniture crowded the corners and clogged the floors—creaky chairs, slanted bookcases, and chipped side tables surrounded a dusty sofa, a bunched-up rug, and a heavy wood coffee table. Two windows overlooked the elevated tracks, and the entire room shook whenever the trains roared by in irregular intervals.

In the center of the room slumped two small boys, still in their nightshirts, on the sofa. In the far corner sat a young man with long hair dressed in a tan suit much too large for him, perched on a wooden chair and staring out the window. All three had white bandages on their hands.

"These are my nephews." Atty nodded to the boys. "The youngest is Rocco, the oldest is Emiliano."

Dash tipped his hat. "Hello, gentlemen. I'm Dash Parker."

"He's Uncle Atty's boss, boys. At the tailor shop." Atty glanced meaningfully at Dash, who got the hint and nodded. No speak talk allowed in here.

Rocco and Emiliano's dark brown eyes, wide and frightened, gazed up at him. Their faces still bore the remnants of the fire, ashy thumbprints on their olive-tinted cheeks. Their dark hair curled in identical waves, the strands curving into a single question mark in the center of each of their foreheads. They sat next to each other, arms intertwined, afraid to let go.

Rocco and Emiliano simply nodded, murmuring a faint "*ciao*" before turning away from him and Atty.

Atty gestured to the young man by the window. "And that's my niece Isabella."

Dash did a double take. She turned her head, and the young man suddenly morphed into a young woman before his very eyes. Of course. If they lost everything, that would include her own nightgowns and dresses, and Atty, a single man, wouldn't have anything other than suits. Dash recognized the one Isabella wore, for he measured it himself.

He stepped forward. "Dash Parker, miss. I am profoundly sorry for your loss."

Her hair was like her brothers', dark and curly. Her face was unadorned, her cheeks having the same rich glow as her brothers. Dark brows furrowed over bright blue eyes, a jolting surprise given the dark browns of her brothers' and her uncle's. They blazed with intelligence as they took Dash in.

When she spoke, her voice was a hoarse croak—damaged from the smoke. "*Grazie.*"

Dash looked over at Atty and said, "And your brother? Where is he?"

Atty raised his chin to Dash's left. "Donte is in there."

Dash turned and saw a narrow hallway leading to a closed door. He walked towards it, the uneven floorboards creaking and groaning. He placed his ear against the wood and heard faint whimpering; the words shapeless, but the meaning crystal clear. Grief. Sadness. Loss.

He gently knocked.

The whimpering stopped.

"Mr. Delucci?"

Silence.

"Mr. Delucci, my name is Dash Parker. I'm a friend of Atticus. He works with me at the tailor shop. He wanted me to talk to you."

A floorboard groaned behind the door. "What do you want?"

"To talk."

Another floorboard groaned. "I have nothing to say to you!"

"That's all right," Dash said. "You don't have to talk if you don't want to. But Atty and I would like it if you opened the door."

"No!"

The sharpness of the word caught Dash by surprise. This man wasn't just in mourning, he was afraid. But of what?

Another train clattered in front of the apartment, its wheels squealing and hissing on the metal rails. Dash waited until it passed before saying, "No one else is here besides us."

What sound was that? Dash squinted. Was it weeping? Yes, yes, it was. Childlike weeping, uncontrolled and unabashed. There was a small thud against the door; Donte slumping against it.

His next words were sloppy and wet. "She said it wasn't her! He said it wasn't real!"

Dash turned his head slightly to the side. What was this man talking about?

"Who did, Mr. Delucci? Who told you these things?"

More sobs. A scratching sound against the door

suggested Donte was sliding down against it towards the floor.

"Mr. Delucci, please open up."

The sobs abruptly stopped. Anger this time. "No! No, you stay out of here! You stay away! Everyone, stay away!"

Dash glanced back at Atty, whose face creased with concern. He returned his attention to the door, pulling out his two narrow nail files. If this was like every other apartment door lock, then it would be a simple bolt. Wordlessly, Dash bent down and inserted the first nail file into the lock to tension the bolt. He then angled in the second nail file to push up the lever in the back of the lock.

"Who taught you that?" Atty murmured.

"My brother," Dash murmured back, keeping his voice low.

"He taught you how to pick *locks*?"

Dash raised a finger to his lips, his head tilting towards the door, indicating Donte might overhear them.

"What are you doing out there?" called Donte.

"We were just conversing, Mr. Delucci," Dash called in response. He then raised his voice to cover the sounds of his second nail file scraping against the lever in the back of the lock. "I understand you're frightened and that this is a terrible time for you and your family. But you must be strong for your children. They need their father now. They are as alone and as scared as you are."

Why was this lock being so damn difficult?

He continued pressing the nail files against the interiors of the lock's mechanism. "You can face this. Your brother is here to help, right, Atty?"

Atty spoke up. "He speaks the truth, Donte. Family protects family."

*Almost there.*

Dash worked the instruments some more until he heard the telltale *click* of the lever finally being undone. The sound was so loud that it reverberated down the hallway. Surely Donte heard it. Rustling followed by the moaning floorboards confirmed it.

"Keep away!" Donte warned.

Dash used the nail file that tensioned the bolt to slide it back, unlocking the door.

Atty crept to Dash's side.

"Mr. Delucci," Dash said, pocketing the nail files and standing up. "We're coming inside. It is all right."

"Stay back!"

Dash muttered under his breath to Atty, "Be ready for anything."

"Yes, Boss."

Dash turned the knob and pushed the bedroom door open.

The room was thick with shadow, and there was no sign of Donte.

Dash called out his name once more before taking cautious steps through the doorway.

Another damnable train roared by, nearly masking the animal-like scream coming from his right.

Dash turned just in time to see a figure lunge at him from the shadows.

## 6

The figure held a large brass lamp above his head and aimed it at Dash's skull.

Dash reached up and seized the lamp base. The lamp's electrical cord whipped past his face, barely missing his cheek. He yelled over the screeching train for Atty as he held onto the lamp.

Atty ducked underneath Dash and grabbed the man's torso.

Dash found purchase with his back foot and tried to push back against the forward motion of the lamp.

The man's mouth was open in a primordial battle cry, his lips pulled back, exposing gray teeth and blood-red gums.

The elevated train hissed and roared around them.

Atty was speaking into the man's ear, but Dash couldn't hear over the el. Dash saw Atty keep one arm around the man's chest while he reached up with his other hand and gripped the man's jaw. He turned the man's face until those crazed eyes were looking into his.

The force behind the lamp relented. Dash took advantage of the opportunity and lowered the blunt brass instrument, so it was no longer aimed at his head.

The elevated train clattered away from the apartment, the ear-splitting squeal and hiss fading into the distance.

Atty's voice murmured, but the pounding of Dash's heart in his ears masked the words. His breaths came out in short, panicked bursts.

He swallowed. "Donte Delucci, I presume?"

Atty looked over his shoulder and nodded.

Dash took the lamp away from Donte's hands and set it safely on the ground. He glanced to the side, seeing the three children staring at them from the other end of the short hallway. Rocco's and Emiliano's faces were white with fear, but Isabella's face was dark with disgust.

"Everything is Jake now," he said, his breathing slowing.

Isabella turned on her heel, pointedly giving them her back, and stormed off. Rocco and Emiliano paused for a second before they followed their sister.

Atty continued to mutter soothing words while Donte stammered incomprehensibly.

Dash steadied himself before closing the door. He turned to see Atty slowly moving Donte backwards to a wrought iron bed. A framed picture of the Madonna hung overhead. The empty bedside nightstand caught Dash's attention, and he bent down to pick up the lamp.

"Nightstand?" he asked Atty, who nodded.

Dash returned the lamp to its rightful place as Atty gingerly set Donte down onto the bed, the metal springs squeaking. Dash got to his knees and searched the baseboards for an electrical plug. He found it and made use of it. The resulting jaundiced light did little to dispel the dank darkness in the room.

As Dash returned to his feet, an anxious thought prickled his scalp. "Where's your pistol, Atty?"

"Bottom drawer of the nightstand, Boss."

Dash opened the bottom drawer and found the gray metal of the Smith & Wesson. Thank goodness Donte hadn't found this; otherwise, they'd have had a different situation on their hands.

He lifted the pistol from its hiding place and opened the chamber, removing the bullets one by one. He handed everything to Atty, saying, "Keep this away from him."

"Youse got it, Boss." Atty placed the weaponry in his pockets.

Dash flicked a look at Donte. There wasn't much family resemblance, other than the bald spots. Whereas Atty kept his black hair cropped short, Donte left his long, resulting in flyaway patches. His triangle-shaped face held a gray pallor to it, the skin sagging around the mouth and wrinkling around the eyes. A dark stubble flecked with white covered his jawline. He wore only a white undershirt, like Atty, and black trousers. His bare feet were pale and crumpled underneath thin, hairless ankles. Fumes of unbrushed teeth and unwashed bodies tainted the air.

"Atty," Dash said. "Does he have a gun as well?"

Atty looked up, puzzled. "I don't know."

Dash searched the top drawer of the nightstand, finding nothing. He went to the closet and opened the door. "Which suit is his?"

Atty looked over his shoulder. "That gray one in the center."

Dash searched the pockets, finding in one a small loaded pistol.

*Thank Heavens he didn't get to this either.*

Dash removed the bullets and placed the weapon in his

own pocket. He continued searching, discovering two other items: a playing card and a folded-up piece of paper.

He held the first item up to the light. No, not a playing card. A tarot card. Used by spiritualists for reading fortunes or some such. The illustration was incredibly vivid. A figure drawn in bright orange and yellow sported a crown of horns, menacing eyes, and a beckoning smile. The entire image promised wicked, lascivious delights which a man might later regret.

A devil.

On either side of the figure were two nymphs kneeling before him, under his control and doing his bidding.

Why did Donte have this?

Dash then unfolded the piece of paper, wondering if it would provide an answer. He stared at the page. It was a letter of some sort made out to "*Signore Donte Delucci*." The ink was smudged and blurry in most places, all the words in Italian, which Dash couldn't make heads or tails of it. The only word he recognized was a name: "*Capellos*." Must've been referencing a family, Dash thought. Seemed ordinary, nay pedestrian, except for the signature.

At the bottom of the page was a crudely drawn hand holding a sharp, pointy dagger.

This was a threat.

Dash held up the letter. "Who's this from?"

Donte rose so fast that Dash hardly registered the motion.

"Thief!" he shouted, spittle flying. "Thief! Going through my things! That's none of your business, none of your business!"

He marched over to Dash and snatched the letter from his hands. "You get outta here! You hear me! Get outta here!"

Atty grabbed Donte by the shoulders and tried to pull him away.

Dash held up his hands in a gesture of defeat. "Alright, Mr. Delucci, alright! I'll leave." He flicked a questioning eye to Atty, who subtly nodded. "Yes, I'll leave. Atty, if you need anything, anything at all, please let me know."

"I will, Boss."

Dash reached into his pocket and removed Donte's pistol. "Should you hang onto this? Or shall I?"

"That's mine!" Donte cried, attempting another lunge at Dash.

Atty grimaced as he held Donte back. "Take it for now, Boss. I can't keep track of two of 'em."

Donte's voice was hysterical with fear. "No! No! I must protect my family!"

"Donte!" Atty said, trying to calm his brother. "Donte! I will protect them. I will."

Donte's anger dissolved into tears. Atty moved his brother back to the bed.

Dash straightened his lapels and his tie. "I'll return it when you're feeling better, Mr. Delucci. I promise."

He looked down at the floor and saw the tarot card. It must've fallen during the minor scuffle with Donte. He pocketed it and left the bedroom.

In the front room, Emiliano and Rocco were back to being intertwined with one another on the couch. Isabella was nowhere to be seen.

Dash said to the boys, "Your father is a little upset, but he'll calm down."

The two young boys were silent.

Dash replied, "You're in excellent hands with your Uncle Atty—" But before he could finish the sentence, another train arrived. The floors shook, and the furniture rattled.

It was just as well. What could Dash say that wasn't trite?

He tipped his hat to the two boys and left the apartment with the train screeching all around him. It was then that Dash finally realized how close he came to being clobbered to death. A sickening turn-of-the-stomach gave way to a burst of white-hot anger. Just what the hell was Donte thinking?! He could've killed his own brother, much less a perfect stranger!

By the time Dash went down the stairs and out the front door, his anger subsided, and the iron banshee mercifully passed.

Two people replaced the screeching and screaming with arguing.

A hoarse voice yelled in rapid Italian.

"Hey!" a second barked in return. "You don't get to talk to me like that, Bella. You *owe* us!"

Dash called out, "What seems to be the trouble here?"

The voices stopped.

Dash took stock of the scene in front of him. Leaning against the building with her arms crossed was Isabella, her face set in a deep scowl. Standing in front of her was a thin, almost sickly looking young man with his hands in his pockets, looking entirely too at ease.

The young man turned and sneered at Dash. "Who are you?"

"I'm a friend of someone who lives here. And I don't think he or his neighbors would appreciate this ruckus." Dash was painfully aware he'd slipped into his "Father Voice," as coined by his late younger sister. It came out whenever Dash dealt with a stressful situation.

*Terrifying that I have even an ounce of bluenose within me.*

Dash raised his chin. "If you'd like to tell me what this is all about—"

"It ain't about nothing, mister. Just me and her negotiating."

Dash regarded the boy. "Weasel-faced" was the first descriptor that came to mind. Sunken cheeks, pointed nose, bony jaw. Yellow teeth hid behind thin, bloodless lips. He wore a dark suit with the tie undone. The fabric thinned considerably at the elbows and the knees, promising patches in the future.

"I see," Dash said. "And what do you want with her?"

Those bloodless lips sneered. "To take her out."

"Why?"

"I want to."

Dash shook his head. "Not good enough, my young friend."

"She's got a debt to pay. And I'm gonna collect."

Isabella growled a curse at him.

Dash stepped closer, situating himself between the two. He kept his eyes on the boy. "What is your name?"

"None of your beeswax!"

Isabella replied behind him, "His name is Vito Beneventi. And he's dogshit on a shoe."

Vito laughed, amused at her insult. He said to Dash, "She's a lively one, ain't she? Pretty too, even if she dresses and sounds like a boy right now."

Isabella's face flushed.

"Mr. Beneventi," Dash said. "The Delucci family is in mourning. This is an inappropriate time to try courtship. Perhaps you can be on your way."

"You don't get to tell me what to do! Not you, not her

old man, and most definitely, not her." He jerked his thumb to his chest. "*We* do. Now I want to take her out, and if I don't get to, I'll get angry. And then Pops will get angry. And when Pops gets angry—"

"That's quite enough," Dash replied. "I'll ask politely one more time—"

"Oh, yeah? Whattaya going to do, High Hat?"

Dash remembered Donte's pistol in his pocket. He knew Donte's pistol wasn't loaded, but the sight of it might deter this rogue.

He pulled it out and aimed it at Vito.

This caused a laughing fit in the weaselly man.

Vito pointed at the pistol. "Oh, look! A dandy with a gun! Now I've seen everything. Whatcha gonna do with that, *sir*?"

Dash cocked the hammer, which made a loud clicking sound. That stopped Vito's laughter.

He held up his hands in defeat, though that sneer remained. "Alright, alright. I'm going." He glanced over at Isabella. "But you haven't seen the last of me, Bella."

Vito turned on his heel and sauntered north on Bowery Street, hands back in his pockets, whistling as he went.

Isabella muttered another curse and spat on the ground.

Dash turned to her, sliding the pistol back into his pocket. "Who is that boy?"

"No one. He's a janitor. He cleans up other people's shit." She turned her head and yelled at Vito's back. "Too bad he can't take himself out to the trash!"

Vito turned on the next cross street and disappeared from view.

Dash focused on Isabella. "Why is he coming around here? How do you know him?"

She abruptly asked, "Do you love your papa?"

Dash inwardly flinched. An unintended, antagonistic question. He hadn't thought of his father in years. Well, that wasn't precisely true. He thought of him at odd moments, moments when he was reminded of how others saw him— Walter Müller, Officer McElroy, the Committee of Fourteen—or when he was enjoying the life he chose with Joe and Finn and Atty. Or at least trying to. The memories he recalled were never fond ones, the voice in his head never loving, always judgmental. Cold. Distant.

He licked his suddenly dry lips. "I suppose—" Good grief, how to answer this without reopening the wound? "I suppose I do but—"

His father's voice roared in his ears: "*Goddammit, son! You will* ruin *this entire family! Did you ever stop to think about that? How other people will suffer because of—because of—this!*"

Dash forced himself to continue. "But I am disappointed with him."

She nodded. "Disappointed. *Si, si,* that is the word for it." She licked her lips, weighing something in her mind. "Vito works at a gambling room called The Smoke Shop on Bleecker Street."

"Really? Do you gamble, Miss Delucci?"

She fervently shook her head and clarified. "Papa."

"Your father?" Dash furrowed his brow as the implications formed fast. "The debts that boy mentioned—"

"Papa owes them hundreds of dollars. *Hundreds.* And now this, this *coglione* won't leave me alone because of it."

"Did your mother know?"

"*Si.* More or less. He used to have his friends over to play cards, but he kept losing more and more money. She said he couldn't do that in our home, so the games stopped. He didn't, though. He only did it elsewhere."

"How about your Uncle Atty? Does he know?"

She shook her head.

"Why haven't you said anything?"

"Because who would believe me?" Isabella said sharply. "Eh? Who would believe a girl who's being followed by this boy, who comes to her one day and tells her that Papa owes the Spinellis money?"

"The Spinellis?" The name in the letter from Donte's pocket was different. "Are you sure it isn't the Capellos?"

"No, no, Vito says it's the Spinellis. The father who owns it, his name is Gianni. Vito calls him Pops, though they're not blood related. Vito thinks he can become one of them if he proves himself. Bah! Vito is a fool. They'll never see him as anything other than what he is."

"Which is . . . ?"

*"Testa di cazzo."*

"What does that mean?"

A half-smile formed on her face. "A louse."

Dash cocked his head. "Is that really what you said?"

The half-smile turned into a full one. "No." As quickly as the smile went up, it dropped. "I went out with Vito. The night of—the night of the fire. He came around that day, saying he knew I was Donte's daughter because Papa waved around my picture one night when he was winning. Saying how I brought him all the luck. Vito said if I went out with him, he'd get the Spinellis to forget about Papa's debts."

She looked down at her feet.

"Stupid! I believed him. How dumb was I, eh? I thought he was some big shot, that he worked with the Spinellis. *Cazzo!* He's a fucking janitor." She glanced up at Dash to see if he'd react to her language. When she saw he didn't, she went on. "So. Now he comes back because I didn't give him what he wanted that night."

"And he keeps mentioning the debts."

"Si, si. Always the debts. The hundreds of dollars Papa pissed away."

Dash thought of the letter and the devil card he pulled from Donte's suit pocket. "Have the Spinellis been sending your father threatening notes?"

Isabella frowned. "I—I cannot say for certain. Papa gets some letters that make him angry, but he doesn't say what they are. He didn't share them with Mama before she . . . They looked similar, though, when he opened them. Same envelope, same paper."

"When did they start arriving?"

She scrunched up her nose while she thought. "A few weeks ago? Near the beginning of the month."

"And when was the last one he received?"

She avoided his gaze.

Dash said, "Miss Delucci?"

She raised those blazing blue eyes to his. "The morning of the fire."

## 7

A jack-o'-lantern grinned at Dash from the corner of the rough-hewn bar of the Greenwich Village Inn.

He pointed to it. "Where did that come from?"

Emmett, the snowy-bearded owner of Dash's usual food joint, stood behind the bar, arms crossed, a frown firmly in place. His uniform resembled his no-nonsense personality: a starched white shirt, a white apron, and a pair of dark gray trousers. He looked up at Dash's question, then waved his hand as though swatting away annoying gnats.

"Your *friend*."

On cue, the kitchen door in the back flew open and in swept Finn, whose grin mirrored that of the jack-o'-lantern.

"Good morning, dearie!" he said, still dressed in his dockworker outfit from last night. His eyes twinkled as they dipped down to Dash's trousers, and his voice changed to the bouncing cadence of Mae West. "Is that a pistol in your pocket, or are you just happy to see me?"

Dash looked down at himself. There was no outline of the pistol that he could see. "How on earth did you figure that?"

"I can identify what's in a man's trousers from at least twenty paces away. It's a special gift of mine."

Dash rolled his eyes while he signaled Emmett for some black coffee. That's when he noticed Finn's arms were full of a hodgepodge of paper shapes—moons, more pumpkins, the pointy ends of devil's horns.

Finn waltzed into the center of the room, where a collection of tables and chairs rested in front of a fireplace. He dumped the decorations onto one, which was scarred with etched epithets.

Dash pointed to the pile. "What's all that?"

"Nonsense," Emmett replied, taking a carafe and filling a mug.

"No," Finn said. "Not nonsense." He turned around to face them both. "Can you believe it, Dash? It's almost Halloween, and this Father Time wasn't planning to have a single festive thing up anywhere. I've been trying to help the ungrateful old man." He gestured to the jack-o'-lantern. "What do you think, Em? Isn't it marvelous?"

Emmett finished pouring Dash his coffee and handed over the steaming mug. "It's ridiculous. And stop calling me Em."

Finn was aghast. "It is *not* ridiculous! How can you say such a thing?"

"It's a goddamned squash."

"It's an artistic *masterpiece*! Do you have any idea how long it took me to carve the blasted thing?"

"I didn't ask ya to do that," Emmett said, returning the carafe of coffee to the counter behind him. He gestured impatiently to the pile of decorations on the table. "I didn't ask ya to do any of . . . *this*, whatever the hell that is."

"No, you've just been complaining nonstop about how

that 'damnable Pirate's Den' is taking all your customers. How do you think you're going to win them back, Em?"

*Volley, volley, point,* Dash thought, as he settled onto the barstool and took his first sip.

Emmett was clearly not ready to concede the point. "It'll rot soon."

"Not as soon as your precious Inn if you don't do something about it. Honestly, it's Halloween next week! The whole Village will be full of ghosts and goblins, especially on Mischief Night. Every place will have something special going on. Even Dash has the infamous Harlem singer El Train performing at his place."

Dash nodded. Somehow, he managed a miracle by talking his friend El Train into performing at Pinstripes for the very first time. With a voice as loud as her personality, El made a name for herself singing at the Oyster House on 133rd Street. She'd since moved over to the J.A. Watkins Hotel, owned by its namesake, a Black woman millionaire. The hotel was for Blacks only, so Dash lost the opportunity to visit his friend regularly and see her perform. Asking her down to the Village was, admittedly, a purely selfish request on his part.

"Everyone is buzzing about it, Em," Finn continued. "People want an Event with a capital E. An *experience.* And if they hear that the old Inn is a haunted house, why, they'll come in droves!"

Emmett scowled. "Why can't people just want food and drink?"

Finn rolled his eyes. "Stop being a grumpy old man."

Dash chimed in. "He is a grumpy old man, Finn."

Emmett nodded with appreciation. "That I am. I worked hard to be an old man. I avoided plague, war, and women. The secret to a long life."

"Well," Finn said, "it's hard to argue with logic like that."

"Especially since you do the same," Dash quipped.

Finn stuck out his tongue at him and returned to the pile of decorations on the table. He began sorting them.

Dash finished his coffee and motioned for a refill. As Emmett poured, he asked, "How is business, Emmett? Any better?"

It was true what Finn said. *The Pirate's Den* opened on Christopher Street less than two months ago and was highly popular amongst the Villagers. How could it not be? The three floors were built to resemble the three levels of a ship with a large elevator moving an orchestra between floors. Waiters pretended to be pirates while they handed out menus that looked like treasure maps. It spoke to the Village's need for the unconventional *and* the dramatic.

Emmett nodded to the room. "Look around."

Dash did. The place was empty, save for the three ex–Wall Street traders they called the Ex-Pats. The three men hardly said a word while they sipped in their back corner. Nobody knew what happened to them on the trading floor, but their bloodshot eyes and trembling fingers told a terrible tale. They never spoke about it and no one dared to ask.

Dash's eyes met Emmett's. "Perhaps our friend has a point, then. I'll spread the word. 'Come to the Greenwich Village Inn for a *spooktacular* good time!'"

"Now ya sound like those dandies in advertising."

Finn called from across the room. "Did you find out what happened to our precious Atty last night?"

Dash turned on his barstool to face them both. "I did. And it wasn't the clams."

He told them about the fire, though he kept the part about the hysterical Donte almost braining him with a lamp to himself. He spoke about the strange, threatening letter found in Donte's pocket, the tarot card with the devil drawn upon it, and the gambling debts owed to the Spinelli family.

He then said that after speaking with Isabella, he visited the scene of the fire. He wasn't entirely sure why. Perhaps to see the destruction and devastation for himself.

The sight on Elizabeth Street left him speechless.

Where once was a building, now there was none. A sudden hole in the solid wall of tenements, like a gapped-tooth smile. The ground was covered in charred rubble, and the standing supports were like blackened bones. The stench of burnt wood and melted plaster hung over the street, a cruel reminder of Saturday's nightmare.

What it must've been like to witness this sudden fiery destruction in the dead of night. And what a horror for Isabella, Emiliano, and Rocco, narrowly escaping death themselves only to see their home obliterated with their mother trapped inside.

"No wonder the boys are mute," Dash said, as he finished his recount of the morning. "And I don't blame Isabella for being as closed off as an angry fist."

Finn was aghast. "How *dreadful!*"

"Atty is in a state of shock."

"No wonder. And those poor children!"

Emmett snorted. "Damn tenements. Nothing but kindling."

Finn was shaking his head in disbelief. "I didn't know Atty even *had* a brother."

"He does," Dash said. "Older by a good ten years, maybe a little more. Atty's always been a little fuzzy with the math. He doesn't say much about him or his family unless he's had a few. I don't get the sense they're very close."

"How do you think Atty will react to his brother being a gambling fiend? Because we have to tell him, dearie, we *have* to. Especially with what that boorish Vito is trying to do with Isabella."

Dash hesitated. "You're not wrong, Finn, but you know Atty's temper. Once we set it off—"

"—he's a regular Mount Vesuvius, yes I know. When you do tell him, make sure he's not anywhere near his brother. Or that blasted pistol of his. Do they have other family in the city?"

Dash shook his head. "Atty and his brother Donte were the only ones to stay in America; the rest of their siblings and parents returned to Sicily. Atty said they felt unsafe with all the gangsters and whatnot."

"Hard to argue when tragedies like this happen." Finn held out his hand. "Let me see the tarot card you found."

"Why?" Dash asked, though he removed it from his pocket and passed it over to Finn.

"Because I'm curious, silly." Finn's eyes widened when he saw it. "Oh my."

"Do you know what this means? It's been a while since I've had a reading." It was months after his younger sister Sarah died from the influenza outbreak. Dash, like many, sought out a spiritualist to try to reach his lost loved one— and, like many, came away vaguely dissatisfied.

Emmett grumbled. "Spiritualism is nothing but a bunch of bushwa."

Finn frowned. "No, it isn't! Every reading I've ever had has come true." He held up the card. "Now, this, dearies, is the devil card. It's a good one. It references the devil that's inside all of us, the parts of ourselves we hide from everyone, especially the people we love and trust the most." He placed a fingertip next to one of the kneeling nymphs.

"These little ones are slaves to the devil inside themselves. Bound and chained to the dark forces they cannot control."

"A hell of their own making."

"Yes!" Finn smiled with approval. "The darker side—the shadow side—has taken over. If the devil is turned upright, you're held back, kept from the light, because you keep doing the same hurtful things over and over again. If the card is *reversed*, the meaning changes and you are being called to a higher purpose. It is a call you must answer, but you can only answer it if you let go of the forces that bind you." Finn gave Dash a curious glance. "When you found this card, was it like this? Or was it reversed?"

Dash shrugged. "I can't remember. Why? Does it matter?"

"Of course, it matters! Athena preserve me. You're either being called to free yourself or to help someone else."

*What if it's both?* Dash wondered.

The three of them stood quietly for a moment.

In his mind, Dash heard Joe saying, "*Bloody hell, lassie, just leave this fire business alone!*"

Finn broke the silence by clapping his hands together. "Well, enough talk. It's time to get back to work. Alright, Em, let's whip this place into shape. We've got a business to save!"

Emmett scowled. "Stop calling me Em!"

---

Fully fortified with coffee and breakfast, Dash left the Inn to open Hartford & Sons. It was well past its nine o'clock opening time, though Dash didn't mind. "Village Time" was usually slower than the rest of Manhattan.

While he'd been in the Inn, a rain shower had dumped onto the streets, leaving behind the smell of musty, wet earth. *The Times* weather page forecasted a strange gale that would soar up from the southern parts of the country and roar through New York sometime tonight. The rain showers were the precursor to the main event.

Puddles collected in the creases between the road and the sidewalk. A veritable lake lay placid in front of his shop, forcing Dash to leap over it. He jammed the keys into the lock and stepped inside a small square with cedar floors and parlor green–painted walls. The shop featured a variety of discarded furniture collected from sidewalks and alleys: a wardrobe, a mirror, a writing desk and chair, a sewing machine and stool, and a hat rack.

Dash settled onto the writing desk chair with a groan, opening the desk's compartment and placing Donte's pistol and bullets inside of it. The devil tarot card was about to join them when Dash spied something odd scribbled at the top above the devil's crown of horns. "T.S.S. *WEDNESDAY 9:00*."

Was "T.S.S." someone's initials? Or was it a place?

*The Smoke Shop?*

Was Donte going to meet with a spiritualist there? What for?

Dash placed the card inside the desk and closed it up. He glanced over at the drawn hunter-green curtain covering the changing area in the back right corner. It was there that savvy customers at night would pass through the curtain and push the mirror embedded in the back wall to enter their club Pinstripes.

He fondly remembered the first so-called degenerate club he ever visited. It was after his first lover Victor Agramonte, the original owner of Hartford & Sons, left the United States because the new immigration laws prevented his family from coming over from Catalonia. He bequeathed the tailor shop and its one-room apartment behind it to Dash. Dash hardly left their bed until one night, the urge to be around people—or at the very least, be around men like him—overruled the need to wallow.

He found a small place called On the Fringe near the western border of Bohemia. He was nervous. Victor never liked going to clubs like this, fearful he'd be caught by the police, not an altogether unjustified fear. Dash remembered taking a deep breath and entering the hidden club.

The emotions he felt the moment he stepped inside were so powerful, so visceral, they still tingled his skin to this day. The excitement, the atmosphere, the *freedom*! He could let his voice, his walk, his hands, wrists, and hips all be natural. Be *relaxed*. He hadn't realized how tense he'd been in the jaw and in the shoulders walking down the streets or chatting with "normal men" in stodgy parlors or at restaurant counters. He had to be so careful. One wrong slip, one wrong gesture, and it was dismissal and disgust, at best, or violence and prison, at worst. The release of that tension was nothing short of euphoric. Rapturous. A delirious joy. He never wanted to leave! But he couldn't very well *live* in an invert speakeasy . . .

. . . or could he?

What if he could build a similar space? Where the Village men could visit and converse, flirt, and dance without fear or shame. Safe from the outside world. He would name it after Victor's suit of choice: Pinstripes.

The front door opened with a sudden rattling of the brass knob and a squeal of the hinges.

Dash looked up and cursed.

Officer Cullen McElroy strolled in, as if he owned the place, a yellow-toothed grin stretching the greasy skin of his flushed cheeks. "Good morning, Mr. Parker."

## 8

McElroy closed the door behind him.

Dash ground his teeth. What he hadn't realized when he built Pinstripes was that his safe space was always going to be under threat—from American "super patriots," from moral busybodies, from the Volstead Act enforcers, and most *definitely* from the police. Case in point, this odious globe of a man.

McElroy first extorted Victor, because he was a "dirty Spaniard," ("*Catalan*," Victor would correct), and then Dash, because he was "the new boy on the street." McElroy likely suspected Dash was into something illegal, but he never knew with certainty about Pinstripes or its clientele.

*And it must stay that way.*

McElroy reached into his uniform trouser pocket and pulled out a gold-plated pocket watch, regarding the time with a theatrical eyebrow raise.

"You're opening late, I see."

He snapped the watch shut and began slowly pacing around the small room, taking in the modest space with a bemused eye.

"Had a bit of a morning," Dash replied, his voice tight. "My friend's brother lost his home to a fire."

McElroy clicked his tongue. "Shame, that."

He passed by the wardrobe, glancing with interest at the changing area curtain. He reached up to scratch his head, knocking his police hat askew and exposing his straw-like hair.

Dash's pulse beat against his temples. "Something I can help you with, McElroy?"

McElroy held up a finger, wagging it from side to side. "Now, now, Mr. Parker. It's *Officer* McElroy." He straightened his hat and continued his slow pace, his heavy boots thumping against the wood floors.

"Right. I apologize, *Officer* McElroy."

McElroy smirked, then went back to looking at the hunter-green curtain.

*He cannot poke around here. If he finds my club—*

Dash stood up from the writing desk, scooting the wooden chair backwards with an ear-splitting screech.

McElroy turned his gaze to him.

Dash tried to recover. "What can I do for you?"

"You been minding your business like I told ya? You haven't been trying to find my witness?"

"Why should I bother? After all, you said I'd never be able to find him . . . or her."

McElroy observed him. "Uh, huh. And where were you last night?"

"I was at home. Why?"

"Someone tried to see my witness while I was out."

"It wasn't me."

"Right. Well. I had him moved again. Just in case."

*Damn!* Now how was Dash going to let Peter Fraker know he'd gotten the evidence of Peter's adultery?

McElroy chuckled, pleased with himself. "But that's not the reason I stopped by. You know why I'm here today?"

"To get a new suit, perhaps?"

McElroy's grin widened. He sauntered towards Dash. "Ah, now, Mr. Parker, we both know you're not a tailor. You've got that little Sicilian lad who sits in that window there"—he pointed to the empty sewing machine—"and does all your work for ya. At night, which is queer."

Dash shrugged. "Not uncommon for one man to be the face of the business and for the other to be the labor."

"You're a factory man, now?"

"A modest one."

"I could use a new suit, but I don't think I can afford ya."

"I'll give you one. On the house."

"I wouldn't want to be accused of taking a bribe from a shopkeeper, now, would I?"

Dash couldn't help himself from saying, "And the so-called donations I used to give you? Those weren't bribes?"

"You said it yourself: they were *donations*. And besides —" McElroy now stood directly in front of Dash. He leaned forward, his hands gripping the sides of the writing desk, his voice plummeting into a growl. "—you don't pay me no more. You've got some 'representative,' as he claims, who greases my palm."

"Why do you care who provides the sugar?"

"Because it makes me wonder about you. Why a 'tailor' needs protection. And let's not deny that's what your 'representative' is paid to do. Heard from Walter Müller recently?"

"Who?"

"The blond kraut fella who seems to have disappeared;

who seems to have a brother murdered and a mother that committed suicide; who paid me to find out where you lived, and you paid me not to tell him."

Dash knew all these details, but he still inwardly flinched hearing them said aloud. "I told you. I don't know—"

"You're lying! You're lying, Mr. Parker, through your precious white little teeth, and we both know it."

Dash's mouth was desert dry. He licked his lips. "Why would I lie?"

"Because you killed Walter, that's why."

Dash forced a laugh. "Why on earth would I kill him?"

McElroy held up a finger. "Ah, that's where this gets interesting. Walter Müller used to work for the Committee of Fourteen. You know what that is, don't you? An anti-vice organization. They root out speakeasies and degenerates. In August, Walter's no longer employed by the Committee, and come to find out his younger brother Karl was a little faggot and got himself arrested in a raid. *Tsk tsk tsk.* Next thing ya know, Karl's found strangled in Central Park, where all the little fairies go to do unspeakable things to one another after dark, and Walter comes here, to this shop, to have an argument with *you.*"

*Dammit to hell!*

McElroy was putting together the story faster and more accurately than Dash thought possible. Karl was a patron at Pinstripes and Walter had followed him here. In an attempt to rescue Karl from the hands of his bluenose brother, Dash hid the shy boy up in Harlem. The plan went wrong. Karl left Harlem and ended up murdered, and Walter blackmailed Dash into an investigation, of sorts. An investigation that left Walter, and a few others, dead.

"Now tell me, Mr. Parker," McElroy sneered, "why was an anti-vice man arguing with you? Huh? An anti-vice man with a fairy for a brother? And why do you have a protector —ah, let's call him for what he is—a *gangster* watching over you?"

Dash swallowed a large lump in his throat. "I'm sure you have a theory."

"I do, I do." He turned his attention back to the hunter-green curtain. "What's behind here?"

Dash kept his voice light. "A changing room. I can't have my customers dropping their trousers for all West Fourth Street to see."

McElroy looked over his shoulder, then pulled the curtain open with a high-pitched *ring!*

Dash flinched.

McElroy turned and examined the space, which held only a wooden chair and the mirror embedded in the back wall.

"See?" Dash said, gesturing to the space.

McElroy nodded to himself and strolled to the back wall. "But methinks there's something behind here." He patted the parlor-green surface before pressing his ear against it. "A speak, perhaps? Is that what Walter and you were arguing about? You breaking the Volstead Act laws? Maybe even the cabaret laws against dancing? Or even—" A faux-surprised gasp. "—the degeneracy laws? Got that little faggot brother to account for, now, don't we?"

Dash concentrated on his breathing. The club was closed, so McElroy wouldn't hear any noise. And even if the club *was* open, Dash and Joe had placed so much insulation inside the walls that only a faint murmuring snuck out. Like tenants from upstairs, or ghosts from another world.

"Seems like a bunch of guesswork to me," Dash said. "As far as I can tell, you don't have a body. Walter Müller may even be alive and well, for all you know. Perhaps *he* killed his brother and his mother and fled the city. Would explain why you haven't seen him again."

"That doesn't smell right to me, Mr. Parker." McElroy straightened up. "I see all kinds of strange things on this beat. So many hidden rooms. Secret doors. Hidden stairs. Clever compartments cut into the floor."

He stomped the cedar boards with his foot.

"And despite what they all say, everybody's got one. Where is yours, Mr. Parker? Where is *your* secret? The secret Walter Müller knew. The secret you killed him over."

A coldness settled into Dash's chest. He tried to form a reply, but it died on his dried-out lips.

McElroy cupped a hand behind his ear. "Hmm? What was that?"

Another damnable chuckle.

He raised a finger. "I'll tell you where I think it is." He turned slowly on the balls of his feet and pointed. "I think it's right here."

He placed his hand on the changing room mirror and slid a slippery glance over his shoulder. "What happens if I push? Hmm? Well. Let's give it a go, shall we?"

The tailor shop door burst open behind them.

Dash whipped his head around to see a tall, thin man clad in a dark gray suit hurry inside.

"Excuse me," the man rasped. "I apologize for being late for our appointment, Mr. Parker."

In Dash's frantic state of mind, he thought, *I don't have time to deal with a customer; I need to get McElroy the hell out of here!* Then he realized he didn't have any appointments lined up for the day. He turned to the man for an explanation.

And found one.

Pinpoint eyes. Pinched mouth. A red, angry scar across his throat. Makowski, one of Nicholas Fife's "clean-up" men, stood in the center of the shop. Dash had first met him when he needed a body removed from his club—a flapper poisoned by bad booze—and the two had never truly gotten along. In fact, the two had had a screaming argument on the midnight streets. An argument that should have, and would have, ended with Dash's release from this mortal coil had Fife not intervened.

Needless to say, they weren't the best of friends, so why was Makowski here?

"Y-y-yes," Dash replied. "That's no trouble at all, my good sir." He faced McElroy. "I am terribly sorry, but I do need to tend to a customer. Could we continue this conversation at another time?"

McElroy's grin hardened. His eyes flicked over to Makowski and back again, his palm still maddeningly placed on the mirror, his fat fingers splayed out.

"I see." He removed his hand, leaving behind a stain of sweat on the glass. He sauntered towards Makowski. "How long have ya been a customer of Mr. Parker's?"

Makowski narrowed his eyes. "What business is that of yours?"

"Curious to hear about his work. See if he's worth my time and money."

"He's not. I'd leave him alone if I were you."

"Is that so?" McElroy lobbied over a mean grin to Dash. "Not that good a tailor, huh?"

Makowski sniffed. "I didn't say that. I meant he doesn't

do lost causes. And if you don't mind me being frank, you're a lost cause."

McElroy stepped closer to Makowski, saying, "Oh ho! We got a regular comedian here!"

"If you know what's good for ya, I'd spend my time and my money elsewhere."

Makowski's pinpoint eyes never wavered from McElroy. Dash could see it was dawning on the copper that this man was not a rude customer and that his words were not idle suggestions.

"You work for him, don't ya? The one who protects this business; protects this man."

Makowski didn't respond.

"Is this when you tell me never to come back here again? Hmm?"

Makowski remained silent.

McElroy watched Makowski's face before giving a curt nod. "I'll be on my way then." He walked to the front door, pausing with his hand on the doorknob. "Don't underestimate me, gentlemen. That would be a very costly mistake."

He wrenched the front door open before slamming it shut behind him.

Dash watched through the windowpanes as the odious man sauntered down West Fourth towards Seventh Avenue. Rain began falling again, gently tapping on the windows and darkening the street.

Dash looked at Makowski. "Thank you," he said, meaning it.

Makowski pursed his lips. "You let him push you around too much."

"Nothing I can do about it right now."

"Yes, there is, but you don't want to do it."

"You're correct. I don't. I have my reasons for it. You

might not understand them, but they're my reasons and they're good ones. And I'm working on a plan that will stop him from bothering me."

Makowski adjusted his lapels and his hat. "You better get to it quick." He strode over to the front door, opening it. "Seems to me you're running out of time."

## 9

"Dammit to hell," Joe groused. "He's not wrong, lassie. We *are* runnin' out o' time."

"And *I* am running out of patience!" El Train retorted back.

They were all inside Pinstripes a few hours before opening. Dash and Joe were at the bar, Joe standing behind it counting bottles, while Dash sat on a barstool nursing a gin rickey. He'd just told Joe about McElroy's visit, something Dash would've waited to do until after El's rehearsal with his band. But Joe took one look at Dash's face and asked what was wrong, and Dash couldn't lie or even deflect. Not since the events of last month, when they both vowed to keep each other informed—especially if something bad had occurred.

"My apologies, El," Dash called over his shoulder. "We'll be quiet."

"You damn well better!" she replied. "It's bad enough I gotta come all the way to downtowner's-ville. I don't need to hear your beating gums either."

Dash turned to see El standing in front of his mixed-race band. The men—two Black and one white—were dressed in their usual sleek black tuxedos, while El had packed her large, broad-shouldered frame into a hound-stooth jacket with mud-brown vest and matching trousers. It wasn't her usual performing outfit, which was a white tuxedo with tails and a top hat, but she said she was changing into that once when she got to her gig at the Watkins Hotel.

"Where the hell was I?" El said. "Oh, the stops! Now when I sing '*I could tell her miles away from here*,' I want the drums to hit on the three. Everyone stops and holds it for three-four. And then come in on the '*Yes, sir, that's my baby*.' You got it?"

The bass player, Vernon, the only white man on stage, raised his hand and said, "Hey, El, you liking that bass line I was doing before?"

El nodded at the tall man with lanky limbs but a round center. "Uh, huh. You can make it walk a little more, Vern. Put a little jaunt in its step." Her lips spread, exposing a snaggletooth dead center in her grin. "Like when you're coming back from your pansy's bed."

The cornet player Julius scoffed, "Oh man, be careful, El. Vern here is insufferable when he's been freshly loved. He smiling and whistling to himself, practically skipping down the sidewalk like a schoolgirl in pigtails!"

"Let the man be happy, Jules. I'm frankly proud of him for swinging on both sides of the fence," El replied. She then pointed to Julius. "Besides, *you* jealous 'cause nobody wants all your knees and elbows."

"Hey, now!" Julius pointed at himself with his brass instrument. "I got some muscle on me."

The drummer Calvin, a man who was all syncopation and curves, said, "Ha! Not where it counts."

"Is that right, Cal? And what exactly are you bringing to the table, except for another plate?"

"Some girls like a little extra meat. Your mama sure did last night."

Cal and Vernon cackled, while Julius just shook his head.

"I see I'm getting the horns tonight," he said.

El replied, "You *wish* you were getting some horns. Alright, enough chin music. You three think you can keep up with me now?"

"Yes, ma'am!" they replied, settling into their positions.

"I told you, cut out that ma'am shit." El turned on her heels to face the front of the stage. "Alright, let's do it, babies." She stamped the floor and snapped her fingers. "A-one, a-two, a-one, two, three, four!"

The music started, a popular English cabaret tune that El and the band remade into a bluesy, greasy shuffle. Her big, expansive voice filled up every inch of Pinstripes. It even vibrated against Dash's chest as she sang:

> *Who's that coming down the street?*
> *Who's that looking so petite?*
> *Who's that coming down to meet me here?*

> *Who's that you know who I mean,*
> *Sweetest "who" you've ever seen,*
> *I could tell her miles away from here!*

The band hit the downbeat, held, and came in just as El hit the chorus:

*Yes, sir, that's my baby,*
*No, sir, don't mean maybe*
*Yes, sir, that's my baby now.*

*Yes ma'am, we've decided,*
*No ma'am, we won't hide it,*
*Yes, ma'am, you're invited now.*

*By the way, by the way,*
*When we reach the preacher I'll say,*
*Yes, sir, That's my baby now!*

Dash smiled and tried to get lost in the music, to ignore the anxiety sickening his stomach.

He glanced around the club. Blue-painted walls surrounded six tables and chairs, three on each side. The dance floor, now empty, stood in the center and would soon be filled with neighborhood men dressed in their finest glad rags. The band and El hugged the far-left corner, the WC the far-right. Two large floor lamps gave most of the light while a table lamp held court at the far side of the bar.

Like what Finn planned to do with the Greenwich Village Inn, Halloween decorations filled every available inch of space. A crepe paper black cat with orange eyes and an angry mouth screeched from the center of the ceiling, its whiskers long and extending well past its face. More of its feline cousins hissed from the walls, their backs arched upwards, their tails like exclamation points. Behind Dash, on the rough-hewn bar, lay a few gourds and one jack-o'-lantern carved by Finn. The back of the secret door—the mirror in the tailor shop's changing area—featured a scowling moon bidding patrons goodnight.

The song ended with loud high notes from El and Julius and an ear-piercing cymbal crash from Calvin.

Dash applauded the foursome. "Excellent!" he called. "Really well done!"

The band smiled and nodded at him.

El frowned. "Something's still off. Vern, let me hear that bass line again at the top of the turnaround."

Dash swiveled back to facing Joe as the sounds of a plucked bass thumped behind him.

"Listen," he said, keeping his voice low. "I'm not too worried about McElroy. We've got his address, so it's only a matter of time before we break in there and get Peter Fraker's photographs."

"But he's moved that Fraker fella. How are ya gonna tell him the evidence is gone?"

"I'll find a way. Maybe Peter left behind a note like he did for his neighbor the first time McElroy moved him."

"It's a long shot, lassie."

"Joe, this whole mess has been one long shot. I just need our luck to hold out for a little while longer."

"I don't understand why ya don't turn over McElroy to Fife," Joe said. "It's what we pay him fer. He's supposed to protect us from coppers and the Feds and the like."

"But Fife will kill McElroy."

"Ya don't know that."

Dash gave Joe a long look.

"Alright, he would. But would that be so bad, lassie? I mean, why should ya protect McElroy when he's a piece of *shite*?"

It was a good question.

"Because I don't want more blood on my hands."

"Ya don't have blood on yer hands. Ya didn't even kill Walter. That Prudence Meyers did."

Not only that, but she also stripped Walter's body of all identification so that when the police arrived, they found a John Doe, an opened safe, and a ransacked law office. They determined it was a robbery gone wrong, one partner shooting the other and leaving with the loot.

"Yes," Dash said, "but . . . I was there. I saw it. And I can't unsee it."

Joe's voice softened. "I know, me boy, I know. Ya saw somethin' terrible and ya don't want to inflict that on anybody else. Even a slimy eel like McElroy."

Dash nodded, feeling cold and small. El and the band continued to murmur in the background.

Joe reached across the bar and held Dash's hand. "The nightmares have been gettin' less and less, though, haven't they?"

"Yes, thankfully."

"But this time, ya won't see it. Ya won't even be there."

"I'd rather take away McElroy's witness and see where we stand. I've also got Pru working some angles on her end, which may help us out even more." Dash looked up into Joe's emerald eyes. "I want to defeat McElroy my way, not Fife's."

"We gotta work faster, then. McElroy almost found our club and now we learn that Atty's got a gamblin' dolt of a brother who's getting threats. Have ya told him?"

"Not yet. I don't have any proof other than the word of his niece, and it would be too easy for Donte to deny it."

"Aye. Men don't believe women."

"Though they should believe them. There's something else. I don't want to come between two brothers unless I have to."

"Whattaya mean, unless ya have to?"

"Right now, we know nothing for sure. I just saw the

flash of a letter. That's all." Dash sighed. "It would help immensely if I had it. Not only would we avoid a he-said-he-said fiasco between me and Donte, but then we'd know who and what exactly we're dealing with. Perhaps even go to the police."

Joe scoffed. "Coppers won' do *shite*."

"But in this instance, maybe they can. They just need proof of the threats. As do we."

They fell silent.

Behind Dash, Calvin added a swirl of brushes to the snare with El going, "That's it, that's it. Nice and easy . . . "

Joe's voice was quiet. "What if Atty's in danger, lassie?"

"Even more reason to get proof."

Dash stood up.

Joe eyed him warily. "Whattaya schemin'?"

Dash smiled as he left the bar. "Don't worry."

"Uh, huh. When ya say tha', tha's exactly *when* I worry."

Dash pulled open the secret door and stepped into the tailor shop. Beyond the green curtain was the pounding of the sewing machine. Dash checked his wristwatch. Atty was early.

He opened the curtain and saw the man sitting at his post.

Atty turned around. "Hiya, Boss. I'm just catching up on the alterations I missed last night."

Dash pulled out the chair from the writing desk and sat. "How are you doing, my friend?"

Atty licked his lips while he considered his reply. "I'm still in shock, Boss. I don't know how this happened."

"Did you know Maria well?"

Atty nodded. "She's . . . she was . . . a good woman.

Strong, smart, tough. She and Donte met at a schoolyard fight, youse know."

"Really?"

Atty's laugh was bittersweet. "Yeah. We was coming out of the school, Donte and I. I must've been about, oh I don't know, five or six; Donte was seventeen. Anyways, we got to the street and there was a gang of Irish fucks—" His eyes widened. "I meant no offense, Boss! Joe and Finn are swell, stand-up fellas, but back then, the Irish? They hated us Italians. Said we were barely better than gutter trash."

Dash sighed. The irony of it all. For it wasn't too long ago when New Yorkers said the same thing of the Irish. In fact, some of them still did.

Atty continued with his story. "We walk onto the street and they throw things at us. Gravel, rocks, empty soup cans, spoiled vegetables and fruits. At small children, Boss!"

"Heavens."

Atty shrugged, nonchalant about the abuse. "We weren't white, Boss. That's how it is here. The Irish may be red with freckles, but at least they're pale enough."

"I see."

"One of the Micks—I mean, Irish boys—picked up a rock and tossed it in the air, catching a young girl in the face. Donte saw that and charged the boy, taking him down. That girl picked herself up and marched over to the boy. After Donte finished working on him, the girl wound up her leg and kicked the boy in the crotch so hard, he vomited."

"And that girl," Dash finished the thought, "was Maria."

Atty smiled. "Yeah. I told youse she was tough. They married a year later. Bella was born soon after that. Then Emil and Rocco."

"How are the children doing?"

Atty's smile faded. "Not well. The boys are being brave, of course, but Isabella? She's . . . she's angry."

"That's understandable. She's just lost her mother."

"Eh, there's something different about it, Boss. It's like she's blaming Donte for it, but he wasn't even home for the fire."

"Perhaps that's why."

Atty considered that. "I'm sorry about earlier, when Donte tried to hit youse."

"No harm done." *Thankfully*.

"He's been afraid ever since the fire. Like those soldiers who got shell shock, youse know?"

"Is he still locked in your bedroom?"

"I've got the keys now, so I's can get in."

"That's good," Dash said. "Atty, what did he mean when he said, 'she said it wasn't her' and 'he said it wasn't real?'"

"I don't know, Boss. I asked him about it after youse left and he said it was none of my business."

"What about the letter I found in his coat pocket? The one he snatched out of my hands?"

"Like I said, Boss, he won't tell me anything. He wouldn't let me see it, so I don't know what it says."

"Has he ever mentioned a place called The Smoke Shop? Maybe seeing a spiritualist?"

"No, but then again . . . he don't really talk to me. I mean, I can't tell him what I do here, so it makes conversation difficult." Atty hesitated. "He always keeps me at arm's length, though. Even staying in my home, he won't say what's bothering him. Maybe it's 'cause I'm the little brother, and he's the oldest and he can't allow himself to be —I don't know what." Atty flicked a glance over to Dash. "Youse was never close with your brother, right?"

"On the contrary," Dash replied. "Max and I were very close. We did everything together. Played all over the house. Invented games. Caused all sorts of trouble." He chuckled. "One game we loved to play was hide and seek. We'd sneak into cabinets, wardrobes. About scared our mother half to death when she opened them and there we were. Heavens. He was my best friend until—until we got older. Until I got different. It . . . changed. Subtly. Something I can't quite put my finger on. But there was a shift, a reversal in the tides, and we started drifting further and further apart. And when my family found out about—about me—the look of disgust on Max's face was far more hurtful than anything he could've ever said."

"That's not right, Boss. I don't understand it, why youse feel the way you do, but I saw boys like that in the trenches in the War. They weren't hurting nobody. Tell the truth, I'd rather see that than the other things I saw there." Atty's face darkened. "It was an awful place, Boss. A terrible place."

"I know." Dash let a beat pass before carefully asking, "Atty, I know you won't take payment for not being at the door—"

"Boss, I'm working tonight. Okay? I'm working. Period."

Dash studied the man. "Do you mind if I go over to your apartment and check in on the children? I don't have to be at Pinstripes tonight. Mondays are usually mild for us, so it won't be too hard on Joe or Finn."

"But Isabella's watching the boys."

"Yes, but Isabella also lost her mother. And I mean no disrespect to your brother, but I'm not sure Donte is in the best frame of mind to care for anyone at the moment."

Indecision creased Atty's forehead. Dash could see the man wanted to say he could handle it, that he could simultaneously earn his coin and be the guardian of the Delucci family, but both knew he could not.

Dash added, "I can also take over some spare clothes. Finn's got a few dresses he no longer likes, and Isabella can't go to school wearing your suits, you know."

Atty blew out a sigh. "Alright, Boss."

He reached into his pocket and pulled out his keys.

## 10

The scene in Atty's front room was the same as that morning.

Rocco and Emiliano curled up together on the sofa in Atty's white shirts, sleeping; Isabella, still in Atty's suit, remained seated by the window, the glass dotted with droplets. The rain had returned tonight with a vengeance; the wind beginning to whip and roar.

Dash placed the dripping umbrella in the bronze can by the front door and inspected the cuffs of his trousers. Damp but not soaked through. He glanced down the hall and saw the bedroom door was closed.

Isabella rasped, "He's not home." Her poor vocal cords still sported the scars of being seared by the smoke.

"Where did he go?"

She turned away from him.

He set down the suitcase he brought with him full of items he scrounged up from the Cherry Lane Playhouse and Finn's discards. "I brought you some clothes."

She didn't seem interested.

"Well. When you're ready, they're in here," he said, patting the suitcase.

He paused, unsure of how to proceed. He glanced down the hallway again towards the bedroom before looking up at Isabella. She stared at the window, her eyes and face averted from him.

Dash's attention returned to the hallway and the bedroom door. If he wanted proof of threats, it would be in there.

He strode towards the door, only to find it locked.

*Not very trusting, are you, Donte?*

Using Atty's keys, he opened the door and stepped inside the bedroom. It was dark still. Dash brought out his brass lighter and used the puny flame to walk his way towards the nightstand. He clicked the light on, returning his lighter to his pocket, and looked around. Bed unmade, dirty underclothes strewn about the floor. The closet door hung open. Dash went to it. The gray suit was gone, as was the mysterious letter he'd pulled out of Donte's pocket.

*Dammit.*

His eyes scanned the room. Would he have hidden the letter elsewhere? What else could Donte be hiding?

Dash gently closed the door. No reason for Isabella or the boys to witness this. He first searched the closet, sliding his hands through Atty's clothes, slipping his fingers into all the pockets. He ran his hands across the upper shelf before dropping down to the floor, where he lifted all of Atty's shoes, checking the soles, and examining the baseboards.

Nothing.

Next was the bedside nightstand. He pawed through the two drawers.

Snake eyes.

He looked underneath the bed, then angled his head to

look above at the springs and the underside of the mattress. A faded envelope was lodged in between near the center. Dash scooted further under the bed, then gingerly pulled it free. He looked inside. Stacks of bills. Dash thumbed through them. About twenty dollars' worth. Not bad, but not nearly enough to pay off his debts—if they were truly in the hundreds, as Isabella claimed.

Dash returned the envelope to its spot and slid out from under the bed. He pulled back the blankets and the sheets. Nothing. He checked the pillowcases, then the pillows themselves. No odd stitching to suggest hidden pockets inside the pillows. Still, he patted and squeezed them. Deuces.

He tossed pillows and blankets to the side and pulled off the bottom sheet. His eyes scanned the topside of the naked mattress for any slits. He circled the bed, checking all sides of the mattress for the same thing. Other than general wear and tear, the mattress remained untouched.

He remade the bed and paused his searches to think.

"Do you have a safe, Atty?" he murmured to himself.

He ran his hands on the walls, knocking occasionally, and listened for the telltale echo of a hollow space. Solid.

He pulled back the chest of drawers and saw nothing but dust bunnies gathering in piles. He searched each of the drawers, careful not to disturb Atty's personal items. No surprises in here. He even checked the backs of the drawers to see if anything had been secured there. Nothing.

He shut the last drawer and spun in a slow circle, his hands on his hips.

*If I wanted to hide something,* Dash thought, *where would I put it?*

His eyes fell upon the bed again, and the framed painting of the Madonna hung above it.

"Huh," he said out loud.

He went over to the painting and freed it from the nail. Though dusty, the wall behind it was unblemished. Dash turned the frame over and inspected the back.

"Pay dirt!" he said.

He extracted several folded squares of paper before returning the painting to its perch on the wall. He unfolded the papers and his brow furrowed in confusion when he saw what was printed on the pages. These were invoices from a shipping company called "MANHATTAN TRANSIT & FREIGHT." It was for shipments of "TOSCANO OLIO D'OLIVA." Olive oil.

What the hell was this? And why did Donte have these?

"I told you he wasn't here."

Dash whirled around to see Isabella standing in the doorway. She'd somehow opened the door without him noticing.

He pointed to her. "Shall I get you something for your throat? Tea? Honey?"

She ignored his question with one of her own. "What are those?" She pointed to the papers in Dash's hand.

"Invoices."

"For what?"

"For . . . tailor shop deliveries." He quickly folded them and placed them in his inside coat pocket. "Your Uncle was keeping them for me." He felt lousy lying to the girl, but he didn't want to add a spark to her kerosene.

She was relentless with her questions. "Why are you here?"

"I told your Uncle Atty I'd stop by to make sure you all were Jake."

"Jake?"

"Jake. Uh, as in fine. Okay. Alright."

"*Si.*" Isabella then eyed him suspiciously. "Why doesn't Uncle Atty work during daylight, like other people?"

"Ah. Well . . . he's a night owl. He was always late in the morning," Dash said, making his answer up as he went along. "But his work was outstanding. Instead of firing him, I just changed his hours and lo-and-behold! Everyone is happy."

"Bosses don't do that. They don't care about what makes their employees happy."

Dash smiled. "I'm a different boss."

She sniffed. "You don't look like a tailor."

He spread his hands wide. "What does a tailor look like?"

"*Non lo so.*"

An awkward silence settled in between them.

"How do you know my uncle?" she asked.

Dash licked his lips while he thought. The truth was likely something Atty wouldn't want his niece to know.

"We met at a restaurant called the Golden Swan," Dash lied. The actual place was The Golden Goose, a mixed-sex invert club. "It was here in Greenwich Village." That part was true.

"And, eh, what happened that made you hire him?"

"How did that happen? Hmm." Dash was thinking fast, trying to mix the truth of the past with the lies of the present. "I remember now," he said with a smile. "At the restaurant, Atty mentioned doing repairs for a fellow waiter whose waistcoat got torn."

*Close enough.*

That night at the Goose, a "normal" snuck in, and this zozzled man kept harassing a young woman, who wanted nothing to do with him. Or with any man, for that matter. Atty was cleaning up empty glasses and wiping down surfaces. When the zozzled man didn't quit, Atty simply walked around the bar, dumped the man from his barstool, and laid a few punches to him before tossing him out. The scuffle tore a seam in his waistcoat, causing him to yell at the fleeing man, "*I just fixed this, youse drunken bastard!*"

Dash went on. "I inquired if he was good with needle and thread. He said he was, and what of it?"

Isabella barked a laugh. "Ah. Sounds like Uncle Atty."

"I asked if he could show me his work sometime, because I was desperately looking for someone to help me at the shop."

In actuality, Dash had asked Atty if he wanted to make some easy, but unconventional, money.

"*As long as it's not tending bar,*" Atty had replied. "*I'm tired of spilling drinks on myself.*"

Isabella crossed her arms. "What work did he show you?"

"Hmm? Oh. His own clothes, of course." This part was also true. Dash needed to make sure Atty was competent in his seamstress work. He learned Atty was far more than competent; he was masterful.

"I see. He impressed you, eh?"

"He did," Dash answered truthfully.

Isabella's expression softened. "My grandma taught him how to do that. There were eight boys and no girls, and she couldn't keep up with all of them tearing their knees and ripping out their seams. Atty was the only one interested."

"Atty's the second oldest, behind your father, yes?"

Isabella nodded. "According to Mama, Papa was apprenticing with Francesco Barone and didn't have time. Atty wasn't very good with his schoolwork. He had a quick temper and everybody says he would've made a noble soldier, but his aim?" Isabella screwed up her eyes in a theatrical display of shock and disappointment.

Dash laughed in response. "I know. He'd hit his fellow men instead of the enemy."

"Si, si. Grandma taught him, and then she moved with all the others went back to Sicily. Except Papa and Uncle Atty. They were left behind."

"That must've hurt."

"Papa? Perhaps. Not me. I wasn't born yet. But sometimes Papa talks about it. He tries to make it sound easier than how it was. He says, 'They did what they had to do. And Atty and I? We do what we must.'"

"I see."

Isabella cleared her throat, wincing as she did so. "You met Uncle Atty, you saw his work, you hired him, si? Why does he work all the way across town? Why not here among his people? You're not Italian. Why should he trust you?"

Isabella had a point. Not only was Dash white, but he was also an invert. And though Atty worked at The Golden Goose, he wasn't like Dash or Joe or Finn.

"Well, Miss Delucci," Dash replied, "we told each other the truth."

"You would still work for a speak but only on the outside," Dash had said to Atty, "You watch the door while you do the alterations. The Village will wear your work, and I'll be glad to let them know it's yours."

"And I'm not serving booze?"

"Not a drop."

Atty had considered the request. "I think I can do that."

In the present, Isabella frowned with skepticism. "The truth?"

"Yes," Dash replied. "The truth is a powerful thing, Miss Delucci."

Her face darkened. "My Papa wouldn't know anything about the truth."

The front door to the apartment rattled, turning both of their heads. As if cued, Donte, dressed in his rumpled gray suit, stumbled into the front room. His gray hair had escaped the brim of his black fedora in thick tufts. He turned and shuffled down the hallway. When he entered the bedroom, he wrinkled his nose and squinted his eyes, staring at Dash and Isabella.

"What are you doin' in my place?" he demanded. "What are you doin' in my *room*? Get out, get out!" He charged forward, grabbing Isabella's arm.

Isabella spoke up as he dragged her out into the hallway. "It's Uncle Atty's place, Papa! This is his friend! They work together at the tailor shop!"

Dash followed them. "I'm Dash Parker, sir. I told Atty I'd help Isabella watch over the boys. We didn't mean to upset you."

Once they were in the front room, Donte let go of Isabella's arm. "Don't you *ever* go in my room again!"

Isabella whirled around on her father. "Where have you been, Papa?"

Donte glared at her with cold eyes. "Watch your mouth, girl. You don't speak to your father like that."

Isabella's face wrinkled with disgust, and she stormed off into the kitchen.

Donte stared after her, confused, hurt, then angry. "All I do for her, this how she treats me? Bah!"

He dismissed her with a wild shake of his hand. He hustled past Dash and stomped off to Atty's bedroom, slamming the door behind him. The lock turned with a forceful click.

Dash looked from the bedroom door to the kitchen,

where Isabella remained hidden. Then he saw Emiliano and Rocco staring up at him from the sofa with questioning eyes.

He smiled. "Gentlemen, would you like to play a game?"

A floorboard creaked on the other side of the apartment front door. Dash turned his head just as an envelope slid underneath with such force that it flew across the entryway and bounced off Dash's heels. He bent down to pick it up. Someone addressed the envelope to Donte Delucci. No mailing address, no return address, no postage stamp.

He peered down the hallway towards the bedroom. Donte showed no signs of leaving.

Dash opened the envelope and slid out a folded letter. The paper was the same type as the letter he found in Donte's pocket this afternoon.

His heart thudded. He unfolded the letter and saw the same cursive script, the same smudged black ink, the same blurry, slanting letters. The words were all Italian and undecipherable except for one, the name "Capellos." At the bottom of the letter was a drawn dagger dripping with blood.

Without thinking, Dash unlatched the front door and stepped into the hallway.

Empty.

The sound of running footsteps echoed from the stairwell.

With the letter still in his hand, he closed the apartment door and gave chase. He tried not to slip on the water-soaked stairs, gripping the banister as he descended. He was nearly at the bottom when he heard the front door bang open.

Dash picked up his speed and ran into the first-floor

hallway, where his soles found a surface slick enough that his feet went out from under him. His ankles lifted skyward as if invisible strings pulled them straight up. His back hit the tiled floor, the impact knocking the wind out of him.

He lay there for a couple of seconds, heart pounding in his ears, before he rolled over onto his stomach and pulled himself upright again, the letter crinkling in his hand. He shook himself off and surged forward, trying to regain his speed.

He burst out into the storm. He halted in place, searching for a running figure.

To his right was nothing but the sight of rain tossed sideways by the fierce wind. The droplets stung like needles on Dash's face, the gale in full force.

To his left, he heard the clickety-clack of hard heels on concrete. A shadow ran down Bowery away from Atty's building. Dash thought about running after it, but what was the point? Whoever the letter-deliverer was, he (or she) had a monumental head start on him.

The wind howled, nearly blowing Dash down. He returned to Atty's building. Once inside, he glanced down and swore. The letter in his hand was destroyed by the rain.

## 11

The next morning, Dash awoke with a sneeze.

And another.

And another.

He always sneezed in threes.

"If ya got a cold runnin' around last night," Joe grumbled from his pillow, "I'm never lettin' ya outta my sight again."

Dash found a handkerchief in their nightstand drawer. "It's only the dust of this place."

Joe rolled his eyes. "Dust, me arse. Ya looked like a drowned water rat when you got back from Atty's place." A baleful look. "And all for nothin'."

Dash blew and wiped his nose. "I know, I know. I was a dumb Dora." He folded the handkerchief and stood up, stretching his arms upwards.

"Yer not dumb, lassie. Ya just acted in haste. But that water-logged piece o' paper won't help ya convince Atty, that's fer sure."

"What's more disturbing is that whoever is threatening Donte knows where he's staying now."

"Aye. Someone's been watchin' him."

"Or asking around the neighborhood. I'm sure it's no secret Atty and Donte are brothers."

"Either way, it looks like Donte's bringing trouble to Atty's door. First that snake Vito tryin' to get at Isabella. Now this letter writer tryin' to spook Donte."

"We've got to find out quick who it is before this gets worse."

"*We?* Oh no, lassie. Yer not goin' off half-cocked like a virgin runnin' towards a whore house with his trousers down 'round his knees, dick flappin' in the wind."

"That's certainly an image."

"I mean it. Whatever this is, it's no laughin' matter. Ya still got Donte's gun?"

"In my writing desk at the shop."

Joe gave him a long look before saying, "Might be time to learn how to use it then."

It was with that morbid thought that Dash finished dressing in a light gray plaid suit and firework red tie. Something ugly swirled underneath the surface of Donte Delucci's world. Did Dash really want to see what was below?

*But what about Atty? He could be in danger! Do I really have a choice?*

He suffered another trio of sneezes before refocusing on the task at hand. Yesterday, McElroy said he moved Peter Fraker from the American Seamen's Friend Society to another location. This morning, Dash needed to catch George Talbot, the front deskman, before he left his shift.

Dash bid farewell to Joe and stepped out into the hallway, finding it empty. No telling where Finn ended up after they closed Pinstripes.

Outside, the full effects of last night's gale were on display. Tree branches, leaves, trash, rocks, and gravel all tossed and strewn about, covering the road, the sidewalks, and any other available surface. Deep puddles covered the streets and spilled over onto the sidewalks. The air was sharp with cold, and the sky above was shockingly blue. Dash always thought the sky appeared clearer after a storm, as if the clouds had scrubbed the atmosphere clean.

He tightened a red plaid scarf around his neck and set off north.

Several blocks later, the American Seamen's Friend Society rose before him, looking even more upscale in the growing daylight. The tower on the corner rose majestically into the pink sky. Several bell bottoms in uniform were coming out of the entrance portico, chatting, their breaths coming out in thick clouds of smoke. Following them in a giant gray overcoat was George Talbot.

Dash called, "Mr. Talbot! Mr. Talbot!" He rushed up to the entryway steps.

The owl-like man looked up. He touched his glasses, straightening them on his face. Confusion furrowed his brow before recognition lightened it again. "Oh. Yes. Finn's friend."

He turned towards town and kept walking, putting distance between him and his workplace.

Dash trotted to his side. "Mr. Talbot, I was wondering if I can speak with you."

"You sound sick. Kindly turn your head when speaking to me. I don't want whatever that is."

"Apologies, Mr. Talbot, but I do really need to speak with you."

"I'm not getting into a lover's quarrel."

"A lover's, what?"

Dash didn't understand. Then he did. He and Finn had pretended to be lovers to get into the Society, and now

Finn was obviously there visiting Borden. That George found out about it didn't surprise Dash. George looked like a man who knew everything that happened on his watch. Even those events that occurred on someone else's watch.

"Oh, that. No, no, it's not about—well anyway, I know all about it, to tell the truth."

"Do you? Either way, I will not confirm or deny anything. My job depends upon discretion, something I'd think *you* would appreciate, given whose bed you rolled around in."

George made an abrupt turn onto an avenue, heading downtown. Dash followed, keeping pace with him.

"That is admirable," Dash said. "And I hate to ask you to break any confidences—"

"But you are anyway. Excuse me," George said to a passerby who was walking their dog. He stepped over the mutt and its leash.

Dash sidestepped around both, coming back to George's side. "Yes. That is true. It's for a good reason. The safety and wellbeing of my friend Peter Fraker."

"Ah, yes. Also known as Mr. Jonah Collins. Queer, being put into the Society with a false name. By a cop, no less. Almost as if he was being protected from someone. Pardon me." George pushed through a couple, a bell bottom in blues and a woman in reds. Both turned to glare at him.

Dash excused himself and pushed through after him. "I can promise you I'm no threat to Mr. Fraker. I'm trying to help him, in fact."

"Wouldn't an assassin say the same thing?"

"Assassin?" Dash laughed at the image of him in such a role. "I'm no more assassin than I'm a—" He almost said 'sailor' but caught himself in time.

Unfortunately, not in time to stop George from making the same leap.

"A man of the sea?" he said with a smirk. "I knew you were a land animal."

"Mr. Talbot, I implore you. It is imperative I find this man. He is being held hostage by that cop. You're not a big fan of them yourself. I believe you called them 'elephant ears.'"

"Oh, trying to use my own words against me, are we?" George shook his head. "You need to get better at negotiations."

"I have information that will free him. Mr. Fraker, I mean." In a desperate move, Dash attempted the same rationale that Finn used on Peter. "Don't you want to help a fellow Villager? After all, we need to stick together."

George abruptly halted.

Dash skidded to a stop, almost running into his back.

George turned on his heel and faced Dash. "What are you up to?"

Dash tried to appear innocent. "Me? I'm not up to anything—" A trio of sneezes interrupted him, causing George to lean away. "—other than trying to help a poor, innocent man."

A thick crowd of people started bumping into them, but George didn't seem to notice. He wagged a finger in front of Dash's face.

"No, no. You're behaving just like Finn Francis, and we both know that little imp causes more trouble than Puck in midsummer."

Dash took George's elbow and moved them to the side, so they weren't standing in the middle of the foot traffic. "I promise you, Mr. Talbot, I am not looking for trouble."

"Oh, really?"

"Yes, really."

George glanced around, studiously avoiding Dash's gaze. "You know, it *is* rather chilly, and I would like to take the train home. But it is *so* expensive these days." He then looked meaningfully at Dash.

Dash smiled and reached into his pocket, hoping he had enough sugar to fill George's bowl. It took fifty cents.

"An expensive subway ride," Dash remarked.

"Yes, the prices are just outrageous in this city, aren't they?" Satisfied with the amount, George said, "I never liked that brute, the copper. He checked out Mr. Fraker the morning after you and Finn did your little act for me. That was quite a show, I might add. Not Broadway-worthy. More off . . . *off* Broadway. At any rate, this copper was quite rude and shockingly ungracious." Meaning McElroy hadn't tipped him.

"Did the copper say where he was taking Mr. Fraker?"

"No."

*Damn!*

"Did Mr. Fraker leave a message by any chance?"

"A message?"

"Yes. A note? A letter? Something to be picked up later?"

"I see." George sniffed several times, then cleared his throat. "You know, I think I'm fighting off a cold. The same cold you have, I daresay. A hot soup and some warm bread might serve me well."

Dash eyed the man. "Will it?"

"Oh, yes. I tend to get rather hoarse when I'm ill. Won't be able to utter a single word before too long. For days, even *weeks* at a time."

Dash stifled his irritation, and once again, reached into his trouser pockets. After the last dime Dash had on him was in George's outstretched palm, he asked, "And the note . . . ?"

---

Dash grinned the entire way back to West Fourth. Peter Fraker indeed had left word of his whereabouts: the Roberts Hotel on Bleecker between Sullivan and Thompson Streets. How he finagled the location out of McElroy spoke to Peter's nervous but determined nature.

"Mr. Fraker," Dash said to himself. "You are one clever customer." He also thought of McElroy's smugness from yesterday. "And take that, you odious fiend."

He returned to the Cherry Lane Playhouse and, using Finn's skeleton key, snuck into the box office once again. He dialed the telephone, and the operator connected him to McElroy's precinct, where he made certain the man had shown up for roll call. The squad was getting briefed. Should take a half hour, give it or take, said the bored voice over the line.

Just the time Dash needed to scout out McElroy's apartment.

He severed the connection, locked up the office, and rushed over to Downing Street.

The building was the saddest Dash had ever seen: two squat stories, uneven roof, misshapen windows, leaning doorways. It was like a gingerbread house that some spiteful child had knocked askew. Steam thundered out of a round metal chimney on top, and with it came the smell of hot, dirty laundry water, sour onions, and fetid beef.

A dog barked incessantly behind one window while a man's voice shouted, "Would you shut that mutt up?! I'm tryin' to sleep here!"

A woman's voice retorted, "It's your dog, you deal with it!"

Dash rang the buzzer by the front door.

A man in an undershirt opened the door, trousers unbuttoned, big toes poking through gigantic holes in his dark navy socks. He was mostly bald on top with curly salt-and-pepper hair sticking out on the sides. A pair of spectacles rested on the edge of his nose, and his pale eyes peered over them.

"Excuse me, sir," Dash said, "but I—"

"Who are you? A bill collector, a lawyer, or a page for the landlord?" the man asked, his breath laced with whiskey undertones. "I'll save you some trouble. If you're looking for Mr. Pitts, he's at work at the Selvin Printer Company, the lucky son of a gun. Though, maybe not so lucky. I worked there until the bastards fired me for taking a, and I quote, *'an unscheduled and unsanctioned urinary break on company time.'*"

He snorted.

"That's capitalism for ya. The socialists got that part right, at least. These holier-than-thou businessmen don't see you as a human being, just a machine they can work day and night, night and day, greasing the wheels of their fortunes, which they'll be damned if they'll ever let you have an extra penny or two. But I digress.

"If you're looking for Mr. Mulgrave, he's dead. If you're looking for Mrs. Mulgrave, she's in prison for killing Mr. Mulgrave. We all think Mr. Mulgrave asked for it. Mean son of a bitch, he was, but that's juries for ya.

"And lastly, if you're looking for Mr. and Mrs. Conrad, they're in there arguing about their goddamned dog. Seems it barks all the time. I say it's only joining in on whatever else those two are carrying on about, which, best as I can tell, is a lot of nothing. They like the sounds of their own voices, though God knows why. He sounds like a braying horse, and she sounds like a shrieking cockatoo. You looking for any of these people?"

Dash was partially stunned by the soliloquy. "Thank you, no," he finally replied. "I'm looking for Mr. McElroy."

The man cupped a hand behind his ear. "What was that?"

Dash raised his voice slightly. "McElroy. I'm looking for Cullen McElroy."

The man cocked his head. "No one here by that name."

"Are you certain?"

The man laughed. "I should be, son. Been here all of twenty years, back when this dump was—well, it was still a dump, but it was a newer dump. Realtors keep threatening to tear this place down, but I refuse to move. The way they want to raise the rents 'round here, none of us will be able to afford to live in New Rich City. No, sir, I was here twenty years and I've never seen a—what was the name again?"

Dash repeated it.

A fervent shake of the man's head. "Nope. You got the wrong address."

"Perhaps he's here under a different name? He is a police officer, and he may not want people to know where he lives." Dash described the man, attempting to be kind but accurate and ultimately failing.

The man had pulled at his lip, his expression skeptical. "A corpulent blondie with hair like old straw and teeth like a corpse? Nope, nobody here who looks like that. Mr. Mulgrave is—I should say, was—a thin man with a sunken chest. Mr. Conrad is short, like circus short, which explains why he's so loud. You ever notice it's the small dogs that bark and growl the most? Men are the same way. This

McElroy that short? No? Alright. Pitts is in his fifties and has white hair. This McElroy white-headed? Blond, right? Yeah, not Pitts then."

The old man rubbed his chin. "He was never a woman, though? God bless her, but Mrs. Mulgrave was a bit on the thick and rotund side with whiskers on her chin. But it sounds like your McElroy fella is free as a bird and not in Sing Sing? Yeah, that's what I thought. No sir, no McElroy here."

Dash thanked the man for his time and left, walking slowly down the sidewalk. Had Dash gotten the address wrong?

After zig zagging his way eastward, he saw a public telephone booth, entered, and dropped two cents into the slot. He reconnected with the precinct and repeated his landlord vetting act, though making up a different company name, as though McElroy had applied to several buildings. Nope, the bored Personnel clerk confirmed the Downing Street address.

Dash hung up the receiver.

What the hell was going on?

## 12

Questions and sneezes followed Dash all the way back to West Fourth Street. He spied the placard for the Greenwich Village Inn and smiled, cheered with the promise of a cup (or three) of coffee.

Only the Inn was closed when he arrived.

And Emmett stood outside of it, scowling.

"Emmett," Dash said. "Why aren't you open?"

Emmett pointed to the sign on the door, which read: "*TEMPORARILY CLOSED FOR HAUNTINGS. COME BACK SOON FOR MISCHIEF!*"

Dash recognized the handwriting. "Finn?"

"That goddamned little—"

The front door suddenly opened, and Finn stuck his head out. "Oh! It's you two! Come in, come in. I'm almost finished!" He opened the door wide.

Emmett roughly pushed past him.

Dash took his time, muttering to Finn, "What did you do?"

"I saved him from himself."

"Someone should do the same for you."

Dash entered the Inn's tavern and was rendered speechless.

The space had been completely transformed.

A grinning paper moon, complete with orange and black streamers, dangled from the center of the cracked plaster ceiling. Pasted on the walls were paper pumpkins, paper witches flying on broomsticks, paper black cats screeching, and paper skeletons dancing in a line. Scarecrows with sightless eyes and stitched mouths held court behind the rough-hewn bar. A painted devil's head laughed maniacally from the fireplace mantle, with a red sparkling pitchfork resting beside him. Piles of creased orange muslin paper formed undulating patterns to give the illusion of crackling eternal hellfire. And witches' cauldrons filled with green paper rumpled to look like boiling potions stood in the center of all the tables.

The three Ex-Pats stared at theirs with a mix of confusion and horror.

Dash asked why Finn allowed them inside and not Emmett.

"Because they didn't leave," Finn muttered. "I tried to explain to the dears that they needed to go home, but they didn't seem to understand my request."

"More likely, they were worried you'd lock them out, and they'd never get back in."

"I suppose."

Dash peered at Emmett, who surveyed the alteration.

Finn wiggled in place with glee. "I think he loves it."

*I don't think so,* Dash thought.

Finn asked, "Did you tell Atty about his gambling brother?"

Dash sighed. "It's not the right time. He's trying to keep his brother, niece, and nephews afloat. It's bad enough he knows about the threatening letters and that he knows Donte is lying to him. Adding this on top of all that?"

"Hmm, yes, I see your point. And the letters seem to be the bigger concern."

"Agreed. And I stupidly ruined the latest one, so we still don't know what exactly they're threatening and why." Dash took out the invoice sheets. "I found these hidden in Atty's bedroom. I'm not certain what these are or what they mean. Could be unrelated to the letters."

Finn scanned the first two sheets before handing them back to Dash. "It seems an odd item for Mr. Delucci to have. You're sure they're not Atty's? He could have an extra job."

"The thought crossed my mind."

The two of them watched Emmett circle around his place. He hadn't yet said one word about the decorations.

*Worrisome,* Dash thought.

Finn leaned in close. "I paid Borden a visit last night."

"Oh?"

"I couldn't very well leave Borden at half-mast, could I? I have a reputation in the navy yard to protect."

"I know, I know. All flags raised and flown."

"Exactly!"

"You're going to see him again tonight?"

"Why, yes! Frankly, it's been a little . . . quiet . . . since Reggie."

"Ah, the acting Don Juan." Dash smiled. "Well, I'm happy for you, Finn. I think Borden is a stand-up gentleman."

Finn's face brightened. "You do?"

"Absolutely! And he's clearly quite smitten with you."

"Of course he is. Why wouldn't he be?"

"And," Dash said, leaning closer to his friend, "you're quite taken with him, too."

Finn waved him off. "Stop that! It isn't like that between us. It can't be."

"Why not?"

"Because he's a bell bottom! Always in another port with another fella. Or gal, if they're not discriminating. Goddess knows when he'll be back in New York again." Finn shook his head more fervently. "No, no, no. It can't be more than what it is."

"Which is what?"

Finn gave a beleaguered sigh. "A holiday."

Dash watched his friend's face.

*You liar*, he thought.

He said, "Well. A holiday is still worth celebrating."

"Cheers to that."

Emmett was still doing a walkabout, gazing at the pumpkins and witches with a pinched expression on his face.

Finn said, "Joe told me about McElroy's little visit yesterday. How *beastly*. I don't understand why he's so fixated on that despicable Walter. It feels so . . . personal to him, as if somehow you've wronged him in some way."

"What concerns me is McElroy tying Karl to degeneracy."

"Thereby connecting us to the same so-called sin." Finn sighed. "Honestly, I don't know why these bluenoses care so much about what *we* do with our lives. Who's in our arms, what kind of outfits we have on. It's just love. It's just clothes. In a world riddled with disease and war, what does any of it matter? And who are we hurting, I ask you!"

"No one," Dash replied. They were silent for a moment. "I did discover something interesting about McElroy this morning." He told Finn about the Downing Street address. "Either Personnel didn't update their records, or—"

"Or he lied about where he lived," Finn said, completing Dash's thought. "You thinking what I'm thinking?"

"He's been spending his 'donations' on someplace expensive and wants to keep it quiet."

"How will we find that out?"

"Simple. You're going to follow him. See where he goes when he clocks out from his shift and leaves the precinct."

Finn's eyes widened. "You mean donning disguises? Oh, what fun! It's so deliciously cloak and dagger. I can't decide if I'll go with my favorite, an old, addled aunt, or my second favorite, a roustabout."

"Whichever you decide is Jake," Dash replied. "Just don't get caught."

Finn sighed. "It is utterly tragic how much you underestimate me. Perhaps I can borrow a few items from Borden. I'll look like a true bell bottom then."

At this point, Emmett stopped wandering about and turned to stare at them, his eyes wide and blank.

Finn was oblivious to the man's genuine reaction.

Dash, filled with trepidation, asked, "What do you think, Emmett?"

"Yes," Finn said, "what do you think, Em?"

Emmett took a moment to respond. When he finally did, he simply said, "Hell."

Finn clapped his hands happily. "Exactly what I was going for!"

While Emmett and Finn squabbled behind him, Dash read the morning *Times*.

It was a heavy news day.

The Romanian Queen visited New York and Philadelphia (stately, polite, and dreadfully boring). A private detective named Felix de Martini that was hired by the defense in the Hall-Mills case was released after spending a night in jail for failing to comply with a subpoena. The contentious, and increasingly ridiculous, governor's race had the challenger doubling down on his claims that New York had widespread tainted milk while the incumbent said it was all poppycock. Even last night's gale got a prominent mention: several boats capsized, eighteen people injured, three people sadly killed.

On page six, he found a follow-up on the Elizabeth Street fire. Laboratory tests showed traces of kerosene and the components of dynamite where the boiler used to be before the tumbling building crushed it. The fire investigator officially ruled arson, and the NYPD was now actively involved. They questioned the landlords about their insurance policies and business solvency to determine, or rule out, their potential motive.

Dash looked up from his paper. Who demolished Donte's building intentionally? He thought of Donte's gambling debts. In the hundreds, according to Isabella. Would a gambling den owner burn down a building full of people over an unpaid debt of one of its tenants? It seemed extreme in Dash's opinion, but he'd since learned that violence was the common currency of the underworld. Next to dollars, that is.

He finished his breakfast and returned to Hartford & Sons. He opened the writing desk, seeing Donte's pistol and bullets. Would he need to learn how to use this blasted thing?

The devil tarot card grabbed his attention. He picked it up, reading the scribbled note again: "*T.S.S. WEDNESDAY 9:00.*" Tomorrow.

He slipped the card into his pocket and concentrated on taking measurements and giving out the secret knock.

To his surprise, Atty showed up in the mid-afternoon.

Dash glanced at his wristwatch, noting the time—almost three o'clock—and placed his hands on his hips. "Atty. You're here early."

His friend was ill at ease. Eyes darted about. Fingers snapped to some internal rhythm. His feet tapped to a different tune altogether.

"Yeah, Boss," Atty replied. "Um, somethin' I want to talk to youse about."

"What is it?"

Atty glanced away. "It's Donte. He told me he don't like youse watching the boys and Isabella. Says you're not family and youse shouldn't be there."

"Ah."

"He says you're spyin' on him too. Watchin' him when he comes and goes. Is that true, Boss?"

"Spying?" Dash shook his head. "I watched over the boys and talked with Isabella. That's it."

Relief eased the wrinkles in Atty's forehead. "That's what I told him! He didn't believe me."

"I see." Dash wondered if Donte discovered the olive oil invoice sheets were missing. "And what do you think?"

Atty released a long, heavy breath. "I don't know, Boss. I know you, but Donte doesn't. He don't trust many people. Frankly, he don't trust me."

"He still won't tell you about the letters?"

A sad shake of Atty's head. "No. Says it's none of my business."

"Has he mentioned The Smoke Shop to you at all?"

"The Smoke Shop? What's that?"

Dash shrugged, keeping himself noncommittal. "A cigar shop on Bleecker," he replied truthfully.

"No. Why?"

"Isabella says he goes there a lot."

"Maria didn't like cigar smoke in the apartment. That's probably why, Boss."

*Damn.*

"Yes," Dash said. "That makes sense. Is Donte's only job at the bank?"

"Yeah, Boss. Moreno Bank & Trust. Why do you ask?"

"Have you heard of Manhattan Transit and Freight? They're a delivery business."

"Never heard of them." Atty frowned. "What's goin' on? Youse askin' questions like a detective." He crossed his arms over his chest. "*Were* youse spyin' on Donte?"

"No, no. This is . . . unrelated." Dash fumbled for a convincing lie. "I'm wondering if Fife has a new cover business. That's all. You know he often he likes to change it up."

Atty stared at him for a moment before dropping his eyes. "Right, Boss. Um, I never heard of 'em." He took a deep breath. "Anyway, I appreciate youse watching over Bella and the boys, but I think it might be better if you don't anymore. Until Donte calms himself."

Dash nodded. "Understood."

They said their goodbyes and Atty left the shop.

Dash tapped the surface of the writing desk. Donte strategically placed him in a tough spot. If Dash told Atty the truth about Donte, it would prove Donte's accusations about him and Atty might side with his brother rather than with his friend. The unlucky gambler was shrewder than Dash thought.

By four o'clock, the walk-in trade had slowed, and the unanswered questions continued to irk Dash. He closed the shop early and grabbed a cab to take him to Little Italy.

The Smoke Shop on Bleecker Street was suspiciously nondescript. Just another store on the ground floor of a tenement.

Inside, dark wood and heavy burgundy drapes created a dusk. A glass case stretched across the entire width of the shop, displaying cigars of varying styles and lengths. The case ended at a waist-high wooden door, and a curtained-off doorway laid just beyond it. Nothing about the décor suggested a gambling den nearby.

Dash glanced at the curtained doorway again. Perhaps it was beyond there.

A young man in his twenties perched on a stool behind the glass case of cigars. Beneath dark, curly black hair was an unblemished face with thick lips. Muscular shoulders, chest, and arms filled out the white shirt and tan vest. A tie the color of spilled red wine twisted down his front.

"Good morning, *signore*," he said, his voice deep and pleasing. "How many I help you?"

Dash smiled and said the first lie that came to mind. "Good morning. I am looking for a gift for a friend, a cousin, rather. He loves his cigars, but unfortunately, I don't know the slightest thing about them."

"Do you know what brand he smokes?"

"Not a clue," Dash answered truthfully.

"We only have one here: Toscano. That's all there is in Italy. It's a, how do you say, monopoly."

"Ah."

"They're still good, though. Excellent quality."

On the street, a set of brakes squealed behind Dash. A motor idled, rattling and coughing.

The shop keeper asked, "Does your cousin like strong cigars?"

Outside, voices shouted at each other. Not a fight. Only to be heard over the motor.

Dash shrugged. "I assume so. He likes the darker ones, if that helps."

The shop keeper smiled. "It's not so much color as age." He gestured to the cigars in the display case. "They vary in color, size and shape, but they are all strong, very robust. No sweetness, like some other cigars. Notable tastes are coffee, wood, and pepper."

"I see," Dash said.

The door opened behind him. He turned to see a young man very similar in appearance to the shop keeper. Same face, same hair, same coloring. Only his eyes were a luminous green, like Joe's. He wore a white shirt, open at the collar, exposing silky dark hair below the collarbone, and a tan vest with matching trousers. A heavy-looking wooden box was resting in both of his hands.

"Renzo," he said, then spoke in Italian, nodding his head to the box.

Dash noticed that someone had stamped "*FRAGILE*" in the corner and branded "*TOSCANO OLIO D'OLIVA*" onto the sides of the box.

Olive oil.

Renzo the shop keeper turned his gaze from Dash to the young man carrying the box. He replied in Italian, the words tumbling over themselves, the only one meaning anything to Dash's ear was "Berto."

The man Renzo called Berto glanced over his shoulder at Dash and smirked. He continued conversing with Renzo and then nodded to the curtain. Renzo refused to get up. Berto barked a few more words in Italian and eventually Renzo rose. With one hand, Renzo pulled open the waist-high door, allowing Berto access, and with the other, pulled back the curtain. Berto ducked slightly underneath it and entered what appeared to be a back stairwell.

Dash peered through the curtain and saw Berto take the first step.

Renzo closed the curtain and gave Dash a baleful eye. He returned to his perch behind the glass counter.

"The aroma is very distinct," he said, returning to the subject of cigars. "Very acidic. Some people enjoy it; others call it 'stink weed.'"

"That's not very polite."

"I tell you this to give you the correct impression of our cigars. So," Renzo said, "do you think your cousin would like them?"

"Let's give it a go," Dash replied after a suitable pause. "I can tell him it's exotic. He goes for that sort of thing."

Renzo arched an eyebrow but didn't say a word. He reached into the glass case and removed one cigar. The paper was rugged, the bumpy wrapper veiny. The cigar was surprisingly short, given what Dash had seen others smoke. If Finn were here, he'd make the sort of comment that would no doubt offend Renzo and land himself in jail.

There were some transaction words, a slight haggling over price, but within five minutes, Dash possessed a Toscano cigar he had no intention of smoking.

During all of this, the man called Berto carried in

multiple crates, all marked the same: *"FRAGILE"* and *"TOSCANO OLIO D'OLIVA."* Dash turned during one of his trips and saw the idling truck outside. *"MANHATTAN TRANSIT & FREIGHT"* was emblazoned on the side. The same name as on the hidden invoice sheets.

When Renzo had wrapped up Dash's newly purchased cigar into a paper bag and handed it over, Dash thanked the man and then said, "Sir, one other thing. I was wondering if I could play around with Chance this afternoon? You know? Dance with Lady Luck?"

There was a flicker in Renzo's eyes, but otherwise his face betrayed nothing. "What do you mean, sir?" he asked.

"I mean—oh my, this is awkward—but I would like to play some cards."

"Cards," Renzo repeated.

"Yes."

They locked eyes.

Dash pointed to the curtain. "Is it just back there?"

Renzo held out his hand. At first, Dash didn't understand the gesture. Renzo cleared his throat and wiggled his fingers.

"Ah," Dash said, reaching into his trouser pockets and pulling out a nickel. He placed it into Renzo's palm, who then stood and went over to the waist-high door. He held it open and gestured to Dash to walk through.

"Next time, the password is *dado*," Renzo said as Dash passed by him. "Means dice."

"Thank you."

Dash pulled the curtain to the side and saw a steep set of stairs. He followed them down until he came to a closed door. Voices murmured behind it, urgent and anxious. He took a deep breath and opened the door.

## 13

Immediately, a cacophony of noise and smells washed over him.

Raucous laughter, tumbling dice, tinkling ice.

The calls for numbers, the calls for bets.

Sweet perfume and musky aftershave underlaid with spilled liquor and sour sweat.

The place wasn't fancy by any stretch of the imagination. It was a basement with no attempt at flash or style to conceal what it was. Concrete flooring, bricked columns, exposed bulbs hanging from the ceiling by rusty chains. A construction scene more than a club. Dash could even spy the building's boiler in one of the far-off corners.

Fanning out across the floor were tables hosting several games of chance. Above them all, thick clouds of cigarette smoke. A noisy crowd of men and women played craps to Dash's left, a man shaking his dice before letting them fly in an aggressive throw. The dice hit the far end of the table. Half the crowd cheered; the other half groaned. Dash couldn't see if the dice-thrower had his pile of money doubled or taken away.

The harsh rattle of the roulette wheel turned Dash's head to the right. A blond woman in a blue dress, complete with lace collar, clasped her hands together. Hopeful, she and her table companions watched the small black ball bounce over the grooves until it landed on a number.

She shrieked and jumped up and down. A winner.

"Oh, that's wonderful!" she said. "Isn't that wonderful? I knew it would go to that number, I just knew it! It's my mother's birthdate and wouldn't you know? She was born early, and the doctors didn't think she'd survive. But she did, and ever since, I've had that be my lucky number. Isn't this grand? Oh, thank you, sir, thank you. Look at this pile! My stars, I've never seen that much mo—Yes, I'd like to bet again. Let's try a different number . . ."

Dash turned his head, continuing to scan the room. What struck him was how *early* it was in the day. This was well before noon, yet these gamblers were dressed as if it were midnight. Perhaps they'd *been* here since midnight.

A figure stepping through a doorway in the far-left corner caught his eye. The area was mostly in shadow and partially obscured by a collection of potted palms. The man called Berto used a key to lock the door before turning around and entering the main room. There was a hitch in his step when he sensed Dash's gaze. The two locked eyes for a moment, then Berto sauntered over to him.

"Good morning, *signore*," he said. "Welcome to The Smoke Shop. Is this your first time here?"

"Indeed, it is."

"Excellent, excellent! What's your game of choice? Poker? Blackjack? Bridge? Perhaps you'd like to try our roulette wheel? That cute blond over there is having the game of her life."

"I can see that." Dash placed his hands in his trouser

pockets, hoping to look nonchalant. "I was wondering if I could speak with someone about a debt."

Berto's smile dimmed a wattage or two. "A debt?"

Dash nodded.

Berto asked, "What's your name?"

"Max Bennett."

"Well, *Signore* Bennett, why are you inquiring about a debt? Is it yours?"

"No, it belongs to a fellow named Donte Delucci."

Berto's lips twitched. "Ah, yes, *Signore* Delucci. We know him well." Berto pointed to a card game occurring near the potted palms. "He loves to sit over there and draw losing card after losing card. He is not very lucky."

"That's what I've gathered."

"Are you a friend of his?"

"Of his brother."

"And do you wish to pay his debt?"

"Perhaps," Dash replied carefully. "How much are we talking about?"

"How much did he tell you?"

At that moment, a woman's voice from behind Dash called out to Berto.

A flicker of annoyance crossed his face. He muttered a curse as the determined click of heels on concrete came towards them.

Dash turned to find a lovely creature in an olive dress with a plume of peacock feathers in blue and green bursting from one shoulder. The hemline, stopping just beyond the knee, featured beaded feathers in the same colors. Her dark, slightly curled hair and blue eyes with black "Egyptian-style" eyeliner were striking.

"Berto, we need to talk," she said.

"Not now," he growled.

"Yes, *now*." She glanced over at Dash and dismissed him with a blink of her eyes. She turned back to Berto. "I'm supposed to do this séance and I have no earthly idea what day he scheduled it."

"I thought you didn't deal with earthly ideas; only spiritual ones," Berto replied.

She pursed her lips. "Very funny."

"He didn't schedule it, Miss Sams. *I* did. I run this entire floor. Or did you forget that?"

The woman smirked. "I can't forget it when you mention it every minute. Now if you can't tell me when *you* scheduled the damn thing, I'll—"

"Wednesday. Eh? Wednesday night. Tomorrow night, *capisci?*"

The woman smiled sweetly. "Thank you. Was that so hard?" She then eyed Dash uneasily and said, "And, uh, there's something else I need to speak with you about."

"Later."

"Berto—"

"I'm working, Delilah!" Berto cleared his throat and lowered his voice. "I'm discussing something with a potential customer."

Dash took this break in the hostilities to extend his hand to the woman. "Max Bennett, a pleasure to meet you."

The woman frowned and gave him a palm full of wet noodles. "Charmed. I'm Delilah Sams, speaker to the underworld."

Berto explained, "Miss Sams does tarot card readings and seances."

Dash looked at her with interest. Donte's devil card was with him now. The one with a scribbled date and time for tomorrow at nine o'clock. "Really? Tarot? How very fascinating."

Delilah smiled. "Care to learn about your future?"

"Possibly. You know, I recently found a tarot card in someone's pocket. A devil card. You wouldn't be missing it, would you? This man is a frequent patron here. Donte Delucci?"

A flash of her eyes belied her calm demeanor. "I see so many people here, I confess all their names blur together."

"I can describe him for you—"

Berto intervened. "I believe Miss Sams has a pressing appointment. Perhaps we can continue this discussion at another time. Thank you, Delilah."

"Very well. We'll talk later." She removed her limp hand from Dash's and slinked off to the bar.

Berto muttered another curse and gestured towards her. "And that, Mr. Bennett, is the famed Delilah Sams. Mysterious, wondrous, and a pain in my ass." He shook his head. "Now, where were we?"

"Mr. Delucci's debts."

"Ah, yes. Why are you so interested in them, *Signore* Bennett?"

"Because he's been receiving letters."

"Letters?"

Dash nodded. "Threatening ones."

"And you think, what? That we're sending them?"

Dash shrugged. "He has debts."

A wintry smile erased any warmth from Berto's face. "Who are you? Why are you here? You *polizia*? Eh?"

"I am most assuredly not the police. I can't stand the crooked assholes myself."

"Then why are you asking me about such letters?"

"I told you. I'm a concerned friend."

"Okay, okay. Let's say I believe you." Berto crossed his arms over his chest. "What did these letters say?"

"Unfortunately, I don't know. They were written in Italian," Dash replied. "There was a name in the letter. Capello. Or rather, 'the Capellos.' Does that mean anything to you?"

"No. Should it?"

A loud shout went up from the roulette table.

The blond in the blue dress leapt up and down, screeching with laughter. "Oh my, will you look at that! I doubled my winnings! I doubled them! Champagne for everybody! Champagne for—why, thank you, thank you. Yes, I'll take it now. My stars, can you believe it?!"

Berto leaned in close to Dash. "Unless you're here to play, I kindly suggest you leave." His eyes bored into Dash's before sliding over to a spot over Dash's shoulder. He cursed.

Dash turned and saw Vito Beneventi, the weaselly boy who harassed Atty's niece Isabella yesterday. He was standing near a craps table and invading yet another poor girl's space. She was trying to shrink into herself, which he took as permission to advance. She kept averting her face, her eyes looking around desperately for a way out.

*She should throw her drink in his face and make him pay for a new one,* Dash thought.

He looked up at Berto, whose eyes had narrowed, his jaw clenched.

Dash said, "You don't care much for him, do you?"

"Because he's not one of us. He tries, god help us, he tries, but he'll never, ever be." Berto looked down at Dash. "Excuse me."

Berto left him, marching over to the bar where he grabbed Vito's shoulder, pulling him away. Vito squawked in protest, and the shrinking girl took this moment to escape.

Dash turned and was about to take his leave when a man in a brown suit bumped into him and spilled the contents of his highball glass onto Dash's suit. The sharp juniper smell of gin mixed with the citrus of lime wafted over Dash's face as the man spoke.

"Oh jeez, will you look at that? I am so sorry, sir, so sorry. Here, let me clean that up." The man's words were ever so slightly slurred at the edges. He pulled out a handkerchief and started dabbing ineffectually at Dash's coat.

Dash took out his own handkerchief and did the same. "My apologies, my good man. I didn't see you there."

"No, it's my fault, my fault." The man looked at the mess on Dash's suit. "I seem to be making it worse." He blotted some more of the stained fabric before stopping. "I'm so sorry, sir. I'll pay to have it cleaned."

Dash was about to refuse out of politeness, but then thought, *if he's offering* . . .

"Thank you. That's quite considerate of you."

"Least I can do, least I can do." The man looked down at his soaked handkerchief. "Let's go over to the bar and see if they have a towel or something. The name's Gus, by the way. Gus Brown. Like my suit."

"Pleasure meeting you, Mr. Brown. I'm Max Bennett."

They went over to the bar where, despite the morning hour, several patrons sat nursing their cocktails. From the looks on their faces, they hadn't been winning.

"Hey, Johnnie!" Gus called. "I made a mess over here. You got a towel?"

The bartender Johnnie, his expression bored, passed over a cloth.

"Thanks, Johnnie. Johnnie, this is Max; Max, Johnnie. Johnnie takes good care of us, don't ya, Johnnie?"

"Somebody's got to," Johnnie replied. "You want another?"

"How d'ya know?" Gus handed the cloth to Dash, who blotted at the damp fabric. At least it was gin and not whiskey or bourbon.

Johnnie pointed at Dash's suit. "Unless you spilled someone else's drink on him, I figured your glass would be empty."

Gus guffawed. "Oh, yeah! I'm such a dope. Yes, Johnnie, I'll have another. I'll buy this chap a round too. Whatcha drinking?"

Dash held up his hands. "It's a little early for me."

"Don't tell me you're a teetotaler. That would make you an awful bore. I always say, life is too short; the last thing any of us should be is *boring*. Right, Johnnie?"

Johnnie nodded as he mixed the gin and seltzer before throwing in a splash of lime. He handed Gus his drink while glancing over at Dash, who shook his head.

"Cheers!" Gus said, holding up his glass before drinking half of it down. He smacked his lips. "That hits the spot. Oh, before I forget." He reached into his trouser pocket and pulled out a quarter. He placed it on the bar, nodding to it. "That's for the suit cleaning."

Dash slid it off the bar and into his own pocket. He thanked Gus again.

"Don't mention it. My fault entirely, my fault. Say," Gus said. "Did I overhear you talking to what's-his-name— Bezo? Bruno? *Berto*! That's it—did I hear you talking to Berto about Donte Delucci?"

"You know Mr. Delucci?"

Gus's grin was wide. "I should say so! He and I are buddies. Pals. We met in this joint, ya know."

"How long have you known him?"

"A month or so."

"Only a month?"

Gus got a little defensive. "I don't see how the length of time pertains. But we look out for each other, yes indeed, we do. I heard about what happened to him. Losing his home, losing his wife. It's not fair. Why couldn't those lazy firemen put it out, huh? What we pay taxes for if they can't do the one thing they're supposed to?"

"I don't know," Dash replied. "Perhaps the firemen got there too late." He gestured to Gus. "You mentioned you and Donte are friends."

"Yessiree. We look out for each other," he repeated. "You have to in a place like this. Those Spinellis are no joke. Keep your nose clean and your tab paid. Otherwise . . . it ain't good."

"I understand Donte isn't doing the latter."

Gus looked down at his shoes. "Yeah, yeah. I feel bad about that. I was supposed—" He hiccupped. "—I was supposed to look after him. That's what buddies do. Only he can't—can't stop." Gus looked up and leaned with his elbow on the bar. He held up a pointer finger like a teacher giving a lesson. "There comes a point, winning or losing, when a man has got to walk away from the table. You know what I'm saying?"

"Sure, sure."

"And Donte, he doesn't know when to quit. He keeps going until the money's gone."

"How much is he in for?"

Gus leaned in close and whispered, "Six hundred dollars."

Dash whistled. "That's a lot of sugar."

"You're telling me! I don't know how he's gonna come

up with it, to be honest. The bank doesn't pay him that much, even if he is a manager."

"He's in banking?"

Gus nodded. "Yes, sir, he is. Works at Moreno Bank & Trust. Been there a couple years. Used to work at Francesco Barone's Bank." His eyes were sliding around in his sockets. "You don't know who that is—" Another hiccup. "—do ya?"

"I'm afraid I don't."

"*Well.* Mr. Barone, see, he was one of the richest men in Little Italy. (This is what Donte told me, you understand?) Set up one of the most successful banks here. Anyone who was anyone had their money in his vault. Donte and his best friend Ro—Ro—Rodolpho." Gus grinned sloppily at his eventual successful pronunciation of the name. "They both worked at the bank." Then he frowned. "Sad story, though. When the Great War started, he and Rodolpho went off to the trenches. Only Donte came back. That was Nineteen-Seventeen."

"How tragic," Dash replied, meaning it. It was a common story among many men in this city.

"Yeah, tragic." Gus took another healthy sip of his cocktail. "Anyway, we met at the craps table. I was having an okay night. Him, though? He was on top of the world! Every card hit. It was incredible. We went to celebrate here with Johnnie and we've been pals ever since." He finished his drink and held up his empty glass. "Johnnie! I'm dry, Johnnie! Can't have that."

"Mr. Brown—"

"Gus. Call me Gus."

Dash smiled. "Gus. Has Donte mentioned receiving threatening letters recently?"

Gus's mood darkened. "Yeah. He mentioned 'em. I told him they were fake."

Dash remembered Donte's hysterical rantings: "*He said it wasn't real.*" He supposed Donte was referring to Gus.

Gus asked, "How do you know about the letters?"

"I saw one when I stopped by his brother's apartment yesterday."

"That how you know Donte? You friends with—" *Hiccup!* "—his brother?"

Dash nodded. "Donte's staying there for the time being until he's back on his feet."

"Oh yeah? That's good. Good he has family to lean on during rough times. His brother in this neighborhood, too?"

"On Bowery and Hester."

"Nice." Gus cleared his throat and got serious. "This letter? Where d'ya find it?"

"In Donte's coat pocket. The signature was a drawing of a hand holding a dagger."

"Yeesh! That's omi—omi—ominous." Gus paused. "Say, I remember now. Yeah, yeah, he told me about someone dropping off notes. Made him real upset."

"When did he start getting them?"

"Oh. I'd say the first day or two in October. Ever since he's been getting one every week."

"And what did the letters say?"

"Pay up or else. Donte wouldn't go into specifics."

"But it was a threat."

Gus confirmed it was.

"What was the amount?"

Gus held up his palm with all five fingers splayed. "Five thousand dollars."

Dash stared at Gus. "Really?"

"I don't need to tell you he didn't have that. Not like he's a Rockefeller."

Dash thought for a moment. "Gus, was Donte in debt to the Spinellis when the first letter came?"

Gus opened his mouth to respond, but stopped himself. He tilted his head first to the right, then to the left. "You know . . . I believe so," he drawled. "Yeah. *Yeah*. He was racking up some debt, though back then, it was just a hundred dollars."

Johnnie set Gus's second cocktail onto the bar.

Gus instinctively reached over and picked up the glass. "Say, you don't think the Spinellis sent him those letters, do ya? Cause the amounts don't match. Six hundred dollars. Five thousand dollars. It doesn't make no sense."

"You're right," Dash admitted. "But who else would be threatening him?"

Gus stroked his chin while he considered Dash's question. "I don't know, Max, I don't know. One thing Donte told me the other day. He was going to see if it was some woman who was sending them."

"A woman?"

"Yeah, yeah. She and him have a history. Not a good one, from how he tells it. He said she was trying to get back at him."

Donte's ravings came back to Dash: *"She said it wasn't her!"*

"Were the letters signed with her name?"

"No. Anonymous."

"Then how does he know it's her?"

"He didn't say. Only he knew in his gut."

"I see. And you wouldn't know her name, would you?"

Gus nodded vigorously, which caused him to grip the sides of the bar and moan, "Oh, I shouldn't have done that. Now the room is spinning." He took a moment to compose himself. "That's better. Whew! Thought I was gonna pull a Boone there."

"Mr. Brown—Gus. The woman. Did Donte say who she was?"

"Sure did! Said her name was Carmela Fiore. She owns a restaurant around here. On Mott and Kenmare. Fiore's." *Hiccup!* "I've been there before. Good raviolis."

"Did Donte say how he knew this woman?"

Gus started to shake his head again, but caught himself. "Nope—wait. Wait, wait, wait. Yes, he did. How could I forget that?" He tapped his glass. "Too many of these, I think. So! Carmela? She was married to Ro—Ro —Rodolpho."

"Donte's friend who died in the war?"

"Yessiree. After he died, something happened and Carmela and Donte weren't friends no more."

"And he wouldn't say why?"

"Nope. Just said that widow was, and I quote, '*a vengeful bitch.*'"

Something about this scenario didn't feel right. "Why send him an extortion letter?" Dash asked. "That threatened violence, of all things."

"Are you sayin' a girl can't beat up a boy? Cause I know plenty who—" *Hiccup!* "—can."

Dash smiled. "So do I. Statistically, though, it's not a woman's style to use brute force."

Gus mouthed the word *statistically* to himself, fascinated by the shape of the word in his mouth. Then he said, "Then what is a woman's style, Max?"

Dash thought of all the clever women he knew. "Cunning."

"Ah. Well *maybe,* just maybe, writing a letter like a man would *is* cunning."

"Fair point. But there's still something else that's off."

"Oh?"

"Why, after all this time? It's been almost a decade since Rodolpho's death and the parting of the ways between Carmela and Donte. Why now?"

Gus shrugged. "Maybe she's been holding a grudge all this time and finally snapped."

"Why do you think Carmela was angry at Donte?"

Another *hiccup!* "Don't know," Gus replied. "But if there are arguments between a man and a woman, I have my guesses."

## 14

Fiore's was at the bottom of a department store boasting clothes, makeup, and hats. A green awning stretched over part of the sidewalk with the name stitched into the front and sides.

Dash paused for another trio of sneezes before pocketing his handkerchief and entering the restaurant.

Inside, the air was thick with garlic and onions. Small round tables dotted the floor, and cotton curtains of a colorful green-and-white print draped the two front windows. A brass chandelier hung over the center of the room, lit candles flickering against the metal. A gramophone perched on a built-in shelf against the far wall was playing a gentle piano waltz featuring a lilting violin.

Seated in the right corner nearest the door were a group of men having a lively debate in their native language. They halted when they caught sight of Dash, who tipped his hat to them and continued walking forward. Their boisterous voices dropped to indistinguishable whispers behind him.

A woman was leaning against the doorframe at the far side of the dining room that presumably led to the kitchen.

She was older than Dash by maybe ten years. She wore an ankle-length dress done in red, its drop waist secured by a sash and its hemline decorated with embroidered swirls and curls in an amber thread. A pair of pearls, blindingly white, circled her neck.

She looked at him with interest. "We're not open, *signore*." Her voice was higher pitched than he expected. A clear soprano.

"I'm not looking to dine. I'm actually looking for someone. Is Carmela Fiore here?"

Her guard instantly went up. "What do you want with her?"

The whispering behind Dash stopped. He could feel the men's eyes on him.

"To talk about an urgent matter that's come up."

"Who are you? You're not from this neighborhood, that I know, so don't lie. Why is a stranger coming around asking for a woman he doesn't know?"

A chair scrapped the floor behind him.

*Diffuse this now or they'll toss you out on your ear.*

Dash cleared his throat. "My name is Dash Parker, and I'm a good friend of Atticus Delucci. His brother has been receiving threats, most recently last night. We don't know who's threatening Donte's brother, and we're worried his children might be in danger."

The woman measured him up.

Dash attempted to look as unthreatening as possible.

She ran her tongue over her teeth. "You dine?"

Dash hesitated for only a second. "I thought you weren't open."

"I thought you wanted to speak with Carmela."

The chair behind Dash creaked as its occupant settled back down.

The woman gestured to a table nearest her and farthest from the men in the corner. Dash sat while she handed him a handwritten menu. She pointed to a dish at the very bottom.

"I think you should have *spalla di vitello primavera*. Is very good."

Dash noticed it was the most expensive dish on the menu. He looked up at those clear eyes. They stared back with defiance. He nodded. "Then I shall have to have it."

She took back his menu. "I'll also bring you some *cappelletti al consommé*. The raviolis, they are very fresh. *Vino* as well, *si*?"

She didn't wait for a response. She went through the doorway back into the kitchen.

The four men in the corner went back to their conversing and teasing, no longer speaking in whispers.

A moment later, she returned with two glasses of what looked like red wine. The very sight of it filled Dash with melancholy. He remembered the wine and spirits of old before the Volstead Act, how unique and flavorful they were. Now they had to settle for cheap imitations, grape juice mixed with rubbing alcohol. Dash hoped what she poured wasn't the horse liniment he'd had in the past. She set the two glasses down on the table and then sat down across from him.

He gestured to the wine in front of them. "*Grazie*."

She raised her glass. "*Salut*."

He raised his in return. "*Salut*."

The glasses clinked, and Dash took a sip. Dear heaven, it was *real* wine! Before he could stop himself, he moaned out loud.

The woman chuckled. "Is good, *eh*?"

"*Si, si*, very good." He took another sip, savoring the

notes of cherry and plum, the creamy thickness of the liquid. "How—how do you get this?"

"Eh, how do you say? Loophole in the law. Families can grow it for religious or cultural purposes. Our family is in California. They grow it there and ship it here."

"Why don't more people know about this?"

"They don't like us immigrants all that much." She shrugged. "Their loss."

"Their loss, indeed."

A moment of silence passed between them.

The four men in the corner continued their conversing and teasing. Two of them were in a fit of giggles so pronounced, their faces dark red, their laughs high-pitched whistles.

"So," Dash said, after taking another sip. "How long are you going to pretend you're not Carmela Fiore?"

She smiled. "Do you have this letter you claim you saw?"

"Unfortunately, no. It got destroyed."

"Oh, too bad. Perhaps there wasn't any letter at all."

Now it was Dash's turn to smile. "Perhaps not. Unless you saw the one Donte claimed you wrote?"

Her eyes flashed. "Why do you say that?"

"When I first met Donte, he was yelling *'she said it wasn't her.'* I met another friend of his who confided that he thought you were responsible. Were you?"

"Of course not."

"Why would Donte think you did?"

"You'll have to ask him."

"I'd rather ask you."

She avoided his gaze and drank more wine, her jaw tight, her brow furrowed.

Dash changed tacts. "You were friends once. You and Rodolpho. Donte and Maria. What happened?"

"What happened? The War happened! Rodolpho killed, Donte returned a changed man, and nothing could go back to the way it was."

Dash understood that. He'd seen many a boy return from the trenches looking like a ghost. Hollow eyes. Vacant stares. Pale, white skin and trembling hands. It made him wonder if the survivors received significantly less mercy than the dead.

He asked, "How did you all meet?"

"We were neighbors across the alleyway. We met while sitting out on the fire escape during the hot summer nights. Smoking cigarettes and drinking *vino*. This was before Volstead, you understand. We got to talking. Where we were from, our path to get here. Donte got my Rodolpho a job with him at Barone's bank. Francesco Barone," she added for clarity. "Very famous. Anyone who was a success in our part of the city put their money in Barone's bank." Pride filled her voice, as sparkling and rich as contraband champagne.

"I've heard about the prestige of the Barone bank."

"It's tarnished over the years, but back then? It was beautiful. They were both tellers, Donte and my Rodolpho. They worked at Barone's bank for many, many years. Until . . ." She trailed off.

"Until the war," Dash finished for her.

She nodded, taking another hasty sip of wine. Her glass was almost empty.

"When my Rodolpho died, I hadn't the heart to—to keep up the friendship. Perhaps I feel guilty about that, I don't know. It was too difficult to do."

Dash couldn't put his finger on it, but he felt that

Carmela Fiore was lying. There was another reason behind the split. He just knew it.

"I take it you haven't remarried?"

A bitter smirk. "No. Nobody wants a widow."

"How did you get into the restaurant business?" Dash asked, gesturing to the surrounding space.

A passive shrug. "It's the only thing I knew how to do. I had to put the restaurant in my husband's name on all the papers. All because a woman can't own, can't do for herself. What nonsense. I'll check on your food."

Carmela left the table and went to the kitchen in the back.

The four men in the corner were really getting worked up over some woman. Out of the corner of Dash's eyes, one man held his hands out far in front of his chest. The words were unintelligible to Dash, first for the language and second for the sputtering laughter, but he got the point.

Carmela returned with a carafe of red wine to refill their glasses and a steaming bowl of tortellini soup, which was, Dash had to admit, delicious.

"Tell me about Rodolpho?" he asked in between bites.

"He wasn't the most attractive man, nor the most interesting, but he was predictable and stable. A man with excitement is a man with problems."

"Like Donte."

She hesitated. "Sì, like Donte."

"Do you know about his gambling problem?"

Another flash of the eyes, but she didn't answer.

"I know about his debts with the Spinelli family. Several hundred dollars, or so I've heard." Intuition inspired his next question. "Did he ever come to you for money?"

A patch of pink appeared on the side of her neck. It was as solid as a verbal confession in Dash's book.

"I'll take that as a yes," he said. "Did his problems start before the war or after?"

Carmela studied him over the rim of her glass. "He'd always loved 'dancing with chance,' he used to say. The fool thought he could win. And sometimes he did. But after the war, it got worse. I remember one time he and Maria were flush with money. This was the year after the Armistice. A bonus from the bank, he said. Although I suspect he got it in other ways. He could buy her jewelry, buy his children new clothes, get them an expensive apartment. They moved away from our tiny buildings and our tiny fire escapes. Then, over time, he lost it all. The apartment, the clothes, the jewelry." She cursed under her breath. "Stupid man."

"Had you seen him often in the neighborhood?"

"Seen him? *Si*. Conversed with him? Ate with him? Kept his company? No. No, *Signore* Parker, I have not."

She excused herself, taking away Dash's soup.

The four men in the corner had calmed themselves after hilarious stories of voluptuous women. Now their voices were serious and low. In the steady flow of Italian, Dash picked up the words "Hall," "Mills," "Felix de Martini," and "Senator Simpson." Even the immigrants were following the exploits in New Jersey.

Carmela returned with the veal shank. Dash didn't think he could fit more food into his stomach, but he figured the moment he stopped eating would be the moment Carmela would stop talking.

She sat across from him, refilling their wineglasses. How many glasses had it been now? Dash lost count.

"Mrs. Fiore, do you know who the Capellos are?"

"No."

She answered a little too quickly for Dash's taste.

He observed her. "Are you certain? Are they a prominent family around here?"

"I said no, *signore*."

"I find it curious that the letters mention them. Could the Capellos own a gambling den, some other place where Donte racked up debts?"

"No."

"Could the Capellos be the Spinellis? Perhaps Spinelli is a fake name to avoid—I don't know—the cops, the feds, creditors?"

Dash's persistence annoyed her. "I already *told* you; I *don't* know who they are. And if you don't stop this insulting round of questions, I will have to ask you to leave."

Dash stared at the defiant face. Her chin slightly raised, her eyes narrowed and intense, her shoulders drawn back. Defensive. Determined. Ready to fight.

She was lying.

Dash used a smile to unarm Carmela. "I see. Forgive me, sometimes my curious nature gets away from me." He stood. "May I use your WC?"

"Of course." She pointed towards the back left corner. "It's behind that partition there."

Dash walked towards and around the wooden partition and found the door labeled "WC." He used the facilities. He also took the time to blow his nose for the umpteenth time that day. Frankly, it was a miracle he hadn't sneezed through the entire conversation with Carmela.

He left the WC and stopped. A bright yellow card had fallen to the floor and wedged itself underneath the boards of the cheaply constructed partition. He reached down and picked it up, seeing a fancy script mixed with blocked printing.

The fancy script spelled the name "*DELILAH SAMS*."

The type face promised "LITTLE ITALY'S MOST FAMOUS SPIRITUALIST. TAROT. SÉANCE. CRYSTALS."

Now where did this card come from? A patron? Delilah herself?

More importantly, did Carmela and Delilah know each other?

## 15

Dash eventually found his way to the Village after considerable time and money. The island of Manhattan wasn't that wide; why the hell was it such a complicated equation to get crosstown? It was a mystery Dash couldn't solve.

He left the Sixth Avenue el station and walked down West Fourth. A purple truck with gold lettering parked in front of Hartford & Sons. Dash glanced idly at it. CALLAHAN CREAMERY, the side of the truck boasted. ALL THE SWEETNESS THAT'S FIT TO LICK!

The rhythm of the tagline felt familiar, but by the time it finally registered, the back door swung open. Two men dressed in dark-gray suits calmly got out and surrounded him. The man behind Dash hooked his hands under Dash's armpits and lifted him backwards and upwards. The man in front of Dash reached down and grabbed his ankles.

The movements were so swift, he only managed to yell out a "Hey!" before they threw him into the hull of the truck.

The doors closed with an ear-splitting *clang!*

The darkness was absolute. Dash could barely see a few inches in front of his face.

"What is the meaning of this?" he demanded, his voice echoing off the metal sides and doors.

The man behind him still held a grip on him and kept pulling him backwards. Dash's heels scraped on the metal floor.

Eventually, the man stopped. A rough hand from presumably another henchman inside this truck patted his pockets. Dash was then dropped into what felt like a hard, wooden chair with wide arms and a high back. The air was frosty, nipping his nose and burning his cheeks.

"I demand you let me go!" he called out, his voice echoing off the metal walls and ceiling.

A familiar voice behind him chuckled. "Oh, but why, Mr. Parker?"

Dash's stomach dropped.

"It's been so long since we had a friendly chat."

The buzz of several lanterns igniting crackled the air, lighting the darkened space. A tall shadow loomed on the truck's back door, standing larger than life. Soft heels clicked on the metal floor as they circled slowly around the chair and inched towards the front.

"I must say, I have missed your presence terribly. Have you missed me?"

Dash looked up.

Nicholas Fife, the gangster known as "Slick Nick," grinned down at him.

Dash stared at the warm chocolate eyes set underneath gentle brows. "Mr. Fife. How good to see you."

Those pink, thick lips twitched with amusement. "Believe me, Mr. Parker, the pleasure is all mine."

Though the lighting was poor, Nicholas Fife still

painted an attractive picture. Brown hair in gentle waves lapped at his pixie-like ears and broad forehead. A long neck led downward to a moderately sized chest and torso—not broad, like Joe's, but not weak either. He wore a dapper tan suit accented with a red-striped scarf and a pair of expensive tan leather gloves, which were politely folded in front of him. The epitome of good breeding.

Fife held his gloved hands open. "I hope you don't mind the surprise visit or the location. You have been all over the city as of late, Mr. Parker. So very difficult to track down."

"Yes, well, I've been busy." Dash forced a smile, trying to look nonchalant. "I see you have a new cover business."

He gestured to their surroundings. Solid hunks of ice rested on the floor to create the refrigeration needed to transport the dairy products. Barrels lined the walls, with ice cream flavors printed on their sides.

He returned his gaze to Fife. "Wasn't it Danziger Paper last time?"

"'The classiest of salutations with the best of regards,'" Fife said, quoting the tagline. "I did indeed enjoy that one. But now I'm in the world of creameries. Just in time for that half-wit Ogden Mills to challenge the current governor with a so-called milk crisis in New York. Tainted, adulterated milk. Please. The lying fool."

"Why ice cream?"

Fife leaned down towards Dash. "Because who doesn't love a little sugary sweetness on their tongue?"

Dash found it difficult to respond, especially with those warm, chocolate eyes staring into his, so he simply nodded.

Fife's smile widened. "Would you like one?"

"No, thank you."

"Pity. I'll have one for you then." Fife straightened up and held out his hand. A shadowed man placed a cone with a scoop of what looked like vanilla ice cream into Fife's palm. Fife gripped it, raised it to his lips, and began licking. "Mmm, mmm, *mmm*. I know it's not the season for it, but I love it so! Do you prefer chocolate or vanilla?"

"I, uh, well . . . I like both?"

Fife chuckled. "My, my, my. You're so eager not to offend, aren't you? Here, let's do a taste test."

He snapped his fingers, and another cone appeared, this time with chocolate. Fife gripped the cone and leaned down again, extending the chocolate cone in front of Dash's mouth.

"Lick it," he whispered.

Dash glanced up at the gangster's face. A bemused smirk spread those thick lips even further apart. He sat forward in the chair, opened his mouth, hesitated, and then licked a small sample of ice cream. He sensed the cold, but not the taste.

"Oh come, come," Fife said. "Really get in there, Mr. Parker!"

Dash flicked a wary look, opened his mouth wider, and got a sizeable chunk of chocolate ice cream. Now he could taste it—but he didn't enjoy it.

"Excellent," Fife purred. "What do you think?"

Dash swallowed. "Lovely."

"Now try mine." Fife meant the vanilla cone.

Dash clamped down his anger at Fife's showboating, at that damn smirk. The gangster enjoyed this too much.

"Come on," Fife cajoled. "I know you've wanted to taste mine ever since you saw it."

Dash glared at the gangster. Why did the man insist on peacocking every single time they met? Fife already proved his power over Dash months ago!

*Oh, just do it, Dash. The sooner you bite, the sooner you*

*get out of this truck.*

He leaned forward and licked off a considerable chunk from his vanilla cone.

"Oh, my!" Fife said. "I wasn't expecting such . . . such *fervor* from you." That smirk was now a full-blown grin. "Tell me, which did you prefer?"

Dash knew what answer Fife wanted him to give, but he'd deny Fife that satisfaction. "The chocolate," he lied.

"Pity." Fife stood back up again and returned the cone to his own mouth. "I'm a vanilla man myself," he said, smacking his lips. "I know some people consider that boring, but I find the vanilla flavor to be oh so much more complex than simple chocolate. Don't get me wrong. Chocolate can be delicious and decadent. But there are *layers* to vanilla— hidden treasures, secret pleasures, naughty nuances—that require one to pay absolute attention to the sensation that is occurring in their mouth. Why were you closed on Sunday night?"

Fife delivered the question in the same easy, flirtatious way as the short monologue on ice cream that Dash almost missed it.

"I—excuse me?"

"The club. Pinstripes. It was closed on Sunday night. I would like to know why."

"Oh. Well. An emergency came up."

"This wouldn't have to do with a certain Officer Cullen McElroy, now, would it? Because I am curious why you'd allow such a man to not only threaten you, but to take time away from *our* business."

"I've got a plan—"

"You have a plan? Oh, *do* tell."

So Dash did. Peter Fraker, the photographs, and the idea of stealing them.

"I see," Fife said. "Do you honestly think *you* will be able to stop a man like McElroy? Because, forgive me, Mr. Parker, that seems a touch naïve."

"Maybe not in the long run," Dash admitted, "but definitely in the short term."

"I offer a permanent solution."

"Yes, I know. And I'm trying to avoid that. I—I don't want his death on my conscience."

Fife's smile was tight. "A man with a strong moral center. I admire that, Mr. Parker. I don't understand it, but I do admire it."

"And as for last night, Joe and Atty, my doorman, were to run the club—Sunday nights are typically slow for us—but Atty had a family emergency and couldn't get word to us in time."

"What emergency?"

"A fire burned down his brother's building."

"Oh, yes. I read about that. Tragic thing. Likely arson, don't you agree? But by whom, I wonder?"

"I wonder as well," Dash said. He looked at the gangster and suddenly felt compelled to ask this next question: "Do you know a Gianni Spinelli?"

Fife paused, watching Dash with a curious expression. "Why do you know that name?"

"My friend's brother apparently owes him gambling debts. He runs a room behind The Smoke Shop on Bleecker. I went there yesterday and confirmed the brother's situation."

"I see. Are you interested in gambling, Mr. Parker?"

"Not in the slightest."

"Good. A gambler is perhaps the biggest fool of our species, next to the churchgoer. And anyone who owes the Spinellis sugar is a damned fool, as in condemned."

"So you know Gianni?"

"Oh, yes," Fife said, finishing his ice cream cone, his teeth crunching. "I know Gianni. Know *of* him, I should say." He swallowed, then wiped the crumbs from his hands. "Nasty character. He grew up down at Coney Island when it was first starting out. He was an apprentice to his father, who was an electrician for the amusement parks. Gianni learned how to shock unsuspecting patrons for a laugh, how to light the circus and freak shows, how to power the rides. More importantly, he learned how to rig the midway games, which is why so many of his marks—I mean, customers— lose all that they have and more at his tables." Fife held up a pointer finger, like a schoolteacher wanting to make his point very clear. "And you do *not* want to be in his debt."

"What does he do to you?"

"He owns you."

*Like how you own me?* Dash bitterly thought.

Fife must've read his expression, for he chuckled. "Now, now, Mr. Parker. Such a rude insinuation."

"I didn't mean—"

"*We* have a *partnership.* After all, I allow you to run your club in any way you like. Have any customer you want. Have any entertainment you prefer. All I ask in return is a small percentage of the profits in exchange for that freedom and the security of safe, drinkable booze. I think we both learned a month ago how valuable that last part of our agreement is to you."

Fife meant the tragic story of a young woman who died in Dash's club from ingesting tainted liquor. Granted, it wasn't Dash's booze that had done it—thankfully—but it showed the value of Fife's liquor supply, which was double-checked by a chemist he hired.

"Now Gianni?" Fife said, continuing with his lecture.

"You wouldn't be able to go to the water closet without his permission. He owns men and women who can do things for him. Policemen looking the other way, men of industry giving him a deal, Wall Street traders giving him insider tips. What does your friend's brother do?"

"He works as a manager at a bank."

"Interesting. I wouldn't be surprised if Gianni was laundering some money through that bank. So you see, Mr. Parker, *not* our arrangement at all."

Dash nodded. "Do you know of anyone who sends threatening letters?"

"What do you mean by 'anyone'?"

"I'm not entirely certain, to be honest, Mr. Fife. My friend's brother has been receiving threatening letters for at least the last several weeks. Demanding an exorbitant sum, I might add. Way more than his gambling debts, so I don't believe they're related."

"You believe correctly. Gianni isn't the type to send such things. If he wanted to deliver a message, he'd have one of his worthless sons stop by. Gianni never liked to put anything in writing, and I agree with his approach. Papers get you caught and thrown into prison."

"Who could be sending these letters then?"

Fife shrugged. "Perhaps someone in this man's life. What did the letter you saw say?"

"The letter was written in Italian, so I unfortunately don't know the contents of it. I could only decipher a name, 'the Capellos,' and the signature was quite memorable: a drawing of a hand holding a dagger. And someone else said my friend's brother told him each letter demanded the same amount: five thousand dollars."

Fife was silent.

Which worried Dash. "What's the matter? Do you know them, the Capellos?"

"No. Never heard of them before in my life."

"Then . . . what is it?"

Fife's expression was a mix of surprise and shrewdness. "As avid a newspaper reader as you are, I'm surprised. They were all over the papers the first two decades of this century. Those newshawks practically clucked themselves to death writing stories about them. Of course, you might've been too young when most of the paper's ink went to them."

Dash said, "Who are the 'they' you're speaking of?"

"In the early days of this new century, there was a group of Italian criminals extorting other Italians. Shameful, really. To do that to one's own countrymen. They would demand money, such as you've apparently seen, in crude but effective letters. Often they had illustrations of skull and crossbones, daggers, droplets of blood, stick figures with x-s for eyes, etcetera to underscore the point that if you didn't pay, you'd die."

"And would you?"

"Sometimes, yes. This group, for lack of a better word, was ruthless. Stabbings, shootings, hangings. And then one day, they discovered dynamite."

Dash's hands went cold, and he was reasonably sure it wasn't from the icy air inside this truck, but from the obvious implications.

"Dynamite," Dash repeated.

"Oh yes. Crude but effective, like those letters. They bombed storefronts, vendor carts and motorcars. Sometimes the louses threw a lit stick into the street, landing right at the feet of their intended target. Before anyone could react, *BOOM!*"

Fife's voice echoed off the steel walls.

Dash's heart jumped into his throat.

"The other nasty thing they did," Fife continued, "was kidnap children for ransom. Most of the time, the parents paid, and most of the time, the children returned. But some disappeared forever."

"Did the police do anything about them?"

Fife chuckled. "I swear, Mr. Parker, your naïveté astounds me. This was occurring in the Little Italies! Immigrant-on-immigrant crime! No one cared as long as it stayed away from the wealthy and the white. And mostly, these crimes did."

"As many Italians as there are in this city, surely they put *some* pressure on Tammany Hall."

Fife yawned. "Eventually. And Tammany's solution was pitiful at best. One squad of seven men. All Italians. Led by Joseph Petrosino, who I must admit, was a wonder. Do you know about him? A man of such dichotomies and odd juxtapositions. He was an absolute bruiser, could win any fight, even if the other man had a pistol. Perhaps *especially* if the other man had a pistol. But then he was also a lover of opera and music and the theater. A shy, sensitive man. A master of disguise as well, so he could sneak into any criminal lair, gather evidence, and have the culprits arrested."

"Was he successful in taking down this, this group?"

"In some ways, yes, but mostly no. This group wasn't like today's syndicates. They didn't have a figurehead running the organization. Oh, sure, there were a bunch of little 'leaders' running around. But mostly, these scoundrels worked on their own and they knew how to emulate the group's calling card."

"How?"

"My dear Dash, the newshawks all reported the modus

operandi. Everyone knew what to do."

"You're saying that people would write and sign a letter the same way as this group did, and get the same result?"

"Of course! My dear Dash, the Italians *feared* them! Feared them more than any prejudice or government. This group had eyes and ears seemingly everywhere. No one knew if their neighbors, shopkeepers, bankers, teachers, even priests were involved."

Dash recalled the shouted hysteria of Donte in Atty's bedroom. "And they didn't trust the police?"

Fife had a jaded look. "If you knew half of what went on in Italy—hell, what *still* goes on in Italy with their police and *secret* police—you wouldn't trust them either. But the few who did trust the police ended up regretting it. What vexed our brave Petrosino was the silence of the citizens he was trying to protect. No one would talk, because any witness who came forward was silenced by threats . . . or worse."

"Jesus," Dash muttered.

"He had nothing to do with this, of that, I assure you," Fife replied.

Something was off. "You said Petrosino *was* a wonder. What happened to him?"

"They killed him. The poor sap went to Italy on an undercover mission and never returned. He was shot to death. That was in Nineteen-oh-Nine, I believe. This group reigned terror for at least ten more years until . . ."

"Until what?"

Fife shrugged. "Until they disappeared. No one's truly heard from them in the last five, six years."

"What happened?"

"No one knows. The War likely did them in like it did many. The Volstead Act shifted priorities of the more enterprising members towards a more lucrative business. Quenching a man's thirst earns more consistent money than hoping the man you've targeted can pay the demanded amount. Whatever the cause, they have made little noise." Fife pointed at Dash. "Except apparently to *you*. Or rather, your friend's brother."

Dash squirmed in his seat. "I'm not entirely certain this is the same thing."

"Yes, you are. Don't doubt yourself! You saw a drawn dagger in a letter written in Italian, yes or no?"

"Yes."

"And you believe this friend that each letter demanded money, yes or no?"

"Y-yes."

"And your friend's brother lost his building to dynamite, yes or no?"

*Shit.* "Yes."

Fife held out his hands. "What other conclusion could there be?"

"Perhaps it's an old letter?"

Fife abruptly shook his head. "No. It would be an incredibly *odd* memento to keep around. Most of the Italians I know would've burned it, said fifty Hail Marys, and crossed themselves until the last ember went out."

"How did this group find its victims?"

"They aimed for the newly arrived in the city, the prominent, and the wealthy."

Strange. Donte was neither of those things. "And this group. Did they have a name?"

"Did they have a name?" Fife repeated. "Oh, my yes. A name that will still strike terror in the heart of any Italian in New York City." He leaned down, his manner intense, his eyes flashing with flint. "*La Mano Nera.*"

## 16

"I'll bloody kill him!" Joe bellowed, smacking the wooden rough-hewn bar with his opened palm.

El shouted back. "And I'll bloody kill *you* if you interrupt me again! We've only got a few more nights to get this right." It was their second rehearsal and to Dash's ears, it wasn't going as well as last night.

El turned on her heels with her hands on her hips. Joe was behind the bar counting bottles while Dash sat on his barstool, sipping his rickey and reading his newspaper.

She pointed a finger at Joe. "Listen, that little High Hat there may think your gospel pipe's the best damn sermon on the mount he's ever had, but *I* don't give two rat's asses how big and mighty your testimony is. Cause it sure Lord can't hold a candle to mine, you understand me?"

For the first time in Dash's life, he saw Joe back down and look . . . *contrite*.

"Yes, ma'am," Joe replied meekly, lowering his eyes and his head.

"I *said* cut out that ma'am shit!"

"El," said Calvin from behind his drum kit. "You alright? You a touch more bearcat than usual tonight."

El turned back to the band, waving him off. "Mind your business. Now this number's gotta swing and I don't feel any swing, boys. It's too straight. That might work for these downtowners, but it will not work with me."

Julius cut in. "Oh come on now, El. If we swung any more, we'd flip ourselves right out of the seat."

El glared at the cornet player. "I said swing it, dammit."

Julius mumbled under his breath.

"What was that now?"

"Not a goddamn thing, El."

"I thought not."

Vernon shyly raised his hand.

El, with an exaggerated sense of patience, said, "Yes, Vern?"

"Can we take a break? I'm sorry, but we've been at this for almost two hours and I had an entire pot of coffee, so—"

"Jesus. Shit. Fine. Go. All of ya's."

The band laid down their instruments while El stalked off to the bar. Joe was already pouring her whiskey, which she took and downed immediately and asked for another. Joe eyed her warily, but did as she asked.

Vernon went to the WC while Calvin and Julius went out the secret door to hang out in the tailor shop, putting some distance between them and El.

Dash closed his newspaper and looked over at her. He cleared his phlegm-filled throat and said, "Everything Jake, El?"

"No. Yes. Why's everyone asking me that?" She took her second drink from Joe, but to Dash's relief, she only sipped this one. After a moment, she sighed. "I don't mean to be hard on them. They are an excellent group, Dash. I wouldn't sing here if they were lousy."

"I appreciate that, El."

"It's just—" She took a deep breath. "It's Leslie."

"As in Leslie Charles?"

"The one and only."

Leslie Charles was the owner of the Oyster House, where El used to play her shows. He didn't like inverts as a rule, but he knew the drawing power of El. Things had come to a head last September, and when J.A. Watkins herself asked El to perform at her hotel, El jumped at the chance. Needless to say, Leslie was not happy about El's decision.

"What's he up to now?" Dash asked.

"Oh, he's saying we had a contract, and he's trying to get me to fulfill the rest of it."

"You're kidding! How long is the contract?"

El waggled her head as she calculated the dates. "Let's see, I used to do four nights a week, two shows a night, so he's asking for about a month's worth of performances, give or take."

"Goodness. What does Miss Watkins have to say about it?"

El smirked. "She said she'll break that contract, come hell or high water. I don't know, though. He might get his way, the vain, glorious bastard. If there's one thing I learned about Les, it's that he may be a knuckleheaded Normie, but he knows business. And he knows how to swing things in his direction." She pointed to the *Times* that was opened in front of Dash. "Anything good in there?"

Joe scoffed. "Not hardly. Nothing but bad news."

"Yeah, but it's all the bad news that's fit to print. They learn more about what caused that Little Italy fire?"

Dash replied, "Atty's brother's building is officially an arson. They've ruled out the landlords. The poor fools didn't insure their building, so they lost everything."

"Damn. That's gotta hurt. Now they're looking for a random fire bug? Shoot. Good luck. That'll be finding a needle in a haystack in this city. I bet they shut down the investigation before too long. Immigrants don't warrant much time or resources."

Joe said, "Then what the hell do we pay taxes fer?"

"To keep politicians in the lifestyle to which they've become accustomed! Shit, O'Shaughnessy, you a genuine believer in America or something?"

Joe leaned forward, his eyes glinting. "The only thing I'm a *genuine* believer in is whiskey."

El raised her glass. "Amen to that."

They sipped their respective beverages.

El pointed to Dash's paper. "You mind if I see that? I want to read the latest on the Hall-Mills case."

"Oh no, El," Dash said. "Not you, too."

"What? I want to see if that murderous white woman gets what's coming to her. You *know* she did it. And you know she'll get acquitted. Wealthy white women always do. You hear she's worth almost two million dollars? *Two million.* No wonder that lying, cheating Reverend put one hand up her dress so he could put his other hand into her bank account."

Joe nodded. "Now we know where her hired private dick de Martini was gettin' his sugar to bribe those witnesses. They say he was offerin' them twenty-five hundred *a piece.*"

"Makes you wonder what old Frances Stevens Hall was worried they'd say."

Dash, who normally enjoyed a good scandal, particularly in the upper class, was tiring of this one. He handed El the *Times.* "Go to town."

"Thank you." She took the paper to one of the empty tables to read it while she sipped the rest of her whiskey.

Vernon exited the WC and asked where Calvin and Julius were. Dash pointed to the secret door and Vernon left through it.

Dash turned to Joe. "Listen, Joe, Fife was just peacocking again."

Joe leaned on the bar. "Yeah, well, someone needs to pluck his feathers."

"I'm safe. Nothing bad happened to me."

"I hate the fact tha' man can do whatever he wants to ya whenever he wants."

"I know," Dash said. "Only you should have that privilege." He aimed for levity, bouncing his eyebrows Groucho Marx-style.

It earned a slight smile from Joe before he turned serious again. "Whattaya gonna do 'bout this *La Mano Nera* business? What the hell does it mean again?"

"The Black Hand. And I'm not sure. I want to think Atty will believe me, but it's almost too fantastical to believe. Why would a secret society that's been dormant for years suddenly come back and threaten a broke man like Donte? Fife gave the impression the Hand handpicked their victims."

"Yeah, well, they sure futzed this one up. Unless it's someone pretendin' to be 'em. Didn't ol' Slick Nick say people used to do tha'?"

Dash nodded. "That he did."

"So it's this Spinelli family."

"He owes them six hundred dollars. Why ask them for five thousand?"

"Maybe someone's gettin' greedy."

"Maybe . . . "

"Could be Delilah Sams. Donte probably looks like an easy mark and besides, those bloody spiritualists are all grifters anyway."

"Of course, Donte could've been right when he told his barfly friend Gus that Carmela Fiore wrote the letters. There's certainly no love lost between them, and if Carmela ran into some money trouble . . . " Dash trailed off.

Joe nodded. "Aye, and it looks like Carmela knows Delilah. Maybe they're in on it together?"

Dash shrugged. "What I don't understand are the hidden invoices of olive oil."

"Betcha it's not olive oil."

"Goes without saying. Did Donte discover something he shouldn't have? Maybe the motive isn't money; maybe it's trying to scare him into silence."

"Then why burn his building down?"

"Maybe he didn't stay silent." Dash tapped the bar with his palms. "I sure would love to know who the Capellos are. They may be the key."

"Lassie, yer gonna have to tell Atty 'bout all this."

"I know, I know." Dash ran his hands over his face and groaned into his palms. He looked up at Joe. "Donte's already painted me as an untrustworthy spy. I'm going to need paper proof for Atty to accept the truth about his brother."

The sound of a chair tumbling to the floor raised both their heads.

El was staring down at the newspaper, her mouth open, her eyes wide.

"El?" Dash said. "What's the matter?"

"I don't—*fucking*—believe this! I don't—I mean—why would she—just what the *hell* is doing on?"

Joe echoed Dash's concern. "Whattaya talkin' 'bout, lass?"

El didn't reply, just stormed off to the WC, the door slamming shut.

Dash and Joe looked at one another and shrugged. Dash went over to the table where El was sitting and peered down at the newsprint page. It was the society section, which featured the usual announcements of births, deaths, funerals, engagements, and weddings. He checked the obituaries. Had someone she had known died? The names listed meant nothing to him.

When El returned from the WC, she wouldn't answer them. She tore out a jagged square from the paper and stormed out of the club.

Dash glanced at the missing square. To his surprise, it wasn't the obituaries she'd torn off. It was the engagements.

———————

The next morning, Finn burst into the bedroom, jolting Dash and Joe awake.

"Success!" he said. He strolled into the room with a practice sway of his hips, all smiles, his face positively glowing.

"For the love of Saint Peter, Finney," Joe growled as he rubbed the sleep from his eyes, "why the hell do ya burst in like a bull at Barce-fucking-lona?"

"They run in Pamplona, you ignoramus. Now, be nice to me, because *I* have news!"

Dash sat up in bed. "Is it about McElroy?" Overnight,

his cold had moved into his chest, dropping his voice an octave.

"Oh, my!" Finn said. "Someone sounds like the bruiser he's always wanted to be."

Joe warned, "Finney."

"Alright, alright. Yes, in-deedy do, it's about McElroy. You won't believe what I found out!"

Finn told them that last night, he dressed as a roustabout and went to McElroy's precinct. He struggled to stay on McElroy's tail—"One wouldn't think it, but he moves quite fast!"—but his quick-footedness and brilliance saved the day, for he discovered McElroy's correct address.

"Any guesses about where he's living?" Finn asked.

"The Dakota."

"Not quite." Finn beamed. "At 277 Park Avenue, that new luxury building near Grand Central Terminal. Where the prices *start* at over two thousand dollars to buy!"

"Heavens," Dash replied as he rubbed his chin. He looked over at Joe. "We're in the wrong business."

"And not only did I find that out," Finn continued, "I also made friends with one of the front desk men. A lovely creature named Danny Kingman. Although I remembered him from a club near the docks, where he went as Danny Boy. A nervous nellie, but well-meaning all the same." Finn dropped his voice into "chin music range." "I hear he's got double-jointed hips. 'The Pliable Pelvis' is how the bell bottoms refer to him."

"Christ Almighty," Joe moaned.

"Oh, stop being a flat tire! He's willing to meet with us to discuss our plan tomorrow morning at ten o'clock, when McElroy is on duty."

Dash grinned. "Excellent news, Finn, excellent news! We're one step closer to getting McElroy off our backs."

"From your mouth to Athena's ears. Now," Finn said. "What's happening with Atty and his gambling louse of a brother?"

Between throat clearings and coughs, Dash got Finn up to speed.

"The Black Hand?" Finn said once Dash finished. "I seem to recall a Latin lover of mine who murmured about them in his sleep. Nightmares, of course. They sound positively *beastly*."

"Yes, Finn, they are. Or were." Dash tried to shake the sleep from his head. "We need more proof to tell Atty, and even then, I'm not sure how to broach the subject."

"Quickly. Rip it off like a bandage."

Dash winced as he swallowed what felt like broken glass in his throat. "You're probably right."

Joe replied, "Lassie, ya should stay in bed. Yer gonna bloody kill yerself runnin' 'round like this!"

"We have too much to do. I can't stay in bed for days on end.

"Jesus Chri—ya so bloody stubborn, ya know that?"

Finn muttered, "If that isn't the pot calling the kettle black."

"Finney!"

Dash raised his hand. "I don't want to argue about this. If I feel any worse today, then I'll take the rest of the day off." He looked at Joe's concerned face. "I promise."

He dressed and shuffled his way to the Greenwich Village Inn, surprised to find it nearly full, which was a stark improvement from the last few weeks. He had to wait for two men to vacate their barstools before swooping in to narrowly beating out a scowling man in a green suit.

Emmett came over. "Usual?"

Dash nodded, then gestured to the surrounding crowd. "I see Finn's little tricks worked."

Emmett rolled his eyes. "Ayuh. Finn will be insufferable once he sees this."

"He deserves to gloat a little, Emmett. He's turning this place around."

"Still think it's ridiculous." Emmett flicked him a look. "I'll come back with your coffee. *Times*?"

"Yes, please."

Emmett reached down underneath the bar and removed the paper he'd already read. He laid it on the bar and left to fetch the coffee carafe.

Dash unfolded the paper, the creases not quite aligned as when first pressed, and scanned the pages. Emmett came by with a filled mug.

"Emmett," Dash said. "What do you know about The Black Hand?"

"Excuse me?"

"The Black Hand," Dash repeated. "*La Mano Nera.*"

"Huh, hadn't heard that name in a while. They terrified everyone for nearly twenty years. What of them?"

"Have you heard any rumors about them coming back?"

Emmett squinted. "Coming back? As in, sending letters and killing people and such?"

"Put bluntly, yes."

Emmett scowled while he thought. He shook his head. "I've heard nothing. Why? You getting letters?"

"No, but someone I know might be." Dash took a sip of coffee, grateful for the soothing, hot liquid on his cold-ravaged throat. "How often were Black Hand letters fake?"

"What do you mean?"

"Letters written by people who weren't officially part of the Hand."

"I'm not sure anyone knew. There were obvious ones, of course. A few spouses trying to get back at each other, that kind of thing. One time there was a publicity stunt for a play about the Hand. The producers sent a bunch of letters to high society types, scaring the life outta them, only to reveal it was all an advertisement for the damn show."

"How did the play do?"

"Sold out. Once the upper crust stopped pissing themselves." Emmett crossed his arms over his chest. "But it was hard to tell what was real and what was fake, at least to most coppers and newshawks. That Joseph Petrosino, though. You know about him? He claimed to recognize a fake from the Real McCoy. Rumor was he kept every Hand letter he ever found. File cabinet after file cabinet of the damnable things. Too bad the thugs murdered him. He might be able to help your friend."

"He's not my friend," Dash corrected. "Brother of a friend, but that's beside the point. Those letters wouldn't still be available, would they?"

"Doubtful. Once Volstead passed, the Italian Squad focused less on the Hand and more on the liquor syndicates. It's speakeasies and bootleggers all the time. American Tunnel Vision at its finest. Speaking of America's finest." Emmett tapped the paper in front of Dash. "Just wait until you read what's happened next in the Hall-Mills grand jury deliberations."

Dash rolled his eyes. "I'm getting sick of the naughty Reverend and his equally naughty choir singer."

"It'll be the trial of the century, my friend, the trial of the century."

Dash finished his coffee and breakfast, paid Emmett, and left the Inn. His throat felt somewhat better, but it was still raw and irritated.

He was half a block away from the shop when he saw a familiar figure pacing in front.

"Mr. Delucci," Dash said.

Donte looked up. He was dressed in his gray suit, the one Dash found hanging in Atty's closet. The one where he found the threatening letter and the devil tarot card.

"Mr. Parker, is it?"

Dash nodded.

"I'd like to speak with you. Please."

## 17

Dash unlocked the door and let them both inside. He went over to the writing desk, keenly aware that Donte's pistol rested in its closed compartment. Was he here to retrieve it? He felt another cough coming on, so he turned his head and brought up his handkerchief to his mouth.

Once that was done, he said, "How can I help you, Mr. Delucci?"

Donte paced slowly around the room, his eyes scanning every inch of Dash's shop. His eyes rested on the sewing machine. "Is that where my brother works?"

Dash glanced over to the left side window where Atty perched every night. "Yes, it is."

"I don't understand it."

"Understand what?"

"Why he sits there and works for someone else. He's a Delucci. He should be running his own business. Giving the orders, not taking them."

"Do you give orders at the bank?"

Donte's hand swatted the air with impatience. "Don't you insult me, *signore*. I have people working under me. *For* me. What does my brother have, eh? A sewing machine in a tiny window in a tiny shop on a tiny street."

Dash looked around at the space that Donte insulted. "I grant you it's no Moreno Bank and Trust, or even Francesco Barone's Bank. But it's an honest living in a wonderful neighborhood."

"Across town from him. Why couldn't he find work among his people?"

Dash shrugged. "Perhaps he wants to be here." He shifted the conversation topic. "Why haven't you told your brother about the letters?"

"What letters?"

"The letter I pulled out of your pocket the other day. The letter I saw come sliding under your door two nights ago."

That got Donte's attention. "Another letter came?"

"Ah ha! So you *do* know what I'm talking about."

Donte waved him off again. "It's none of his business. None of yours either. Why you both keep asking me about it? Bah! It's disrespectful. Disrespectful to a man of my position."

Dash crossed his arms over his chest. "When a letter might be from *La Mano Nera*, it deserves a few questions."

"You're crazy! No one has heard from *La Mano Nera* for years!"

"I know what I saw with my own eyes. You still wish to deny it?"

Donte gritted his teeth and stared at Dash, silent.

"Alright," Dash said. "Tell me why you went to Carmela Fiore and asked if *she* was the one who sent it?"

"You spoke with Carmela?"

"I did. She wasn't exactly forthcoming as well about the

letters or why you came to her, but she suggested I ask you about it."

"The bitch," Donte muttered.

Dash studied him. Gus Brown, the Smoke Shop's resident barfly, thought Carmela and Donte had an affair. Could this vitriol be the symptom of a broken heart? A betrayed lover?

Or something else?

Dash asked, "Why did you go to her about the letters?"

No response.

"Why did you think she wrote them?"

More defiant silence.

"Alright," Dash said, pivoting. "Who are the Capellos?"

"I don't know." Like Carmela, he answered too quickly.

"I will find out eventually, Mr. Delucci."

Donte shook a disapproving finger at Dash. "This is a family matter. And as close as you think you are to my brother, *you* are *not* family."

"If you're putting my friend in danger, Donte, I want to know."

"What do you mean? Eh? I'm not risking Atty any harm!"

"That's bushwa. Someone *deliberately* burned down your old building and if you were their intended target, they'll try again. If you're not concerned for yourself, at *least* be concerned with the safety of your children."

"They are *my* children and *my* concern!"

"Donte, your sins hurt more than just you."

"My . . . sins?" Donte sputtered. "What are you talking about?"

Dash placed his hands on his hips. "I'm talking about Gianni Spinelli. The Smoke Shop? On Bleecker? Cards, roulette, tarot, séances? Ring any bells? You owe them hundreds of dollars and one of their workers, a louse named Vito Beneventi has been using *your* debts to get dates with *your* daughter."

A string of Italian curses flew from Donte's mouth, sprinkling spittle across his lips. When he finally returned to English, he said, "I'll kill that little shit!"

"No, you won't, Donte, because then you'll be in even *more* trouble than you already are." Dash shook his head at the angry man. "You need to tell your brother the truth. He loves you. He may be angry with you or disappointed, but he is loyal and he will try to help you."

"Maybe that's why I don't want him involved," Donte replied. "Atty is many things, but clever? Sneaky? Strategic? No, that is not my brother. *I* am the thinker of the family. I have a plan and it doesn't involve him or you."

*A plan?*

Dash glanced down at the writing desk, thinking of the tarot card with a meeting place and time.

"What's your relationship with Delilah Sams?"

"Del—who?"

Dash grinned. "Not quick enough, Donte. You have her tarot card in your possession. A scribbled note of a meeting place and time. Does your plan involve her?"

Donte held up a finger. "If you say anything about this, *signore*, anything at all, the letters, the Hand, Delilah, I'll deny it. I'll deny it all. I'll not only deny it, but I'll tell Atty you've been harassing me, harassing my children, that you steal from him, stole from me. Eh? I'll make sure you won't ever *see* my brother again."

Dash glared at Donte. "He won't believe you."

"Oh, he won't believe me? His big brother? The one he looks up to? We stick together, Atty and I. We are family.

You are an outsider." Donte jabbed a finger into Dash's chest. "And don't you forget it, *signore.*"

———

Dash steamed for the better part of the afternoon. How dare Donte threaten him? He was only trying to help, for Heaven's sakes! And what did he mean when he said he had a plan? The thought of Donte attempting any form of cleverness or trickery filled Dash with dread. The man wasn't exactly the pinnacle of good luck.

When Joe came by the shop to check in on Dash and see how his cold was doing, Dash told him what had happened. In between coughing fits, of course.

Joe replied, "Goddammit, lassie, ya should be restin'!"

"I don't have time to rest," Dash said. "I need to figure out how to outmaneuver Donte."

Joe's eyes narrowed. "Yer not outmaneuvering anybody."

"What do you mean?"

"I *mean,* it doesn't matter what Donte said he'd do. Yer gonna tell Atty. Tonight. Before ya lose yer nerve. I don't care if ya have the proof or not. He needs to know. And whatever happens happens."

Dash tried to argue, but the fight died before it left his lips. He sighed. "You're right, Joe. It just feels…crummy, you know? To help Atty, I have to hurt him. What kind of bum deal is that?"

Joe gave Dash a sad smile. "A deal we sometimes have to make with the people we love."

The day passed slowly. A few measurements, a few secret knocks. A lot of waiting around.

Dash felt fatigue settle in like a damp fog. The gray,

rainy weather outside did little to energize him. He laid his head down on the writing desk and promptly fell asleep.

The tailor shop front door jangled open, startling Dash, and he almost fell out of his chair.

"Oh! Sorry!" a youthful male voice said.

Dash steadied himself and saw a small newsboy standing in the center of the shop.

"Are you alright?" the boy called out.

Dash raised a hand. "Yes. I'm fine. Jake as Jake can be." He shook himself awake as best he could and focused on the boy.

He wore a light gray flat cap, matching pants and vest, white shirt, no tie. Bright eyes, engaging smile with crooked teeth. A smooth face smudged with the remnants of a chocolate bar hastily devoured. He couldn't have been over eight or nine at the most.

Dash felt himself smile. "How can I help you, my friend?"

"Pardon me. Are you Mr. Dash—Dash—Dash-ee-yell Parker?"

"Dash, and yes, I am."

The boy reached into his pocket and pulled out a note. "This is from Pru."

Prudence Meyers. Had she finally found something of use for him about McElroy?

"Thank you," Dash said, taking the note from the boy. The edges of the paper were sticky with sugar and melted chocolate, and Dash tried to avoid smearing more of it across the page.

He read:

*Meet me at MacDougal Alley across from the Hotel Earle at six o'clock tonight. Make sure you're clean shaven and*

*not followed. Bring a lavender handkerchief, if you have*
*it. ~P*

Dash looked up at the boy, who stood shifting his weight from foot to foot. Dash smiled and reached into his pocket and pulled out a nickel.

"This is for you," he said, placing it into the boy's sticky palm.

The boy grinned. "Thank you, sir! Thank you, thank you!" And he raced out of the shop.

Dash closed the shop early and sprinted to the Carmine Baths, where he bathed and shaved. He dressed in his finest pinstriped suit, though he couldn't find a lavender handkerchief to save his life.

"How does *Finn*, of all people, not have one?" he muttered to himself. He hoped Pru had a backup plan.

He took the most circuitous, serpentine route to his rendezvous destination, with constant changes of directions, in case McElroy was following him. He transferred north, doubling back south, going west before changing his mind to return east, passing through Washington Square Park, where he side-stepped around the drunkards, the homeless, and the so-called degenerates meeting one another in the shadows, before turning and tracking north again.

The Hotel Earle stood on the corner of MacDougal and West Eighth Street. Across from the lobby doors was MacDougal Alley, a dead end where backdoor shops and secret studios hid in plain sight.

Dash peered down the narrow path, the shadows thick with the darkness of the departing sun. He glanced around. No one was staring at him or pointedly turning their heads away. The wind bit further into his skin, and he pulled up the collar of his raincoat. He slowly entered the alleyway.

His heels clicked on the concrete and echoed off the walls. The distant hum of MacDougal Street murmured behind him. Above and around him were the clangs of pots and pans of those residents cooking dinner. Voices conversed back and forth. A cat squealed somewhere in the alley and Dash's heart leapt into his throat.

He whirled around. No one was behind him.

Someone whispered his name.

He spun around again, squinting in the darkness. "Pru?"

She stepped from the shadows.

Prudence Meyers, one of the three partners of the all-women's law firm Meyers, Powers & Napier, cut a striking figure in her tailored suit. Tall and trim, like himself, she was nearly his height of six feet. Short-cropped black hair exposed a long, patrician neck and delicate, almost elfish, ears. Dark lipstick colored her lips, and dark brows arched over sparkling, intelligent eyes, which he knew to be lavender.

"Were you followed?" she asked, her voice a rich, honeyed alto.

"I didn't see anyone, so if they're here, they're good."

Pru considered his response. "If that's the case, we're sunk anyway."

"Your faith is touching."

"Just being practical." She frowned. "You sound ill."

"Only a cold."

"Whiskey and honey. That always does the trick for me." She reached into her inside coat pocket and removed a cylindrical tube. There was a slight popping sound as she broke the tube into two parts. "Now, to work. Pucker up."

At first, he was confused; then he understood. Lipstick. "What's that for?"

"Where we're going, you can't be a man."

A self-conscious laugh. "Had I known, I'd have gotten something from Finn's closet. Though it's a dress on him and it would be a slip on me but—"

"With all due respect, we have little time and I want to get out of this urine-soaked alleyway, so purse your lips, please."

Dash did as instructed. She grabbed his chin and tilted it slightly up. He felt the waxy end trace several lines around his lips. Once done, he smacked his lips together, as he'd seen Finn do. Pru judged him with a critical eye.

"Good," she said.

She capped the lipstick and returned it to her inside pocket. Reaching into the other inside pocket, she removed a brass-plated circular compact, which she opened it and lifted a tiny brush. With her pinky finger, she dabbed into the compact and smeared rouge on Dash's cheeks. She then used the brush to blend in the sticky powder. A nod of approval and the compact disappeared into her pockets like the lipstick.

"And now the eyes." She brought out a dark pencil. "Look up. And whatever you do, don't blink."

Dash focused on a lit window three stories above them. He saw a woman chopping root vegetables with a large, flat knife, her face frowning in concentration. If she at any moment looked down, she'd see a most scandalous scene, this changing of the sexes. The thought amused Dash until the tip of Pru's pencil caused him to jump.

"Don't move either," Pru said.

He murmured his apologies. The pencil was scratchy against his lower eyelids. He kept watch of the woman above them, who was now transferring the vegetables to a giant copper pot. She glanced over a shoulder and started speaking to someone just out of view. A smile formed, then a soundless laugh escaped her lips.

"Close your eyes."

The woman disappeared and Dash felt that scratchy tip once again on his upper lids.

"Open them."

Dash did, blinking. "How do I look?"

"Not bad," Pru replied. "Now there's just one more thing."

"The dress?"

"Your suit is fine. Perfect, actually. Did you bring a lavender handkerchief?"

"I couldn't find one."

"Not even among Finn's things? No matter. I have a second one. Open the top of your coat, please."

Pru brought out a handkerchief and stuffed it into his front breast pocket, fluffing it in a jaunty manner.

"Wonderful," she said. "Shall we go? I could sorely use a cocktail."

They emerged from the alley and joined the steady flow of people on MacDougal. One block down, Pru turned and descended a set of metal steps to the basement level of a nondescript building. At the bottom of the staircase was a metal door. Pru raised her hand and knocked. A rectangular brass plate placed at eye level opened, and a pair of sapphire irises stared at them.

Pru murmured, "Lilith was right."

The sapphire eyes stared for a moment longer, then the brass plate closed. A lock unlatched with a loud *clang!*

Pru glanced backwards at Dash. "Are you ready?"

The door opened, and they stepped inside.

## 18

The crowded club was narrow and long, with tables and chairs on one side and a bar on the other. Halloween decorations filled every inch of the space: ghosts and witches flew across the walls in undulating patterns; devil pitchforks crisscrossed in the corners; paper lanterns in the shape of jack-o'-lanterns stretched across the tin ceiling, their orange skins casting a sunset glow over the entire space.

He saw women of all shapes and sizes dressed smartly in tuxedos and dark pinstriped suits. A few wore monocles whose tassels gently shook from their chatting and laughing. Not a single dress in sight. And all wore lavender handkerchiefs in their front breast pockets.

Pru pointed with her chin towards the bar. They squeezed past a trio of tuxedos, one of whom was telling a ribald story involving a woman, a first-class train compartment, and a long, dark tunnel. They settled beside a couple, who ignored all the surrounding noise and got lost in each other's smiles.

The bartender, a short, round-faced woman with close-cropped hair, came over to them. "What'll it be, ladies?"

Pru replied, "Two gin rickeys, Lou. Make them doubles, but pour them like triples."

A mock offended gasp. "Miss Meyers, would I *ever* skimp on your gin?"

"*You* wouldn't, but we all know Miss Who-Shall-Not-Be-Named would charge triple for a single and the single would be at least half."

Dash assumed Pru meant the owner of the club.

Lou chuckled. "You sure got her number. Last week, I tried to comp a lost little lamb fresh off the bus. Ya know, to make her feel welcome and such. Miss I-Needs-All-The-Dimes said no can do; she pays or she ankles. I tried to tell her, 'look, if we treat her right, she'll come back repeatedly. Then your precious dimes are gonna come rollin' in on the regular.'" Lou shook her head. "She don't understand people, that's her problem. And I'm outta limes, that's my problem. Tonight, at least. Lemons Jake? Makes it more a Bee's Knees, I grant ya."

"Bees or rickeys, the important part is the gin. Am I right, Lou?"

Lou was already mixing ingredients into her shaker. "You're always right, Miss Meyers."

Pru laughed. "Now you're just flirting."

"Glad you're picking up the cards I'm laying down. Maybe one night, I'll get a straight flush and you'll come home with me."

Lou bounced her brows with a smile as she added ice into the shaker. She slapped on the top with her palm, raised it to her ear, and shook. The familiar rattle followed.

"Then again," she said, "I think I'm playing with a busted deck." Lou raised her chin towards Dash. "Who's the new doll?"

Pru placed a hand on his shoulder. "Another lamb fresh

off the bus. This is an old friend of mine visiting from out of town."

"Showing her the ropes, huh?"

"She wanted to see the best Manhattan had to offer. Naturally, I had to have her see you."

"*Now* who's flirting?"

Pru laughed. She said to Dash, "Lou here is the best bartender in town. She pours with a heavy hand, offers brilliant advice—"

"Which you never take."

"—and is cool as a cucumber during a raid. What did you say to that cop last week?"

Lou set the shaker onto the bar, popped off the top, and began pouring its contents into two glasses. "I told him not to worry. We weren't old suffragists, just a bunch of women who needed to get out of our husband's hair."

Dash couldn't help but blurt out, "And that worked?" He stopped, realizing his voice would give him away as a man, especially now that his voice had dropped an octave from its normal range. He cleared his throat and raised his pitch as high as he could, which wasn't more than a fifth. A raspy fifth. "I mean, and that worked?"

Pru suppressed a smile.

Lou smirked as she topped off the two drinks. "Well, that and the card I gave him for a certain hotel with certain ladies who love the attention of cops, if you get what I'm saying. And you know what he said to me, Miss Meyers? Hand-to-God, he said, 'Hey, I've never been to this one.'" Lou smacked the bar with her palm, laughing. "I tell ya, these coppers are something else."

She gathered up the two glasses and placed them in front of Dash and Pru.

"That'll be a dime, please."

Pru placed a quarter on the bar. "Keep the change, Lou."

Lou slid the quarter into her palm. "Appreciate it, Miss Meyers. You're my favorite customer."

"And you're full of bunk."

"I'll tell ya's who's full of bunk. That Frances Stevens Hall lady. You been following the trial, Pru?"

Pru smiled. "I don't have to. Everyone follows it for me."

Lou jerked her thumb towards Pru while she said to Dash, "This one is a little jaded about our judicial process. Can't imagine why, can you?"

Dash smiled but didn't reply for fear of his voice giving away his sex.

Pru said, "I'm not cynical, Lou, I'm just a realist. And this case is a cockup of the utmost proportions. They should've been able to land charges back in 'Twenty-Two but the coppers were bribed by that Felix de Martini fellow, the medical examiner screwed up the autopsies, and the district attorney was too busy raising money for his re-election that he missed a murder conviction. Now we have Senator Simpson, who's only reopening the case because of political pressure, which, in my experience, doesn't lead to good results. No, I suspect that unless there's a literal smoking gun in Mrs. Hall's hands, she'll get away with it."

"I don't know. The papers have been having a field day. That should sway some jury members, shouldn't it?"

"Grand juries are fickle. They're like pussycats."

"Hey, you rub 'em right and they purr all night."

"But you rub them wrong and they'll scratch the shit out of you."

Lou found this hilarious and moved down the bar. She was still cackling when she greeted another customer with,

"Joanne! Hey, Joanne, when are you gonna make me an honest woman and take me away from all this?"

Pru shook her head, smiling. "Lou is a character."

"That she is," Dash said.

They held up their glasses and clinked the rims before taking their sips. The strength of the gin hit Dash across the mouth like a fist.

"Goodness!" he said, his voice tight and thin. A shudder traveled down his spine. "You're not wrong about Lou's heavy hand."

"Being a woman requires extra fortification. Especially when talking about the man we're here to discuss."

She cast a careful eye to their surroundings, and Dash did the same. Satisfied no one was eavesdropping, they turned to one another.

Pru raised her glass to her lips as she said, "You go first, Mr. Parker. What did you find out?"

The entire tale took a good ten minutes: Peter Fraker, the damning photographs, and their presumed location; McElroy's fake address on Downing Street and his actual address on Park Avenue South.

Dash finished his account with, "This Peter Fraker says if the photographs are gone, he'll take great pleasure in thwarting McElroy. And now, we have evidence that ol' McElroy isn't being honest with the city government about where he's living. If we can get his bank statements, the rental agreement, the deed, if he bought. If we can get any of those things, we can prove graft as well."

"Not a bad strategy." Pru stroked her chin while he nourished his parched throat with another sip of his cocktail. "Has McElroy threatened you lately?"

Dash felt himself turn grim. He told her of his latest

threats, primarily that of turning Walter Müller's disappear-
ance into murder.

"His obsession with Walter Müller matches what my
sources have heard," Pru said once Dash finished. "Apparently, Officer McElroy ran afoul of the Alderman some
years back."

"Back when he was a detective."

A respectful flash of her eyes. "You've been very busy
indeed, Mr. Parker. Yes, that is true. He was in the detective's bureau before being demoted to street patrol duty."

"How in heaven's name did he anger the Alderman?"

"He had a dalliance with the Alderman's daughter."

Dash winced. "I don't want to think about that odious
man having any sort of relations with . . . well, anybody."

"There's no accounting for taste, though I hear the
Alderman's daughter was looking to stick a finger in her
father's eye. The Alderman isn't exactly known for his
female sensitivities. Needless to say, the Alderman demoted
McElroy, and our nosy flatfoot beat cop has no hopes of ever
being anything other than what he is. Do you see now why
he's so interested in Walter Müller?"

Dash did. "He might undo the Alderman's shunning if
he solves a major case. Would that work?"

"Fifty-fifty odds. And my source says McElroy is
desperate to get back to where he once reigned."

Dash sipped the remaining part of his rickey. Fife and
Joe were right; they were going to need more than just Peter
Fraker's photographs.

"Miss Meyers, how difficult would it be to get McElroy's financials?"

"How do you mean?"

"If we can show how much money he has in relation to
his salary, then we can show the evidence to someone,

maybe this Alderman, who can use it to get rid of him for good."

Pru considered the situation before draining the last of her drink as well and signaling Lou for another round. "It might work, Mr. Parker. Besides the Alderman, the sergeant of Mr. McElroy's current precinct is also no fan of his."

"Saving that, we could always go to the papers. They love to expose corruption."

"I might have a contact in the banking world. Let me see if she can peek into McElroy's accounts. We could get a thorough history of his financial situation before official subpoenas."

"Is that legal?"

Pru gestured to the surrounding room. "I bend the rules when it suits me. The so-called normal world doesn't play fair with us inverts; why should we give them the same courtesy? Isn't that right, Lou?"

Dash looked up to see Lou had returned to their place in the bar.

"You got that right, Miss Meyers," Lou said, the shaker once again rattling in her hands.

Pru set her empty glass next to Dash's, and Lou filled both to the brim. "Thank you, Lou."

"This round's on me," Lou replied, then winked at Dash. "If Pru here won't pay me any mind, maybe you will, dolly."

Dash, although he wasn't Lou's type, still blushed. Embarrassment tied his tongue, which amused Lou to no end. She slapped the bar with her opened palm.

"Ha! I've struck another one dumb by my beauty. Maybe my luck is finally changing!"

Still crowing, she left Dash and Pru to attend another couple.

Pru turned her attention back to Dash and raised her glass. "To getting that bastard McElroy."

"Amen," Dash replied as their glasses clinked.

———

It was long past sundown when Dash exited the Third Avenue el at the Canal Street stop. Lou's heavy pours helped to dull the anxiousness he felt about crushing Atty's illusions about his brother.

He was almost to Atty's building when he heard two arguing voices. One was a familiar nasally whine, the other a familiar rasp. He saw a young man standing on the sidewalk pleading up to Isabella, who was shouting back from Atty's window in fiery rebukes.

*Vito.*

"I thought I told you to postpone your courtship for another time?" Dash called to the weaselly boy.

Vito turned around. "Huh?" He squinted to see Dash in the dark. "Oh, it's you. Mr. High Hat. You sound like her," he said, pointing at Isabella. "Say, you still got that pistol?"

*I sincerely wish I did.*

Dash looked up at the window. "Miss Delucci, is your father home?"

She shook her head. "He went off with Uncle Atty. They needed to talk, they said. In private."

*Damn!*

Dash returned his attention to Vito. "I apologize Mr. . . . Beneventi, is it? Miss Delucci isn't available for an evening out."

"Says you."

"You are correct. That is exactly what I say."

"Beat it, mister."

Dash called up to Isabella. "Would you mind using the neighbor's telephone to call the police? Please report a disturbance to the peace." He sincerely hoped there was a telephone somewhere in the building.

Vito tried to call his bluff. "Oh, come on! There ain't no telephone in that dump!"

Isabella called down. "I'll use Mrs. Lombardi's next door."

Dash said to Vito, "Think your employers will mind if you miss your shift tonight because you're in jail."

Vito leered at Dash. "What do you want?"

"I think you and I ought to have a little conversation."

If it was possible, Vito's voice got even more nasal. "I don't wanna talk to *you*!"

"Too bad. That's all you're going to get this evening."

"I ain't no fairy!"

"And I'm not really wanting to talk to you."

Vito's voice cracked. "Say again?"

Not only was the boy dogshit on a shoe, to quote Isabella, he also had as much smarts.

Dash replied, "I want to speak with your employer Gianni Spinelli."

## 19

They walked uptown, Vito's pencil-thin legs taking large strides and trying to outpace Dash. Dash mentally rolled his eyes. The pathetic tactics insecure men resorted to when threatened.

Or dismissed, as when they turned to leave Atty's building, Isabella called out, "Say hello to Pops for me!"

Vito murmured, "Ungrateful bitch."

"Strange reaction to someone you claim to like," Dash said as they strolled.

"I like her. Why don't she like me?"

*Do you have an hour for a list?* Dash thought.

"Treat her with respect, and she will be more likely to respect you."

"You some kind of suffragist? Think women are equal to men?"

"I think they're superior."

Dark eyes, black in the night, narrowed. "Huh. You're a queer one, alright."

*In more ways than you know . . .*

They tacked their way north, taking lefts onto cross

streets and rights onto uptown avenues. Dash glanced over at Vito, who kept his hands in his trouser pockets, his bony arms looking like wire coat hangers.

He said, "You got a name, mister?"

Dash paused, remembering that at The Smoke Shop, he was Max Bennett. He gave Vito his brother's name, then asked, "How long have you been in the neighborhood, Vito?"

"None of your beeswax."

"I understand you had a date with Miss Delucci the night her home burned down."

"Yeah, what of it?"

Dash shrugged. "Nothing. Just . . ." How did he want to play this? ". . . impressed."

Vito snapped his head to look at Dash. "You makin' fun of me?"

"I wouldn't dream of it, Mr. Beneventi. No, truly, I am impressed. Miss Delucci is a beautiful young woman. Smart. Swift. Strong. And brave? Imagine going down a fire escape while a building burns all around you and jumping onto a sheet several stories below. The girl has got nerves of steel."

"She's pretty. I don't know about the other parts."

*Of course, you don't.*

"Regardless," Dash said, "it speaks to your—your prowess that you snagged an evening with her."

"Wasn't no—what was that high hat word you used?— prowess? Wasn't nothing like that. See, I *made* her go out with me."

Never before had Dash wanted to slug someone so badly. "Is that the debt you were mentioning back there?"

"Sure was." Vito faced forward again, but Dash caught sight of a satisfied grin stretching bloodless lips. "Her father owes Pops money, and nobody skips out on a debt with Pops. No, sir. And Mr. Delucci, he is one unlucky devil. He in the hole six hundred dollars. That's right. Six hundred. No way he can pay that, no way."

"And when you learned this, what did you do?"

Vito dared to smirk, and his chuckle filled the air with a mocking tone. "I gave Bella a preposition."

"You mean, *propo*sition."

"What?" Vito's expression changed abruptly, his smirk replaced by a menacing scowl. "Hey, you listen here, high hat, *I'm* tellin' this story. You wanna hear it or what?"

Dash held up his hand. "My apologies. Continue on."

Vito fumbled with his tie, his fingers clumsily tugging at the knot and causing it to become even more crooked. "Like I was saying. I made her a *proposition*, and said if she went out with me, I'd see what I could do to lower her father's debt. Maybe even put in a good word with my Pops."

*And I bet you had no intention of doing either of those things . . .*

"And did you?"

That infernal snicker yet again. "Of course not! Pops doesn't listen to me! Why would he? I'm just a no-account, according to him. I'm not family."

"Why do you call him Pops?"

Vito replied, as if Dash was a fool. "Cause he's old! Jeez! You slow?"

Dash stifled his anger. "But you're going to use Mr. Delucci's debt to keep going out with Miss Delucci."

Vito feigned the voice of a pompous dandy. "Why yes, yes, I do believe you are correct, old chap. That's exactly what I intend to do." He returned to his nasal whine. "She gave me icy mitts a few nights ago, but I'll thaw her."

Bitter anger hardened Dash's words. "Do you often

pressure women like that? Use their father's debts to make them more amenable to your advances?"

"Wouldn't you? I mean, come on, mister, all us men have an angle. You know what yours is?"

"No, but I'm sure you'll tell me."

"You got fine clothes and fine manners and some fancy school learning. Your *propositions* and your *amenables*. You're also handsome, though I ain't no fairy, you understand. It's all pressure, just a different kind. The pressure that if she don't throw her legs around you and get your money, some other woman will." Vito eyed him with suspicion. "Assuming you want a woman's legs around you. I still think there's something fairy-like about you."

Dash ignored the degeneracy charge and replied, "And because you don't have education, style, and culture, you resort to other tactics."

"What?"

Dash took a deep breath. "You're not handsome, rich, or clever, so you have to use other means to get the ladies."

Vito's mouth opened in outrage. "Did you just insult me?" he sputtered.

Dash couldn't help himself. He laughed, which led to another coughing fit. He wiped his mouth with his handkerchief.

"Vito," he eventually said. "I couldn't possibly insult you when you've already insulted yourself. But that's neither here nor there. You went out with Miss Delucci and dropped her off at her apartment last Saturday night, yes?"

Vito scrunched up his brow, wanting to return to Dash's assessment of him, but either thought better of it or, more likely, couldn't figure out what to say next. Isabella, however, provided him with plenty of words.

"Yeah," he said darkly. "We had dinner and some dancing. Then we went to an after-hours club, and I tried to get a little check cashed, if you know what I mean? But she—she was one cold teller. Wouldn't allow me to open any accounts."

"Then you brought her home."

"Yup. Tried to get a little kiss goodnight, but she ducked out on me." Vito's voice simmered with fury. "All them girls trying to duck out on me. Why do they do that? Huh? I like them. That should count for something."

There wasn't an answer Dash could give that could make this selfish boy understand, so he simply asked, "While you were there, did you see anything odd?"

"What do ya mean, odd?"

"Her building burned to the ground, Vito, right after *you* dropped her off. It's quite possible you saw what caused the fire. Or who."

"I didn't see nothing."

"Oh, come now, Vito. Think."

*If that's even possible for a pea-brain like you.*

Vito flashed a devious smirk. "I think—I think I *might've* seen something."

"What was it?"

"How much is it worth it to ya?"

"I'm not going to *pay* you money, Vito."

Vito shrugged. "Too bad. What I know is pretty interesting. And a high hat like you enjoys *interesting* things, don't ya?"

"Vito, you just admitted you had no intention of following through on your deal with Isabella, so why should I believe you'd keep your end of the bargain with me?"

Vito stopped abruptly. "We're here."

Dash turned on his heels and looked up. The Smoke Shop was right in front of them. He half expected the curtains to be drawn across the front windows, as it was far beyond closing time for a normal shop. But the windows remained naked, exposing a dimly lit young man behind the glass display case. Renzo. Still at his post. Still concentrating almost single-mindedly on the rolling of another cigar.

Vito looked over at him. "You ready?"

Dash swallowed a cough, his throat scratchier than ever, and gestured for Vito to walk in ahead of him. "After you."

They entered the shop with a jangle of the door.

Renzo kept his eyes on the neat line of tobacco. "Evening, Vito."

"Hello, Renzo. How's tricks?"

The man shrugged as he rolled the paper over the brown leaves. "Same as always. Who's your friend?"

"Oh, him? He ain't no friend of mine. He wants to see Pops." Vito glanced back at Dash. "This is Renzo. He the baby of the family, isn't that right, Renzo?"

Renzo Spinelli looked up. "Good evening, sir," he said. His eyes sparked with recognition. "You were here before. How was the cigar for your . . . cousin, was it?"

It took a moment for Dash to recall the reference from when he first visited this place. "Ah, yes. He enjoyed it very much."

Renzo kept his gaze averted, his voice a gentle hum. "Your name is Max Bennett, *si*?"

"Word gets around."

"Are you looking for another . . . cigar?"

"Actually, I'm hoping to dance with Lady Chance once more. I believe the password is *dado*."

Vito waved them both off. "We don't need passwords. He's with me."

Renzo gave Vito a stern look. "Papa doesn't like it when you bring people to show off."

"Geez, 'Renzo, when'd you get to be such a bluenose?"

"I'm no bluenose. I just know what Papa says. You keep disobeying him, he's gonna throw you out on your ear, and I don't want to hear any whining from you."

Vito rolled his eyes. "Renzo tries to keep me in line," he said to Dash.

Renzo snorted. "A lot of good I do." He returned his attention to Dash. "My brother says you're much too—how did he put it?—*invested* in the debts of someone else."

"Word really does get around," Dash replied. "I am concerned on behalf of a friend of mine. His brother has been receiving threats."

Renzo finished rolling the cigar and began the process for a new one. "I see. Who are these threats from, if I may ask?"

"We're not entirely certain, but they're signed from *La Mano Nera*."

Renzo's hands stopped. "You should be careful with that name, *Signore* Bennett."

"So I've been told."

"And yet, you throw out their name so carelessly." Renzo returned to rolling the second cigar. "If it is truly *La Mano Nera* targeting your friend's brother," he said, "then he is in serious trouble. More trouble than his debts."

"I agree." Dash glanced around the shop. "Have you heard of a Black Hand resurgence in your neighborhood? Among your patrons, perhaps?"

Vito scoffed. "Oh my god, we're back to talking about the boogie man. The Hand wasn't real, folks. Nothing but a scary story to frighten children."

Renzo pounded the glass case with a fist. "The Hand

was real, Vito! It was real!" His face flushed red, his eyes bulged in their sockets. Thick veins pulsed against the sides of his neck. "You are far too ignorant to say such things. I saw with my own eyes what the Hand can do. I saw buildings, motorcars, *people* blown apart by their bombs. Terrified to leave their homes, to have their children leave their homes. I saw families decimated, fortunes lost. So no, Vito, the Hand wasn't a fairytale. It was a *nightmare.*"

An uncomfortable silence settled into the room.

Finally, Vito held up his hands. "Jeez, Renzo, I'm sorry. Gosh. So sensitive." He looked at Dash. "Renzo's always been the more fragile of us all."

Renzo ignored Vito and said, "Mr. Bennett, is that why you wish to speak with my father? *La Mano Nera?*"

"Perhaps."

Renzo studied Dash intently. "I'll see if he's available to see you."

Vito cut in. "All hail Renzo, the gatekeeper." He nodded towards the curtained off doorway. "C'mon. Let's get ourselves a drink."

## 20

It was as if Dash had never left.

Rattling of balls on roulette wheels, flicks of cards, tumbles of dice and cheers, jeers, shrieks, and moans. All under clouds of smoke, cologne, and perfume.

Vito muttered, "Shit, here comes Berto."

Dash saw Vito staring off into one of the far corners. Berto sauntered over, a smirk creating half-moon dimples on either side of his thick lips. He was dressed in a black tuxedo complete with tails, white waistcoat, and white bowtie.

For the first time, Vito wasn't so cocky. He didn't even bother to sneer.

"Hello, Berto," he said, his voice flat.

Berto bared his teeth like a shark happy to find new prey. "Hello, Vito. What brings you in tonight? Usually, you're out trying to land yourself a girl and failing every time." He glanced at Dash. "Gave up and went with a fella, did ya?"

"I told you, I'm not no fairy," Vito growled.

Berto's laugh was mean. "So you say, pansy, so you say."

He finally gave Dash his full attention. "Hey, I remember you. You're the one who was asking about Donte Delucci. Mr. Bennett, isn't it? You promise to mind your own business this time?"

Dash smiled. "Tonight, I'm interested only in the world of chance." He suddenly remembered that the date and time on the devil tarot card in his writing desk was for tonight. He looked at Berto. "I may also be interested in the spiritual realm. Is your spiritualist here this evening? Miss Delilah Sams, is it?"

"I regret to inform you it's an invitation-only event tonight." Berto turned his head towards Vito. "That means private."

Vito scoffed, "I know what it means!"

Dash replied to Berto, "Oh? That's such a shame. Especially since I was *very* interested in seeing her." Dash removed a few coins from his pocket and held them up.

Berto's grin grew more predatory. "I can see that." He took the coins from Dash's hand. "Seance is at midnight. You can stick around and play some games, if you'd like."

"Thank you. I appreciate you squeezing me in."

"Not a problem." He jerked his chin towards Vito. "How do you know this little runt? You really his friend?"

"Vito and I know each other because he's been trying to court the daughter of a friend of mine."

Berto barked a harsh laugh. "Oh, really? And how is he doing with your friend's daughter, what with his charming personality and good looks and all?"

Vito glowered at Berto.

"I can't speak to young love," Dash said, wanting to get out of this shoving match between the two men. "I wonder if I can get a drink."

"You certainly can," Berto replied. "Bar is over there."

Vito said, "I'll join ya."

Berto held out his arm, blocking Vito from moving. "You are coming with me."

"Why?"

"Because there's something we need to discuss." Berto nodded to Dash. "If you'll excuse me for one moment, Mr. Bennett. I need to speak with Vito in private."

Berto grabbed Vito's arm and lead the protesting, whining man away.

Dash let out a sigh of relief. Good lord, the two of them were tedious! He went to the bar, where he ordered a gin rickey. It was going to be a long couple of hours.

He half turned, surveying the room. Some gamblers tonight looked familiar, including the blonde who was in blue yesterday and was in gold fringe tonight. Last time Dash saw her, she was winning big. That wasn't the case now. She wore a decidedly more serious expression, biting her thumb as she placed her bet and watched the wheel turn, turn, turn. The bouncing ball stopped. She cursed and left the table.

None of her table companions won on that play as well. Among them was Gus Brown.

Gus sensed Dash's gaze and looked up. The two of them locked eyes, and Gus gave a sad wave before shuffling over to him.

"Can you believe it?" he slurred. "Not one number. Not one goddamn number."

"I'm sorry to hear that," Dash replied.

"I need a drink." Gus ordered a gin and soda. He turned to Dash. "You want anything?"

Dash held up his mostly full cocktail. "I'm Jake, thanks."

The bartender set Gus's drink in front of him. He flicked a nickel through the air and the bartender caught it with ease. "I don't get it. The last time I was here, every number hit. Every. Single. One. Best night of my life. Paving the way for the worst night of my life." His eyes brightened. "Hey! You were there before! You were the fella who was askin' 'bout Donte. What's your name again?"

"Max Bennett."

"*Bennett.* What a name. Sounds like a lucky name. Too bad I can't bet on names. Only numbers. Goddamn, my numbers are lousy tonight."

"Why not use the same numbers you used the other night?"

Gus was appalled. "Mister, you can't reuse lucky numbers!" He set about explaining the convoluted rationale as if Dash were a slow student. "Lucky numbers only have so much luck in them. Every time you bet on them, a little luck goes away. It's like sugar, you see? I put in some coins, and I get something in return. Only instead of a new hat, a new suit, or a fresh drink, I get a win."

"Does the winning replenish the luck?"

Now Gus was even *more* appalled. "Oh, boy. You got a lot to learn. Luck doesn't get *replenished*, it gets spent. You use it up, then it's gone. Especially if we're talking numbers. They're lucky no more. Now they're *un*lucky. If I were to use those same numbers tonight, I'd be losing even *more.*" He took a healthy swig of his drink.

"I see."

"You talk to that widow woman Donte was raving about?"

"Carmela Fiore? I did."

"And . . . ? Come on, don't hold out on ol' Gus! Did she write those nasty letters?"

"She says she didn't."

"She's lying!"

Dash shrugged. "Too early to tell. Have you ever seen her in this place?"

"Here? The Smoke Shop?" Gus thought about that one. "I don't . . . I don't think so. Why do you ask?"

"I found something that suggests she and Delilah Sams know one another."

"Ah, *De-li-lah*. There's another one I don't trust."

"Really? Why's that?"

Gus shook his head. "No. No, no, Gus, you say too much. I'm sorry, mister, I got a big mouth and I really shouldn't gossip."

Dash leaned his head in close. "I promise I won't tell a soul I heard it from you."

"You swear?"

"I swear."

Gus nodded his head fervently. "Alright, alright. I know a doozy about Miss Delilah Sams. Did you know none other than Houdini exposed her as a fraud?"

"*The* Harry Houdini?"

"The one and only."

"Wow," Dash said. "I knew Mr. Houdini had been disproving spiritualist after spiritualist, but I never thought I'd run into one. And the Spinellis still hired her?"

"Well. They didn't hire *Carrie St. Cloud,* but they sure hired *Delilah Sams,* if you catch my drift."

"She changed her name."

"Changed everything. Dyed her hair, bought new clothes. I even heard rumor she had some surgery, but I can't confirm that."

"When was this?"

"Oh, a year ago, I think." Gus leaned closer to Dash and lowered his voice. "You think she's been sending the letters? I bet her business dried up after Houdini did a number on her and I know for a fact the Spinellis don't pay her near what she used to get."

"Does she have debts?"

"Mister, *everyone* who works for the Spinellis has debts. Even Johnnie, our friendly bartender."

"I see."

At that moment, Berto returned to the main floor. Without Vito, Dash noticed. He asked Gus where Vito might be.

Gus was perplexed. "Why on earth would you want to be around that little runt?"

"Because he said to me a little while ago that he saw something the night of the fire."

"The night of the . . . you mean, Donte's building?"

Dash nodded. "He wouldn't say what it was, though."

"That's cause Vito's the biggest bullshitter that ever lived. Isn't that right, Berto?"

Berto walked up to the bar, at first ignoring Gus and speaking to Dash. "Good evening. Mr. Bennett? Vito will return shortly. He has some tasks to complete."

Gus cut in. "Got him on latrine duty again, Berto?"

Berto glanced over at him with the patient tolerance one gives a drunk. "Hello, Gus. How's your luck tonight?"

Gus's mood dropped again. "Terrible."

"Maybe it'll turn around."

"Maybe you're right." Gus finished his drink in two gulps and stood up. "Gentlemen. The tables are calling me."

They both wished him well and watched as he swayed back into the fray.

"Gus is an interesting character," Berto said.

Dash feigned agreement.

"As I was saying before Gus interrupted, once Vito is

done with his tasks, he will take you to the seance. You won't be able to sit at the table, I'm afraid—Miss Sams's orders—but you can observe from the outer perimeter. I hope that will suffice."

"It will."

"Until then, have a drink, have a game. Good luck, Mr. Bennett."

Hours later, Vito found Dash at the bar and nodded over to a curtain hanging in an archway across the room to their right. "Let's go. And you better not cough during this. You'll scare the spirits away."

They passed by more gambling tables before coming to a curtained-off doorway. Vito pulled open the curtain, and they both ducked under the archway.

This was an abandoned corner of the basement with hardly any of the previous room's harsh light or jubilant atmosphere. A drip pinged a puddle in the darkness. Faint murmurings occurred in the distance.

Vito glanced back, that irritating sneer stretching those weasel cheeks, and led Dash forward.

Up ahead were flickers of light. Candles—dozens of them—lined the edges of the room. In the center was a group of men and women sitting at a table. A black cloth embroidered with white lattices around the trim covered the entire surface. It took Dash a moment, given the dim light, to realize it wasn't embroidery at the edges. Rather, the "lattice" design was human hands. Several sets of hands.

At the head of the table sat Delilah Sams. She wore a funereal black dress with a lace top exposing her shoulders and breastbone. Her hair was dark and slightly curled, her eyes painted a thick lavender. Plum lips set in a serene smile, perfectly at rest, perfectly at ease, like a cat having mouse dreams.

On either side of her were two couples. There were excited giggles from the two young women and slight discomfort from the two young men. They were dressed in their glad rags, the men in tuxes, the women in feathers and fringe.

Delilah said, "Tonight, we are gathered to call upon the spirits of Jack Tolliver and Oscar Anello." She took a deep breath and then a low chant in a monotone vibrated from her lips. "Beloved Jack, we bring you gifts from life into death. Be guided by the light of this world and visit upon us . . . Beloved Oscar, we bring you gifts from life into death. Be guided by the light of this world and visit upon us . . ."

She repeated the incantation several times. Then she stopped.

"We all must say the incantation together."

The two couples began the incantation, reciting it with her.

"Beloved Jack, we bring you gifts from life into death. Be guided by the light of this world and visit upon us . . . Beloved Oscar, we bring you gifts from life into death. Be guided by the light of this world and visit upon us . . ."

Vito snuck a leering glance at Dash. It was clear he thought it was all a bunch of bunk. For the record, Dash did as well. Yet listening to these men and women repeat these words, it was difficult not to get caught up in the moment.

"Beloved Jack, we bring you gifts from life into death. Be guided by the light of—"

Something heavy and loud struck the wood table.

## 21

The two women shrieked a simultaneous "Oh!"

Their two men looked up, alarmed.

Only Delilah remained calm.

Dash checked the table. No one's hands had moved. How did Delilah do that? Nicholas Fife's words came back to him, how Gianni was raised by an electrician to perform tricks and illusions at Coney Island. Was he adept at trickery in seances too and Delilah was using his techniques?

Delilah slowly raised her eyes. "To whom am I speaking? Knock once for yes, twice for no. Am I speaking to Jack?"

Nothing.

The other two women glanced at one another, the feathers in their hair vibrating with anticipation. Their dates forced a smile, trying to look brave.

Delilah intoned again, "Who is here? Are you Jack?"

Dash concentrated on his own breathing, embarrassed that he, too, was getting caught up in the theatre of it all.

Two loud knocks startled the group.

"It is not Jack," Delilah said. "Is it Oscar? Oscar? Are you here with us now?"

The four guests looked excitedly at one another.

Vito's shoulder shook, as if suppressing a guffaw.

A single knock struck the table this time.

The foursome murmured to one another.

Delilah replied, "Quiet. We do not want to scare away the spirit."

The foursome got control of themselves.

"Oscar. Can you see your friends? Your friends who are here tonight?"

A pause, then a mighty knock followed.

"Do you feel their love for you, Oscar?"

Another knock.

"Do you feel they miss you, Oscar?"

*Knock!*

"They are sad they didn't get a chance to say goodbye to you. You went off to battle, fought bravely, but didn't return. They wish to give you a message. Will you hear it, Oscar?"

*Knock!*

Delilah looked over at one of the girls and nodded.

The girl visibly swallowed a lump in her throat. She spoke in a halting voice. "Oscar. Dearest Oscar. I can't stand the fact that we had to do that stupid, useless war, and that you had to go off and fight it. We had such grand plans, didn't we?"

The boy sitting next to her shifted in his seat. Dash regarded him with interest. He must be the current beau. How strange it must be to listen to your lover profess their love to someone else.

"I want you to know, Oscar," the girl continued, "that even though I'm marrying another man, there will always be a place in my heart for you. A place no one can else can fill, noble as they are. I know this might upset you, but I need to know, Oscar, if you will be at peace with this. If you will be happy for me. For us."

She looked over at the boy next to her and smiled. He gave a pained smile back. Then she looked over at Delilah, who nodded.

"Oscar," Delilah intoned. "Mildred loves you, but she must move on in this life. Will you let her go? Will you give her your blessing to wed?"

A long pause.

"Oscar? Are you still with us?"

No one seemed to breathe. Dash saw the foursome shift nervously in their seats.

A mighty knock shook the table, causing the boys this time to shout, "Oh!"

Delilah said, "Oscar, do you give Mildred your blessing to wed?"

No response.

"Oscar, again I ask, do you give Mildred your blessing to wed? Knock once for yes, twice for no."

Dash glanced over and saw Vito with his hand in front of his mouth, his eyes twinkling in the dark.

*He knows what's coming,* Dash thought.

And then the table vibrated from the force of the blows. *Knock! Knock!*

The girl named Mildred cried out: "No! No, no, no! Oscar, please! I must be married. I *must* be!"

"Silence!" shouted Delilah. In a calmer voice, she said, "You will scare Oscar away before we can ask him why you shouldn't marry Stephen."

Mildred sniffed back tears as she nodded.

"Oscar. Do you see the paper in front of me?"

Dash stood on his tiptoes and squinted. He spotted the

faint glow of white paper resting on the tablecloth.

*Knock!*

"Do you see the pencil next to it?"

*Knock!*

"Tell us, Oscar, why Mildred should not marry Stephen?"

Mildred whimpered. The boy next to her—her fiancé, Dash presumed—scowled. The couple on the other side of the table looked on with discomfort. Whatever they signed up for, it wasn't this.

"When you have finished giving us your answer, Oscar, knock once."

*Knock!*

Another jolt to the table.

Delilah slowly stood up, her hands leaving the edge of the table for the first time since Dash had arrived. She reached towards the center and gingerly picked up the piece of paper. The top side remained blank. She inspected the underside.

"What does it say?" Mildred blurted out, which prompted a "Millie!" from her fiancé.

After a dramatic pause, Delilah read, "He is a cheat."

"What?!" The fiancé stood up, almost knocking over the table. "Now see here! I will not be slandered by some—some *charlatan*!"

"Stephen!" called Mildred.

"Millie, I have entertained this for long enough. There is no ghost, there is no spirit of Oscar, and we do *not* need his permission to be married!" Stephen rudely gestured to Delilah. "Let me see that paper. I'll bet you my entire trust it's blank."

The woman shrugged and handed it to him.

He snatched it out of her hands and turned it over to see

the underside. He froze.

"What is it, Stephen?" Mildred asked, standing up from her chair. "There's something written on there. There is! Let me see it."

Stephen spoke in a milder voice. "Millie—"

"Let me see it!" She took it from him and gasped. "There is writing on here! But—but there wasn't when we arrived." She pointed to the couple sitting across from them. "You saw it! You both did! It was blank and now—now—there's a note from Oscar. From *my* Oscar." She then turned to Stephen. "Who calls you a *cheat*! Who is she, Stephen? Who *is* she?"

"Millie, calm down! You are making a spectacle of yourself."

"Silence!" Delilah held up a hand and looked around the room. Once she finished scanning the candle-lit area, she closed her eyes and took a deep breath. When she exhaled, she said, "The spirit is gone. The veil has been lifted."

Vito snuck up to Dash. "Let's ankle and wait for them to clear out," he murmured in Dash's ear.

---

"How does it work?" Dash asked once they were back in the main gambling room.

"I'm not gonna tell you! You're a rule-follower; you'd blab to everyone. Besides—" He leaned in close to Dash's ear, his foul breath wafting over Dash's face. "—it's magic."

Dash scrunched up his nose. "I thought it was spirits."

Vito stood back, waving him off. "Same difference."

"I appreciated the theatrics—very effective—but what you're doing to that young couple is cruel."

"Seems to me we're doing her a favor. Her man's a cheat. Her dead boyfriend says so."

"Perhaps, perhaps not. I'm sure she'll come back and want to question her Oscar further. With the help of Miss Sams. After paying your father a hefty fee, of course."

Vito grinned. "Don't feel too sorry for poor old Stephen. If he were straight, she'd never bat an eyelash at the charge, so she must know he's rotten *some*where. That's how the game is played, Mr. Bennett. You make suggestions and zero in on their reactions. People always give themselves away."

The curtain parted and out walked Stephen, Mildred, and their two friends. None of them looked happy. Soon Delilah appeared. Dash was going to introduce himself to her when he felt a tap on his shoulder. He turned.

Renzo.

"Father wants to see you. Now."

---

Renzo led Dash up the stairs, but instead of turning left into the Smoke Shop, they turned right, rounding a corner, and ascending another flight of steps.

At the top was a closed door.

Renzo knocked and murmured, "Father. He's here."

A muffle voice said, "Show him in."

Renzo opened the door and gestured for Dash to enter.

Inside was a small foyer with a coatrack and an umbrella stand. Beyond that was a darkened sitting room dominated by old carved-wood furniture, heavy drapery, and a flickering fireplace to the right. The fire crackled and popped.

"Good afternoon, *Signore* Bennett," a voice said.

Dash turned, scanning the room. Fireplace, easy chairs,

a sofa, end tables, coffee table, lamps with dusty shades, walls with dark wood. A man sat in a large leather chair with rounded arms and a high back smoking a cigar and watching him with cobra eyes.

Dash stepped forward. "Mr. Spinelli, I take it?"

"*Si, si.* Please. Have a seat." Gianni Spinelli gestured to one of the easy chairs directly across from him.

Dash sat, taking in the features of the man: gray hair, wide face, crooked nose, thick neck, and broad shoulders over a solid torso. A bruiser. A man not to be trifled with.

He stared straight at Dash, his gaze unwavering and unmoving, illuminated by the flickering light of the flames.

Dash could hear Joe say, "*What on earth are ya doin', lassie?*"

Gianni drew a long drag on his cigar. "Why did you want to talk with me about *Signore* Delucci's debts? A puff of smoke accompanied every word he spoke, forming a thick cloud around his head.

Dash took a shaky breath. "His brother is a friend of mine. And Donte received what appeared to be a threatening letter from The Black Hand."

"*La Mano Nera. Signore* Delucci is truly unlucky."

"Yet I understand the Hand has been largely dormant the last few years."

"That is also true."

"Have you heard in any of your circles of the Hand returning?"

"My circles?"

*Careful, Dash.*

"Business men, such as yourself."

Gianni gave another bemused grin. "No. No, *Signore* Bennett, I have not heard of the Hand returning. As far as I, and others, are concerned, the Hand is no more."

"Then who is sending the letters?"

"I do not know."

"Have you been sending them?"

Gianni found this amusing. "Why would I do such a childish thing?"

"To scare him."

"I don't need to scare him with cheap parlor tricks. My *name* scares him." Gianni knocked a tumblerful of ash into a black marble tray. "Why do you care about these letters so much? Eh? What's it to you?"

"They burned his building down."

"Perhaps so, perhaps not."

"If they did, they may try again with my friend's building."

Gianni placed the cigar between his teeth. "Such is life, my friend."

"Wouldn't you want to find out? I mean, someone else is trying to take away Donte's money. The money he owes you."

This got Gianni's attention. "How much are 'they' asking for?"

"Five thousand dollars."

Gianni whistled. He took another puff on his cigar and Dash saw a begrudging respect lightening up his face. He removed the cigar from his teeth.

"In that case, you are correct. I would be interested in knowing that. How are these letters delivered? What do these letters say?"

Dash shared what he knew, which wasn't much, but when he said the name "Capellos," Gianni's eyebrows flicked upwards.

Dash caught the expression of surprise. "You know who they are?"

"*Si*, I do. Or did. They owned a construction business here. Very successful. They got contracts with the city to do all the tunnels for the railroads."

"And how did you know them?"

"From my father. Tragic story, what happened to them."

When he didn't go on, Dash tried to prompt him. "And what happened to them?"

"How much is it worth to you?"

Dash paused, unsure of how to respond. Part of him was incensed at the offer, the other part of him afraid of it because he would've taken the gamble.

Gianni laughed, a wheezing sound which led to a fierce bout of coughing. He reached over to an end table and picked up a glass filled with a brown liquid that Dash guessed was either whiskey or scotch. The coughing fit passed, and he returned the glass to the side table.

"Oh my, you should've seen your face, *signore!*" He shook his finger at Dash. "You do not have a poker face, if I may be so bold to say. You should never sit at one of my tables. You will lose worse than Donte."

Despite the coughing fit, he took another puff on his cigar. "Alright, alright, I tell you. It is a sad story, though. Umberto Capello was the owner of a very successful construction business in Harlem's Little Italy. Given how fast the city was growing, Umberto was making money hand over fist. He couldn't send out invoices fast enough before the next bid came in. He specialized in tunnels."

"Designing them?"

"Clearing the way for them."

Something stirred in Dash's chest. "Clearing the way," he repeated.

"*Si, si, si.* Until one day, his fortune was lost. Their main warehouse caught fire and all their supplies and machinery went up in smoke. And then Umberto was arrested for arson. It seemed he was having what we respected businessmen would call a cash flow problem, and so he took matters into his own hands."

"He was hoping to collect the insurance money."

Gianni nodded. "But Umberto was no a criminal, so he didn't know how to cover his tracks. He increased the insurance coverage of his warehouse one week before it caught fire. Poor man. They arrested him within two days of the fire. He thought if he pleaded guilty, the judge would go easy on him. But the *polizia,* the judges, they don't like us Italians. We're all dirty, rotten criminals to them. Immoral Catholics with our rapist popes and lesbian nuns. A scourge that will corrupt the pure soul of the United States and plunge it into ruin."

Gianno scoffed and muttered something in Italian. "Umberto? He forgot about that. And so, the judge sent him to prison for the maximum sentence." A sad shake of his head. "He didn't last. He hung himself in his cell after a month."

"Heavens."

"Not where he went for committing a mortal sin." Gianni glanced over at the flickering, cackling fireplace. He pointed to the flames. "He'll be somewhere like that. His wife Mia, she couldn't take the loss. They had to pay restitution to the insurance company for the fire, so by the time ol' Umberto hung himself, Mia was bankrupt. Had to move to a slum where all she could afford was a hot bed, not a rented room."

Dash shook his head. Hot beds were a tactic used in many of the slums. Tenants would literally rent out their beds for either the day or night whenever they weren't home. This helped the tenant pay the rent while also providing a place to sleep for those who could not make even the cheapest of rents—which, of course, were hardly cheap to begin with.

Gianni continued. "Mia got ill and died some months later. She was always sickly, that one, always needing doctors and medicine of some sort."

"Is that what caused their cash flow problem?"

"Likely, I think."

"Did they have any children?"

"Only one, though I can't remember if it was a boy or a girl. Whoever it was, they were sent to an orphanage. I never heard what happened to them after that."

Gianni paused his tale to relight his cigar.

Dash watched the man perform the ritual, waiting until Gianni finished. "And how do you know the Capellos?"

"Ah. How much do you know about my father?"

"I know he worked in Coney Island as an electrician."

Gianni smiled. "Someone has told you about me, then. No, no, it's alright. It's not a secret; everybody knows. Yes, he worked the amusement parks out there. And Umberto's company supplied one of the Parks with supplies for a fire show."

A sizzling pop from the fireplace startled Dash. He felt his hands go numb as the implications took shape.

"Fire show?" he said.

Gianni nodded. "The park would set a building on fire and the firemen would come to put it out. People loved watching it. Sold out every time."

"And what did Umberto's company provide for the parks? Specifically, I mean."

Gianni gave him a long look. He eventually said, "Dynamite."

## 22

*Dynamite?*

Dash muttered the word to himself as he left Gianni's office.

What the devil did this all mean?

He made his way back down to the gambling den before he realized where he was going. He looked up, surprised to see the men and women cheering on the roulette balls or the thrown dice. The ever-present cigarette smoke gave the room a hazy, dreamlike quality, as if nothing down here was real.

*That's the point. None of this is real. It's all an illusion of chance, of choice, but the tables are wired and the games are rigged and the outcome is always loss.*

Like the stock market.

As he tried to rouse himself, he saw Delilah Sams quickly cross the room to the far left side. She gave a furtive glance over her shoulder and disappeared into a corner behind the pair of potted palms.

Now what was that all about?

Dash instinctively followed her. The corner was far

enough away that the noise of the main room diminished by half. The fat, drooping leaves of the palms provided a bit of cover from any prying eyes. A door was ajar. The same door Dash saw Berto exit from and lock during his first visit to The Smoke Shop.

Dash paused outside of it, listening. A murmur. Shapeless and sexless. Someone muttering to themselves, perhaps.

He peered around the edge of the doorframe. A faint light glowed inside the room. Shadows of what looked like piled-up tarps had been strewn about the floor.

The murmuring continued, followed by a whisper of "Goddammit, where the hell *is* it?"

Dash waited to see if anyone would respond, in case there were two people inside this room instead of one.

No reply.

Dash took a deep breath, pulled open the door, and strolled inside.

This was a storage closet. A small lightbulb buzzed above him. Lining the walls were tall stacks of wooden crates with the same markings on the ones Dash saw being delivered during his very first visit to The Smoke Shop: "MANHATTAN FREIGHT & TRANSFER," "FRAGILE," and "TOSCANO OLIO D'OLIVA."

And Delilah Sams was standing over an opened one, her arms elbow-deep inside.

Her head turned, those heavily made-up eyes staring at him.

Dash expected a shriek of surprise. Instead, Delilah Sams remained cool as a cucumber.

"What are you doing back here?" she asked.

Dash replied, "I was looking for the water closet. Someone pointed me in this direction."

She arched her thickly painted brow. "Someone told you wrong."

"It would appear so." He gestured towards the opened crate. "Do you need any help?"

"No, thank you." She lifted her arms out of the crate. Her hands were empty, but Dash didn't think they always had been. She quickly secured the clasp of the fringed purse dangling from her shoulder. "Water closet is on the opposite side. Go out this door and keep going straight. You can't miss it."

Dash nodded his head. "I appreciate that." He took in the surrounding room. More concrete flooring and walls, more wooden ceiling. Those wooden crates filled all the nooks and crannies, half of which were covered with tarps. Dash guessed the tarps thrown onto the ground covered the stack Delilah was currently rifling through.

He nodded towards the uncovered crates. "Does this place serve food?"

"Hmm?"

"These crates. They're full of olive oil, aren't they?"

She hesitated. "Yes, yes they are."

"Strange," Dash said. "I wouldn't expect a cigar shop with a gambling casino underneath it to have so much of it. They're not putting it into the drinks, are they? Passing it off as liquor?"

"No, the liquor they serve is enough to keel over a horse." Delilah looked around the room, as if seeing it for the first time. "And you're right, Mr. Bennett, to outsiders it looks strange." She faced him. "It's also nobody's business but the Spinellis."

Dash laughed. "I'm only making conversation. I didn't mean any offense. Oh, I believe you dropped this." He reached into his pocket and pulled out the business card he found in Carmela Fiore's restaurant.

Delilah gave it a quick glance. "You can keep that. In case you need my services."

"Don't you want to know where I found it?"

She shrugged. "I leave cards everywhere. You never know who will call."

"I found it at Fiore's restaurant. Owned by Carmela Fiore."

She stared at him. "Is that name supposed to mean something to me?"

"Oh, I don't know. Maybe. After all, Carmela used to be good friends with Donte Delucci. You've heard of Mr. Delucci, right? He's apparently well known in this establishment, though not particularly in a good way."

"First the Spinellis, now this Carmela person and Delucci fellow. You're much too inquisitive to be—how did you phrase it?—'making conversation.'"

Dash gave what he hoped was a disarming smile. "I'm an inquisitive man, I suppose."

Her lips pressed into a tight smile. "Well, I would temper your curiosity lest you get into trouble."

"What trouble would I get into?"

She didn't answer him.

"What's odd is that Donte had a stack of invoice sheets about these very deliveries right in here," Dash said, pointing to the wooden crates. "Why do you suppose that is?"

"You should go." The look she gave him was hard and unyielding. She wouldn't answer him. Not here.

"Well," Dash said, "it's been a pleasure chatting with you. Good afternoon, Miss Sams."

As he was turning to leave the storage closet, he saw

that the clasp of her purse had come undone. He spied an odd silhouette protruding from its mouth. Rectangular, fairly thick in the middle, slightly wrinkled like paper. A package of some sort. It could've been something she'd carried with her into that storage room, but Dash doubted it.

But for damn sure, it wasn't a bottle of olive oil.

***

"What do ya think it was?" Joe asked after taking a lengthy puff.

They were both standing by the opened window of their bedroom, sharing a cigarette. Joe was wearing his undershirt and brown trousers and matching suspenders. Dash was in a similar state of dress.

"I'm not sure. Booze perhaps? It wouldn't surprise me if those bottles of olive oil held gin, bourbon, or whiskey instead."

"Stealin' from the management. No good employees anymore." He took another drag and exhaled. "Ya think it's tied to this Hand letter business?"

"If it is, I can't see it," Dash admitted. "This Capello piece bothers me. How is Donte connected to this disgraced family? Who specialized in explosives, of all things."

"It's none of our business, lassie. Our business is keepin' ourselves and Atty safe. That's it." Joe gave a warning glance to Dash. "It was foolish of ya goin' in there by yerself a second time. Yer lucky that Gianni Spinelli or his sons didn't teach ya a lesson. Hell, even this Delilah Sams sounds dangerous."

Dash gestured for the cigarette. He placed it between his lips and inhaled deeply.

"I'll admit it, I overstepped," he said, exhaling smoke. "I

was trying to get Vito away from Isabella and it seemed like a splendid opportunity to ask some questions."

"Uh, huh. Next time ya go, yer takin' me or Atty. Even Finn would be better than by yerself. I mean, askin' if they sent the Hand letters and droppin' names like bombs. Jesus H. Christ."

Joe snatched the cigarette out of Dash's hands and took a hasty puff.

"It wasn't all for naught, Joe. We're learning the components of Donte's letters bit by bit. First, the nature: threats and extortion. Second, the sender: The Black Hand, or someone pretending to be. And now the third, this family name: the Capellos. We just need—" Dash was interrupted by a coughing fit.

Joe gave him a baleful stare. "Godammit. Yer gettin' worse."

"I am not," Dash lied.

Joe wasn't buying it. "I love ya to pieces, but sometimes yer just so . . . *careless*."

"Me? Careless? When am I ever careless?"

Joe gave him a knowing look and extinguished the cigarette in the teacup. With one deft motion, Joe slid the suspenders off Dash's shoulders and pulled the tails of Dash's undershirt out of his trousers.

"See?" he said. "Careless."

"Oh?" Dash looked up into those emerald eyes, sparkling with mischief. "Oh. Oh, I see. How utterly, utterly careless of me."

"And that's not all." Joe quickly grabbed the undershirt's tails and pulled them up and over Dash's head. "Yer reckless too." He tossed the undershirt onto the floor.

"Some might argue I'm brash as well."

"Aye, let me show ya how *brash* ya can me."

Joe undid Dash's trousers and they fell to the floor.

Dash kicked them away. "Don't forget negligent."

Joe's fingers found Dash's underwear drawstring. "Aye. Complete and utter disregard for yer safety." He loosened the drawstring, and his underwear joined the discarded trousers, suspenders, and undershirt.

Dash replied, "Irresponsible."

He pressed his naked body against Joe, the fabric of Joe's undershirt and trousers delightfully rough on his skin. He leaned in for a kiss.

Joe's mouth was hot and wet, a stark contrast to the cold air seeping in through their window. Dash shivered, the hairs on his arms and the back of his neck standing straight up—among other things. He stared into Joe's eyes, getting lost in those sparkling emeralds. He reached down into Joe's trousers, and his hand gripped what he knew he'd find.

A grin twitched Joe's lip. "My, my, my, how *imprudent* ya are."

"I see someone's been reading the dictionary."

Joe reached behind Dash and playfully smacked his bare ass. "Don't be insolent, me bonnie boy."

"My apologies." Dash began stroking Joe. "Allow me to be *indecent* instead."

Joe's breaths were getting shallower, his eyes glazing over. The hand that smacked Dash's ass was now gripping it tighter and tighter. "Now ya just bein' *foolhardy*."

Dash felt electricity buzzing through the air, a powerful current igniting the base of his spine and burrowing into his core. "Allow me to show you how *heedless* I can be."

Joe gripped the back of Dash's neck and pulled him to his chest. "Ya *feckless* wench."

The heartbeat under Dash's ear matched the rhythm of

the throbbing in his hand. He picked up his pace, making Joe's pulse beat faster.

"Careful," he said. "I'm about to make things *sloppy*, you big timer."

Joe grabbed Dash's wrist and removed Dash's hand from his trousers. "Don't be impatient," he purred. "No need to be *hasty* when we have all night."

"Do we? Have all night?"

Joe pulled Dash's head from his chest and kissed him hard, his lips opening Dash's mouth so his tongue could snake inside.

An unintentional moan escaped Dash's throat, inspiring the same from Joe.

They parted, staring at one another. Joe's cheeks were bright red. His naked arms and the part of his chest uncovered by his undershirt were splotchy as if from fever.

Joe said, his voice hoarse, "Ya wanna keep playin' dictionary? Or do ya wanna play a different game?"

"I think what we were playing before was *thesaurus*."

"Tha's it."

Joe put his other hand on Dash's ass and lifted him up. Dash wrapped his legs around Joe's wide hips as Joe growled into his ear, "I'm gonna show ya what happens to high hats who think they're so clever."

"You're going to teach me a lesson?" Dash whispered wetly.

Joe carried him to their bed. "I'm gonna teach ya several lessons, lassie." He laid Dash down onto the mattress and rolled Dash's hips up, fully exposing him.

"Starting with this one," Joe said. Then he placed his mouth on him.

Dash awoke the next morning re-energized, his cold reduced to mere sniffles and a light cough. Amazing how a night of intense physical activity followed by the deepest of sleeps restored a man. He grinned, aware of the whisker burn he sported, which was noticed immediately by Finn barging into their bedroom.

"Well," Finn said. "I see *someone's* felt the power of healing hands."

"Shut it, Finney," Joe growled.

"What? You healed the sick, O'Shaughnessy! Now if only you can turn water into wine—"

"That's enough, lad. We've got more important things to do."

It was true. They were to meet with Finn's newly gained contact Danny Kingman, also known as "Danny Boy," at McElroy's actual residence.

Within the hour, a cab dropped Dash, Joe, and Finn off in the center courtyard of 277 Park Avenue.

Dash exited the cab first, with Finn and Joe behind him. Joe forked over the money to the driver while Dash roamed around, astounded at the magnitude of the place. Numerous stories ascended into the sky, a perpetual array of windows gazing upon the park below. Towering, slender fir trees and lush bushes surrounded him. A peculiar stone well adorned with square, featureless faces on its sides was crowned by four curved black iron bars. Beyond this court-yard, Dash spied a rounded archway at least thirty feet tall cut into the heavy brick and limestone, leading towards another lavishly landscaped park. "*An acre of garden*," the New Yorker ad boasted and for once, it wasn't an exaggeration.

The building surrounded them completely, effectively cutting them off from the city. One would never know that the busy Park Avenue traffic motored outside, honking, cursing, and swearing their way to Grand Central Terminal.

"Impressive, isn't it?" murmured Finn behind him.

Dash turned and nodded. He'd grown up with wealth, but it wasn't as flashy nor as large a scale as *this*. Self-conscious, he adjusted the lapels of his overcoat. Underneath, he'd worn his finest: the Banff-blue pinstripe with white shirt, bright red tie, and light gray Homburg. He even brought a mahogany wood cane and wore light gray gloves.

Finn, reading his mind, said, "Don't worry, dearie. You look like a regular billboard." Finn preened himself. "As do I." Underneath his overcoat, he'd gone with a flashy pink plaid suit with bright yellow bow tie in polka dots.

Joe finished with the cabbie and grumbled his way over to them. "We're gonna go broke payin' fer all these bloody cabs."

"We couldn't arrive on foot, Joe," Dash replied. "Look around you. The residents arrive by motorcar, either their own or someone else's."

Joe pulled at his collar. Dash and Finn had picked out his suit, a green plaid number with an orange tie, and Joe was *not* thrilled with the choice. He preferred his white work shirt and brown trousers; or at the very most, his simple dark gray suit.

"Why do I have to dress like I'm a bloody garden?" he said.

Dash explained, "This is a new building full of the nouveau riche."

"Won't we stick out being all dandy-like?"

"On the contrary," Finn said, "we'll blend right in, O'Shaughnessy."

One glance around the men and women stepping out of

their motorcars or out of the building lobbies showed they were right. Brightly colored suits in pinstripes and plaids topped with fedoras, Homburgs, and trilbys; fringe dresses with thick fox fur collars and peacock feathers complemented by cloche caps, French berets, and beaded toque hats. Even the doormen wore done up in black satin with bright gold buttons and stiff hats ornamented with gold thread.

"I can' imagine a slob like McElroy in a place like this," Joe muttered.

Finn shook his head. "Nor can I."

Dash said, "I'm hoping that makes this Danny Boy more amenable to helping us."

He reached into his coat pocket and withdrew his cigarette case. He offered to Joe and Finn, who took them gratefully, and lit his own. They paused a moment—stalling, in truth—until the flames had whittled down the while cylinders to nubs.

"Alright," said Dash. "Let's go meet our Danny Boy."

This inspired Finn to sing the old Irish dirge, prompting Joe to growl, "Stop bein' bloody cheeky, Finney!"

They left the center courtyard and walked into the grandeur that was 277 Park Avenue. Vaulted ceilings, giant rounded columns, potted palms, expansive Oriental rugs, asymmetrical vases and lamps were all surrounded by brass sunbursts, jade walls, and geometric-tiled floors. Men and women strolled about in their finest clothes, pausing in intervals as if for unseen cameras.

This place boasted wealth with a capital W.

They searched for and found Finn's contact.

Danny Boy turned out to be a nervous, twitching bird all of nineteen years old. Long, frail limbs impossibly thin. Beak of a nose. Pencil for a neck. The boy tried to shrink inside a uniform that already swallowed him whole. A canceled stamp, if Dash ever saw one.

"Mr. Francis says I should assist you," Danny Boy said, his voice cracking every other word.

Dash and Joe glanced over at Finn. *Mr. Francis?*

Finn said in a soothing voice, "It's Jake, dearie. You will not get into trouble."

Danny took off his cap, running a shaking hand through his short blond hair. "It's just that I need this job and if anyone hears about this, I'll be—"

Joe replied, "We're not gonna get ya fired, lad. Not if ya play it right."

The boy put his cap back on. "Why do you need to get into this fella's place, anyway?"

Finn replied, "He's a wicked man, and that's all you need to know."

"But he's a—" Danny leaned forward, dropping his force to a whisper. "*A policeman.*"

"Trust us, lad," Joe said. "Coppers are as bad as gangsters."

"Maybe even worse," Finn added.

Dash nodded more encouragement at Danny. "We're helping an innocent man. Don't you want to help him out, too?"

Danny twitched some more. "I don't know."

Finn said, "Danny."

"Alright, Mr. Francis, alright. I'll do it."

Joe raised an eyebrow. For that matter, Dash did too. This boy was . . . *afraid* of Finn.

Danny looked around again. "Come back Sunday. My boss doesn't come in on Sundays. I'll give you a skeleton key to get into Mr. McElroy's room. He always goes to Mass, so you'll have the entire morning to yourselves."

"Thatta boy," Finn said, nodding his approval.

Danny replied, "It would serve that man right, though. He's a lousy tenant. Neighbors complain about him constantly. Treats us staff like the lowest of the low. Who does he think he is, anyway?"

Dash replied, "A flat foot with too much money and not enough class." He placed a hand on the boy's shoulder. "Thank you, Danny. We'll be here Sunday."

They turned and nonchalantly walked away.

Finn murmured, "That went well."

"Easier than I expected," Joe added. He looked over at Finn. "*Mr.* Francis? What on earth did ya do to tha' poor boy?"

"I did *nothing* untoward! I can't help it if some boys find me . . . awe-inspiring."

They pushed through the double doors and re-entered the expansive courtyard.

"Inspiring, my arse. He was terrified of ya."

"He probably saw me defending myself on the docks. You know, it's not a gentle playground down there. In any event, we have what we need, a way in to McElroy's apartment, and I say that's cause for a celebration."

Dash said, "We'll need to hold off on that party." He glanced over at Joe, who nodded.

Finn frowned. "Why is that?"

Joe replied, "Because we need to check in on Atty and tell 'im about those bloody Black Hand letters."

"Oh, dear goddess. Do we have to? I thought we were waiting for more proof."

"If we wait any longer, his place might go up in flames, lad."

Finn sighed. "Let me pray to Athena now."

"But first," Dash said, "on our way there, let's pay a brief visit to Carmela Fiore."

"Why?"

"Because she knows something, and I'm going to find out what it is."

## 23

They returned to Little Italy, though Dash had Finn and Joe wait in the cab. He remembered Atty saying how antagonistic the Irish and the Italians were to one another, and he didn't think two very Irish fellows—albeit fine, upstanding men—would be welcomed in the restaurant.

Especially if Carmela Fiore proved to be difficult.

As soon as Dash stepped out of the cab, he heard the frantic, manic chatter of gossip in the neighborhood.

It was the lunch rush, and Fiore's was filled to the brim with men and women. Conversations echoed off the walls and the ceiling, adding to the cacophony of rattling silverware on plates, poured water and wine, sizzling dishes, and chairs scooting back from the table to allow full bellies to breathe easier.

A maître d' strolled up to Dash and asked if he would mind waiting? Dash shook his head and said he needed to speak with Carmela Fiore as she was expecting him, which was a lie bolstered by the coin in his hand. That got the maître d' to say she was out back taking a break. Dash thanked him, dropping the coin into his palm.

The maître d' murmured, "Follow me."

They snaked their way through the dining room before passing through a doorway. The kitchen was as chaotic as Times Square. Men barked orders at one another, cooks and waiters ran to and from countertops, one side dropping off orders, the other picking them up. Dish washers plunged discarded plates into tubs of soapy water and stacked them to be dried. Hot oil sizzled, broths boiled. Utensils clanged against metal pots and pans while steam rose to the ceiling and hovered above them like cigarette smoke. The sticky air was thick with sweat, herbs, and garlic.

Dash and the maître d' sidestepped their way through the chaos and arrived at the back door. The maître d' nodded, turned on his heel, and cut his way back through the chaos. Dash stepped through the back door and into the alleyway. Blessed relief. The air was much cooler out. Pungent tobacco greeted his nose, as did Carmela's voice, which asked him what he was doing here.

He turned to her. She was leaning against the brick of the building, cigarette to her lips, arms crossed over her chest.

"You again," she said.

"Yes, me again."

"What do you want?"

"What do you know about the Capellos?"

Carmela glared at him. "Who's that?"

"I think you know."

"Why? Because I'm Italian and they're Italian?"

"Because that name is in Donte's letters and that family dealt with explosives."

"So?"

"So that family sold dynamite to the Spinellis back in the day to set buildings on fire for Coney Island shows. The family somehow lost their money, resulting in the father committing arson for the insurance, getting caught, and being sent to prison, where he died. His wife succumbed to an illness, leaving an orphan behind who disappeared."

Carmela shrugged. "What does any of this have to do with me? Or Donte?"

"*Someone* is threatening Donte with that name, Mrs. Fiore. He is somehow connected to them."

"Ask him about it."

"I'd rather ask you."

"Why is this *any* of your business?"

"Mrs. Fiore," Dash said, his frustration mounting. "I'm Atty's friend, and he is in danger, too. Not to mention Donte's children. Don't you care about them?"

"Don't play cheap games with me."

"This isn't a game."

Carmela's gaze was fierce, her expression unreadable, the glint in her eyes like striking flint. "No, *signore,* it's not."

"What really happened between you and the Deluccis? It wasn't just Rodolpho's death, was it?"

Carmela took a long drag on her cigarette, her fingers trembling.

Dash filled in the blanks. "Donte asked you for money in the past. How many times?"

"He didn't ask me, *signore.*"

"Alright, he asked your husband, Rodolpho. How many times?"

"Four times. That I know of. There were probably more."

"It was for his gambling debts, wasn't it?"

"*Si.* He had a problem even back then. He kept asking and asking and finally I told Rodolpho we give to him no more! That Donte was just using him. Rodolpho didn't believe me, but he did as I said. Well. Rodolpho says, no more, and Donte disappears. Eh? What did I tell him? Donte is a leech."

Something wasn't right. "But then Donte came into some money. Pockets filled with sugar. What happened to the debts?"

"I suppose he paid them off."

"How?"

Carmela glared at him. "I do not know."

Dash stared at the defiant face. Her chin was slightly raised, while she narrowed her eyes and drew her shoulders back. Defensive. Determined. Ready to fight.

She was lying.

She knew.

Dash said, "It involved the Capellos, didn't it?"

She twisted her head away from him. A confession, even if she didn't intend for it to be.

Dash said, "Mrs. Fiore, what did Donte do to get that money?"

She never answered him, despite him pleading with her. "I have to get back," she said, nodding towards her restaurant. "You? You should go."

Dash returned to the cab, more confused and frustrated than ever before.

---

Moments later, Dash rang Atty's buzzer, with Joe and Finn standing behind him. When Atty arrived at the front door, Dash instantly knew something was wrong.

"Boss," he said, his voice shaking. "Joe? Finn? What are youse doing here?"

"Atty, we need to speak with you."

Atty glanced around, his eyes bouncing with anxiety. "Yea, well, I gotta talk to you, too."

"What is it, my friend?"

Atty could hardly catch his breath. "It's Donte. I don't know what's happening or why he won't talk to me and he's saying crazy things, like youse spying on him and me being a busybody who needs to mind his own business, but something's goin' on and I—"

Joe said, "Lad, slow down!"

Dash gripped Atty's shoulders and stared into his panicked eyes. "Take a deep breath. With me. In and out. That's it. In and out. Now. Tell us what happened."

Atty bit his lip. "He got another letter."

---

"Tell us what happened," Dash said.

They were sitting in Atty's front room. Dash and Atty were on the couch in Emiliano and Rocco's spot, whereas Finn was in Isabella's chair by the window. Joe leaned against the wall across from the couch.

"I was sitting in the living room," Atty replied. "I'd just gotten back from dropping the children off at school, and suddenly, I heard this swishing sound. I looked down and saw that someone had slid an envelope under the front door. It was addressed to Donte, but it was odd, Boss. There was no postage stamp and no return address."

"It wasn't sent through the postal service."

"Right. I opened the door to see who was there, and all I heard were footsteps on the stairs."

*Just like a few nights ago,* Dash thought.

"They was running, Boss, so I chase after 'em. I don't know, but I *knew* they was up to no good. I get all the way down there and out front the building, but I don't see anybody. I look right, I look left, I look across the street and scan underneath the el. Nothing. Whoever it was just—just disappeared! I don't know how. I was right behind them. At least . . . at least I thought I was."

Atty ran a frustrated hand over his mouth and looked over at Dash, then Joe and Finn with guilt-ridden eyes. "Anyways, I go back upstairs and I tear open the envelope. And I read . . . this."

Atty holds up the letter for them to see.

Dash said, "What does it say?"

"It—It threatened Donte for not paying some ridiculous amount—"

"Five thousand dollars?"

A curious tilt of Atty's head. "How did youse know?"

Dash waved him off. "It doesn't matter. And was it signed with a drawing of a hand holding a dagger?"

Atty's eyes widened. "Seriously, Boss, are youse a magician? How'd youse do that?"

"It's the same as the letter I saw in your brother's suit pocket. Only I didn't see who it was from. Did you? Was their name in the signature?"

Atty's face fell. "Yeah."

When Atty didn't continue, Finn prompted, "And . . . ?"

Atty licked his lips, as if his mouth was suddenly dry. "How much—" His voice was weak. He cleared his throat again. "How much do you all know about *La Mano Nera*?"

Joe replied, "We've recently been educated on 'em."

"Then youse know they was bad. The worst of the worst. Why are they going after my brother? What did he ever do to them?"

Finn asked, "Can you read the letter to us?"

"Yeah, sure." Atty held it a good ten-to-twelve inches from his face. "'*Signore Donte Delucci, you have not brought us the five thousand dollars as we demanded. You have continued to ignore our demands, so now you will feel the cold steel of our blades and you will splash the sidewalks with your own blood. But not before we make you suffer. Do not go to the police. They will not help you. We have men who are in the police. They will tell us if you go to them, and we will destroy you like we did the Capellos. Vengeance shall be delivered soon. Signed, the Black Hand.*'"

"Good heavens," Dash muttered.

Atty folded up the letter and quickly shoved it back into his pockets, as if he couldn't bear to touch the paper anymore. His brow wrinkled with confusion. "What has Donte gotten himself into?"

Joe replied, "Gamblin', lad. He goes to a casino in the basement of a cigar shop. He apparently owes a fella named Gianni Spinelli over six hundred dollars."

Atty's mouth dropped open. "No." He looked desperately at Dash. "No, no, that isn't right. That isn't right, Boss. Tell me Joe's wrong!"

The sight of Atty's crestfallen face saddened Dash. "I spoke to Gianni Spinelli myself," he said. "The casino and his debts are real."

"Well then, this Spinelli fella sent these letters!"

"The amounts don't match. And Gianni is extracting payment in other ways, likely using your brother's position at the bank for financial favors. Hidden accounts, secret loans, who knows?" Dash pointed to the letter in Atty's pocket. "What about the name listed there? The Capellos. Does that sound familiar to you? Anyone you know? Anyone Donte knows?"

Atty shook his head. "Doesn't ring a bell, Boss." His

heavy breaths came out like long sighs before he struck his palm with his fist. A sputtered Italian curse flew from his lips before he said, "Youse don't lie to family, Boss! Family is everything! Everything! Donte knew that and he still—he still *lied*. He—he—"

Atty suddenly stood up and stormed to the rack, pulling off his raincoat with such force, it fell to the ground with a *thwack!*

"Atty," Joe said, "where are ya goin'?"

Atty hastily pulled on the coat. "To Donte. At the bank."

Dash stood, calling out, "Wait, Atty!"

Finn left the chair. "Take a moment, Atty! Don't do something you'll regret!"

Atty either didn't hear them or didn't care. He threw open the apartment door and stormed off into the stairwell.

Dash glanced at Joe and Finn, and the three of them grabbed their own coats. Joe went after Atty while Dash and Finn paused just long enough to lock the apartment behind them.

"What do we do?" Finn asked.

"You go to the bank and try to get Donte to—I don't know—go on break or something. Joe and I will try to slow Atty down."

"Done."

They spiraled down the stairs.

Outside, they saw Atty turn the corner on Hester and charge forward with Joe trying to hold him back. Even though Atty was more than half the size of Joe, he managed to break free of the ruddy man's large arms.

"Go, Finn!" Dash said.

Finn took off, passing by Atty and Joe in a blur.

When Dash caught up with them, he heard Joe saying, "Atty, what in bloody hell are ya doin'?"

Dash and Joe flanked either side of Atty as he walked in double time to most pedestrians on the street at that hour. Finn was already a block ahead of them and gaining ground.

"Goddamn liar," Atty growled. "That goddamn liar!"

"Atty," Dash said, "perhaps it's not a good idea to confront the man at his job. You might get him fired."

"Serves him right, Boss. Serves him right!"

Joe replied, "Aye, but lad, if he gets fired, how's he gonna pay back his debts? How's he gonna get a new home for his children?"

They turned onto Mulberry Street. Dash found he was having trouble catching his breath. Who knew a man so short could take such long, quick strides?

"I know it's difficult to be disappointed with someone you love," Dash said. "But your brother, however flawed, is in serious trouble."

"He got Maria killed!" Atty replied. "And he almost got Isabella, Emil, and Rocco killed! That son of a bitch. That son of a *bitch*!"

They crossed an intersection, moving too fast for Dash to catch the name of the cross street. How far were they from Moreno Bank & Trust?

The ground beneath him shifted, like someone trying to pull a rug out from under him.

He stumbled as a loud rumble moaned its way down the street. At first, Dash thought, *Another train? A large truck?*

When he saw debris flying a block ahead of them, he finally understood.

## 24

Wooden boards, glass shards, splintered plaster, even an entire window frame and door, arced upwards and downwards like tossed rag dolls. Smoke trailed behind them, black and ugly. Screams soon followed.

The three men stopped.

Whatever anger seethed through Atty's veins turned to immediate concern. "Donte," he said before breaking into a run.

"Atty!" Joe bellowed. "*Shite!*" He looked over at Dash. "Christ, lassie, did they just blow up the bank?"

"I don't know!"

They took off after him.

A half a block away, pulsating in the distance, was a shattered building ablaze with fire.

When they got closer, Dash saw it was Moreno Bank & Trust. Dash and Joe reached Atty and the three of them stood at the edge of the destruction, staring up at the building with horror. The bomb blast had ripped the face clean off the front, littering the street and sidewalk. Fire raged from its gaping wounds as smoke spilled upwards into the dirty gray sky.

"Telephone," Dash said quietly, before raising his voice. "Telephone!" He pulled at Joe's arm. "We need to call the fire department!"

Joe, frantic, searched for a public booth. "I don't see one!"

Dash felt a sudden, jolting panic. "Finn. Oh my god, Joe! Where's Finn?"

They searched the fiery scene.

Joe called out, "I don't see 'im!"

They stumbled their way down the sidewalk opposite the Bank, careful to step over the jagged and burning debris. Smoke settled over them like a grimy fog, bringing with it a pungent, scorched smell that sickened Dash's stomach. Coughs erupted from his chest, and his stinging eyes spilled tears down his cheeks. He dashed at them with his coat sleeves, bewildered by the destruction surrounding them.

They made it through the worst of it and came to the other side. No sign of Finn or Donte. A crowd of people settled into the street, cries of alarm filling the air like the black smoke. They saw Donte, his face smudged with soot, his suit torn at the seams. A trickle of blood slid down his right cheek, his mouth opened, his eyes wide, transfixed on the crackling flames in front of him.

Joe shouldered his way through the bystanders. Once he got to Donte, he shook the shocked man's shoulders, yelling, "Where's Finn?"

Donte didn't understand. "Who?"

Dash came to Joe's side. "A small Irish man! Dressed in a fancy suit!"

Donte tried to speak, but no words came out. His eyes froze on something just over Dash's shoulder.

Dash turned his head and saw Atty a few paces behind him, eyes dark with anger as he glared at Donte.

Before Dash could react, Atty marched his way over and grabbed Donte by the lapels, lifting him off his feet.

"Youse son of a bitch!" he screamed, spittle spraying Donte's surprised face. "Youse got Maria killed! Youse almost got your children killed! Youse son of a bitch!"

Donte finally found his words. "I did no such thing!"

"Liar!" And with that, Atty released Donte's lapels and punched him square in the face.

"Atty!" Dash called.

His friend didn't hear him. He advanced towards Donte, ready to inflict more violence. Luckily, Joe stepped in between the two men.

"Stop it, lad!" Joe bellowed.

Atty tried to go around him, but Joe simply wrapped his arms around the man's chest, effectively pinning his arms down and holding him in place. Atty squirmed in vain, yelling curses at his brother.

Dash went over to Donte and helped him up.

"W-w-what was that for?!" Donte yelled to Atty.

"The Hand, Donte!" Atty replied, still trying to escape Joe's grasp. "Why didn't youse tell me 'bout the Hand?! Youse been getting Hand letters, and you didn't tell anybody?! You didn't tell me, your brother? And they blew up your building like they blew up your bank!"

Joe kept a firm grip on him. "Calm yerself, lad!"

Dash asked Donte, "Are you hurt?"

Donte shook his head.

Over Donte's shoulder, a crowd had formed, panicked men and women, crying, shouting, embracing. Those older stood still just as Donte was, frozen, shocked, afraid.

*They remember.*

Though they didn't speak a word, Dash felt he saw the phrase *La Mano Nera* flash across their eyes like Times Square billboards.

"Joe!" Dash called.

Joe raised his head. The fight was trickling out of Atty, but Joe still kept his arms locked tight.

"We need to find Finn!"

Joe nodded.

That was when Dash saw a small, lithe figure pushing his way through the throng, covered in dust and soot, his bare head missing his hat. He shuffled his way over to them, swaying with every step. Dash's recognition was as sudden and jarring as a bolt of lightning.

"Finn!"

Superficial cuts crisscrossed his cheeks and forehead, his wide blue eyes dazed and unseeing. Blood trickled out of one ear while the other was covered in soot.

Dash grabbed his friend's shoulders and repeated his name in the ear that wasn't bleeding, hoping to rouse him.

Finn tilted his chin up and attempted a smile. "Oh, wonderful! I guess I'm not meeting the goddesses today."

Alarmed, Dash looked him over. The sleeves and shoulders of his coat were singed, the once-colorful fabric now blackened and torn. Blood dripped down his left hand. Dash tore off Finn's coat and saw the left shirtsleeve was dark and crimson. He lifted Finn's arm and peeled back the shirtsleeve to examine it. A long gash split the forearm in two from wrist to elbow.

By this point, Joe had spotted Finn and came over.

"Bloody hell!" he said when he saw Finn's injuries.

"We need a doctor, Joe. *Now.*"

Sirens made their way towards them.

Joe looked over the crowd's heads and nodded. "I see an ambulance. Follow me!"

Dash gently maneuvered himself until he was under Finn's good arm. He glanced over at Atty.

"We're going to an ambulance!" he said. "Bring Donte!"

Atty charged forward and snagged his brother by the arm, looking more like a copper arresting a criminal than a brother.

Dash focused on Finn. "Can you walk?"

Finn's glassy eyes rolled over to him. "I'll certainly do my best, dearie. Five, six, seven, eight—"

They advanced forward. The crowd was getting thicker by the second. With one arm, Dash stabilized Finn; with the other, he pushed people out of the way.

"Pardon us! An injured man is coming through!"

"My hero," Finn murmured with a chuckle.

*I've got to keep him talking, keep him awake.*

"What happened, Finn?" he said into Finn's good ear.

"I went to get Donte at the bank, like you said. He was coming out for his lunch break to go to a deli across the street. I introduced myself and said Atty was coming to see him and he might not want to be at his post when it happened. Well, then Donte went into a screaming rant. Very argumentative and so *defensive* and quite, quite rude."

"I've experienced that firsthand myself."

"Ah. Then you *know*."

"Oh, I know."

Dash saw they were ten, maybe fifteen feet from exiting the thickening throng of spectators.

"I tried to get him to walk away from the bank," Finn replied, wincing. He coughed and spat phlegm onto the ground, barely missing a crowd member's shoes. The man glowered. Finn glanced up at him. "Pardon me, I know that isn't very ladylike."

Dash steered him away from a possible confrontation. "It's Jake, Finn. Keep going."

"While we were arguing, this bicycle flies up from out of nowhere." Finn lolled his head towards Dash. "Pardon *moi*. I'm mixing my verbs. A bicycle doesn't fly, does it? Not like it has wings or a beak and calls out, '*caw! caw!*'"

"Yes, Finn."

*Four more lines of people and then we're set.*

Finn went on. "It *rolls*. Yes, that's what a bicycle does. So. This bicycle *rolls* from out of nowhere, someone pedaling fast. I see this, this shadow fly across Donte's face." Finn frowned. "A shadow can fly, right? I know a bicycle can't, but I believe a shadow might."

The crowd started pushing back against them, trying to see the cause of the noise and smoke. More sirens joined the initial chorus, and they were all singing three-part harmony.

"Don't worry about it, Finn," Dash said, resisting the crowd's motion. "What happened next?"

Finn scrunched up his brow. "Well, dearie, from then on, it's a big blur. The shadow crosses Donte's face—I think something had been thrown behind me—and then there was a *very* loud noise. Next thing I knew, *I* was flying through the air." Finn stopped. "No, I'm wrong. A shadow can't fly. It *crosses*. Yes, that's it! A bicycle rolls by, a shadow *crosses* Donte's face, and then I, Finn Francis, son of the goddesses, *flew*."

It sounded to Dash as if the bicyclist threw a stick of dynamite.

*Hadn't Fife said the Hand used the same tactic?*

He gave one final push, and they made it through to the other side.

"Did you see who was riding the bicycle?"

Finn didn't answer.

Dash looked over. Finn's eyes were closed.

"*Finn!* Finn! Wake up, Finn! Wake up!"

But the little man's eyes remained closed.

From Dash's peripheral, he saw two ambulance workers appear on either side of them. One worker murmured Dash could let go of Finn, but Dash couldn't. Dash wouldn't.

Joe came up behind him and said, "It's alright, Dash. Let 'im go. They can help 'im."

Dash glanced up at Joe. "What if they can't?"

"Me boy, let 'im go."

"But what if they *can't*?"

"Ya'll never know if ya don't let 'im go."

Joe gave him a nod and Dash removed Finn's good arm from his shoulders. He expected Finn to be whisked away to the ambulance, but one of the two men stood there, arms crossed, glaring at Finn.

"No," he said, his Italian accent thick with anger.

Joe stepped forward. "Whattaya mean, no? Can't ya see the lad's hurt?"

"I can see that. I can see he's a Mick and I don't help no Micks."

Dash said, "Why not?"

The man turned his angry eyes to him. "Because they never helped us. Why should we care if they live or die when *they* never did?"

The other ambulance worker tried to intervene, but the angry man was insistent.

Joe was incredulous. "I can' fuckin' believe this! Ya not gonna at least take this man to the hospital?!"

The angry man sniffed. "There are others who are hurt.

I'll tend to them first. I'll get to *him*"—he said, stabbing the air with his finger— "when I'm done. Let's go."

The other ambulance worker, nothing more than milquetoast, Dash saw now, looked on helplessly before following his colleague.

Joe swore several strings of curses.

Dash looked around, trying to think of another plan. There were bound to be more ambulances, but would they all take the same tack? The sinister Hand and the apathetic Irish NYPD were less than a decade ago. Not enough time for those wounds to heal. And speaking of time, they were running out of theirs.

"Joe," Dash said. "Find a cab."

Joe whirled his head in Dash's direction. "Wha'?"

"Get a cab! We might get luckier."

"Where are we gonna go? If the fuckin' ambulance won' take 'im, neither will the hospital in this neighborhood!"

"I know, I know," Dash replied, thinking fast. An idea shone like a light in the fog. "I know where we can take him."

"Where?"

Dash put Finn's good arm back around his shoulders. "We've got to get to the West Side."

## 25

Borden swore to both Dash and Joe that Finn would have the greatest of care.

"I know these doctors, sir," he said, the slight lilt of his accent tracing his vowels and soothing Dash's nerves. "They will treat him well."

The three of them were sitting in Borden's room at the American Seamen's Friend Society, Borden having coffee, Dash and Joe having something stronger after they'd slipped the waiter in the downstairs café a few extra coins. It was bad gin, but at least it was that.

Joe frowned with every sip, as if offended he wasn't tasting his usual whiskey.

"How do ya drink this swill?" he murmured to Dash. "Tastes like a fuckin' Christmas tree."

"It's a magical holiday in every glass," Dash replied. "Besides, it's better than that burnt lighter fluid you usually drink."

"My whiskey's not *burnt*. It's smokey."

"There's a difference?"

"One's accidental and the other intentional."

"And that matters?"

Joe grumbled and waved a gruff hand at him. "Drink your tree, lassie."

"I will." Dash brought his teacup to his lips, his pinky raised as he took a sip. It felt good to joke, good to be absurd, even though at his core, Dash was scared to death for Finn.

Borden sniffed a laugh. He wagged his finger at the two of them. "You are very close, yes? Finn talks of you both constantly and with such great affection. And I can see why. He loves you two dearly."

Dash set his teacup down onto its saucer and looked at the giant man across from them. "And we love him just as much."

Borden smiled, his teeth a flash of headlights. This morning, he wore a white shirt bulging at the arms. An opened collar showcased a jaunty red ascot. A tweed vest and dark blue pants pulled tight by his monstrous thighs completed the ensemble. His bald head reflected the light coming in from his window overlooking the street and the river. A small gold hoop dangled from one of his ears.

*Leave it to Finn to land himself a pirate,* Dash thought, before adding, *Please let him pull through. I know I don't pray often, but please—*

"Did Finn tell ya anything 'bout what happened?" Joe asked.

Dash was suddenly exhausted. He bolstered himself with more gin and repeated what Finn had said before he passed out. Dash felt strangely disconnected. He was aware his mouth was moving, his lips, tongue, and teeth forming words, and yet, he wasn't paying attention. His eyes scanned the room. Unlike Peter Fraker, whose room was barely six feet wide, Borden had a larger room, with a bed all to himself, as well as a small Juliet balcony that over-looked West Street and the Hudson River.

Dash was suddenly aware he'd stopped talking, and both men were looking at him expectantly. "Hmm?" he asked.

Joe replied, "I said Donte's at the tailor shop. Atty's holdin' 'im there 'til we get back."

"I see." Dash finished his drink and said to Borden, "We'll be back in a day or two to check on Finn."

Borden nodded. "Of course."

"Thank you, Borden," Dash said. "You're a godsend."

Borden chuckled. "I don't know about *that*. But Finn has a gentle soul, and this world is often not kind to those who are gentle. I shall protect him as best I can."

"Finn would tell you he can take care of himself just fine."

"Yes, yes he would," Borden said. "But no one can make it through this world alone, no matter how strong they are."

Dash looked over at Joe, the two of them locking eyes. "You speak the truth, sir." He stood up. "Joe, let's go talk to Donte."

"Aye," Joe said, standing up as well. "Time to get some answers from tha' little liar."

---

Donte sat in the wooden chair in the curtained-off changing area of Hartford & Sons with his arms crossed. A pugnacious petulance replaced the shock and fear from before. His swollen lip from where Atty punched him added to the overall aura of obstinance. He didn't know what they were talking about and how dare they keep him here? Dash and Joe were lying about what they found and what they saw, and he couldn't fathom why his own brother would even believe such lies.

"You turned him against me," Donte said. "I see now. You fill his head with lies and you—"

Atty stepped forward. "Enough, Donte! We are trying to help youse, understand? You've lost your home to dynamite; another bomb almost killed youse—"

"That had nothing to do with me."

"Oh, it didn't, eh?" Atty put his fists on his hips. "I'll bet youse a day's pay the fire inspector finds the same traces of explosives in the bank that they found in your old building. Whatta youse call that?"

With a condescending expression, Donte replied, "A coincidence, of course."

Atty cursed and returned to his usual perch at the sewing machine.

Dash stood in the center of the shop, his arms also crossed. Joe remained slightly behind him, leaning on the wardrobe. All the shades of Hartford & Sons were drawn, and a note was placed in the front window: "CLOSED DUE TO FAMILY EMERGENCY." Only the lamps on the writing desk and the sewing machine provided light. Shadows danced around the room, and darkness streaked across Donte's face.

"Tell us about the letters," Dash said.

"Bah! What letters?"

"Atty?"

Atty pulled from his pocket the letter that had been dropped off at the apartment today and handed it over to Dash.

Dash, in turn, gave it to Joe. "Would you do us the honor?"

Joe flicked a questioning glance, but then held the pages

out a good distance from his face so his eyes could focus. And then he read the Italian words of the first letter, his thick brogue stumbling and halting over the alien words. It was, frankly, abysmal to the ears. As Dash had intended. Not only was Donte hearing his language butchered, but butchered by an Irishman.

Donte put his hand up. "Please! Please. I've heard enough."

Joe stopped.

Donte took several shallow breaths before saying, "Your Italian is terrible."

Dash swallowed his impatience—as well as a cough gurgling up. "The letters," he said. "How many did you get?"

"Four."

*Five, counting the one I accidentally destroyed in the gale,* Dash thought.

"When did they start coming?"

Donte licked his lips, which were dried and cracked. "Beginning of October."

"How did you receive the letters? In the mail? On your doorstep?"

"Slipped under the door."

"Did you see anyone suspicious on the days you received the letters? Any person watching your building? Leaving the vestibule? Walking down the street?"

"No, I didn't see anyone. And believe me," Donte said, "after the second letter, I looked. I *watched*. I saw no one."

"Did you report them to the police?"

"What are those bastards gonna do, eh? They did nothing before. Why would they now?"

"Fair point. Who are the Capellos?"

Donte glared at Dash in response.

Atty lost his temper. Again. "Come off it, Donte! Youse almost died today for lyin', so youse better start talkin'. Or I'll make youse talk."

To demonstrate his promised methods, Atty cracked his knuckles and tightened his hands into fists.

The two brothers glowered at one another.

"Alright!" Donte conceded. He spoke a fast line of Italian before switching back to English. "The Capellos were a family in my neighborhood ten years ago. Before the War. They were very rich, very successful."

"Making explosives," Dash said, hoping to speed him along. A trio of sneezes burst through, interrupting him. He wiped his nose with his handkerchief and ignored Joe's concerned look. "Until one day, they weren't successful and Umberto, the head of the family, torched his own warehouse for the insurance money. He got caught and died in prison. His wife Mia soon after. Their child was sent to an orphanage, and that was the end of the Capellos."

Suspicion wrinkled Donte's forehead. "Why do you know so much?"

"Immaterial. Why was that family name in your letters? What connects you to them beyond proximity in the neighborhood?"

Donte stared at the floor.

"Mr. Delucci," Dash said. "People are dying. More people are going to die unless you speak up."

They waited.

Donte's weary sigh echoed through the quiet room. He looked up at Dash, studiously avoiding Atty's gaze. He kept his voice in a low monotone. "I gamble. Sometimes I do okay. Other times? I had debts. Back then. Before the War. I had no way to pay them back and the bank wouldn't give me, one of their own employees, a loan." A burst of energy raised his voice. "Can you believe that? One of their own and they don't help!"

Donte glanced around for sympathy and when he found he received none, he lowered his gaze again and returned to speaking quietly.

"The family who owned the room threatened to hurt me. Hurt Maria. I couldn't have that. I couldn't let them do that."

Dash said, "So you asked Rodolpho Fiore for money, and he gave it to you."

"Until the damnable bitch Carmela cut me off! Why she do that, eh? It's not her business. It's not her money. It was her husband's, and her husband can do whatever he wants. Why he listened to her, I'll never . . . I thought Rodolpho had more stones than that."

Dash didn't think it was the time to admonish such old-fashioned beliefs. "Then what happened?"

Now Donte wouldn't meet anyone's eyes. He spoke the next part of his tale to the floor. "*La Mano Nera*, they were everywhere. It seemed like everyone got a letter. I knew how much money the Capellos had because I saw their accounts, I saw their balances, and I thought—I thought, they won't miss some of this—"

Atty couldn't help himself. "You *stole* from their account?!"

Dash looked back and patted the air, warning Atty not to interrupt. Intuition gathered in the back of his mind like whispers. They grew in number and in volume until they shaped into words and formed an idea.

"No," he said. "Your brother didn't embezzle from the Capello accounts." He turned back to Donte. "He sent them a letter. A Black Hand letter. Didn't you?"

The silence in the shop was profound.

Donte's voice was small, barely above a murmur. "*Si*. I sent them a letter signed *La Mano Nera*. I asked for the amount I owed, plus a little more. What I didn't know . . . was that Mia was ill. Her medicine was very expensive, and they had to pay so many doctor's bills. The bills and my letter? Umberto paid us all, which devastated them."

"Forcing Umberto to arson and insurance fraud to gain back the money he lost," Dash said, finishing the sad story.

Joe whispered, "Jesus."

Dash faced Atty, whose face was dark, his body hunched over, closed off. He'd never seen his friend so angry and so hurt.

Atty clenched his teeth. "Youse lyin' bastard. Youse pretended to be the most despicable society this city had ever seen to pay off your own *debts*?"

Donte tried to defend himself. "I was desperate! I couldn't let them touch Maria! They would've done unspeakable things to her—"

"So you did unspeakable things to someone else? You're pathetic, Donte! *Pathetic!* A small mouse of a man who can't take care of himself, much less his family. You bring shame to the Delucci name."

"Atty," Dash said. "I know this is difficult for you to hear, and you have every right to be angry with your brother over what he did. But right now, there is someone trying to kill him who doesn't care if other people get hurt. Donte's bank, his apartment building. Perhaps even in yours."

Atty understood. "Boss! Bella! The boys!"

"We'll protect them." Dash glanced at his wristwatch. "School is about to be let out; someone needs to get the children. And it can't be you, Donte."

Joe added, "Ya've got a bloody target on yer back."

Atty stepped forward. "I will get them. You, Donte, stay

here. *Stay* here, *comprendo?*" Atty looked at Dash and Joe. "That okay, Boss?"

Dash nodded.

Joe cut in. "Ya can't take 'em back to yer place, lad. If they tried to get Donte at his bank, then whoever *this* is has been watchin' him."

"And with the new letters being slipped under your door," Dash added, "they know he's staying with you."

Atty's eyes widened with fear. "What do I do?"

Dash hesitated briefly before making a decision. "Bring them back here."

Joe's face twitched with surprise. "Yer not suggestin'—"

"If this is the work of the Hand, chances are, they're concentrated in those Italian neighborhoods. We haven't heard of anyone getting letters around here, right?"

"Right, but—"

"There's always a chance they'll follow Atty here, I know, which is why," Dash said, turning to Atty, "you need to be very careful. Take circuitous routes. Take multiple cabs if you have to. Keep your eyes open."

Atty nodded, his face grim. "Where are we gonna put 'em, Boss?"

"There's an empty set of dressing rooms in the Playhouse right now. We can house them there for a short period."

"Are you sure? If you take them back to the Playhouse, they might see—you know—actor-type things."

Dash caught the warning. "We'll make some adjustments," he replied, coding his intended meaning. "The most important thing is to make sure those children are safe. Go. School is about to let out."

Atty gave Dash one last look and then left, the tailor shop door squealing and rattling in its hinges.

Dash and Joe stared at Donte.

"Who else knows about what you did?" Dash inquired.

"No one."

"Apparently not, given the name in these letters."

"I don't know!" Donte replied. "I don't know *who*, I don't know *why*. You can ask and ask and all I can say is, I don't know." He slapped his own thighs with his palms, muttering in rapid Italian.

"What's going on with the olive oil?"

"Eh?"

"The olive oil. The crates being delivered to The Smoke Shop. Yes," Dash added, "we know all about that place—the Spinellis, Delilah, Gus, all of it—so spare us another denial." Another cough cut into Dash's interrogation. "Excuse me. Now. The olive oil."

"That has nothing to do with these letters."

"How can you be sure?"

"Because I *know*. That I know. Those crates have nothing to do with this."

"What's being smuggled through The Smoke Shop, Donte?"

"You can't make me talk."

Joe stepped forward. "Aye, but I might, lad."

Donte smirked. "Big talk comin' from a Mick."

At that point, Dash started coughing and couldn't stop. The cold that seemed to have subsided this morning was back in full force.

After almost a full minute of coughing, Joe said, "Tha's it. Yer goin' off to bed. No ifs, ands, or buts." He then pointed to Donte. "And yer comin' wit' us."

The rest of the day passed in a blur of sleep, sneezes, and coughing.

Joe kept watch over Donte in the hallway where Finn's bed stood.

Atty was able to get the children with no issues. He swore no one followed them as he got Isabella and the boys set up in the empty Playhouse dressing rooms.

Isabella did not want to be here, but it thrilled Emiliano and Rocco to run around the back of a theater. According to Atty, they found one of the costume drawers and began trying on the various hats, mustaches, glasses, and bow ties kept in storage. Isabella's icy pouting eventually thawed and joined in on the fun.

That left three sulking men—Atty, Joe, and Donte—and one sniffling, sneezing, coughing mess—Dash.

Atty put Donte in the dressing room to give Dash some space, swearing he wouldn't let Donte leave his sight.

Joe went to the Greenwich Village Inn and brought back a thermos full of Emmett's chicken soup, as well as the *Times*.

"You're a prince, Joe. Truly."

Joe chuckled. He glanced around to make sure no one was in the apartment with them and kissed Dash's forehead before leaving the bedroom.

Dash leaned back in the bed and read the front page.

The bank bombing hadn't yet made the headlines, but would undoubtedly be above the fold, page one tomorrow morning.

The latest development in the Hall-Mills murders involved the slimy private investigator hired by Frances Stevens Hall. Felix De Martini had once again eluded extradition from New York to New Jersey, where Senator Simpson hoped to cross-examine him on the stand.

Deeper into the paper was another follow up on the destruction of Donte's former building. Investigators were expanding their search for a suspect, yet the newshawk was doubtful about their chances.

El's words came back to Dash: *"Finding a firebug in this city is like searching for a needle in a haystick."*

It seemed the *Times* agreed.

He thought about her strange reaction the other day to what had to be an engagement announcement in the social section. Was she having an affair with a woman who later accepted a proposal from a man?

The room spun a little, and Dash set down the paper onto his lap. He felt his head drop, and he drifted off to sleep.

A creak of the floorboards roused him. Dash struggled to sit upright and reached for his pile of handkerchiefs on the nightstand. The room was dark and cold. How long had he been asleep? Past sundown, from the looks of it. He blew his nose hard, sounding like a rusty cornet.

"My goodness," said a voice that wasn't Joe's. "That is one nasty bug, Mr. Parker."

Dash froze.

*Oh, no. Not here. Not now.*

He slowly reached for the bedside lamp and flicked it on. Pale light flooded the room.

Nicholas Fife, the notorious gangster and Dash's liquor supplier, stood at the foot of the bed.

## 26

A look of bemusement played on the round, smooth face, his thick lips closed in a Cheshire smile. He wore a three-piece, high-waisted suit in a blue-plaid pattern that fit his six-foot frame rather well.

It should. After all, Dash had measured him for it and Atty did the alterations.

A red polka-dotted tie sparked from the blinding white shirt. A matching vest did much to hide some of the man's bulk, but it still allowed the power of his body to come through. He leaned on a bamboo cane like a Broadway dancer waiting for his cue.

"H-h-how did you get here?" Dash asked. He wildly looked around. "Where's Atty and Donte?"

Fife frowned. "Your doorman and his brother, if I'm not mistaken? They're still safe and sound in the dressing room. The children are taking a nap, I believe. I wouldn't make any sound to wake them. It would be so rude, wouldn't you agree?"

"Where's Joe?"

Fife raised a hand. "Calm yourself, Mr. Parker. No

harm has come to your precious bartender. He's currently sitting in the Greenwich Village Inn's tavern. Should he leave early, I've hired a few well-meaning citizens to distract him. Tourists asking for directions. A child falling off his bicycle. A nun asking for donations. We have plenty of time to chat."

Fife reached over to the wooden chair in front of the window and dragged it over, the legs screeching against the floor. He settled the chair right next to Dash's bed and sat down, crossing his legs, leaning his cane against his hip.

Dash warily asked, "About what?"

"Tut, tut, Mr. Parker. Or should I say Mr. Bennett? My, you've been dropping that name around Manhattan. Oh, don't look so worried. I come bearing good news! I saw in the papers about another bombing in Little Italy, and it got me to thinking about our last conversation. Do you remember it?"

"Being forced to eat cones of ice cream? Hard to forget that." A string of sneezes interrupted him.

"That is a *nasty* bug." Fife reached into his inside coat pocket and pulled out a thermometer. "Let's see how high your fever is. Open wide, please."

"Mr. Fife—"

"I said, open wide."

Fife waited, his chocolate-brown eyes warm and inviting, his smile mischievous.

Dash's distrustful gaze never left Fife as he slowly opened his mouth.

Fife gently slipped the thermometer under Dash's tongue. "Good boy," he purred.

Dash ignored him. "How did you know to bring a thermometer?" he asked, the glass tube bouncing up and down in his mouth.

"I know everything about my business partners. And please, don't talk. We wouldn't want to get a false temperature read, now do we?"

Dash nodded, clamping his lips down onto the thermometer.

"As I was saying, I saw in the newspapers about the second Little Italy bombing, and I started thinking of your Black Hand letter situation. I thought, could this be connected? And then I recalled the name you asked me about. The Capellos, wasn't it?"

Dash nodded again.

"I thought it was strange as well that a seemingly random family name was dropped into the center of a threatening letter. The name must've been significant to its recipient."

Dash couldn't stop himself from saying, "I know why. Atty's brother forged a Black Hand letter himself ten years ago to the Capello family as a ruse to pay off his gambling debts."

Fife wagged his finger. "Now, now, Mr. Parker. If you insist on talking, I'll have to stick that thermometer in a place that's more . . . compliant."

Dash clamped down on the glass tube again.

"It appears you've done some fine detective work," Fife continued. "I shouldn't be surprised. You have a knack for this. I gather you know all about Umberto and his warehouse fire and the insurance fraud, and poor Mia and her illness?"

Dash nodded.

"Did you find out what happened to their child?"

Dash shook his head.

"Ah. Then you *will* find this interesting. My visit here wasn't a waste after all! How delightful."

Fife suddenly reached out and pulled the thermometer from Dash's lips. He brought the glass tube up to his eyes. "One hundred and one. Yes, that is a fever to behold!"

He wiped the thermometer with a handkerchief before pocketing it. From another pocket, he produced a jar.

"This ought to do the trick."

The label read: "VICKS VAPORUB SALVE, SPASMODIC GROUP, CROUP, COLDS, AND INFLAMMATION."

Dash stared at it with trepidation. "What is it?"

"You can trust it," Fife said. "It's made by Presbyterians. If the Baptists made it, that would be another story." He opened the lid and held it under Dash's nose.

The aromas were sharp and slightly pungent, like chopped rosemary. Hints of mint, honey, and citrus all blurred together to create something that immediately opened Dash's nose and brought tears to his eyes.

"See?" Fife said, bringing the jar closer to himself. "Already working. You rub this salve every few hours on your neck and chest and you'll be right as rain, Mr. Parker." He dipped two fingers into the salve. "Now. Undo your pajamas, please."

Dash hesitated.

"Oh, come now. I've seen you in the baths, if you remember."

Dash did. When Fife snuck into his bathing booth at the Carmine Baths and washed Dash's body, all the while giving him orders.

Fife said, "No reason to be shy. Besides, you have *nothing* to be shy about and I have more to tell you about the Capellos."

Dash kept his eyes on Fife while he undid the buttons of his pajama top. He exposed his chest and Fife reached over and gently spread the salve across Dash's skin. It was cold to the touch and Dash flinched at the first bite of it.

Fife smiled. "Silvano Capello was Umberto and Mia's only son. Quite uncommon for anyone to have single digit progeny, especially amongst the Catholics. He was, by all accounts, eight or nine years old when his parents died."

Fife's fingers moved over to the left side of Dash's chest, paying particular attention to the nipple.

Dash sat straight up, the tingling sensation of the salve and the rubbing of Fife's fingers causing a confusing but urgent chain reaction. Dash sincerely hoped Fife didn't glance down at his waist to see the bed covers slightly moving.

"After Mia died," Fife said, "Silvano was sent to live in an orphanage until his aunts and uncles in Italy saved enough pennies to bring him home."

Fife's hands moved from the left side to the right side, slathering a thick layer of Vicks onto Dash's pec and nipple.

Dash, once again, stiffened. The juxtaposition of cold and hot on sensitive skin was almost too much to bear.

Fife got another dollop of salve from the jar and began rubbing it across Dash's throat.

Dash, slightly recovered, said, "What's so interesting about that? It sounds like a happy ending to an otherwise tragic story. I assumed they lost the child forever to the streets."

Fife's hand went up to the top of Dash's throat, gripping him firmly around the glands.

Dash held his breath. Would Fife squeeze? Cut off his oxygen supply? He glanced upwards at Fife's face. Those warm chocolate eyes hadn't changed into the dark fiery coals that normally marked his change in mood.

Fife's fingers slowly massaged the glands and sides of

Dash's throat. To be honest, the motions felt marvelous. The aromas of the Vicks penetrated Dash's nose and throat, and the hot-cold sensation soothing against his sore, swollen glands.

"His family in Italy," Fife said, "belonged to a certain secret society that specialized in using dynamite."

They held eyes.

"*La Mano Nera*," Dash said.

Fife nodded. "I bet you can guess the next part."

Dash could. "Silvano Capello returned to New York City."

Fife grinned. "Very good. Now all you have to do is find an Italian boy of about eighteen, maybe nineteen years of age."

Dash immediately thought of Vito Beneventi.

A high-pitched whistle came from outside the bedroom window. Someone in the alley behind the Playhouse.

"Our time is up," Fife said, removing his hand from Dash's throat and standing up. "Your Irish setter will be home any moment now." He screwed the lid onto the jar and placed it on Dash's nightstand. "Remember, put that on every four hours and you'll snuff out this cold in no time."

Fife wiped the salve from his fingers with his handkerchief, grabbed the bamboo cane, and placed his hat on his head. "Good day, Mr. Parker. And once you're well, I fully expect you to be at your tailor shop, earning us more customers. As talented a detective as you are, let's not forget what your *true* occupation is, hmm?"

Then he left the bedroom, his footsteps gently clicking away, unhurried and unbothered. In the distance, he heard the apartment door open and close. Dash half expected to hear an altercation between him and Joe, who'd soon be coming up the stairs, but there was nothing. Only a silence like a held breath.

A few minutes later, Joe's heavy stomps filled the stairwell. The apartment door opened, and Joe called for him. "Ya still alive?"

Dash gave an uneasy laugh, considering what had just transpired. "Yes," he replied, "for now, I am."

"I got ya the rabbit stew from Emmett," Joe said, his footsteps heading towards the bedroom. "Sorry I was late, but I swear to the Holy Mary, every man, woman, and child asked for my help today."

He entered the bedroom with a thermos in hand and stopped. He sniffed. "What's tha' godawful smell?"

Dash looked down at the jar again. "It is Vicks salve."

"What the bloody hell is tha'? And where did ya get it?"

Dash forced a smile. "Our friendly benefactor."

Joe was confused, but only for a moment. His eyes flashed with fear, followed by anger. "I'll bloody kill 'im."

## 27

The rest of Thursday night and all of Friday, Dash spent in bed.

As predicted, the newshawks squawked loudly about the bombing at Moreno Bank & Trust. A few other witnesses saw a bicyclist ride up and toss something into the air seconds before the explosion. No motive identified, no suspects identified. That two bombings occurred in the same neighborhood within the same week had the article's writer wondering if the same person was behind them.

*Silvano Capello.*

Dash didn't want to believe all the things that people said about the Italians: their fiery tempers, their loose morals with sex, their ability to hold grudges for years. And yet, he couldn't deny this situation felt absurdly Italian. A boy who lost both his father and his mother, condemned to an orphanage only to be saved and, presumably, trained by a terrorist organization. All because of one man's desperate actions to repay his gambling debts.

The question was, how did Silvano know about Donte?

Dash had Atty ask his brother.

After several shouted exchanges in Italian, Atty came back with an answer. Umberto always brought Silvano to Francesco Barone's Bank with him, so the little boy likely saw Donte working as a teller during those visits. Atty also discovered that Donte dropped off the letter himself late at night at the Capello's address, so if Silvano peered out his window, he'd have seen the mysterious teller on his family's stoop.

A long shot that depended on a lot of things happening at just the right moment.

"Good grief," Dash said to himself. "Donte's luck *is* truly awful."

Dash also had Atty ask if Donte knew a Vito Beneventi. Only at The Smoke Shop, Donte said, and no, he'd never seen Vito before then and no, Vito had no resemblance to the Capello family.

Still. Familial similarities fade over time. And it had been ten years. Would Donte even recognize a Capello if he saw one?

By Saturday morning, Dash felt mostly human again. He and Joe visited Finn at the American Seamen's Friend Society, where Finn was recuperating in Borden's room.

"Don't you worry," Finn told them as he patted Borden's thick, muscled arm. "This man is a most *excellent* nurse."

Borden said, "The doctor says he has a few more days before he'll discharge him."

"Which I am *devastated* about! I won't be able to sneak into you-know-who's place. Oh! And I was so looking forward to seeing how nice the apartment is."

Dash replied, "The number one priority is to get you healed up and back on your feet. Joe and I can handle you-know-who."

After they left the Society, Joe said he'd return to the Playhouse to watch after Donte and the children. "Remember, we've got Mischief Night tonight with El."

"I almost forgot about that." Dash pinched the bridge of his nose and shook his head. "What a week it's been."

"Aye. And listen to me, lassie, don't do anything foolish," Joe warned. "We don't want to accidentally lead the Hand, or whoever is behind these bombings, back here. Don't go anywhere near Little Italy. Yer stayin' here and that's final."

Dash raised his hand. "I swear on my honor, Mr. O'Shaughnessy, I will simply take measurements at my tailor shop."

Joe responded by giving Dash's behind a good swat. "Don't make me teach you any more lessons," he growled.

Dash felt his cheeks flush. If they hadn't been in public, god knew what would've happened next.

As it was, Dash returned to Hartford & Sons and spent a mostly uneventful day taking measurements and giving out the secret knock.

Halfway through the day, the front door jangled open and in stepped a barrel-chested man in a brown suit and brown fedora.

The man looked around. "Is anyone else here?"

The voice was curious. Low, but not exactly masculine.

Dash shook his head. "How can I help you, sir?" That's when he recognized the man standing before him.

Or rather, the woman.

It was Lou, the bartender from the lesbian club he had gone to with Pru a few nights back.

"Fantastic!" she said, her voice bellowing as if she were still behind the bar. "You Mr. Parker?"

"That I am."

"Nice to see ya again."

"See me . . . ?"

Lou laughed. "Oh yeah, you and Pru didn't fool me one bit. That shoddy makeup job. What did you all do? Put it on in an alleyway?"

Dash couldn't help but smile. "As a matter of fact, we did."

Lou's laugh turned into a cackle. "I knew it! I knew it! I may be getting old, but I still got the eyes of a cat. Unfortunately, I got the joints of a rusted-out jalopy. Here ya go."

She handed Dash an envelope.

"When did she give you this?"

"Last night. Told me where to find ya." Lou placed her hands on her hips and looked around the tailor shop. "Not bad, not bad. A little small, but you've got some good-lookin' stuff in here. You, uh, think I could be a customer of yours one day?"

"I don't really know—well, yes, I think so."

"Listen, you can cut the suit like you normally do. Ya just gotta make the chest a little wider." She glanced down at her bosom. "No matter how hard I pray for them to stop, these buds just keep on growin'. At this rate, I'll soon be all tit and no torso."

Dash smiled and opened the envelope, finding a stack on papers. On top was the following note :

*M has been with Empire State Bank for close to four years and is a tenant of 277 Park Avenue South for close to two years. Account balances and apartment deed included along with salary details. Original copies are all safe. Also, heard M is into something very secret and very heavy. No clues as to what yet. Be careful.*

*∼P*

With all the commotion surrounding Donte, Dash almost forgot about her. He stared back at the note and thumbed through the sheets of paper included with it. Here it was. Confirmation that McElroy was living well above his means. Now all they had to do was grab the photographs and free Peter Fraker from that odious globe's extortion.

Dash looked up, watching Lou saunter around his shop. "Lou? Can you do me a favor?"

"That depends. Do I get that hat?" She pointed to a chocolate-brown felt trilby perched on the top of the wardrobe.

Dash walked over to it, reached up and grabbed the trilby. He handed it to Lou, who took off her fedora and placed it on her head. She admired herself in the mirror.

"Very smart," Dash said.

"Yeah," Lou replied, turning her head this way and that. "Yeah, this is the one. How much?"

"On the house."

"Oh, I can't do that. Ya got a business to run."

"If you give Pru a message, we'll call it even."

Lou considered the offer. "Sounds Jake to me." She took off the trilby and put on her fedora. "I gotta say, this espionage stuff is cracking me up. What the hell are you all up to?" She immediately held up a hand. "No, don't tell me. I'm having too much fun guessing."

Dash returned to the writing desk and pulled out a sheet of paper. He scribbled a note, folded the paper in half, and handed it to Lou, who, of course, immediately opened and read the note.

Her brow furrowed. "What's this mean, '*Acquiring items soon. Will contact you afterwards.*'? You two's playin' spy?"

"Something like that."

She glanced down at the paper once more, shrugged, and placed it in her breast pocket. "Whatever floats your boat. You sure you don't want any sugar for this hat?"

Dash shook his head. "Besides, it looks too good on you to take it back."

"It does, doesn't it?" She held up the trilby, a wide grin on her face. "If this don't break a few fillies' hearts, then I don't know what will!"

---

Mischief Night.

Pinstripes was like an over-poured cocktail: impossible to walk with without making a gigantic mess.

Musky cologne, cigarette smoke, and sweat filled the air as masked men mingled, chatted, guffawed, and flirted. The dance floor was a sea of blue, gray, and tan pinstripes. Splashes of color blurred with their movements—pink, green, yellow, and red, the colors coming from their ties, handkerchiefs, and socks. The men at the side tables had their heads bent close to one another, sneaky hands rubbing knees and thighs underneath the tabletop. The bar was stacked at least two men deep, each shouting drink names over the urgent band. Dash pushed his way through and gave Joe, who was covered in sweat and moving as fast as possible, another order.

Joe said, "This fer one table?!"

"It's a party, Joe. Everyone's removed all the stops."

"Mary Mother of Christ."

At that moment, El Train hit the stage, and the entire room shook as if from an earthquake. Dressed in her all-white men's tuxedo, complete with tails, top hat, and cane, she surveyed the room, seeing if the audience was worth her time. After a moment, she counted off the band and Julius, Calvin, and Vernon—all wearing black masks themselves— began a lively number. The thick throng of men broke out into their best Charleston. It wasn't quite on par with the dancers in Harlem, Dash noted, but it was respectable, nonetheless.

After the instrumental introduction, El belted out:

> *Hey! Hey! Women are going mad today!*
> *Hey! Hey! Fellers are just as bad, I'll say!*
> *Go anywhere, just stand and stare,*
> *You'll say they're bugs when you look at the clothes they*
> *wear.*

All the men in the crowd knew the song by heart, so they sang along with her:

> *Masculine women, feminine men,*
> *which is the rooster which is the hen?*
> *It's hard to tell 'em apart today!*
> *And say!*
> *Sister is busy learning to shave,*
> *Brother just loves his permanent wave,*
> *It's hard to tell 'em apart today!!!*

El called out: "Any sisters in here tonight?!"
The men hollered they were.
"Now listen," El said, before singing:

> *Girls were girls and boys were boys when I was a tot,*
> *Now we don't know who is who or even what's what.*
> *Knickers and trousers, baggy and wide*

El pointed to her own wide and baggy tuxedo, then widened her eyes and clutched at imaginary pearls in a show of mock terror.

> *Nobody knows who's walking inside.*
> *Those masculine women, feminine men!!!*

The song was originally written to make fun of Bohemia and the modernization of men and women. But the bohemians—and in particular, the inverts—used it to make fun of the normals who so irrationally and needlessly feared the social changes. As Finn said days ago, "It's just love. It's just clothes."

El was working the room up into a frenzy so that Dash couldn't hear anything but El's voice, the band, and the men singing along:

> *Ever since the Prince of Wales in dresses was seen,*
> *What does he intend to be, the King or the Queen?*
> *Grandmother buys those tailor-made clothes,*
> *Grandfather tries to smell like a rose.*
> *Those masculine women and feminine men!!!!*

The band finished with a squealing, cymbal-crashing flourish. Everyone, Dash included, applauded El, who said, "Well *shee-it!*"

On cue, the crowd repeated her usual greeting. "Well, *shee-it!*"

"I have to say. When Mr. High Hat Dash Parker asked me down here, I thought no way could a bunch of Village fairies keep up with the driving, grinding, huffing, puffing engine of El Train. But here you are, matching me *tit* for *tat,* as it was!" She wiggled her shoulders and adjusted her bosom with both hands, earning a riotous laugh from the crowd.

"Now, we all know tonight is a night for Mischief. Yes, babies, we *will* be misbehaving! Some of you have already started. I see a little indecency going on here in this back corner. Lord, you two keep that up, one of ya's gonna be with child before too long!"

The couple she pointed out was a slight man in a purple mask sitting on the lap of a giant bruiser of a man wearing a face-covering white mask. The man on the lap raised his glass and yelled out, "It's my wedding night!"

"Oh, I see. Well, this night *is* a night for . . . tricks. I hope he paid a full price for you!"

The man and everyone else around him laughed.

"Alright, I feel the need for a love song. Shall we play a love song? To toast the newlyweds!"

She glanced back at the band and Julius nodded, counting them off. It was a slower song, inspiring those on the dance floor to grab each other's arms and sway gently to the music.

*Why do I do just as you say*
*Why must I just give you your way*
*Why do I sigh, why don't I try to forget*
*It must have been that something lovers call fate*
*Kept me saying I have to wait*
*I saw them all, just couldn't fall, 'til we met*

*It had to be you*
*It had to be you*
*I wandered around and finally found*
*The somebody who*
*Could make me be true*

*And could make me feel blue*
*And even be glad just to be said*
*Thinking of you . . .*

Dash turned just as Joe filled part of his latest order. The sweaty, ruddy man placed three filled glasses on the bar in front of Dash. "There's the Bee's Knees. What else?"

"Two sidecars and a gimlet."

Joe set about making the other drinks. "Whattaya think Pru meant by McElroy being into something secret?"

Dash shrugged. "His extortions?"

"Nah, it's gotta be somethin' bigger."

"Well, I'll be damned if I know."

El was now winding up the song:

*For nobody else gave me a thrill*
*With all your faults, I love you still*
*It had to be you*
*Wonderful you*
*It had to be you!*

The band finished the song, and the room erupted with applause. Just before El could introduce the next number, a red light glared in the small room.

Everyone gasped.

Nervous chattering filled the air.

This red light meant only one thing: the coppers were here for a raid.

## 28

Dash and Joe met each other's eyes and nodded.

Joe left his post at the bar and crossed to the secret door, which he secured with several deadbolts.

Dash pushed his way through the dance floor and walked over to the band with a calmness he didn't feel. He ignored El's glare and turned to face the crowd.

"Ladies and gentlemen . . . and those somewhere in between. I regret to inform you that there are coppers outside."

A chorus of boos immediately followed this statement.

"I ask each and every one of you to either drink all of your evidence or calmly go to the water closet and dump the unfinished contents of your cocktails down the toilet or the sink. I know it is a tragedy, but it cannot be helped. And don't worry about the bar. Our knight in shining armor, Joe O'Shaughnessy, is getting rid of the evidence as we speak."

Joe was now dropping liquor bottles down a chute cut into the floor that led straight to the building's basement. There, a giant mattress was collecting the bottles. They'd tried it once as a test run and only one bottle broke. Dash

sincerely hoped that would be the case now. It was imperative that they dispose of the booze, for it was the buying and
selling of alcohol that was illegal. If the coppers bust their
way in, they'd find a bunch of men buying and selling
water.

Of course, they'd also find a mixed-race band and a
bunch of inverts dancing with one another, but Dash
couldn't think of that possibility right now.

He continued. "Please remain absolutely quiet while
we wait for the coppers to move along." He leaned back to
the band and said, "Any whites on this stage need to step
off. Now." An integrated house band would surely have
them all arrested for indecency.

Vernon laid down his bass and stepped aside.

Dash left the stage, pushing through the men, and went
towards the secret door. He stood behind it, placing his ear
against the wood. Muffled voices on the other side, and he
couldn't make out who was saying what.

The club was still vibrating with energy, prompting Joe
to hiss, "Shut yer bloody holes, boys!"

The room finally descended into silence.

Dash heard Atty's voice say, "What brings you by,
officer?"

A murmured response.

"I'm just doing late night alterations for my boss . . . No,
he isn't here . . . it's not against the law to work late, is it,
officer?"

More murmured responses.

Then McElroy's voice shot through the thick door and
the insulation. "I know it's somewhere! It's behind this
mirror!"

There was a thump.

Someone behind him gasped, "They're trying the mirror!"

"Steady now," muttered Dash. He flicked a look over at Joe, who was watching him from behind the bar with shiny eyes.

Some scuffles, more muffled voices.

McElroy again. "Don't look at me like that! I'm telling ya, it's behind here!"

Another thump.

Dash figured McElroy kept pushing against the mirror, but the deadbolts they'd built into the door kept it solid.

Someone in the club began praying a Hail Mary. The high-voiced man got to "Pray for us sinners" before someone shushed him.

Atty's voice raised. "Hey! What are youse doing?!"

There was a resounding crack in the door, followed by a strange, musical tinkling.

*The mirror!* Dash thought with alarm. *He's breaking the mirror!*

Another crack, a bigger shatter.

Atty was screaming at the man to stop.

Just then, Dash heard a booming voice say, "Stop that this instant, McElroy!"

Faint protests on McElroy's part.

"I don't care what you've heard!" the voice shouted. "You have no evidence here, and what's worse, you're making damages that the NYPD will be responsible for!"

"But sir—"

"Leave the premises immediately!"

Silence.

Dash felt as if the entire world was holding its breath.

Someone picked that very moment to sneeze, a loud *a-chew!* which caused Dash to jump. It sounded so loud in the quiet, and about a dozen men all went *sssshhhh!* at the same time.

Dash rolled his eyes heavenward.

*Wonderful. Caught and convicted by a goddamned sneeze.*

McElroy tried to protest further, but then muttered something that sounded like defeat.

Footsteps followed by a mighty slam of the tailor shop's front door.

The booming voice said, "Sir, I apologize for our officer's behavior. He will—he will pay for the broken mirror. Good evening."

Atty's voice thanked the man, and soon, the front door opened and shut again.

They waited.

Before Pinstripes opened, Dash, Joe, Finn, and Atty had discussed what to do if there was a raid. First, the red light would turn on if officers of the law were inside the tailor shop. If Atty could get the coppers to leave, then they would wait for Atty's signal—a special knock against the wall—that the coast was clear. After the knock, the club would count to one hundred to make absolutely certain the coppers weren't coming back.

The seconds dragged by.

Suddenly there was a gentle, syncopated knock on the wall, something too hep for coppers to emulate.

Dash felt an overwhelming rush of relief.

*Thank you. Whoever is up there looking out for us, we thank you.*

A few of the men behind him laughed nervously, the anticipation and dread demanding a release.

Dash held up a warning finger. "Don't celebrate yet,

ladies." He turned around and said to the crowd of men, "Everyone, slowly count to one hundred."

A high-pitched voice said, "One, two, three—"

"In yer head, ya bloody fool," growled Joe.

A few snickered, but then they quieted down. After what felt like an eternity, Dash heard someone say, "One hundred."

Dash knocked on the wall, another syncopated knock, which Atty answered with the code for the coast being cleared.

Dash grinned. "Alright, ladies, we did it. First drinks are on the house!"

The room sent up a celebratory cheer.

Dash unlocked the secret door, pulling it open carefully. A giant gash had splintered the mirror into jagged, spidery cracks, with several errant pieces of glass sprinkled across the floor. Dash stepped over the carnage and entered the curtained-off changing area. After the coppers left, Atty had pulled the curtain back to its original position to hide the door and conceal Dash stepping out of it.

Dash parted the fabric and saw Atty standing in the center of the tailor shop, his expression grim.

"I'm sorry, Boss," he said. "McElroy wouldn't stop!"

"It's Jake, Atty. You did what you could." Dash put his hands on his lips and looked around. "Who was with McElroy?"

"A bunch of rookies, it looked like. Inexperienced."

"Who barged in and saved our skins?"

"I don't know, Boss," Atty replied. "He was older, had white hair. Looked like a lieutenant or something."

"Someone outranking McElroy."

"Youse got that right. And if I had to guess, Boss? He was someone Fife paid."

What Atty said made sense.

There was a sound of more glass falling behind him. Dash turned to see Joe coming through the curtain.

"I gotta get the bottles from the basement. Let's hope to the Mother Mary none of 'em broke." Joe then looked at Dash. "El's right angry at ya, lassie. She wants to know what the hell we're up to and why didn't we pay off the police?"

"We *did* pay off the police! Or rather, Fife did." Dash sighed. "It's goddamn McElroy. This," he said, pointing to the broken mirror, "this was a message."

"What kind of message?" asked Atty.

"The kind we can't ignore."

"Aye," Joe said. "Now those pictures of Peter Fraker dallyin' with his mistress better be at that apartment tomorrow, lassie. Otherwise, we're sunk."

---

It was Sunday morning, and rain thumped against the cab's roof and splattered across the windows. Dash stared out the side while Joe faced the front. Resting on the cab floor at the bottom of their feet were two empty suitcases, ready to be filled with whatever evidence of McElroy's extortion they would hopefully find.

Last night after the police left, Dash and Joe were relieved to find the majority of their bottles had survived the fall from the chute. The rest of the night proceeded without incident, although El gave Dash several glaring looks.

"Damn downtowners," she muttered at the end of the evening, when Dash paid her fee and watched her walk out.

"Ya think she'll ever come back?" Joe asked.

"I don't know," Dash replied. He had the feeling she was upset about more than just the police almost raiding

Pinstripes. His mind went back to that engagement announcement she tore out of the *Times*.

*What* was *that about?* he wondered.

The cab dropped them off in front of the main lobby of 277 Park Avenue. They ran to the double doors, shaking off the rainwater from their slickers, and crossed diagonally towards the far corner where Danny Boy was trying to conceal himself behind a column and a potted plant.

"Took you long enough!" he hissed. "I've got to be back at my post in less than two minutes!"

"Calm down, lad," Joe replied. "It's pourin' outside! Ya know that fusses up the streets."

Danny narrowed his eyes. "Where's Mr. Francis?"

"He's got a cold," Dash replied, skipping right over the truth. "You have the key?"

Danny nodded. He reached into his pocket and pulled it out, placing it in Dash's outstretched palm. "The apartment is on the fifteenth floor. Apartment 15T. The storage closet is at the end of the hall near 15Y. I put in two uniforms of men from the night-shift. I checked on them—the uniforms, I mean—twenty minutes ago; they should still be there." He eyed Joe. "I hope they fit."

Joe grumbled a curse.

Danny pointed to the key in Dash's hand. "That key should also get you into the apartment. Mr. McElroy left for Mass. I saw him leave myself, so he shouldn't be back anytime soon. And I confirmed with our records that Mr. McElroy has put nothing in the building's safe."

"Excellent!" Dash said. "Once we're done, we'll drop off the key at the front desk like we're giving you our room key. It'll look perfectly natural."

Danny swallowed a thick lump in his throat.

Dash gave a reassuring smile. "Like we said before, it's Jake."

Danny cut his eyes over to the front desk, which lay a good thirty to forty feet away. "I need to get back."

Dash gave a nod and said in a slightly louder voice, "Thank you, my good man. We appreciate your help." He winked at the boy, who forced a smile.

"At your service, sir." He left the corner and walked towards his post at the front desk.

The elevator ride up was uneventful and dropped them off in the center of the building at Apartment 15M. They first went in the wrong direction, going towards A rather than towards Z.

They turned around. When they passed by 15T, Dash hesitated, looked over his shoulder to see no one was in the hallway watching him, and then pressed his ear against the door.

"Whattaya doing?!" hissed Joe.

Dash placed a finger to his lips and listened. True, Danny said McElroy left the apartment, but it didn't hurt to be cautious. Either the doors were incredibly thick, or McElroy's apartment was dead silent.

Dash straightened up and nodded. There was still a risk they'd stumble upon someone there, but they'd at least be dressed the part.

After Apartment 15Y, there was the unmarked door Danny Boy mentioned.

"This must be it," Joe said.

Dash took out the skeleton key and placed it in the lock. It turned, and he pushed open the door. A man's voice suddenly rang out at the other end of the hallway, his words formless. A woman's voice laughed in response. Two figures suddenly appeared, making their way towards the center of the hallway, presumably heading towards the elevators. They were looking at one another, conversing animatedly.

"Go, go, go," Dash murmured. He pushed Joe into the closet and quickly followed, closing the door behind him.

The dark was absolute.

"Great," Joe said. "How the hell are we supposed to see?"

"There should be a chain for a light somewhere."

There was a rustling sound as Joe searched in the dark. "Ah ha," Joe said. "Here we go."

He pulled the chain, and pale light flooded the surprisingly large room. Service odds and ends filled the space: dusters, polishing rags, empty trash bins, ashtrays. In the far corner was a tiny desk, on which lay a rectangular piece of paper with angular script in rigid, straight lines. The servants' schedule, no doubt. Hanging on a row of hooks were the extra bellhop uniforms, as Danny boy had promised.

Dash picked one and held it up to his frame. It would do. He glanced at the other and looked at Joe.

"They apparently don't hire a lot of baby grands here," he said, apologetically. "It's going to be a tight fit."

Joe sighed. "Goddamn it."

They changed from their suits, folding their clothes and tucking them into the empty suitcases. Dash's uniform reminded him of the dockworker's disguise from last week: it was mis-cut across his shoulders and neck, causing him to tug repeatedly at the collar. Poor Joe, he saw, threatened to bust the seams of his uniform, what with his barrel chest, broad shoulders, and substantial torso.

"I feel like I'm in a bloody sausage casing," Joe grumbled.

"Well, you *are* a large cut of meat," Dash replied, doing his best Finn imitation.

Joe scowled, but there was a hint of a smile behind it. "Can we just get this over wit'? Ya got the key?"

"I do."

They left the closet, locking it behind them, and walked down the hall, carrying the suitcases. If anyone asked, they were bringing up a guest's luggage.

Two men exited the elevator bank and walked towards them, conversing softly. Dash and Joe stepped aside to allow them to pass.

"Morning, gentlemen," Dash murmured.

Neither one of them responded nor looked their way, just continued down the hall.

"Bunch of impolite asses," muttered Joe.

They turned and went to room 15T. Dash placed the key inside the lock and turned. The lock gave way, and they entered McElroy's apartment.

What they saw stunned them.

"Holy *shite*," Joe breathed.

## 29

Dash knew to expect luxury, but what lay before them was so incongruent with McElroy's personality, it stunned them both into silence.

The archways beckoned upwards to a ceiling that soared fourteen feet high, adorned with a magnificent brass chandelier. Two dozen charcoal lampshades hung over the bulbs, matching the black marble floor. Golden sunbursts spread across the square-shaped tiles in a dizzying array of sunrises and sunsets. Doors layered with dozens of gold and silver geometric designs gave Dash a sense of vertigo.

In the sitting area, couches done up in plush blue velvet were accentuated with amber and gold pillows. Round tables like giant drums stood stoically at the end points, their bodies sapphire, their tops brass. Large windows on the far-right side overlooked the gardens in the center of the property, letting in streaks of sunlight.

Black velvet curtains with golden trim and gold tassels surrounded a rectangular cutout in the far-left-side wall. A silver bar cart stacked with bottles—mostly rum, from the looks of them—stood in front of another sunburst design etched in brass.

Dash and Joe spent a few moments slowly wandering around, their mouths agape.

When they looked at each other again, Joe said, "Fuckin' hell. How much sugar is the bloke stealin' from folks?"

"Pounds of it, obviously.

"Where should we start? Bedroom?"

"I've always had good luck there," Dash quipped.

Joe snorted a laugh in response.

The bedroom was off to the side, tucked into a corner behind the bar. There, they found more sunbursts, more vertigo-inducing layered geometrics, and more velvet curtains with gold tassels. They set the suitcases onto the floor.

"Can ya imagine McElroy with his slimy, dirty hair sleepin' here," Joe said, pointing to the enormous brass bed.

"I'm trying not to imagine McElroy in *any* bed."

"I know, lassie, but it's jus' . . . how does he not feel like a stranger in his own place?"

"Who says that he doesn't?"

Dash knelt by a low-lying bedside table, a spartan black square with white painted drawers. He rifled through each one, finding nothing of interest. Standing up, he walked to the closet and opened the doors, revealing a dizzying array of clothing. Among the items were police uniforms, day suits in various shades of gray and brown, and a few tuxedos for formal events.

Joe started searching the top shelves while Dash knelt and searched the floor.

"Nothin' up here but hatboxes," Joe said.

"Nothing down here but shoes."

Dash stood up, wiping the dust from his hands. If he had incriminating evidence, where would he put it? He looked up at the top shelf to the hatboxes Joe had just referenced.

"Joe," he said, pointing upwards. "Take one of those boxes and shake it."

Joe gave him a queer look, but selected one box and shook it. The box produced a strange noise, like playing cards. Joe raised his brows at the same time Dash did.

Joe took down the box, and the two of them went over to the bed, where they opened it.

Photographs.

Piles of photographs.

"Jesus wept," Joe said. "Look at all this!"

"He certainly has quite the collection," Dash replied. "And look, Joe. They're not just of our poor Peter Fraker either."

"Isn't that the woman who runs the tearoom on MacDougal?"

"Kissing another woman? It appears so. And here's that gentleman who runs the pastry shop on West Third. Looks like he was selling some booze under the counter."

"Christ, lassie, he's got half the Village in here!"

Dash nodded. "Now we know how he can afford all this."

"Is Fraker's stupid visit to the hotel with his mistress in there?"

Dash gave half the stack to Joe and kept the other half for himself. They quickly thumbed through the pages until they found Peter Fraker, looking nearly giddy with anticipation, walking into the hotel room and exhausted when leaving it.

"Oh!" Dash said. Apparently, McElroy had found a

place across the street from the hotel room's window. Peter Fraker, in his zeal for relief, had foolishly left a gap in the window curtains. McElroy found a straight shot into the middle of the bedroom and, with his camera, hit paydirt. For there was Peter Fraker, naked and aroused, while a woman, topless but still wearing her garters and hose, was on her knees, gripping Peter with both hands.

Joe looked over Dash's shoulder and whistled. "Who knew a canceled stamp like tha' would have a big gospel pipe?"

"Better not show this to Finn. He might fall in love."

"Alright, grab his pictures and let's go."

Joe moved off the bed, but Dash stayed put. He looked down at the piles of photographs, the piles of victims. He couldn't, in good conscience, only save one of McElroy's victims—even if saving that one victim was for purely selfish reasons. What had Peter Fraker said that night? *We Villagers need to stick together.*

"Dash," Joe said, his voice wary. "Whatcha doin'?"

"We need to take them. All of them," Dash replied, gesturing to the photographs.

"If we take them all, he'll know we've been here."

"He was always going to know that, Joe. Once the photographs were gone and Peter Fraker changed his tune."

"Yeah, but this is—this is his entire income. He'll come down at us like a ton o' bricks!"

"Which means Pru will need to work her magic fast. It's all about timing, Joe. We take the photographs while she gives McElroy's sergeant the bank statements, the apartment deed, and the salary records." Dash looked up at Joe. "We can't let McElroy ruin more lives."

Joe sighed, but ultimately relented. "Fine, lassie, but we'll need to check the rest of these bloody hat boxes."

Dash left the bed and grabbed the first suitcase. He threw it on top of the comforter and opened it, setting his discarded clothes aside, and began tossing in the photographs. Joe grabbed the other suitcase and did the same. As soon as they finished packing the photographs from the first hat box, they went through the remaining hat boxes in the closet. The next two held photographs; the last two held the negatives.

They arranged their clothes on top of McElroy's evidence and were just about to shut the suitcases when Dash spotted a scrap of paper clinging to the side of one of the emptied hatboxes.

"Wait!" he said.

He reached into the hatbox and removed the sliver of white. It was several pages folded and crammed into the crevices. He unfolded them and saw an odd typewritten report along with invoices. Hotel bills. With dates. And at the top of the page was a name that read very familiar.

"Felix de Martini," Dash said. "I know this name . . . why do I know this name?" Realization dawned, but it didn't make any sense. "Oh. *Ohh.*"

"Lassie. Who's this de Martini fella?"

"The private detective in the Hall-Mills case."

"Wha'? Isn't he the one who's been bribin' witnesses?"

"Allegedly. And the one who's been hiding out in New York City to avoid cross examination in front of a New Jersey grand jury." Dash tapped the pages. "Why does McElroy have any interest in him? Or rather, what is McElroy *extracting* from him?"

"Yer gonna have to think about it elsewhere, lassie." Joe slammed the suitcases shut and locked them. "We gotta ankle."

It felt like Dash was floating the entire cab ride home. They'd done it. They'd actually done it! A glance over at Joe showed the man's face was flushed, relief crinkling his eyes, pride tickling his smile.

Now that they had the photographs, they needed to find a safe place for them so they could sort them out and let McElroy's victims know that his proof was gone. The tailor shop was out of the question. So was their apartment proper. The Cherry Lane Playhouse attic seemed their best bet—for the time being, at any rate.

During the ride home, Dash put it together about Felix de Martini. "Pru's message from Lou the bartender said McElroy was into something very secret and very heavy. I think he's blackmailing Mr. Martini to keep his whereabouts in Manhattan a secret!"

"Tha' seems very much like our McElroy."

"And would get him in loads of trouble. He's interfering with another state's investigation." Dash grinned as he tapped the hotel invoices. "This might be our ace in the hole, Joe. He won't want *this* to get out."

"Aye, and even if his superiors would protect 'im, they're not gonna want to deal with the wrath of New Jersey coppers and prosecutors."

"Exactly."

The cab dropped them off at the Cherry Lane Playhouse. Dash and Joe ran up the stairs to the very top of the theatre, stashing the suitcases behind a set of discarded lights and trunks of old costumes. They were just coming down from there when they ran into Atty, face drawn and pale.

"Boss," he said, his voice tight. "Someone knocked on

the door. I didn't open it, just like youse said. I asked who it was and nobody answered. Then I heard someone running down the steps. By the time I got the door opened, all I found—well, I found—" He couldn't complete the sentence.

Dash felt the coldness of fear press itself against his chest. Instinctively, he reached back and grabbed Joe's hand.

Joe squeezed it back. "What is it, lad?"

Atty reached into his pocket and removed a folded piece of paper.

Dash instantly recognized it as the same paper as Donte's letters.

Atty said, "I got a letter from the Black Hand."

Joe cursed.

"That's not all. While I was reading it, Donte ran off."

## 30

"The crow's curse is upon us," Joe muttered.

"What does it say?" Dash asked.

Atty sniffed as he read. "'*Signore Atty Delucci, you've chosen to interfere in the matters between the Hand and your brother. For that, you must atone. Deliver your brother to the New York City Marble Cemetery tonight at midnight, or you and your friends will cry out in agony as you perish in flesh-scorching fire.*'"

Atty looked up at Dash and Joe, his eyes frantic with fear, his mouth trembling. "What am I gonna do? I can't turn my brother over to those murderous thugs, but I can't have youse hurt or killed too. And I don't even know where the hell Donte would go!"

His face flushed with a sudden rush of anger. "How can this be? How do I *not* know about my brother's life?" He started vigorously shaking his head. "Stupid, stupid! Who doesn't know their own brother?! Huh? What kind of brother am I?!"

"Atty, Atty," Dash said. "This is not the time to blame

yourself. Your brother kept many secrets. From *everybody*. From you, from his wife, his friends."

"Aye, he was a regular lyin' devil," Joe added. "What we need is a bloody plan."

Dash nodded. "Yes. We've got to find Silvano."

Joe replied, "Are ya crazy, lassie? He's bloody dangerous! He's set off two bombs. Christ knows how many more he has."

"This won't end unless we catch him."

Atty wrung his hands. "Why did Donte run? What the hell was he thinking?"

Joe said, "He probably wasn't, lad."

Atty ran a frustrated palm across his mouth. "How the hell are we supposed to find him, Boss? And how are we's supposed to find this, this Silvano fella?"

Dash replied, "We ask someone who also knows this story."

Atty and Joe both asked, "Who?"

"Carmela Fiore. Atty, you and I will pay her a visit at her restaurant."

Joe tried to intervene. "Lassie—"

"You need to stay here and keep an eye on the children," Dash said. "Besides, you're conspicuously Irish."

"Wha' the hell does tha' even mean?"

Atty came to Dash's defense. "It means you'll start trouble without meaning to. No offense, Joe, I think you're a swell fella, but a lot of my neighborhood won't think so."

Dash added, "Remember Finn and the ambulance?"

Joe muttered a curse. "Alright, alright." He pointed a finger at Atty. "You keep watch over this one, ya hear me?"

"Youse got it."

Dash said, "Joe, stay by the telephone at the box office.

Once Atty and I find out something, we'll telephone here." He added in a softer voice, "To let you know we're safe."

Joe nodded.

Dash turned to Atty. "I'll meet you on Seventh. I need to stop by the shop."

"What for, Boss?"

Dash's voice turned grim. "To get Donte's pistol."

Several minutes later, he bounded up to the front door of Hartford & Sons and puzzled, then alarmed, to find it unlocked and ajar. He looked up and down the street. No one was running away. No one appeared to be concerned.

He stepped into the shop, calling out, "Hello! Anyone in here!"

He saw the changing-area curtain pulled back and the secret door gaping open.

Someone had entered Pinstripes.

And was that someone still here?

Dash's breath was shaky. "Hello!"

A shadow darkened the secret doorway and Officer Cullen McElroy stepped out, a self-satisfied grin stretching his sweaty face.

"I got ya," he said. "I got ya, I got ya, and now, nothing and no one is gonna save you." McElroy pointed to the opened doorway behind him. "I found your club, your speakeasy, all full of liquor and cash."

"You're trespassing."

"Oh, no, Mr. Parker. You don't get to accuse me of anything, especially when you're directly violating the Volstead Act."

"Having liquor isn't illegal."

"That lockbox full of money isn't from its sales? Well, the tallies you kept sure make it seem so. You made me look a fool last night! I had them all out here. Wagons, coppers, the works. Only my chief called it off, and we both know why."

Fife. The only logical conclusion.

"I may not get you for Walter Müller, Mr. Parker, but I for *damn* sure will get you for breaking the Volstead Act."

McElroy charged forward, forcing Dash to back away.

"You'll be in prison one way or another, Mr. Parker." He pulled out a pair of handcuffs. "And I'll finally get off this godforsaken street."

Before he could get his hands on Dash, the tailor shop door opened and in stepped Makowski with a pistol aimed at McElroy's gut.

"That's enough, McElroy," he rasped. He separated the copper from Dash and placed the pistol's barrel against the underside of McElroy's chin. "One move and I'll blow your fat, ugly head all over this place."

McElroy breathed heavily. Angry eyes boiled at Makowski. "You're making one helluva mistake," he growled through gritted teeth.

Makowski twisted McElroy's wrists, causing him to cry out in pain and drop the metal handcuffs. Makowski then reached around to McElroy's belt and relieved him of his own pistol. He placed the barrel of the newly acquired gun to the other side of McElroy's chin.

"No, sir," Makowski said, "*you* made one helluva mistake. And you're gonna pay. Boys!"

Dash turned to see three more men step into the shop. The first carried a dark trench coat, the second held a cloth in a tightly clenched fist, and the third stretched a scarf between his hands.

Makowski stepped back as the three men surrounded McElroy. The first man picked up the handcuffs. The second man shoved the piece of cloth over McElroy's nose and mouth. McElroy screamed, but the third man punched McElroy in the gut, silencing him.

"Breathe deep, ya fat fuck," the man with the cloth growled, keeping it securely over McElroy's nose and mouth.

Dash saw McElroy's eyes flutter and then close. McElroy slumped downwards, but was kept upright by the three men.

"What was that?" Dash asked Makowksi, his voice trembling.

"Chloroform," Makowski replied. "It'll give him a pleasant sleep."

The trio of men acted in unison. The cloth was removed from McElroy's nose and inserted into his mouth, while the scarf was tied around his face and the trench coat was wrapped around his shoulders.

Dash heard the squeal of tires out front and looked through his shop's windows to see a CALLAHAN CREAMERY truck.

Makowski's trio opened the tailor shop front door and "walked" the sleeping McElroy out of Hartford & Sons and into the cab of the truck. The whole action took less than ten seconds before the truck door slammed shut and the whine of the gears sent it on its way. Makowski's trio dispersed, each walking in different directions before disappearing into the foot traffic of West Fourth Street.

No one on the sidewalk pointed and screamed. No one turned to their friend and gasped. In fact, no one noticed nor cared that a man was just abducted in broad daylight.

Dash turned back around to face Makowski. "What's going to happen to him?"

"Don't worry, Mr. Parker. Mr. Fife is not having him killed, as you requested." Those pinpoint eyes stared at him.

"God knows why he listens to you. Makes me wonder, though. It makes me wonder." He shook his head. "In any event, that McElroy fuck will wish he was dead."

And with that, Makowski adjusted his lapels and walked out of Hartford & Sons.

Dash stood there for a long moment, his mind swirling. *Would* Fife keep his word? And what did Makowski mean, McElroy would wish he was dead?

No good answers came to Dash. Eventually, he roused himself, refocusing on the task at hand. He had to help Atty save his brother—to save them all, now that the Hand was targeting Dash, Joe, and Finn as well. He opened the writing desk compartment and retrieved Donte's pistol.

------

Dash and Atty made it over to Little Italy in record time. Curiously, Fiore's restaurant was closed. The sign said because of the tragedy at Moreno Bank, but that didn't stop Atty from pounding on the front door until a tired, irritated Carmela opened the front door.

"You're lucky I don't have a pistol, or I'd have shot you by now." She glanced at Atty. "Who are you?"

"I'm Atty, Donte's brother."

Carmela cursed. "What do you want?"

Dash said, "Mrs. Fiore, I apologize, but this is important. May we come in?"

"No, you may not. You have exactly one minute before I call the police."

Dash looked her square in the eyes. "Silvano Capello."

The name hit home. She squinted at first, then her face fell. "Who is that?" she asked, a beat and a half too late.

Atty replied, "Youse know damn well who it is."

Dash touched Atty's arm. "Atty, please." He turned back to Carmela. "The only name that could cause Donte to come up here to visit a woman he hasn't seen since the War and to demand if she wrote these letters. Because only his best friend Rodolpho would know what he did all those years ago. And since Rodolpho never returned from the War, that leaves you."

Carmela scoffed, "Why would I write such things? Such things are the devil!"

"Because the Capellos were the family that Donte extorted with his Black Hand letter."

That silenced her.

Dash went on. "Donte isn't a victim of The Black Hand. He *pretended* to be The Black Hand."

Carmela cleared her throat. "Why would Donte do such a thing?"

Atty said, "Because my brother, the louse that he is, was in debt and his friends, such as your husband, stopped bailing him out. The Black Hand was everywhere by that time. Their exploits, their threats, their letters were all published in the newspapers. The Hand and its tactics were well known."

"So?"

Dash picked up Atty's narrative. "So, the Hand also had counterfeiters. Fake Handers. Copycats. Donte figured he could follow their lead."

Dash watched Carmela's face carefully, and though she didn't lose her temper, her skin paled with each passing word.

He said, "The Capellos banked at Barone's bank. Donte would know how much money they had because he had access to their accounts. Only what he didn't count on was that the

Capellos were significantly short one quarter because of Mia's illness. Paying off the Hand letter cost them everything. Which is why Umberto committed arson and insurance fraud."

A few stray tears fell down Carmela's cheeks. She sniffed. "Goddamn that man. My Rodolpho was so impressionable. He believed everything Donte told him. It was the last time he'd gamble. It was the last time he'd owe money. There was always a 'last time.' And then this—this *scheme*, of his." She raised a pointer finger. "But Rodolpho had *nothing* to do with it, *capisci?* He didn't know what Donte was doing. And when he found out about it, it was done. Nothing more to do."

"And then the War happened."

Carmela nodded. "Rodolpho and Donte go off to the trenches. Only Donte, the bastard, comes back. And he's living high. Mr. Moneybags. Until he gambles it all away."

"The Capellos's son was delivered to an orphanage before being called home to Italy. Never to be seen again. Or so we thought."

Carmela glanced up at him sharply. "What do you mean?"

"Hasn't the timing of all this seemed strange to you? A letter mentioning a Black Hand victim specifically to the man who extorted them almost ten years later?"

Carmela's face paled even more. "He grew up."

Atty cut in. "No shit, he grew up. And he came back. Angry. And he found my brother. The question is, Carmela, did he have help?"

Carmela's fear turned to indignation. "What are you implying?"

Atty advanced forward. "Did you help Silvano Capello find my brother?"

She barked a bitter laugh. "Why on earth would I do such a thing? I, a widow, who's barely scraping by—?"

Dash stepped in between the two of them. "While Donte lives like Mr. Moneybags. You said so yourself the last time we spoke. Donte, the undeserving one, the liar, the cheat, he survives the War while your husband, an honest man, never returns. You've had to watch Donte live the life Rodolpho should've had, the life *both* of you should've had. I wouldn't blame you for being resentful, Mrs. Fiore. I wouldn't blame you one bit."

"I don't need your absolution," she replied, her voice hard and flinty. "Yes, it's true. I hated Donte for all these years, but why would I risk prison and more over a slimy eel like Donte?"

"People do worse for less."

"So, what? You think I burn down buildings? You think I know how to use, eh, explosives?"

Dash shook his head. "No, but Silvano does."

"You think I'd stand by and watch innocent people die? Why should more innocents die because of Donte? After Umberto and Mia and Maria? Donte has hurt so many people! Why would I do the same? Eh? That would make me no better than him."

Dash watched her face. The defiance, the righteous anger, the . . . hurt. She was telling the truth.

Atty demanded, "Where can we find Silvano? Where is he?"

"I don't know."

Dash said, "Mrs. Fiore, if you know anything—"

"I know nothing! Now, if you'll excuse me, I've been insulted enough."

Before Dash could say anything further, she shut the

door in their faces. The deadbolt rattled home, effectively ending the conversation.

Dash stepped back, crossing his arms while he thought.

Atty paced the sidewalk. "Youse right, Boss. She knows more than she's lettin' on."

"Yes, but I don't think it's about this."

"What do youse mean?"

"I can't quite articulate it just yet."

The harsh smell of cigarette smoke mixed with jasmine tickled his nose. He glanced up.

In the darkened window above the restaurant sat the silhouette of Carmela. She was curled up on the windowsill, staring down at Dash. The cigarette end glowed an eerie orange as she took a drag.

Dash was about to call up to her when another silhouette joined her from behind. Thin arms wrapped around her shoulders in a gesture that was comfortable and intimate. A quiet moment between two lovers. The figure leaned forward so Carmela could light the cigarette bobbing in its lips. The sudden flash of the flame briefly illuminated the face of the second silhouette.

The jolt of recognition almost knocked Dash into the street.

Delilah Sams.

## 31

Atty spoke a mile a minute while Dash led them away from Fiore's.

"Carmela and Delilah? What do you think it means, Boss? Are they working together? What are they after? Revenge? For what? And why letters and bombs? That don't seem right, but then, I don't know, Boss, I don't know."

"I don't know, Atty. Things are adding up, but I'm not sure what they mean yet."

"I didn't know Carmela bent that way. No offense, Boss."

"None taken. Listen, Atty, this mess is about to break open. I can feel it. We need to go back to The Smoke Shop."

"Why, Boss?"

"Because we need to know what's in that storage closet."

"Storage closet? What's in there?"

"Olive oil."

Renzo wasn't managing the front this afternoon. Rather, it was an older man, about mid-forties, hair beginning to gray at the temples, round cheaters resting on the edge of his nose. His eyes, a watery blue, peered over the lenses.

"Can I help you, sirs?"

Dash replied he could and gave him the password.

The old man let them in.

Atty's face was stunned when he saw the main gambling floor.

Seeing it for the third time, Dash was less impressed. The same monotonous sights and sounds, the same men and women at the tables, cheering themselves and each other on; the same fog of cigarette smoke that hovered over the room; the same soft flicks of the playing cards and the ever-present rattle of the roulette wheel.

Both Dash and Atty scanned the room.

"Where to, Boss?"

Dash pointed to the black curtain where he saw the séance his first night here. "That's where Delilah does her seances. Let's check there first."

"Why?"

"Because she took something from those olive oil crates. I wonder if she hid it in there."

"Let's go check it out."

They glanced around the room, seeing that no one was watching them, and walked with purpose through the black curtain. The darkness was almost absolute. Dash and Atty both flicked their lighters and used their puny flames to stumble forward.

"There should be a light switch somewhere," Dash said.

"You sure, Boss?"

"How else could they set up the table and whatnot? Someone's got to see in here. Ah, here we go!"

The switch was on the same wall as the curtained doorway and looked like a round gold coin. Dash flicked up the tiny lever in the center and two work lights blasted on, temporarily blinding him. He rubbed his eyes and waited for the black splotches to disappear from his vision. He turned to find Atty squinting.

"Jesus, Boss, it's bright."

"Apologies, my friend."

He looked around the room. The round table with the black velvet cloth stood in the center. Dozens of white candles lined the edges of the room, their dripping wax dried and hardened into streaks, like tear stains. Black curtains hung on three of the four walls, the fabric shimmering slightly under the lights.

Atty took one side of the room, and Dash took the other. They each peered behind the curtains to find only concrete. No hidden rooms or closets in here.

The two of them met at the head of the table, where Dash had seen Delilah give her séance. He lifted the cloth, finding the table top painted black. He studied the base and the underside.

"Whatcha doin', Boss?" Atty asked.

"I want to know how she did it."

"Did what?"

Dash got down on his knees for a closer look. "Get the 'ghost' or 'spirit' or whatever to knock on the table and write the message. Her hands never left the table cloth."

Underneath the table, he found a circular base as the chief support. He looked up, expecting to see a club or a lever, something she could use to thwack the table.

*But her hands stayed visible.*

Regardless, he looked and found nothing. His eyes cast down to the table base again. He frowned. What was this?

There was a square outline at the foot of the base, almost imperceptible. Dash looked to where he imagined

Delilah sat. He let his eye travel from where he thought her legs would be to this square outline. She could've placed her foot easily on top of it.

Dash pushed with both of his hands.

The square went down.

He grinned. It was a pedal!

He pressed it hard, and the table rattled with a mighty *knock!*

"Ah ha!" he said.

There must've been a lever hidden inside the table base that connected to the pedal and, when activated, struck the underside of the tabletop. With the tablecloth down and only candlelight for illumination, no one could see Delilah working the pedal.

"Very clever, Miss Sams," Dash said. "Now, how about the letter? How did you do the letter?"

"Boss, we should go."

"One moment, my friend."

He studied the underside of the table again. This had to be where Delilah—excuse him, the "spirit"—wrote the message to that poor girl Mildred. He followed the line of sight again, from where he thought Delilah sat to where he remembered the piece of paper being.

He didn't see it the first or second time.

But the third time he ran his eye over the underside, he spied a square-shaped hole. He reached up with his hand and found that in addition to the square-shaped hole in the table, there was also a hole cut into the table cloth.

He started laughing.

"Boss," Atty said. "Youse okay?"

"I am. Wow! This is a devious piece of furniture, I have to say."

This must've been where Delilah laid the blank piece of

paper at the beginning of the séance. Again, because of the lack of light, no one would notice the hole when Delilah lifted the paper to show it empty and again to show the spirit's message. But how did she write it?

He looked around the underside again. "The only thing under here would be her knees. Did she attach a—I don't know—a pencil to one and scribble the letters backwards?"

"Boss," Atty hissed.

"Alright, alright. I'm coming out." Dash slid out from under the table. He pointed at it with his thumb as he stood up. "Truly fascinating."

"That's great, Boss, but we didn't find nothing."

"Not true. We learned how devious Delilah Sams is." Dash gestured to the curtained off entryway. "Shall we go?"

Dash flicked off the work lights, and they re-entered the main gambling floor. They flicked their eyes right to left. No one paid them any attention. The gamblers were too engrossed in their wins and losses to notice them.

"Where else, Boss?"

As Dash scanned the room again, he saw Gus Brown sitting at the bar. "There's someone who's Donte's best friend in this joint. Let's see what he knows."

Dash led Atty went over to the bar, where Gus greeted them enthusiastically.

"Mr. B-something, wasn't it? Oh, I'm so terrible with names. Berry? Benson? Bentley?"

It took a moment for Dash to recall that everyone at The Smoke Shop knew him as Max Bennett. He repeated his alias, which earned him a bark of laughter.

"That's right! Mr. Bennett, Mr. Bennett. Say, who's this?" Gus asked, meaning Atty.

Dash introduced him as Donte's brother.

"Nice to meet ya, nice to meet ya. Whatcha drinking?

Johnnie," Gus called to the bartender. "I'll have another Scotch, and Mr. Bennett here will have a . . . ?"

"Gin rickey."

"And you, Atty?"

Atty replied a whiskey.

Gus shouted to the bartender, "You got that, Johnnie? A scotch-ie and a rickey and a whiskey." He held up three fingers. "Three drinkies, pretty please-y." He laughed again, turning back towards them. "I crack myself up. So! What brings you back here?"

"We're looking for Donte. Have you seen him?"

"I haven't. What's happened to him?"

"He got another letter."

"Oh, no! What do the bastards want this time?"

"They want him," Dash replied. "It's a long story, Mr. Brown, but we've found the letters are part of a personal vendetta."

"Jeez Louise! That's terrible! Well, I haven't seen him," Gus said, swiveling his head from Dash to Atty and back again. "Honest, I haven't!"

"What about Vito Beneventi? Seen him lately?"

"That little pissant? Pft! Not lately and I'm not ashamed to say I'm glad. Say," Gus said, cozying up to Dash. "Did Vito ever tell you about what he saw? The night that Donte's building burned down?"

"He didn't."

"Shame. Probably would help you with this letter business. Although . . . " Gus took another gulp of his drink. "That Vito fella? He's real queer."

"How so?"

"Nobody knows where he came from! He just *showed* up. Said his name—though I always thought it was fake, to tell the truth—said he's a hard worker, which was a crock.

But he's real short on friends and long on trying too hard, you know what I mean?"

Dash and Atty flashed a glance at one another. "When did Vito show up?" Dash asked.

"Oh, about the same time Donte did. Thereabouts anyway. It's queer, isn't it? Vito shows up, weasels himself a job, and then Donte gets those letters." Gus shook his head. "Queer business."

"Speaking of business . . . " Dash turned his shoulders slightly towards Gus, his head dropping down as if he were gearing up for spilling a secret. "Do you know anything about olive oil?"

Gus squinted. "Olive oil?"

"Yeah. I've seen crates of them coming into this place."

"Oh, those. Yeah, yeah, I know a bit about them. Donte did too."

Atty said, "My brother?"

"Sure did. One day, Donte was out here, and these two big guys walk in with these large crates. And they said olive oil on the side—or really, the Italian words for olive oil. Anyway, Donte acts like a carnival barker. '*Step right up, step right up, feast your eyes on the eighth wonder of the world!*' And Berto, he was so mad. Wasn't he, Johnnie?"

The bartender had come up behind them and set their drinks onto the bar, murmuring, "Yes, sir."

Gus grinned, his eyes glassy, his grin sloppy. "Isn't he the best? Johnnie takes such good care of me, don't ya, Johnnie?"

"Yes, sir."

Gus grabbed his drink and downed half of it.

Dash and Atty nursed theirs.

"Where was I?" Gus said. "Oh, Berto. Anyway, Berto

was furious. Told Donte to shut the hell up if he knew what was good for him."

Dash took a tiny sip of his rickey. "Sounds a little harsh."

"Yeah, but I think it's because Berto didn't want people to notice the crates being brought in."

"Isn't it a little obvious, them carrying the crates across the casino floor?"

Gus gave Dash a jaded look. "Listen, mister, when you're at the tables, you're *at* the tables. Nothing else matters. Nothing can matter, otherwise you'd lose." He swallowed more Scotch. "But I'll tell you this, though, and you can trust me, I'm a regular. I know all there is to know about this place. And those brothers? Berto and . . . R-R-R—"

"Renzo."

"Renzo, right. They're up to no good."

Atty asked, "Why do youse say that?"

"'Cause those crates come in when Papa Gianni isn't around. I bet ya dollars to doughnuts their Papa doesn't know those shipments are coming in."

Dash glanced towards the corner closet where the crates were being stored. "I see." He laid a quarter onto the bar. "Thanks, Gus. The next one's on me. Atty? Why don't you keep Gus company while I do a little exploring?" He glanced meaningfully at Atty.

Atty nodded. "Youse got it, Boss."

Dash's eyes flicked from one end of the main room to the other. No Spinellis anywhere in sight.

*Now or never, old boy,* he thought to himself.

## 32

Dash left his empty glass on the bar and hurried across the room and past the potted palms. He saw the storage room door, grasped the knob, and turned, only to find it locked.

Damn.

He looked over his shoulder. There was sufficient cover to pick the lock undetected, provided that someone didn't round the corner.

*Let's not think about that.*

Dash removed his lock-picking tools and set to work. He blocked out the surrounding sounds—the laughter, the cheers, the rattle of games—and concentrated solely on the lock.

One tumbler fell almost instantly. Not so great a lock, he thought happily.

The second tumbler was a bit of a trick to find, but he eventually found it.

The lock clicked, and Dash stood up. He glanced over his shoulder again. No one was standing there, watching him, demanding what the hell he was doing. Just shadows on the adjacent wall of the club's guests as they bartered with Chance and Fortune.

He entered the storage closet, locking the door behind him.

It was dark. He fumbled for his lighter and brought it out of his inside pocket. He flicked the wheel until a tiny flame appeared. Meager light, but he'd take it until he could find the overhead bulb.

He slowly inched forward, careful not to trip or run into anything. A tiny flash appeared, then disappeared in midair. Something had caught the light from his flame. He continued forward until he saw a metal chain dangling from the ceiling. Dash grabbed it and pulled.

Light filled the room, illuminating stacks of wooden crates. Dash searched for an open one. All of them nailed shut, which meant a new shipment must've arrived. He searched the closet for a tool, thinking they'd had to have something to open these crates. He found a crowbar standing in the far corner of the room.

He picked it up and went over to one stack, focusing on the top crate. He positioned one end of the crowbar underneath the crate's top and pushed down on the other end of the iron rod. With gritted teeth, he fought with the crowbar until he heard a wrenching sound, followed by the splintering of wood.

The sound was loud, like a gunshot.

Dash's heart pounded. He left the crate, with the crowbar still in hand, and went to the storage door. He unlocked it and cracked it open, peering out.

All he saw were the potted palms and the shadows of the gamblers on the concrete walls. The laughter and gaiety continued on its merry way. No one in the main room seemed to have heard the sound.

Dash closed the door, locking it again, and returned to the crate. He removed the lid, setting it aside on top of a neighboring crate, and looked inside.

Loose straw surrounded bottles of "olive oil." Dash lifted one up and removed the cork. Almost immediately, the overpowering perfume of juniper filled the room. He still sniffed the lip of the bottle, confirming the contents was gin.

Dash frowned. This couldn't be what Berto and Renzo were selling on the side, was it? Hardly transgressive, and not worth the defensiveness of both Donte and Delilah.

Not to mention the shape of these bottles didn't match the shape of the package in Delilah Sams's handbag.

He dug through the straw, his fingertips hitting another layer of glass bottles. He plunged his arms even further into the crate.

*Just like I saw Delilah doing.*

He felt the coarseness of paper. He paused. His fingers slowly traced the edges of a rectangular packet underneath a glass bottle. With one hand, he pushed aside the unseen bottle, and with the other, he extracted the paper package. A few bushels of straw spilled over the lip of the crate as Dash brought it up to the light.

A rectangle, about the size of his hand, maybe a little smaller, an inch thick, perhaps less. There was a flap at one end of the package. Dash quickly opened it and peered inside.

White powder.

And a distinctive smell. Floral underlaid with something astringent. Ammonia? Vinegar?

Dash touched it and brought his fingertip to his mouth. His tongue immediately went numb. The realization flashed before Dash's eyes like a Times Square neon sign: *COCAINE*.

He folded the lip of the paper package to reseal it and placed it in his pocket. Then he quickly picked up all the loose straw and repacked the box. He was putting the lid back onto the crate when there was a scratching sound at the door. Metal on metal, followed by a familiar jangling sound.

Keys in a lock.

Someone was coming in.

Dash glanced around, frantic for a hiding place.

There. A discarded tarp laid in the far corner. He dove underneath it just as he heard the door open. A male voice echoed off the walls, "Berto, did we leave the light on?" It belonged to Renzo.

Dash held his breath. The darkness under the tarp obscured his view, revealing only a small triangular section of the floor. He remained motionless. Sweat trickled down his spine and slipped underneath the waistband of his trousers. He hated this. Hide-and-seek was never Dash's game of choice as a child. Inevitably, he would jump out of his hiding place as though his clothes were ablaze, over-whelmed with the thought of getting caught.

"Why does it matter?" Berto.

"Because Papa's a stickler for utilities. Doesn't want to pay extra if he can help it."

Berto's voice sneered, "You're such a goodie-goodie. Always wanting to be on Papa's good side."

"I haven't told him about what you're doing, have I?"

"What *we're* doing, Renzo. You agreed to this."

"After you'd already made the deal. What was I supposed to do?!"

"Skip it. It doesn't matter—wait, who opened this box? Did you?"

"Why would I have opened it?"

"I don't know, Renzo. To take some for yourself?"

"*Why* would I do that? I don't even like the stuff!"

"You could be lying."

Renzo ignored his brother's accusation and said, "Is there a *reason* you took me away from my post?"

"Your post," Berto scoffed. "Jesus Christ. Well, if you didn't open it, someone else did, because *I* didn't open it."

"Shit," Renzo said, "is someone in here?"

Dash's heart stopped.

Berto replied, "The door was locked. They're long gone. Besides, I know who it was. Which is why I took you away from your precious *post*. That bitch Delilah found out about this."

"I knew it. I knew we'd get caught. Didn't I tell you we'd get caught?"

"Calm down, ya clown. We haven't been caught by Papa, and that's the most important thing. Delilah, we can deal with. We can handle her. *I* can handle her."

"What does she want? Money?"

Berto chuckled. "No, you Dumb Dora. She wants her freedom from Papa. She wants her debts erased. That knucklehead Donte's too."

Dash felt a leap of intuition. The invoice sheets of these crates of olive oil hidden in Atty's bedroom. It didn't make any sense that Donte had them, *unless* he and Delilah were working together to get out from under Gianni by blackmailing his sons about their secret side business.

Renzo said, "Donte? Donte Delucci? Why does she care about him?"

"How the hell should I know? Maybe they're fucking in the back alley in between tarot readings."

"You're crude, Berto."

"And you're prude enough to be a virgin. Jesus, Renzo, the *point* is, they want out."

"We can't convince Papa to erase the debts."

"No shit."

Renzo's voice took on a tinge of hysteria. "If we can't do what she asks, then she'll tell Papa. We're sunk, Berto, we're sunk—"

Dash heard a light slapping sound, an open palm on a cheek.

"Listen," Berto said. "*I* will take care of this. Alright?"

There was a pause.

"Berto," Renzo said, "what are you going to do to her?"

Silence.

"Berto?"

"I said, *I'll* take care of it. *Capisci?* Besides . . . you need to man your post."

There was the click of the overhead light being turned off and the room plunged into darkness. Dash heard two sets of footsteps and the closing of the door.

He finally let out his breath and counted to ten before slowly sliding forward, lifting the tarp so he could stand up. He fumbled for his lighter again, the tiny flame not much of a guide through the darkness. Waving his hands like a blind man without a cane, he inched forward.

Suddenly, the door opened. Pale light drifted in from the other room.

Dash froze, panicking locking him into place. If it was Berto or Renzo, he was as good as dead.

Atty poked his head inside and whispered, "Come on, Boss! Before they come back!"

Dash left the darkened space. His lower back and armpits were damp with sweat, and for a moment, Dash worried his fever was coming back.

"Thank you, Atty," he said.

"Boss, I found out something. I asked the bartender if he knew Vito. 'Course he had not nice things to say about him."

"Of course."

"But I got his address. He's on the other side of Little Italy." Atty's eyes hardened. "Shall we go get him?"

"No," Dash replied quickly. "No, no. Not you."

"Youse sure? I've got my pistol—"

"And that's exactly why you're not going."

"But you can't go there by yourself! He's too dangerous."

"I know," Dash said. "Let's find ourselves a telephone. I have one call . . . " He paused, glancing back at the storage closet. "Correction, I have two calls to make."

## 33

Vito lived on the corner of Crosby and Broome Street, which was on the outskirts of Little Italy.

*Away from prying eyes,* Dash thought.

He and Joe stood on the side nearest the M. Stein Cosmetic Company, its large sign promoting in bold white letters face powders, cold creams, wheat croft, grease paints, lip and cheek rouges.

*I wonder if I should pick up a few items for Finn while I'm here,* he randomly thought.

Dash checked the address the bartender had scribbled down for Atty, glancing up at the M. Stein building's number. He then looked across the street, scanning those numbers, working out where Vito's apartment was located.

There was a small three-story building with its upper-level windows boarded up. That wasn't a good sign. On the sidewalk in front of was a hodgepodge of discarded furniture: a chest of drawers missing one leg, a swivel chair missing one arm, a tailor's dummy horribly stained, a lamp with a fringe shade, and a box of discarded dresses.

Two men stood at the corner of the building, one

dressed in a blinding white butcher's apron, the other in a dark gray vest and trousers. They were chatting amiably while the butcher had his arms crossed over his barrel chest. The man in the vest had one foot on a stoop so he could lean forward.

"Excuse me," Dash said as he and Joe walked over to them. "We're looking for Vito Beneventi. Someone told me he lives here."

The butcher smirked, amused.

The man in the vest replied, "You looking to teach him a lesson?"

"I'm sorry?"

"Most fellas come around here teed off because good ol' Vito went too far with a girl of theirs. He do that to a lady friend? Sister?"

"No, nothing like that. He . . . he left something behind at a club one night and we're here to return it."

"An honest man? In this town?"

The two men hooted some laughs.

Joe said, "He still here, boys?"

The butcher said, "Haven't seen him today."

"Missed his rent payment last I hear," the man in the vest added. "He's out as soon as the landlord prints out the eviction notice."

"That's too bad," Dash replied. "If you don't mind me asking, how long has he been in this place?"

"Far too long," muttered the butcher.

The man in the vest said, "He's a lousy neighbor. Makes too much noise, doesn't keep his place clean, comes in at all hours of the night. No doubt up to trouble. We've been lucky it hasn't been coming here."

"Like them buildings that got blown up."

"Vito got excited about them. Wanted to talk all the details with us, as if we're friends."

The butcher said, "We're not friends."

"Talk and talk and talk. What accelerant was used, what caused the collapse, how many people died, and my, wasn't that all interesting?"

"We weren't interested."

"Wouldn't take a hint, that Vito. No, sir. Wouldn't shut his mouth for all the world."

Dash cut in. "Do you know where he came from?"

The man in the vest and the butcher glanced at each other.

The man in the vest said, "Didn't he say he was in Italy before coming here?"

The butcher shook his head. "Said Little Italy. The Harlem one."

"I think he has family around."

The butcher shook his head again. "No, no family. Said he had none to speak of. Can't recall if they died or if they disowned him."

"Probably disowned him. I would if I were them."

"No, I heard he was an orphan."

*An orphan?*

Dash suddenly remembered something Berto had said: *"Because he's not one of us. He tries, god help us, he tries, but he'll never, ever be."*

Dash cut in. "And you haven't seen him in the last day or two."

The two men squinted at one another before replying they hadn't.

The man in the vest pointed down the sidewalk. "He's at the side door there. You can see if he's in there sleeping."

The butcher said, "Passed out more likely."

"Yeah, he loves his liquor. Too bad he doesn't love a toothbrush as much."

This inspired guffaws from the two men.

Dash thanked them and he and Joe walked past the furniture and the boxes, finding a side door propped open by yet another box. This one contained men's hats.

"Someone's moving out," Dash muttered.

"Aye. Wonder if it's Vito."

Dash pushed open the door and stepped into the foyer. A narrow staircase tacked its way upwards, the boards warped and cracked; the banister leaning unsettlingly to the side. On Dash's right, another door stood ajar.

"This isn't good, lassie," Joe said.

Dash knocked, calling out Vito's name.

The door creaked loudly and swung open, revealing a dimly lit room.

Dash and Joe looked at one another.

"I'll go first," Joe mouthed. He stepped around Dash and slowly entered the apartment.

Dash followed.

Floorboards groaned underneath their feet, announcing their presence.

Dash froze and braced for Vito to lunge out of the darkened corners and attack them.

There was no one.

They waited for a few more moments before determining the apartment was uninhabited.

It was a modest square with two closed closet doors cut into the walls on the far left-side and a galley-style kitchen no bigger than a postage stamp on the far-right. Most of the furniture was missing. Only the bed and the chest of drawers remained. On top of the stripped mattress were piles of unwashed shirts, trousers, underwear, and socks sending up a sour musk that offended Dash's nose. The chest of drawers had more of the same on top of it. Three of the four drawers had been pulled out in haste.

Joe opened the two closet doors. "Watch for me, lassie."

Dash's muscles tensed, ready to react in case Vito—or anyone else—was hiding in the closets.

Joe gently gripped the doorknob, took a deep breath, and pulled open the closet door so fast and with such force, it swung around and banged into the wall.

Dash's heart was hammering in his chest.

No one was in the closet. The only items were discarded packing materials and trash.

"Closet number two?" Dash said.

Joe nodded. He went through the same routine, only this time, he caught the door before it rammed into the wall.

"Jesus, Mary, and Joseph!"

Dash jumped. "What is it?" He stepped forward to see over Joe's shoulder.

Joe knelt and carefully brought up a stick of dynamite. "There's more in there, lassie, plus bags of some sort of powder and wounded wires."

"Nothing on timers that you can see?"

Joe scanned the area. "None that I can see. Though I wouldn't mind gettin' out of here as soon as we can."

"Let's first see if he left any clues showing where he's going." Dash went over to the chest of drawers and peered inside the top drawer. He stopped. "Joe. You need to see this."

Alerted by Dash's odd tone of voice, Joe turned and strode over to Dash's side. He looked into the first opened drawer and cursed.

"Bloody hell, lassie, is that . . . is that . . . ?"

"Rough drafts of Black Hand letters? It would appear so."

Dash reached into the drawer and pulled out several discarded pieces of paper. The paper itself was a match for the letters Dash had seen addressed to Donte Delucci. The text of the letters had several cross-outs and corrections. Edits, which was darkly amusing to Dash in this context. God forbid there be a mistake or an awkward phrase when you're trying to extort someone.

Each draft listed the amount they wanted Donte to pay and the name "Capellos."

Dash closed this top drawer and began looking through the others. He discovered an ID card belonging to Silvano Capello, and a passport with stamps from Italy in Nineteen Twenty and the U.S. in Nineteen Twenty-Six.

Dash passed his findings over to Joe and began slowly pacing around the apartment.

"Lassie, does this mean that Vito is the Capellos's son?"

"It certainly looks that way." Dash spun in a slow circle. "Where's his suitcase?"

"I think he took it."

"But he left his passport behind."

"Maybe he's got a new one. New identity and whatnot."

"Maybe."

Joe frowned. "Ya got that look on yer face. The one that says yer about to put yerself into trouble."

"No, no. It just . . . seems so easy. Why leave the door open and have evidence of your extortion practically in plain view?"

"Didn't ya say this Vito was dumber than a pile of rocks?"

"He's smart enough to do a covert extortion scheme,

complete with dynamite, and dumb enough to leave it here?"

"If he's leavin' town, what else is he gonna do? He can't bring all of it wit' him."

"If he's leaving town, that means he'll have, or be close to, completing his mission."

Dash went back to the chest of drawers and paged through the letters. At the bottom of the stack wasn't a discarded letter like the others, but a list. The hairs on the back of Dash's neck stood on end.

"We need to get back to the Playhouse," he said.

"Why?"

Dash held up the list, which included two items crossed out, and one circled several times. The crossed-out items were: HOME and BANK. The item circled was Atty's name.

## 34

"Atty! Atty, where are ya, lad?!" Joe called as he searched their apartment.

Atty was nowhere in sight.

They went into their bedroom where Dash paced behind Joe. "He's not in the box office nor in the theater itself. Where is Isabella, Emiliano, and Rocco? I don't see them anywhere!"

"*Shite!*"

There was a knocking sound on their bedroom wall. A muffled voice said, "We're in here."

Dash looked at Joe. "The dressing rooms."

They found the door locked and with some convincing managed to get Isabella to open the door. Her face was white as ash.

"Someone came and got Uncle Atty," she said. "He said he knew where his brother was, but I didn't believe him. I tried to tell Uncle Atty but he wouldn't listen to me, he wouldn't listen. I told the boys to come in here and we locked the door in case the man came back here."

Dash and Joe exchanged a look before Dash addressed

Isabella. "It is alright, Miss Delucci. Everything will be alright. Do you know where this man took your Uncle?"

She shook her head, her mouth trembling to hold back her tears.

"It's Jake, Miss Delucci, it's Jake. I think . . . I think I know where Atty will be." Dash turned to Joe. "We need a plan, and we need help." He glanced at his wristwatch. "And we only have a few hours to do it."

⸻

It was midnight.

The moon cast a pale spotlight on the black wrought-iron gate of the New York Marble Cemetery.

Dash and Joe found the gate to be opened.

*Someone beat us here.*

They looked around.

No one.

Not even a late-night stroller.

This stretch of sidewalk on Second Avenue was deserted. Dash attuned his ears to their surroundings, listening for any muffled voices, snapping tree branches, rustling leaves. Anything to indicate whether someone was moving about.

Silence.

Only the whisper of the wind as it blew through the large trees that stood in between the graves. Half of their leaves were gone, exposing gnarled wood and twisted branches. They vibrated more than swayed, causing the shadows on the ground to shimmer and shake.

Joe murmured, "What now, lassie?"

Dash scanned the area again. The wrought-iron gate gave way to a fence that encircled only one side of the rectangular-shaped property. On the other three sides were stone walls. Apartment buildings rose behind them, their windows dark with sleep.

Sleeping buildings. Empty sidewalks.

The only clue that someone was here from the gambling den was the truck that Dash had seen delivering Berto's and Renzo's "olive oil."

There were no witnesses to what was to happen tonight. No witnesses other than he and Joe.

*Thank heavens we have Donte's pistol.*

Before they left for the cemetery, Dash had given it to Joe since the ruddy Irishman had the most experience with firearms.

"I suppose we go in," Dash replied.

He stepped through the opening in the gate with Joe close behind him. The moonlight here was more muted, the large trees blocking most of its beams. A cobblestone path led straight down the middle but most of the property was covered in grass and fallen leaves.

"Stick to the path," Joe muttered. "The leaves will crunch."

Dash nodded and continued straight forward, looking right and left for human-like shadows. The wind bit into his skin. Winter was certainly coming soon, and he wasn't ready for it.

*Assuming I live long enough to see it.*

Headstones dotted the grounds. Some were small rectangles or squares in the ground; others tall pedestals with obelisks. An owl hooted in the distance. Dash shivered. He always found those birds of prey particularly terrifying. Hiding in the shadows or camouflaged in the night sky only to swoop down with sudden speed, sink their talons into flesh, and make off with their victims. How horrifying must it be for those field animals. One moment they're on the ground, the next they're airborne, hurtling towards a gruesome and violent death.

A low moan stopped them.

Dash's eyes darted about. Was he hearing things? He kept still, kept quiet.

Another low moan, muffled but anguished, came from their left.

Dash turned. Where was it? His eyes slowly took in the undulating shapes of the headstones, pedestals, and obelisks.

There! A darkened figure sat at the base of one of the obelisks.

Dash touched Joe's shoulder and nodded towards it. They quickly walked towards it. The figure came more into view.

"Atty!" Dash called out.

The figure jerked its head up. More muffled moans but no words.

*He's been gagged.*

Atty tried to speak but couldn't because of the handkerchief stuffed into his mouth. The moans became more urgent.

Up close, Dash could see someone had tied Atty to the base of obelisk with thick, heavy ropes. Dash rushed towards Atty but was stopped by the tell-tale *click* of a hammer being cocked back on a pistol.

Dash froze.

As did Joe.

Atty's eyes widened.

Dash glanced over his shoulder. The sound came from somewhere behind them.

"Who's there?" he asked.

Only the wind answered, cold and breathy.

"I said, who's there?"

Nothing.

"Vito? Is that you?"

A snicker.

Atty grunted.

Dash turned his head back to his friend.

Atty was jerking his chin to a spot just over his shoulder behind the obelisk.

Dash focused his eyes. At first, he saw a flash of pale white and thought it was a rock or two. He looked closer. A chill seeped into his chest.

It was a hand.

A motionless hand.

Dash stepped forward. The hand was attached to an arm. A white shirt sleeve led to a shoulder.

Dash got closer.

The shoulder gave way to the side of a man's face. A sunken cheek, a sharp cheekbone, and a pointed nose. One would describe it as "weaselly."

Vito.

The glassiness of his eye betrayed his condition.

So did the round hole at his temple.

Joe gasped behind him. "Lassie, if that's Vito, then who tied up Atty?"

Dash stared at the fallen form of the boy he thought was Silvano Capello. It all fit so neatly. The age. The letters in his apartment. The fact he tried to belong to the Spinelli family for he never had one of his own. That no one knew where he came from. He just showed up at the same time as Donte. At least that's what Gus had said.

*Gus.*

The man who knew everything about everyone.

Or did he?

The first time Dash met him, Gus pointed to Carmela Fiore. Then to Delilah, the brothers, and finally to Vito. Why?

*To keep me looking elsewhere.*

Dash whirled around to face behind him. "Gus? Are you there?"

The snicker turned into a familiar chuckle. "I was wondering when you were going to catch on. Honestly, you took a lot longer than I thought." The voice was the same, but the slurred consonants were gone.

*An act. The sloppy drunk was all an act.*

Dash said, "You did do a decent job of sending me down multiple wrong paths."

"I know. That turned out to be incredibly fun, watching you spin and spin and spin. Alright, boys, put your hands up."

Gus stepped forward, brandishing a pistol aimed straight at them. His black suit blended in with the shadows. A swath of moonlight illuminated his pale face, making him appear to be a disembodied head floating in the room.

Dash and Joe raised their hands.

The drunken grin Dash was used to seeing was now replaced by a cunning, fiendish smile. Like a jack-o-lantern's.

Dash nodded down to Atty. "How did you get him tied up?"

"A light chop behind the ear and he was out like a light, weren't you, Atty? I had to use Berto's and Renzo's truck to get him here. Do you have any idea how much cocaine they have in there? I might snag me a bag or two on my way out."

"And you plan on making Vito the fall guy for all this?"

"You gave me that idea, Mr. Bennett. Or shall I say, Mr.

Parker?" Gus clicked his tongue with disapproval. "Such lies. For all the good it did."

"How did I give you the idea?"

"You mentioned that Vito saw something interesting the night I torched the Delucci's building. Turns out the sucker *did* see something, the rat. He saw me leaving the building while he was pouting that he didn't get into that girl's bed. He wasn't swift but he knew an opportunity when he saw one. Of course, I saw an opportunity too, unfortunately for him."

"You planted the letters in his apartment and told me where to find him."

"No, the bartender did, but I told the bartender, so in an indirect way, you are correct, sir," Gus said. "I had to get you fixated onto *someone*. Carmela didn't take. Neither did Delilah. Berto and Renzo looked good, but that whole cocaine business felt too far-fetched to tie to these letters and those bombs. That left good ol' Vito. And I had pressing business with him, he wanting to blackmail me, so two birds, one bullet." Gus tilted his head. "Have you puzzled out the motive?"

"Vengeance," Dash replied. "To systematically destroy the man who ruined your life. Right, Gus? I assume you prefer Gus over Silvano."

An evil grin dimpled his cheeks. "Silvano died when too many people didn't care about him. His father got sent up the river and died there. His mother got sick and died near-about here. He was sent to live in an orphanage, which was hell on earth, until the remaining family in Italy summoned him home. Except they weren't a family. They were a gang. Black Handers. Nasty folk. Silvano's home, his parents, his *future* taken away, and all because one man decided to be clever and send a little letter."

Joe said, "What do ya want, lad?"

Gus furrowed his brow and clenched his jaw. "I want justice! I want Donte Delucci dead and buried. *That's* what I want!" He took a moment to compose himself. "The moment I landed back in the States, I went to every bank in all the Little Italies. And I found him at Morena Bank & Trust. Then I simply followed him to that shit hole The Smoke Shop, where he doesn't have a care in the world. As if he didn't ruin my life with his vice.

"I watched him lose night after night. One night, I figured out how to hurt him. I knew how to take away every piece of his life. I'd use the same tactic he did. Send him a letter signed *La Mano Nera* asking for an amount I knew he couldn't pay and watch him squirm. And my, oh my, did he squirm."

Gus laughed. "He was desperate! I thought he'd steal from the bank, I really did." The laughs stopped. "But when he became defiant about not paying, that's when I knew it was time to have his life go up in smoke. So to speak." Gus grinned. "First, I took his home."

"And his wife," Dash added.

Gus shrugged. "That was by accident, swear to God! I set the fire in the basement so it would give more people a chance to get out. How was I to know that building was nothing but kindling?"

"And then you threw a stick of dynamite at Donte in front of his bank."

"First his home; second his job." Gus glanced over at Dash with fiendish eyes. "And now, his family. The trifecta of a life. A man can't be anything in this city without those three. Now. Where is Donte?"

Joe replied, "We don' know, lad! We've been tryin' to find him ourselves."

"That's unfortunate." Gus lifted up a suitcase. The ticking of a clock could be heard through the leather. He said in a singsong voice. "I'm all packed up with no one to explode." He glanced down at Atty. "Well, I suppose his brother and his friends will have to do. For now, at least."

Dash said, "It's not going to change anything, you know? Killing Donte. Taking away his home, his work, or even his brother. It won't change what happened."

"Yeah, but it'll make me feel better. There needs to be *some* justice in this cockamamie world."

"That isn't justice," Joe said. "Tha's revenge."

"Same thing," Gus spat back. "It's a settling of accounts. And Donte is long past due."

A voice shouted from the entrance: "Silvano!"

Dash and Joe looked at one another.

"Silvano!"

Dash squinted. It sounded like . . . Donte?

They turned toward the gate.

A darkened figure stood there in a trench coat and a fedora.

"Donte?" Gus called. "Is that you, you rascal?"

*He must've found my note.*

Before Dash and Joe came to the cemetery, they left notes at the Playhouse and at Atty's apartment, saying what was about to happen. He hoped Donte would return to one of those places and find it. Apparently, he had.

"Silvano!" Donte called. "I have your money!"

"Bullshit! You don't have that kind of dough!"

A hesitation. "I stole it!"

Gus laughed. "He's bluffing. He was always a terrible bluffer." He glanced back at Dash. "Doesn't matter. I don't really need the money." He returned his attention to Donte. "I have your brother here. Would you like to take his place?"

"Haven't you done enough, Silvano? Haven't you destroyed enough?"

"Well, don't that beat all? Righteous indignation from an incessant gambler. Tell me, how many lives have *you* destroyed, Donte, with your incredible bad luck?"

"Come over here. We can settle this like men."

"Oh, trying to be a big timer now, I see."

"Your fight is with me, not with him."

The ticking in the bag seemed to be getting louder by the second.

Dash pointed to it. "How much time is on the clock?"

Gus looked down at the suitcase. "Eh, about eight minutes, give or take."

Donte motioned Gus over. "You wanted me. Come over and get me."

Dash called out, "He's got a gun, Donte."

"Quiet, you!" Gus hissed. He cleared his throat and said, "Alright, Donte, I'll come to you. I've got a message with your name all over it. But first, these two men are going to lead the way. Wouldn't want them to get any funny ideas." He gestured to Dash and Joe with the gun. "Get moving, boys."

Dash and Joe stepped away from the tied up Atty, shuffled passed the gun-welding Gus, and started towards Donte. Even from this distance, his face was bathed in shadow. Only his eyes, narrow as pinpoints, could be seen under the brim of his fedora.

Joe murmured to Dash, "What do we do now, me boy?"

"I don't know."

Gus said, "Quiet up there! Don't be clever now."

They were now about fifteen feet away from Donte.

"About five more minutes. Any last words, Mr. Delucci?

Any parting thoughts of wisdom before you leave this world?"

Donte didn't say a word.

"What? Cat got your tongue?"

Something was wrong.

Dash felt it the same moment that Gus did.

"Say, what's the big idea?"

No response.

"You're not going to say nothing?"

Silence.

"I took everything away from you! Your home, your wife. I almost took your children. I've got your brother tied up and defenseless, your friends held at gunpoint, and you've got *nothing* to say?"

Donte remained quiet.

"Say something, you bastard!"

A large shadow from Dash's right ran up behind them and knocked the pistol out of Gus's hand. Giant arms surrounded him and lifted him off the ground.

"Grab it!" the shadow yelled, its accent familiar.

*Borden.*

Dash, without thinking, snatched up the pistol while Gus wiggled around and beat at the thick forearms holding him. The ticking suitcase fell to the ground. Dash's heart stopped, waiting for the explosion to carry him away.

None came.

Gus's legs kicked wildly at Borden, eventually making contact with something fleshy and soft.

Borden shouted and let go of Gus, who ran towards Dash.

Dash raised the pistol.

Gus skidded to a stop. He smirked. "You're not going to shoot me."

"No," Joe said, taking Donte's pistol out of his pocket and aiming it at Gus. "But I will."

Another voice said, "And I won't even need a brutish pistol."

A small, impish figure came up from behind Gus. One arm wrapped around his chest, the other around his neck. The flash of moonlight on silver temporarily blinded Dash.

Finn said, "I will make your neck smile all over these lovely cobblestones if you even *dare* to move."

Dash blinked. The silvery blade of a knife was held at Gus's throat.

"Borden!" Finn called. "The suitcase!"

The shadowy form of Borden lifted the suitcase and opened it. The ticking became even louder.

"I don't know how to turn it off!" Borden replied.

Gus laughed, his voice constrained by the pressure of Finn's surprisingly powerful arms and hands on his chest and neck. "What a conundrum. Keep the bomb here, we all die. Put the bomb somewhere else, innocent people will get hurt. What to do, what to do?"

Joe came forward and stuck his face near Gus's. "Ya bloody bastard, turn it off!"

"Nope. I don't believe I will. Tah-tah!"

Joe looked at Dash. "What do we do?"

Dash's mind was a blank. All his thoughts were racing, formless, urgent, messy. He couldn't concentrate and he was running out of time. They all were.

Finn said, "Someone make a decision. *Quick.*"

"I'll take it," Borden replied.

"No! You can't! You'll—"

"Tick tock tick tock tick tock," Gus sang.

Joe grabbed Gus's coat by the lapels and shook him. "Shut up, ya fucker! And disarm it!"

It was enough of a distraction for Gus to break free from Finn's knife. He elbowed the small man in the stomach while stomping on Joe's foot. He tore away from the two men and ran towards the cemetery's exit.

"Get him!" Donte yelled.

Dash and Joe raised their pistols again as all four of them chased after Gus, who was laughing maniacally as he went.

When Dash reached the gated entrance, he saw Gus leap into the Manhattan Freight & Transit truck. The motor started with a chest-vibrating roar and rattle.

Gus leaned out the window gave a little wave. "So long, suckers!"

Joe fired.

The sound of the shot was deafening to Dash's ears. An immediate ringing muffled the remaining sounds around him. He looked up and saw that Joe, unfortunately, had missed.

Gus put the truck into gear and pressed the accelerator down, surging forward. Joe continued firing in vain.

As the truck pulled out into the street, Donte took the ticking suitcase from Borden and ran after it. He leapt up onto the back of the truck, ripping the back door open and throwing the suitcase into the hull before slamming the door shut.

He jumped down from the truck and ran towards them. "Take cover!"

Borden grabbed Finn and pulled him into the graveyard again. Joe dropped the pistol and seized Dash's hand to do the same.

A sudden boom shook the ground beneath their feet. Dash felt an invisible hand lift him into the air a good five or six feet before hitting the grassy ground with a stomach-pounding *whoompf!*

The air was knocked out of his lungs. Stunned, he laid there for a moment, temporarily deaf. He turned his head and saw Joe sprawled on the ground beside him. He felt, but didn't hear, himself calling out for Joe.

Joe slowly turned his head. His lips moved but Dash couldn't hear the words.

Dash eventually turned onto his back and saw a plume of fiery smoke rise above the rooflines of the surrounding buildings.

# EPILOGUE

"Miss Meyers!" crowed Lou, the bartender. "You came back! And look, you brought Missus Mister with ya!"

Dash smiled, aware of how ridiculous he looked with Pru's second impromptu alleyway makeup job. "Lou, nice to see you again."

"Nice to see *you*. And hey! Look at this!" Lou reached down below the bar and removed the hat he'd allowed her to take from his shop. She placed it on her head. "Eh? Eh? Don't I look sharp?"

Pru replied, "An utter billboard."

"That's what I'm talking about! Since I got this thing, I've been fending off fillies left and right. I can hardly walk down the street anymore!" Lou laughed and leaned on the bar. "What can I get ya's?"

They ordered two rickeys and set off towards a table in one of the far corners. The club was nearly empty. A rare slow night, according to Pru.

It was Friday, November 5, and Dash was still battered and bruised from the events of the past week. That Halloween night, Dash and the rest of them fled the New

York City Marble Cemetery before the police and the fire trucks arrived.

The Manhattan Freight & Transit truck was a wall of fire by the time emergency personnel got to it. The next day, the papers mentioned that once the flames were put out, a body had been found in the truck's cab. In the hull were crates filled with booze and packages of cocaine. The newshawks speculated that the recent bombings of late had been over the illegal contraband. Politicians and police captains vowed to crack down on crime. "This time," they said, "we mean business!"

The Smoke Shop was no more. Authorities reacted to the anonymous telephone call made by Dash concerning cocaine being smuggled into an unlawful gambling establishment. A single raid closed it down for good. Shortly thereafter, Berto—who wouldn't get the chance to kill Delilah Sams—and Renzo were arrested for drug trafficking while their father Gianni was arrested for various vice charges related to gambling. It looked like Delilah and Donte's plan worked, albeit not quite in the way they intended. The last Dash saw of The Smoke Shop, there was a FOR RENT sign hanging from the front doors.

It wasn't the only one in Little Italy. Carmela Fiore closed her restaurant and left the city. Her neighbors said she was looking to start a brand new life—they also whispered to Dash that she came into some money, thanks to that spiritualist who was always hanging around. The two of them packed everything up and split. Dash wondered if Delilah had sold a few packets of the cocaine she found that night he caught her in the storage closet. He didn't blame her. Freedom wasn't free, as the Super Patriots often crowed.

If Donte knew about Delilah and Carmela, he never let

on. He admitted he found the cocaine packages by accident, but it was Delilah who decided to use this knowledge to free themselves. Dash assumed Carmela knew about Delilah's scheme. Was this her act of kindness towards Donte? Had she felt guilt for making Rodolpho refuse to give his best friend money all those years ago? Whatever the truth, Carmela and her lady love Delilah were gone, and Dash hoped they would find happiness wherever they landed.

Donte and Atty still fought with one another. Atty was furious his brother would endanger so many lives, including his own, all for a card table. Not to mention Maria lost her life because of what Donte did. It might take years, in Dash's estimation, for that relationship to be repaired, if at all. Then again, the Deluccis' sense of family was strong. It would be bumpy, but their paths might soon intertwine once again.

Speaking of relationships, Borden extended his ship leave so he and Finn could have a few more weeks together.

"I know it's eventually going to break my heart when he finally sets off," Finn said. "But I intend to enjoy every waking moment that I can with him."

"That's wonderful news, Finn," Dash replied.

"Well, dearie, he *did* nurse me back to life. Do you know how attractive a man is once he saves you?"

Dash immediately thought of Joe. They both suffered from superficial injuries, although Dash's ears maintained a low-level hum from the explosion. Doctors said it might take weeks, even months, for it to subside. In the meantime, Joe was applying his own special brand of medicine, which most definitely took Dash's mind off his various hurts.

"Oh yes, Finn," Dash replied with a smile. "I know *exactly* what you mean."

Now in this hidden lesbian speakeasy, Dash and Pru

toasted their success. Pru had turned over the deed to McElroy's apartment and his bloated bank accounts to his sergeant, who immediately suspended the odious man pending an investigation.

*So Fife didn't kill him,* Dash thought with relief.

After their initial sips, Dash slid an envelope from his inside coat pocket and placed it onto the bar.

Pru's lavender eyes removed the contents and scanned the pages of McElroy's evidence of private investigator Felix de Martini's hiding out in Manhattan—and McElroy's subsequent blackmail of him.

She looked up at Dash. "This is incredible. He's meddling with another district attorney's case, across state lines, in point of fact. This is more than just graft; this is interstate corruption." The look she gave him was of admiration. "You certainly did well with your little . . . adventure. Did you also get the photographs of your witness?"

Dash nodded. "And the negatives too."

Peter Fraker couldn't stammer his thanks out fast enough. "I promise, I'll never ever do something like this again. Never ever!"

That wasn't all. Dash and Joe were tracking down all of McElroy's victims and handing over the proof to be destroyed, freeing up dozens of men and women from McElroy's grasp.

Pru folded up the pages and slid the envelope into her coat pocket. "You must be relieved."

"Oh, I am." He let loose an enormous sigh, his shoulders finally relaxing. "Thank you, again, for your help."

"It seems to me you did all the work."

"Not by myself. I had a lot of help." He sat back in his chair. "What's new in the world of Meyers, Powers, and Napier?"

"Quiet, but we're hoping things pick up soon."

"I'm sure a big case will come along at any moment."

Speaking of a big case, the Hall-Mills grand jury returned an indictment of Frances Stevens Hall and her brothers, and the trial began its first day of official legal proceedings on November 3. It appeared the shenanigans of Felix de Martini had little effect on the outcome.

Which left only the matter of Officer McElroy. Dash wondered what Fife had done to the man. He hadn't seen McElroy since his suspension. Odd. Dash fully expected a retaliation.

When Dash asked Emmett about him, the old man grunted. "I don't know where he is, and I don't care. It'd be nice not to lose so much of my profits to that rat bastard."

It was Saturday, November 6, when Dash discovered McElroy's fate.

He was walking from the Greenwich Village Inn, happy to see it was as full as ever, and heading towards Hartford & Sons to open it for the day. Sometimes the tailoring bit was a slog, but strangely, he found himself looking forward to it. Given the last three months, mindless, even boring, activities sounded like a vacation.

He just crossed over Cornelia Street when he stopped in his tracks.

The purple-painted truck, announcing CALLAHAN CREAMERY, idled in front of the shop.

He sighed. Turning around and walking away wasn't an option. Fife would find him—and be more irritated at expending the extra effort to do so. Damn. There was no way out of this meeting. There never was when it came to Fife.

*Let's see what he wants this time.*

Dash adjusted his lapels and the knot of his tie before

strolling forward. After he passed by the cab of the truck, he reached up and knocked his fist on the side of the hull. As he rounded the back bumper, the back doors opened.

He glanced up and said, "Good morning, Mr. Fife."

Nicholas Fife stood in the shadows of the truck's hull. "Mr. Parker." He extended his hand.

Dash clasped it and allowed the gangster to pull him up from the street and into the truck.

Fife closed the back door behind him. The lanterns that were present the first time Dash was back here buzzed from the upper hooks on the sides. His breath came out in puffs of clouds.

"What happened to McElroy?" he asked.

Fife smiled. "All business and no pleasure. I sincerely worry about you, Mr. Parker. A life without a little *fun* is no life at all."

"What I want now is a little rest."

"You've certainly earned that. I read about that truck exploding in Little Italy. Pray tell, does that mean your Black Hand problem is resolved?"

Dash nodded.

"And was it solved to your satisfaction?"

Dash wagged his head. "I suppose, though I wish there hadn't been so much death."

"Ah. Unfortunately, in the shadows, death is a common event." Fife reached into his coat and pulled out an envelope. He handed it to Dash. "For you."

Dash opened it. Photographs.

Fife went on. "I honored your request not to kill him. But his little side business inspired me. He so enjoyed taking incriminating photographs of other people, so I thought it was only fair to return the favor."

Dash's mouth dropped open. "These are . . . these are . .

."

"Scandalous? Shocking? Career ending?" Fife arched an eyebrow. "I sincerely hope so. I was aiming for all three."

"How did you . . . ?"

Fife peered over at the photographs, admiring his handiwork. "Certain chemicals allow a man to be both pliable and, shall we say, alert."

Dash flipped through the photographs. Ten in all.

At one, Fife pointed and said, "I choreographed that one myself."

Dash looked up at him. "Did you now?"

All the photographs were of Officer McElroy in his uniform, posing with naked men. Naked men laughing, kissing, dancing in some, performing sex acts in others. All the while, there was McElroy front and center, grinning from ear to ear, seemingly enjoying it all.

"Does he know about this?" Dash asked.

"Oh yes. I have sent him copies along with an explicit warning that if he ever comes near your shop or your apartment again, these will be sent to every precinct and antivice squad in the city, along with his actual address. He applied for a precinct transfer the next day and wouldn't you know? It was approved instantly."

"Will he try to get revenge?"

"A man like him would never survive in this town if the entire police force saw with their own eyes he engaged in degeneracy. But to be even more certain, I promised to send these photographs to every newshawk and tabloid in town. Can you imagine the scandal?" Fife preened. "I have to tell you, it was quite fun. If you have another officer in need of silencing, I'm happy to repeat my services." He turned his head up slightly. "I could make it another business venture. I'm sure there's no shortage of men and women harassed by the NYPD who would like to see them victimized for a change."

"Hopefully, that won't be necessary for me," Dash replied. He returned the photographs to the envelope and held it out for Fife, who shook his head.

"Those are your copies. Rest assured, I have multiples printed and the negatives are kept in a very safe place."

Dash slid the envelope into his inside coat pocket. This was an unconventional approach to dealing with an odious extorting police officer, but Dash could see the effectiveness of it. If McElroy made one move, he'd be ruined. He'd have to leave the city.

*I wonder if we should leak the photographs anyway . . .*

Dash shook off the thought. He wasn't a vindictive man. He only wanted to be left alone, to live his life in peace.

He nodded at Fife. "Thank you."

"You're entirely welcome." Those warm chocolate eyes twinkled in the lantern light. "Well, I believe this concludes our business. And I hope this means you'll be able to concentrate purely on Pinstripes. I hate to have you distracted. It impedes my . . . *our* . . . profits."

---

"We did it."

Dash raised his glass in a toast to the three men surrounding him. Joe, Finn, and Atty.

Finn said, "Hear, hear!"

Their glasses clinked, and they drank their libations down.

They were sitting inside Pinstripes before opening. Joe was standing behind the bar, as was his usual, while Dash, Finn, and Atty settled on the barstools.

"How are the children?" Dash asked Atty.

"They're doing better. Bella is still angry at Donte. Hell, Boss, *I'm* still angry with him. But he found an apartment a few blocks away, so they'll be moving soon."

Finn leaned on the bar. "Will you miss them?"

Atty smiled. "Yeah, yeah I think I will. They're goofy, youse know? The boys make up stuff that makes no sense. The rules change all the time. And Bella talks like a young woman, which is strange to hear. When did she grow up so fast? They're loud, they argue, they scream, they cry, they laugh until their cute little faces turn purple, they . . . . made my place feel like a home."

Finn patted Atty's shoulder. "It's always nice to have another heartbeat around."

Dash reached over and grabbed Joe's hand. The two of them locked eyes and grinned.

"Well," Finn said. "Now that we're done solving cryptic letters and mysterious packages, I think it's time we solved the biggest mystery of all."

Joe rolled his eyes. "And what's tha'?"

"Getting Atty a woman, of course! You've been living far too celibate a life. It's simply not *natural*."

"Hey, now!" Atty said. "I've had plenty of women. Just not . . . lately."

"Exactly my point. Here you are, strong, strapping, and solid, wasting away in bachelor-dom."

Dash replied, "Says the man who was a proud bachelor until recently."

Finn pursed his lips. "I'll ignore that comment for the sake of our friendship. Atty, let's have a little chat. Tell me about the girls you like." He placed his arm around Atty and led him from the bar to one of the side tables.

Dash looked at Joe. "Finn playing matchmaker? This outta be interesting."

"It'll be a disaster."

Dash tilted his head. "I'm not so sure. I think he might be quite grand at it."

The secret door opened and the large wooden body of the bass walked in with Vernon behind it. He was followed by Julius and his cornet and Calvin and his cymbals. The mood amongst the three men was decidedly sour.

Dash and Joe picked up on it immediately.

"Lads," Joe said. "What's wrong?"

Vernon placed the bass down on the ground. "You haven't heard?"

Dash asked, "Heard what?"

"About El."

Dash shook his head. "Is she alright? What's happened?"

Ever since the club was almost raided on Mischief Night, she hadn't responded to Dash's notes or telephone calls. He figured she was still angry with him about that night, but he never considered something bad had happened.

Calvin shook his head as he settled behind the drum kit. "Not likely. She's in a big mess."

"What mess?"

The three men looked down at the ground.

"Gents," Dash said. "Please. Tell me. What's happened to El?"

Julius tapped the sides of his horn. "She's just been arrested for the murder of her white wife."

Joe's eyes widened. "Murder?"

Dash said, "*Wife?*"

THE 4TH HIDDEN GOTHAM NOVEL

We've had three books of Dash and the boys.

Now, it's the ladies' turn:
Queer performer and force of nature El Train,
dancer extraordinaire Flo Russell,
millionaire Madame J.A. Watkins,
and the mysterious Baroness of Business, Zora Mae.

Their adventure is coming 2024.

# AFTERWORD

*La Mano Nera,* otherwise known as The Black Hand, was a secret society which operated for several decades in the late 1800s and early 1900s. They targeted wealthy Italian immigrants and those who had just arrived in America. Their modus operandi—letters signed with threatening imagery, child kidnappings and ransoms, and the use of violence, particularly dynamite—was the same in real life as it is in this book. They were not constrained to cities, though; there is evidence of their operations in rural areas across the Midwest and Southeast. For a time, they were the most feared group in all of America until the rise of the Ku Klux Klan in the 1920s.

Much of my learning of The Black Hand was from Steven Talty's excellent book *The Black Hand: The Epic War Between a Brilliant Detective and the Deadliest Secret Society in American History.*

Spiritualism was a highly popular and highly contested movement driven by the devastation of World War I (aka "the Great War") and the Influenza Pandemic (1918-1920). The movement was led by none other than Sir

Arthur Conan Doyle, the author of Sherlock Holmes. As is referenced in this book, the infamous escape artist Harry Houdini did indeed set out to debunk and disprove all the spiritualists he could find. A historically detailed account of Houdini's rivalry with a spiritualist promoted by Doyle can be found in *The Witch of Lime Street: Séance, Seduction, and Houdini in the Spirit World* by David Jaher.

The Hall-Mills case, including the sleazy private detective Felix de Martini, are real. The case is so bizarre, it deserves its own book. In 1922, the bodies of Reverend Hall and Eleanor Mills were found shot to death with Eleanor's throat cut and her voice box almost removed. Love letters the couple penned to one another were strewn about the crime scene. The case languished until 1926 when the tabloids picked up the case, writing several articles and drumming up quite a bit of interest, to the point where the district attorney was forced to reopen the case for political purposes. The Hall-Mills trial is considered one of the first examples of the press and the public being obsessed with a criminal affair. Frances Stevens Hall and her brothers were indicted in November and acquitted in December. The case is still technically unsolved.

The Lower East Side Little Italy was larger than it is today, extending from Canal Street up to Bleecker. There were actually several Little Italies in Manhattan, with the largest one being in East Harlem. (The more you know!)

The American Seamen's Friend Society was a real place, and the structure is still standing today as the Jane Hotel. The Society's intent was to prevent sailors from being exploited and taken advantage of, and in the early 1900s, they did indeed house some survivors of the *Titanic*.

For anyone visiting Manhattan, you'll notice that West

Street isn't on the river. That's because the island was extended to make room for the West Side Highway.

In addition to the above sources and historical events, this novel was also informed by the thorough research efforts of George Chauncey (*Gay New York: Gender, Urban Culture, and the Making of the Gay World, 1880-1940*) and James F. Wilson (*Bulldaggers, Pansies, and Chocolate Babies: Performance, Race, and Sexuality in the Harlem Renaissance*). Thanks to *The New York Times* and *The New Yorker* for their archives. And thanks to the *Vintage Dancer* website for its invaluable information on 1920s clothing.

—*Chris Holcombe*

# ABOUT THE AUTHOR

Chris Holcombe is an author of LGBTQIA+ historical crime fiction. *The Devil Card* is the third novel in his Hidden Gotham series, which showcases New York's lively but criminally under-represented Queer world of the 1920s. He is also an award-winning songwriter and an accomplished brand strategist in marketing and advertising. He lives with his husband in New York City, where he is hard at work on the next Hidden Gotham novel.

facebook.com/thechrisholcombeauthor

instagram.com/thechrisholcombe

tiktok.com/@thechrisholcombe

patreon.com/ChrisHolcombeAuthor

goodreads.com/chrisholcombe

Printed in Great Britain
by Amazon

34995983R00209